'A twisty thriller that is immer

'A tense, twisting, international thriller. Deftly written and engrossing, E. C. Scullion's debut *Intruders*, quickly drew me in, and the intrigue and pace kept me turning pages. A talented writer to watch' Adam Hamdy

'A tightly written thriller, with wonderful descriptions that really convey a sense of place... It had me hooked'

'I raced through this book in about 24 hours... I loved it – brilliant characters and a fast-paced plot that kept me guessing throughout'

'Well-written, well-plotted, tense thriller'

'Honestly a very enjoyable and gripping read, from the onset to the final page'

'I absolutely loved this book from start to finish. Five stars'

'This is a really, really good read. Forget all those generic action novels, this is a thriller that delivers – with a plot genuinely new and different from any I've ever read before'

'Loved this book, was completely engrossed by it. A clever plot with unexpected twists as the story unfolds'

'Captivating from the start. Unlike many thrillers the plot developed from the start with many unexpected twists and turns. Difficult to put down'

'A real page-turner'

'Generous and rewarding three-dimensional characters, good pacing and taut plot. Excellent!'

'An incredible debut novel – this is a thriller on every scale – slick, stylish and intriguing'

'This is a seriously impressive debut novel. Highly recommended'

'You will not want to put this book down – I read it in three days… A great read'

'This was a cracking read… Perfect escapism with an intriguing gang of characters to get to know'

'A novel hard to put down… Highly recommended!'

'Got totally hooked on this book, a great story with a great mix of characters. Beautifully written and lovely details of places and a real sense of each character'

'A twisty page-turner which keeps you hooked throughout. Interesting characters, descriptive locations and nail biting situations'

'A rollercoaster ride around London, Argentina and Uruguay. Great characters and twists'

'Gripping storyline, with amazing scenery. Would make an amazing film'

'Brilliant story line, great title, excellent reading'

'Loved this book, I was gripped from beginning to end. So exciting!'

'I absolutely loved this book'

'A triumph in high-octane thriller writing… Entertaining, enthralling and totally gripping, this is a fantastic debut'

'A superb book that had me engrossed from the very first page'

'An absolutely brilliant novel; it's a literary white knuckle ride that had me on the edge of my seat, holding my breath with my heart pounding and my palms sweating'

'And so with a joyous conclusion I cannot give this anything but five stars, this book has definitely earned its place on my bookcase as something to re-read for years to come'

E. C. SCULLION
EVADERS

Red Door

Published by RedDoor

www.reddoorpress.co.uk

ISBN 978-1-913062-73-6

A CIP catalogue record for this book is available from the British Library

Cover design: Tim Barber

Typesetting: Jen Parker, Fuzzy Flamingo
www.fuzzyflamingo.co.uk

Printed and bound in Denmark by Nørhaven

To Penny Thomas,
the best mother a daughter could wish for

Prologue

Barking, England
25 November, 2016

Chief Inspector Neil Rawlins took a drag on the Montecristo No.5 pressed between his lips – Cuba's finest – customary for the occasion, the last Friday of every month spent playing poker in his cramped East London basement. The room was a swirling yellow haze. The boys were all present: white, flabby, off-duty London Metropolitan Police detectives, retired or on the verge, lounging on foldaway chairs around a wooden table and bingeing on the red wine; an earthy Valpolicella. Rawlins, money down, hadn't had a decent hand all night.

'Who's for a refill?' he said, raising his nicotine-ravaged voice over the hubbub.

Cheers went up. He had more stocks in the kitchen. Rawlins stumbled to his feet, gripped the table edge, cheers turning to jeers. He cackled in response, lungs crackling, and gave his chest a thwack with a balled-up fist.

Upstairs, he burst through the door to the kitchen. Outside it was hammering; rain lashed the glass window pane behind the sink which looked out onto a back garden in all-encompassing darkness. Rawlins took two cans of Red Bull from the fridge. He managed to spill an open carton of juice, splattering orange fluid all down the front of his shirt.

He swore, got to the sink, swaying, grabbed a dish cloth and dabbed at the cotton. He switched on the tap, glancing up at the reflection of his weathered face. His neighbour owned a security light with a motion sensor; it'd been on the blink for months, sometimes switching on for no reason and lighting up one corner of the garden. Outside the light flickered. Rawlins peered from his window, rain still belting down. In the same corner, he glimpsed a black silhouette, for the briefest of moments, standing under an umbrella, back to the hedge.

The light cut out. Rawlins held his breath. Ten seconds later, a pale face with hollow eyes emerged from the gloom on the other side of the window pane.

Recoiling, he slipped on the pool of orange juice and plummeted to the floor, landing on his coccyx, cursing out loud. Within his eyeline, he could still see the figure at the window tapping on the pane with the sharp end of an umbrella, a deluge of water drenching the figure's hair, matting it to his forehead. Rawlins gripped his chest, scrambled to his feet. It took him a few seconds to realise who it was that he was looking at.

He switched off the tap. The face behind the glass was cold and impassive; just as Rawlins remembered it.

Snapping from his reverie, he grabbed a towel and went to the back door. He searched around for an umbrella, located a small red one that belonged to the missus. When he managed to get the door open, the figure was already waiting.

'You scared the living shit out of me,' Rawlins hissed. 'You can't be here, I have guests.'

The figure had a dead-centre parting, squashed nose not

dissimilar to a rugby forward, and a square jaw. He stepped inside the house. Water cascaded from his coat, soaking the lino. 'Then get rid of them,' the figure said.

Rawlins gaped at him.

The man was serious. 'Where's the package?'

'It's downstairs, locked in my desk drawer,' Rawlins stuttered. 'I'll need some time.'

'I don't care what you tell them. I need everyone but you out of this house.'

Twenty minutes later, the boys turfed out early in the downpour, grumbling at their host for cutting short their poker night due to a so-called dodgy stomach, Rawlins returned to the kitchen. The man, whom he knew only as Anton – though he didn't know if that was his real name – lingered in the shadows beside the back door. Rawlins raised his eyes. Anton was wearing gloves, just as when he had last encountered him.

Gripping his fists to stop his fingers from trembling, Rawlins ushered Anton down the wooden steps into the fuggy basement, the aroma of cigar smoke clinging to the walls, glasses of wine unfinished on the table, a pile of discarded poker chips where the boys had cashed out in a hurry. Anton removed his coat, hanging it on the back of one of the chairs, having to duck to avoid hitting his forehead on the low ceiling. Rawlins unlocked his desk drawer and passed Anton the unopened package from the international courier company. Anton snatched it, and studied the address label.

'Tell me about the phone call,' Anton ordered, walking

over to the drinks cabinet and pouring himself three fingers of whisky.

Rawlins started talking – too fast, he knew, the words tripping over one another from his lips. 'He wouldn't give his name. Said that he was calling from South America.'

'Where in South America?'

'Didn't say. The postmark of that package is somewhere in Argentina. The sender's name is Thomas Holt. He knew who I was, what I'd done. Said he had some information relating to Clare Buchanan's disappearance that he wanted to send me. He wanted to send it to the Met but I gave him my address here.'

'Did he think that was strange? Sending it to your personal address?'

'I don't think so. I fudged it. He must have bought it, else I wouldn't have it.'

'What else did Thomas Holt say?'

'He told me to write down a name.' Rawlins rummaged around for a small notepad in the bottom of the drawer, consulting the scribbled notes he had made during the phone call days earlier. 'Sabina Cordero. Told me that she lived on a secure compound in Uruguay called *Aves de Las Colinas*. That I should find out what happened to her.'

He saw a muscle in Anton's jaw pulsate. 'What else?'

Rawlins swallowed. 'He mentioned your name.'

Anton raised his eyes, saying nothing, before downing the whisky in one. He took the courier's package, tore it open and reached inside. Rawlins watched him pull out the contents: a small USB flash drive. Anton turned it in his fingers.

'Did he mention anything about a laptop?'

'No, nothing. That was it.'

Anton stood and went back over to his wet coat, sinking his hand into one of the pockets. When he turned again, Rawlins saw that he was holding out a swollen Manila envelope. Rawlins took it with a nod, the bundle of cash he knew it contained a good deal thicker than usual.

'As always, Mr Capricorn appreciates your loyalty, Detective Chief Inspector.'

Rawlins didn't remember ever being given a choice.

Anton was pulling on his coat. Rawlins continued to watch him, fascinated by the darkness of his character. In more than thirty years as a police officer, he'd never come across anyone quite like him. Physically fit yet somehow bruised; a history of damage in his facial features, lithe in his movements, hardened in his stare. He presumed he wasn't British-born. He watched as Anton helped himself to a Montecristo No. 5 from the box in the centre of the poker table, sliding his twisted nostrils down its full length. He spent time lighting it up, taking a long drag before exhaling a thick plume of cigar smoke towards the ceiling.

'I can't stop Thomas Holt from putting in another call to the Met if he senses no action is being taken. How do you propose to keep him silent?' Rawlins asked.

The man he knew as Anton was already half-way back up the basement stairs, holding the package, leaving a trail of cigar smoke behind him.

'I'm going to cut out his tongue,' he said, and was gone.

Part One

Chapter 1

Chile
20 December, 2016

He didn't know the missing woman, but he knew her face.

Her name was Clare Buchanan. She'd been gone more than eleven years.

In the past few weeks, he'd begun to feel responsible for her. For her memory.

When he wasn't required at his job driving holidaymakers around on jet skis out on the lake, he would choose to retreat to the *cabaña*. Inside, the wrought-iron bed was about ten inches too short for his six-foot-two frame. Sometimes he would jolt awake, sick to his stomach and drenched in sweat, dreams still plagued by the events in Uruguay and Argentina. When Tom Holt wasn't thinking about Clare Buchanan, he thought about his friend Anil Choudhury, slumped to the floor in a pool of blood, a bullet in his skull.

The *cabaña* consisted of three small rooms, built on thick struts into the rugged landscape, which led down to the volcanic sand beaches on the banks of Lake Caburgua. The lake was nestled in the mountains, twenty minutes' drive from the adventure town of Pucón, in the shadow of a volcano known as Villarrica. There were no carpets; instead crumbling wooden floorboards, liable to invasion by wasps and a hoard of ants. It wasn't light on the inside, the sunlight only filtered through the windows for a couple of hours in the early afternoon. A light bulb hung from fraying wire on the ceiling in each room. As living spaces went, it was decent enough. It was a place he could hide, for now.

Every day followed a similar pattern. At first light he would doggedly attempt one hundred press-ups before running the steep network of rugged paths leading past the campsite back up to the main dead-end road, a throwback to his days training in the British Army. It was a process he would often try and repeat after dark, keeping up his core strength, lifting cans of petrol for the jet skis in place of weights. He believed he had to stay ready, ready to run, to escape if he needed to. He had lost weight back in Uruguay; if anything, in Chile he had lost a few more pounds. He didn't remember the last time he'd had a shave or a haircut. His face was covered with a full beard, sandy blonde hair curling softly at the edges.

Outside it was dark. He lay with the lights off. When there was a hammering on the door, Tom's hand shot to the jagged kitchen knife he kept under his pillow.

'Holt! You in there?' a voice said.

'I'm sleeping,' Tom replied, relaxing his hand.

'*Ach,* come *ooooon*,' came the retort in Swedish-accented English. 'I've got beers and a campfire going on the beach. You cannot stay in there.'

Tom dragged himself into a sitting position. Aksel hammered again. He got to his feet, unlocked the door. In the dim light, the Swede stood with a grin on his face, his wild, bleach-blonde hair now familiar, clutching a six-pack of local Kunstmann lager.

4

'It's almost Christmas. Have a beer with me,' Aksel said.

'Fine, OK,' Tom conceded.

Aksel was dressed in a shirt for a change, white with short sleeves. Tom followed him out into the darkness, tall trees casting eerie shadows over the landscape. He was sure to lock the door behind him.

'Smoke?' Aksel asked, holding out a packet of cigarettes. Tom took one, borrowing Aksel's lighter, and followed him down the path to the sand. At the water's edge Aksel had lit a small fire. They sat either side of it, smoked cigarettes and sipped at bottles of beer in silence. Tom wanted a drink. He wanted seven or eight, enough to get him inebriated so he could forget about what had happened in Uruguay, and then afterwards in Buenos Aires. But he reined himself in, reminding himself every day that there was a chance, albeit slim or otherwise, that someone could find him. Put a bullet it him, like Anil, and Denham too, the lawyer who had given him the job in the first place, who was now also in the ground. The body count was rising. The things he had done had made him a target.

'That guy I told you about,' Aksel said, looking up at the vast starry sky. 'I asked my friend in Valpo. He says he still runs the office there. He can get you on a boat.'

Tom's eyes shot up. 'He can?'

'For a fee. Mainly the cruise ships from Valparaíso they go to Easter Island, Bora Bora, out west. But there are some that go north, up the coast towards Peru. Some end up in Miami, so they must go through the Panama Canal.'

Tom gave him a single nod. 'Thanks for asking.'

'You never told me what's in Panama.'

Tom finished the last dregs of his beer, helped himself to another. 'Last I heard my father was in Panama City.' He felt he'd already said too much. 'I have to get there without going through an airport or anywhere where I'm traceable. I know things… things I shouldn't know.'

He stopped short when the image of a red-headed woman entered his mind. He tried to push her away but she lingered. She was beckoning to him, like she did in his dreams.

Aksel chuckled, blowing smoke towards the night sky, hugging his knees. 'You remind me of me, you know that? You have that bunny-in-the-headlights look, like when I first discovered this place and didn't know if I could make a life here. Because I was running, like you are. Am I right?'

'What makes you think I'm running?'

Aksel raised his hands. 'See, there you go. You answer questions with questions. You never talk about yourself. Alone, scared maybe, I don't know. You don't sleep, keep your door locked. I remember that about myself, when I first got here, in the days before I realised no one would ever recognise me in a place like this.'

'What were you running from?'

Aksel took a swig from his bottle, relaxed his legs. His gaze shifted from the sky to the sand under his feet. 'Hit and run on a mother and daughter in Malmö, back home. They both died I think. I was high at the time, out of control. It was an accident, of course. I got spooked, I ran, never looked back. Made my way through Europe then across to South America. I'm probably on a list somewhere. Not proud of what I did, but I couldn't go to jail. Wasn't prepared to throw my life away.'

Tom was silent for a moment. It didn't sound like the Aksel he had come to know. 'Think you'll ever go back to Sweden?'

'No. I could never. Chile is my home now. Unless they find me.'

Tom grimaced. 'I can't stay here. I need to get to Panama.'

Another silence. Aksel took another swig of beer.

'Here,' Aksel said, taking a key from his keyring and passing it to Tom. 'This is the spare to my bike. Take it if you ever need to get out of town in a hurry.'

Aksel's motorbike was a banged-up 1999 Suzuki, tied to a tree trunk with a heavy-duty chain in the clearing at the entrance to the main road.

'I used to plan my escape, like you,' Aksel continued. 'Knew exactly what I would need to do, how I would do it, where I would go. What my new identity would be. But that was years ago. If the authorities haven't found me by now, I'm not sure they ever will.'

Tom took the key, pocketed it and thanked him.

'Take her out tomorrow for a spin maybe. You ever ride a bike before?'

'Few times.'

'Take it easy on the corners into Pucón. Hey, look.'

Tom turned his head. In the distance, on the inky horizon, fireworks exploded in a cloud of silence, too far away to be heard over the lapping of the water.

New Year's Day, 2017, a Sunday, was busy at the lake. In cloudless skies, crowds of bodies clad in swimwear lined the beach, wading into the warm waters, dark sand oozing under the toes like silt. Rainbow parasols littered the shoreline, wasps circled open bags and soda cans. He had a sore head, having shared three bottles of Swedish vodka with Aksel and a few others the night before. By the time Tom had opened the door to the *cabaña* soon after 3 a.m., he was swaying on his feet. He had managed to lock the door behind him before puking, making it to the toilet bowl with seconds to spare, then collapsing face down, still dressed, on the bed. His safety on a jet ski was questionable, yet the cool air rushing at his face had eased his hangover a fraction.

On Monday he trimmed his beard and hair, smartening his appearance up one level to swarthy backpacker over dishevelled drifter. After lunch, he climbed the path towards the road, up to the clearing where Aksel's Suzuki was chained to the thick tree trunk, a shopping list and his wallet in his jeans pocket. His passport he kept with his bag under the bed in the *cabaña*. Also inside was the laptop; the laptop he had brought with him from Uruguay, containing Clare Buchanan's video statement.

The helmet was attached with a separate carabiner combination lock. The bike started first time, much to his surprise. Aksel said it usually took several attempts. He took it steady on the road into Pucón. The last time Tom had ridden a bike was over ten years ago on the streets of South London. It was a forty-minute trip to the town centre. The road was lined with *cabañas* for rent as he weaved his way through the queues on Ruta 99, the only road into Pucón that was now clogged with holiday traffic. He parked near a supermarket in town, self-conscious as he removed the helmet, feeling exposed. He replaced the helmet with a cap, pulled down low on his brow, and took a moment to regain his grasp on reality. No one, not even his family, knew where he was. Not that it made him any less anxious as he moved around the harshly lit aisles of the *supermercado*, collecting up a few essentials in his basket, paying in cash at the checkout, loading the food in his backpack except for a long French stick and stuffing a wad of money back into his pocket. He walked to the hostel where he had first stayed on arrival, paying one thousand pesos for thirty minutes of internet use.

He googled Clare Buchanan's name, searching for news stories. Six weeks earlier he had couriered two copies of her video statement contained on separate USB flash drives, copied from the laptop in his possession, one to a Detective Chief Inspector Neil Rawlins of the Metropolitan Police, the other to Diane Cambridge, the head of Insight News International in London.

Frustration gnawed away at his gut. There was nothing. No breaking news stories, no breakthroughs in the investigation into Clare's disappearance. The most recent article was four years old; a missing persons charity interview with her sister. There were no reports of the arrest of Charlie Ebdon – the British businessman who Tom knew also used the name Solomon Capricorn, and the man who Clare had accused of embezzlement on a grand scale. He was also her former boss to boot. She was simply still missing, fading from the collective memory. Internet fodder; forgotten in an ocean of communications data.

He'd spoken to Rawlins back in Argentina. Had the detective ignored the video? Did he think it was some kind of hoax? Tom sat back in his chair, stomach growling. Rawlins had been the Senior Investigating Officer for Clare's case. He would have a vested interest in finding out what had happened to her. It would have reflected well on him.

So why no news?

If Charlie Ebdon had been hauled in and questioned, the British public would be talking about it.

There was no way of knowing what had happened on the night of the twenty-first of February 2005, almost twelve years earlier. The video had been recorded in the weeks running up to her disappearance. Clare had stepped off a number forty-three bus on Upper Street in London's Angel Islington and had never been seen again. She had worked for Elate International, Ebdon's vast conglomerate, as head of its charity arm. Ebdon was syphoning off massive amounts of cash for profit. He only knew snippets of the whole story. But Tom knew he couldn't simply let Ebdon walk away.

He ate lunch in a restaurant called Trawen. Pucón's sky was crystal clear, the main strip still crawling with tourists and holidaymakers, adventurers looking to windsurf on the lake or climb a volcano. Having ordered a simple club sandwich, his supply run coming to an end, he glanced out of the window towards the street. The man he saw, who had his back turned, was thick set, squat with a rounded waistline made wider by the stripes on the pair of long navy board shorts he was wearing, together with a plain black T-shirt and leather sandals. It was the moment he turned around that made the hairs on the back of Tom's neck stand on end. He found himself looking at a man he had seen before, back in Uruguay. Sancho Belosi had been his name, a violent psychopath. Only this man wasn't Belosi, but his spitting image, younger, but with familiar-looking curly black hair shoved underneath a fishing hat. A cigarette was pursed between his lips, and he was talking into his phone. He seemed to be loitering, looking around him.

It couldn't be a coincidence. His meal only half-finished, Tom signalled to the waitress for the bill, sinking lower, keeping his eyes on the man as he reached into his back pocket for the wad of pesos. When she brought the receipt, he counted out the change then and there, apologising to her with a smile that had no feeling. He didn't have time to think about a tip. Pulling his cap down, he swiped up his backpack and the French stick. He left the restaurant at speed and took a sharp right out of the door, sending a few pamphlets flying off their metal stand, keeping his head down as he weaved in and out of the bodies and strollers taking up room on the pavement. His heart hammered as he passed the shop with a giant donut for a sign, dumping the French stick in a public waste bin and crossing at the junction towards the side road where he'd parked the Suzuki. Keys at the ready, he had already fastened the backpack in place when he slung his leg over the saddle and in one seamless motion inserted the key, switched on the choke and pushed through with his foot, kick-starting the bike. Revving the engine as he secured the helmet, he was on the road heading outside of Pucón towards Caburgua within a matter of minutes.

Back at the lake he reached the clearing, removed the helmet, tossing the supplies on the ground. He broke into a sprint, skidding and sliding his way back down the path, tripping over tree roots, smashing through branches, knowing all along that he wouldn't have a chance to say goodbye to Aksel. This was it. Tom's lungs tightened as he took a tumble, somersaulting forwards, regaining his footing. At the *cabaña*, he unlocked the door, snuck inside, reaching for the bag from under his bed containing his passport and the laptop. He grabbed the knife from under his pillow, breaths coming out in ragged gasps. He threw off his top, changed it for a T-shirt and a hooded top he'd had since Uruguay, thrusting his cap in the bag. He stayed to the side of the window, glancing out, seeing nothing through the trees and leaves, only shafts of serene sunlight. Had they seen him leave? There was only one road out of Lake Caburgua and that headed straight back to Pucón. He deliberated, wondered whether to wait until nightfall before making his next move. Outside there was nothing, an eerie silence, rustling in the trees. No voices, a distant whirr of jet skis out on the lake, a girl's laughter somewhere.

The door was kicked open. Tom's eyes shot up. A second Sancho-lookalike entered – a brawler – this one thinner than the one in Pucón but with a thick neck. Tom did a double take, gripped the knife. The brawler wore a black T-shirt, baggy jeans, curly hair growing high up his cheekbones. Tom backed away, knife up, left arm gripping the bag strap. The brawler lunged, menacing, saying nothing at all. Tom sliced, the brawler ducking before coming at him headlong, going for his waist. Tom felt the force in his stomach as he was pinned to the floor with a gargantuan weight, the brawler's face close, sweat dripping, pudgy fingers squeezing the blood from Tom's wrist on his knife hand. Tom knew he was taller, yet he didn't have the momentum he needed to twist out from underneath. He spat in the brawler's face, making the man's fingers loosen for a split second and allowing Tom to free his left wrist and throw it up in the direction of brawler's nose, sending him over. Tom bolted to his feet, slinging both straps from the bag onto his shoulders, freeing his hands. They circled. The brawler let go of his face. His nose was streaming, blood mixing with facial hair; he spat across the room then lunged to throw a punch. Tom ducked, charged again with the knife. The brawler danced back, face expressionless, like it was a walk in the park. Tom felt the sweat dripping off him, breath rasping. *It's you or me*, he thought. *If I stay here you will kill me. Unless I kill you first. You and your twin.*

Tom threw the next punch with his left hand, missed, the brawler ensnaring Tom's curled fist inside his own hand. At the same time Tom slashed low with the knife, didn't hold back, burying it into doughy flesh. The brawler howled, let go, fell back, yanking out the blade from the left of his abdomen and tossing it against the wall, blood splattering against wood. Stunned and out of ideas, Tom threw a second punch, this time with his right, making contact with bone, pain shooting down his veins. He turned and bolted.

Uphill, he willed leaden legs forward, head low, eyes darting left and right as twigs and branches snapped underfoot. A shout went up in Spanish from the direction of the *cabaña*. A voice came back, not too far ahead. The twin. Tom changed tack ninety degrees, decided on a narrower path in the coarse shrub that would take him directly to the road that lead to the Suzuki. The path, whilst visible, was not in use anymore, overgrown and thick with branches that were slowly reclaiming it as another part of the forest. Dry twigs scratched his face. He stumbled frequently, hopped over logs and dead leaves that crunched underfoot, chest heaving, adrenaline in his limbs, willing him on.

At the road, he jumped down a slope, estimating that the bike was about fifty metres away. He stepped out. He could see all the way down the hill, the lake no longer within view. He broke out into a run, hamstrings already burning with lactic acid. He glanced back as a figure appeared at the bottom: the first Sancho lookalike, a man who was now breaking out into a run too.

Tom's fingers shook as he inserted the key into the ignition. He fumbled with the helmet, sweat pouring from his face. In the saddle, he switched on the choke, failed on his first two attempts to kick-start the bike. Gripping the handle bars, grappling with his composure, he remembered something Aksel had said about pushing through with the weight of your body to start it up, not from your hip down. His third kick was a success, the engine thundering into action.

Tom permitted himself a backwards glance only once as he set off out of the clearing. A black pick-up truck had been parked opposite the entrance, the two men not visible. He put his head down, eyes forward on the road, building up speed, glancing at the petrol gauge. The dial showed he had enough fuel to make it a fair distance from Pucón.

Down the hill at Caburgua he took a sharp right on to the 905, leaving the lake behind. Minutes later the black pick-up appeared in his wing mirror, closing the gap fast, a snarl from its engine echoing out through the trees. Tom put his foot down, willing the bike faster, knowing he couldn't outrun a 4x4. The truck soon pulled up level and through the helmet he got a good look at his pursuers: the nearer one, the driver, the man from Pucón, more like Sancho in appearance, the second, the brawler, now in the passenger seat, complexion pallid. They were staring out at him from behind the windscreen and open window, faces impassive, no aggression, as if he was another fly to be squashed, all in a day's work. Without warning the truck swerved, causing Tom to turn the handlebars on the Suzuki too sharply, almost sending him sprawling into a roadside ditch. He regained his balance, moving out in front of the truck, the driver hitting the accelerator until Tom could feel the bonnet bearing down on his back wheel. The next possible turn was still minutes away, an impossible three-hundred-degree left which would take him on a road to nowhere, back up towards the east side of the lake. Remaining on the 905 was about his only option. Tom swerved again, gentler this time, giving him some traction, stopping them from mowing him down. These guys weren't going to give in.

A red convertible was approaching on the left-hand side of the road. Tom pulled out in front of it, putting his foot down, approaching it head on. The convertible's horn blasted, both lanes now blocked, nowhere for it to turn. The driver flashed the car's lights in a panic. Tom glanced back at the driver of the truck, the Sancho lookalike's eyes narrowing, as if assessing the situation, questioning what Tom would do next. Gritting his teeth, Tom ducked further to the left, pushing the red convertible into the centre of the road, over the dividing lines. Red braked hard, causing

Sancho Jnr to slow up, and Tom took his chance then, sticking as far over to the left as he could without veering onto the grass verge. Red swerved centrally to avoid Tom, in turn causing Sancho to move out further to the right. The two cars clipped one another, sending the convertible, by far the lighter of the two, into a spin, causing Sancho Jnr to seemingly remove his foot from the accelerator. In response, Tom put his foot down again, sailing ahead, allowing him to gain a few precious seconds of reprieve. The truck was on him again soon enough, trying hard to plough him over. Tom weaved from side to side, sensing imminent death, visions of him falling headlong into the river rapids at the upcoming bridge clouding his vision. He pushed on, Sancho Jnr's engine growling, the sound of Tom's gasped breaths echoing inside the helmet. As the 905 merged into Ruta 199, he was met with a sight that could just about save his life: the standard traffic jam on the road into Pucón. He pulled out, followed the white lines, sped across the bridge over the rapids, steaming past cars to his right. Sancho Jnr did the same, close on his tail; all Tom needed was another car coming the other way. In the end, he couldn't have hoped for a better kind of vehicle: a lumbering yellow tractor, muddy bucket quaking as it trundled over concrete, up to twenty cars behind it moving at minimal speed. Sancho Jnr was forced to brake, the grass verge not wide enough for a go-around. Tom sailed through on the Suzuki, picking up speed again, leaving the pick-up and tractor for dust, following the line of traffic, the road cutting through a sea of yellow heather, past the local airport all the way to the roundabout at the entrance to Pucón, where all lines of traffic converged on the town.

He followed the road straight over, mentally bidding Pucón a bittersweet farewell, continuing forward on the 199, high above Lake Villarrica.

Tom allowed himself a stop at a service station, after a toll on Ruta 5, twenty kilometres south of Temuco. Removing his helmet, he swung his leg over the saddle and, against a setting sun, heaved the contents of his stomach into the undergrowth. Chile's capital, Santiago, was a good seven hundred kilometres north. It was an eight-hour journey in a car, let alone on a banged-up motorbike. He debated ditching the bike, hitch-hiking the rest of the way, but he thought better of it, not wishing to risk a black pick-up offering him a ride. If he pushed on, he could get to Santiago by three in the morning, get his head down before moving to Valparaíso on the coast and seeking out Aksel's contact. He knew he wouldn't sleep, even if he did stop for the night. He filled the bike with petrol at the service station, paid cash, bought a bottle of water, downed it and took a slash into the undergrowth.

Before getting back on the bike and replacing his helmet, he took a moment to catch his breath, to steady himself, the sound of the passing highway traffic reverberating in his ears.

So Capricorn wanted him dead after all.

Chapter 2

Bangkok, Thailand
22 December, 2016

Nashaly Akinyemi loitered within spitting distance of the seedy neon lights of Soi Cowboy, behind her the frenetic traffic junction of Sukhumvit and Asok. She was wearing a strappy vest and a baggy pair of boyfriend jeans, the strap from her tan leather bag slung crossways over her torso. The local humidity made her Afro hair doubly frizzy, sweat gathering between the tight ringlets on her scalp, the back of her neck drenched in perspiration. The throb of club beats drifted up towards the stars. Somebody had added a flashing Santa Claus to the display. She had laughed off several of the ladyboys' attempts to lure her into one of the venues, her mind fixated on tracking down one man: Dennis Geary.

She had covered the criminal case from the outset, in the days before Geary had been put on trial at Liverpool Crown Court for the murder of twenty-year-old Ashley Adamson-Leith. From the morning Ashley had been reported missing, right through until the trial had collapsed due to mishandled evidence by the police, to the moment thirty-six-year-old Geary had walked from court a free man; she had lived the story.

In her heart, Nash knew he was guilty. Geary's so-called

alibi had always been paper thin; his Thai wife claiming he had been with her at their house in Merseyside all night on the evening barmaid Ashley left work an hour early, only for her body to be found dumped two days later in a shallow grave. The bungled operation to collect evidence from her body following a heavy rainstorm led Geary's lawyers to argue that his status as a regular at the pub where she worked meant that there were other ways his DNA could have ended up on Ashley's clothes.

Nash puffed out her cheeks, all hope fading, when her phone started to vibrate in her pocket.

'My police contact called,' the voice at the other end of the line said. 'They're at a street food stall just off Silom Road. Meet me at Sala Daeng.'

Nash thanked him, racing across the uneven pavement towards Asok Skytrain station, taking the stairs two at a time. One photograph was all she needed. One photograph of Geary enjoying his freedom would make the front page of all the UK tabloids. There was pressure in the local community for a retrial, such was the level of vitriol against not only Geary, but his lying Thai bride, his parents and sister, and Merseyside Police.

Somchai, her contact at *The Bangkok Post* – a man who despite his forty-plus years still managed to resemble a twenty-year-old with a flawless complexion – was waiting for her beside the ticket barriers.

'This way,' he said in English, without greeting her, 'we don't have long.' Nash followed, pushing through bodies coming the other way, sweat drenching her torso. Somchai descended the steps to Silom Road, market sellers out in force, steam rising from manhole covers mixing with the sizzling clatters of the street food vendors. High season meant crowds of eager tourists were heading for the counterfeit watches and handbags sold at Patpong Market. Somchai was moving fast, weaving in and out of the people traffic. Nash danced on his tail, light on her feet, at the same time feeling around in her bag, fingers closing in on a telephoto lens. Three days of hanging around on street corners and she would be damned if she missed her chance.

The delicious aroma of pad thai filled her nostrils. She hadn't eaten since lunch. Somchai took a sharp left. Suddenly the road narrowed, the crowd thinning. There were trees overhead.

'This is Convent Road,' Somchai shouted back, without breaking pace. Moments later he came to an abrupt halt, turning and tugging at her elbow, yanking them both underneath the awning of an antiques shop, rusted bars protecting the windows. 'There,' Somchai said nodding up ahead. 'You see?'

Nash leaned out, gaze settling on a food cart up ahead, a hefty Thai female in a golden-yellow headscarf cooking up bowls of spicy noodles to order. Beyond the cart, under the light of the streetlamps in a makeshift seating area, Dennis Geary lounged on a red plastic stool, a bottle of Chang beer in hand, laughing in between mouthfuls. All the men wore Hawaiian shirts, Geary's wife in a gold-sequined vest, fake tits looking like they might burst free from the constraint. The parents were there too: Geary's mother all bronzer, leathery skin and badly dyed hair.

Nash unleashed the camera from her satchel, set to burst

mode. She captured as many images as she could before pulling out her phone as a backup and taking a few extras where the light felt better. She made sure to get as many faces as she could in one go. With a few taps of the screen, she had sent four shots securely back to London.

'You got it?' Somchai asked.

'I'm good,' Nash confirmed.

Somchai nodded once. 'Time to go.'

They were back out on the street, blending in with the crowd. Something nagged in her chest. How she would have loved to give Geary a piece of her mind.

Nash stopped dead, turning on her heel, walking back the other way.

'Hey.'

Nash's fingers yanked the beer from the Thai wife's grasp and poured the liquid contents into her lap. 'This is for all the lies you told.'

Within seconds, all the Hawaiian shirts were on their feet. The wife was shrieking. Nash brought the base of the bottle down with a smack on the table surface, unintentionally shattering the glass. Geary's father started cursing. She held onto it, jagged glass now her only protection, sweat breaking out on her upper lip. Geary's older brother was on her, bearing down so close she could smell the spicy shrimp on his breath.

'You're that journalist, right?'

'It doesn't matter who I am.'

He bared his teeth, laughing at her. 'Fuck off, why don't you? My brother is a free man.'

Geary's wife manhandled the brother out of the way. '*He no guilteee!*' she was screeching in Nash's face, the sentence resembling one long syllable, her teeth yellowing at the edges.

Nash straightened her spine, tossed the remnants of the bottle. 'You know as well as I do, that man was not with you all night.'

'*Fak yeuww!*' she shot back, shoving Nash backward, as in the distant background she could hear Somchai calling her name. She had caught Geary's eye. He was the only one holding back, the only one who looked perturbed by her appearance.

Nash backed off, flipped the brother the bird, causing a fresh wave of profanity to head her way. No one had thrown a punch at least. Dennis Geary was shaking his head, as though he'd believed his freedom had been guaranteed. The following day, the family of Ashley Adamson-Leith would see pictures of him living it up in Bangkok, increasing their heartache and tripling the level of anger aimed at Geary and his lying Thai bride.

Chapter 3

London, England
24 December, 2016

In Holland Park, Nash grappled with her keys, her entire body shivering. Outside it couldn't have been more than two or three degrees. When she had left England for Thailand four days earlier she had been in such a rush and, knowing her destination, hadn't bothered to pack a coat.

She hesitated, thought about ringing the bell before sliding her key into the lock. It was close to midnight on Christmas Eve and she hadn't bought a single gift. At her mother and stepfather's townhouse in Lansdowne Road there was a single light on in the study. Nash left her suitcase at the bottom of the stairs, tossing her tan leather satchel and keys on the hallway table. Her stepfather, Pete Cambridge, had likely already gone to bed, else he was sitting in a darkened corner somewhere clutching his third shot of whisky, nose buried in a history book. A light in the study meant her mother was still hard at work, the current Head of Insight News International rarely ever taking time off, perhaps three days in her lifetime, Nash contemplated, and even then only to give birth to her three children.

She knocked on the study door and leaned her head inside. Her mother's face was bathed in the glow emanating from her laptop, fingertips dancing across the keyboard. Mid-fifties, wearing a navy jumper over a white open-collared shirt, her hair was dyed ash blonde to conceal her natural grey. Diane had pale English skin, in complete contrast to Nash's dark coffee-coloured flesh inherited from her father. Nash cleared her throat. Diane Cambridge glanced up, peering at her over her glasses.

'Oh, it's you. I thought I heard something.'

Nash stepped inside the room. It felt stuffy, the radiator on too high. She felt awkward. 'Hello to you, too.'

Her mother sat back, removing the glasses, giving Nash the once-over. 'Is this a flying visit or will you be staying for Christmas?'

Nash gave a shrug. 'Is there room at the inn?'

'Your sisters are out on the King's Road. I made up a bed for you in case. So no, you're not banished to the stables.'

Nash looked to her feet. She needed a shower. 'Thanks, Di. I didn't bring any presents.'

'It's covered. I sent the last intern out to Liberty's with a list.'

A small smile spread across Nash's lips. At least her flaky half-sisters would be happy, their primary concern as to where their next overpriced accessory would be coming from. She shuffled closer to the desk.

'I see Dennis Geary made the front pages of the *Mirror* and *The Sun* today,' her mother hummed.

'I saw that.'

'In Thailand.'

'*Mmm.*'

'How *was* Bangkok?'

'Sultry.'

'Are you hungry?'

'Ravenous.'

'Well the fridge is fully stocked. Pete had a ball in the supermarket. Help yourself.'

'What are you working on?'

Diane puffed out her cheeks. 'Clearing a rather large backlog, I'm afraid.'

'Anything I can help with?'

Her mother looked to a pile of mail on her desk. 'Open all that? Christmas cards mainly, I think. Write me a list?'

Nash didn't have the heart to say she had meant something with more meat to it. She picked up the pile of mail and clutched it close to her chest. Picked up the top card and studied the elegant handwriting.

'It's good to have you home, my darling,' she heard her mother say before Nash was closing the door to the sound of Diane Cambridge *tap-tap*-tapping at her keyboard. 'Though I do wish you'd call me Mum.'

'Good to be home, *Di*,' Nash muttered in return.

Nash sat at the breakfast bar in semi-darkness, gorging on a plate of cold cuts and cheese, loading as much food in her mouth as would fit in one go. There was a bottle of red already open. She worked her way through the pile of Christmas cards sent to her mother from the great and good: newspaper editors, TV personalities, publishers and the like, some bland, some too personal, others verging on the intimate. She scribbled a short list on a Post-it, attention drawn to a larger yellow and blue cardboard envelope on the bottom of the pile. She teased it out. It wasn't like the others. She studied the couriered package for a moment, turning it over in her hands. It would seem odd to courier a Christmas card, yet whatever was inside was thin. The documentation said that it had come from San Carlos de Bariloche, in Argentina. There was a scrawled signature at the bottom, the name illegible. Nash frowned, tearing it open. Inside was a scrap of white paper, folded, together with a USB flash drive.

'Sabina Cordero,' she muttered out loud, reading the piece of paper. '*Aves de Las Colinas*. Find out what happened to her. Charlie Ebdon fathered her child. Anton equals dangerous.'

Her heartbeat quickened its pace. Keeping hold of the flash drive, she marched back through to the hallway, yanking her laptop from her satchel. Returning to the kitchen, she opened it, switching it on. The screen burst to life. Attaching the flash drive to a USB port, she ran a basic virus check. From what she could tell, the device was clean. Using the mouse, she opened up the contents. The flash drive contained a video file and two PDFs. Nash frowned, double-clicked on the video file, the plate of food abruptly forgotten.

She flew through the door to her mother's study, still clutching the laptop.

'Clare Buchanan,' she blurted, disregarding her mother's look of surprise. 'Do you remember her?'

Diane removed her glasses. 'Clare Buchanan,' she repeated. 'She disappeared in North London about ten years ago. Police never found out what happened to her as far as I know.'

'You've been sent a video. Clare Buchanan was a *whistleblower.*'

'I'm sorry, what?'

Nash walked round to her mother's side of the desk, swiping aside a pile of papers to make room for her laptop on the desk surface.

'It was in with the Christmas cards. You need to see this.'

Diane replaced her glasses. Nash hit play.

Clare's familiar image arrived on screen. Her face was drawn, skin pallid, brown hair in disarray. It was different from the carefree, pretty file photo that had gone out across the wires after she had been reported missing. This Clare looked nervous, scared. She read from a piece of paper she was holding, fingers trembling.

'My name is Clare Rose Buchanan,' she began on screen. 'My date of birth is the eighteenth of September, 1970. Today is Friday the eleventh of February, 2005. My address is 14a Sicily Street in Highbury Fields, London. I am currently Head of Elate International Charities Division in central London. This is a video statement I will be passing to the police in relation to my work at Elate.'

'Jesus,' Nash heard her mother whisper.

'I am making this video,' Clare continued, 'because I can no longer stay silent. I have recently become aware of my company – of Elate International's – financial dealings. In the face of natural disaster, where tragedy strikes and lives are lost, Elate's job has been to raise funds from the British public, the British taxpayers, to support local charities across the world and to give funds to those who really need it. In recent weeks I have seen documents that show that a large proportion of these funds are being creamed off to charities that on the surface look genuine, but in fact do not even exist. I believe the funds are being accumulated by Charles 'Charlie' Ebdon and his company investors, some of whom I also do not believe exist in the flesh. I believe the money is moved into offshore companies, to shell businesses for their own personal gain, and most never reaches the real victims. In recent weeks I have been followed and I believe my life may be in danger.'

Nash glanced towards Diane. Her mother's hands were covering her mouth. On the video, Clare was crying.

'The proof I have at this stage is limited, but I believe it is enough to warrant an open investigation. I will be sending my statement and the evidence I have to the Metropolitan Police and I plan to hand in my resignation from Elate in the coming days. I can no longer work for a company where syphoning off taxpayers' money has become standard practice. I can no longer stand to watch the likes of Charlie Ebdon get rich from tragedy and desperation across the world. I have to speak out.'

Clare leaned forward and switched off the camera that was recording her. The screen went black; the video file had come to an end.

Nash glanced down. Diane's chest was rising and falling.

'It came with this slip of paper. It was sent to you from Argentina.'

Her mother glanced down at the scribbled handwriting. 'Sabina Cordero,' she said. 'Who is that?'

'Who is she, and how does a video like this end up in South America?'

'Do you think she's alive?'

'Clare Buchanan?'

'She could have sent us this video herself,' her mother said.

'Unless she recorded it, then someone found out about it and killed her. She tried to blow the whistle and failed. Somebody got to her first.'

The two locked eyes for a moment, electricity almost palpable.

'If Clare didn't send it, then who did?'

'There's a name on the envelope. It says Thomas Holt.'

She handed the envelope to her mother. Diane studied the accompanying documentation. 'This was sent in November. Why haven't I seen this 'til now?'

Her mother proceeded to fire off some choice language regarding her latest set of interns before sobering. 'I remember her,' she continued. 'She stepped off a bus in Islington and no one ever saw her again. It was baffling, she vanished into thin air. Police couldn't locate a shred of physical evidence, apart from her phone which was wiped clean of prints. I remember the theory from the police was that she got off the bus two stops earlier than normal, but nobody could work out why that was. There was a man on the bus, someone the police never managed to identify.'

Diane Cambridge inhaled, like a bull warming up to a charge. She had already started pacing. 'Why not go straight to the police with this?'

Nash was staring at her. 'Let me have this. Let me find out what happened to Clare Buchanan.'

'Darling, this is…' her mother said. 'You get too involved. I should call—'

'Who? Who should you call? I came to you with this. You wouldn't have found this if it wasn't for me.'

'Nashaly,' her mother whispered.

'Stop doubting me.'

'I don't doubt you, my darling.'

'Stop calling me that. Treat me like an employee!'

'Fine.' Her mother stepped forward. 'Know this. We went after the money. There were rumours about Charlie Ebdon's finances. We found nothing. I had a guy going through the Panama Papers with a fine-tooth comb for months trying to unearth something on Ebdon. We came up blank. So I will let you investigate this. But if you're going to be the one to do it, you'll do it with Miles to back you up.'

Nash's stomach performed a flip. 'What? The Italian guy?'

'He's not Italian, he's from Middlesex.'

'No.'

'He's good. He could help you.'

'I don't like him.'

A smile tugged at her mother's lips. 'You don't like anyone.'

Nash stood her ground. Diane looked back at the laptop. 'Find this woman, Sabina Cordero. Find out who and where she is and what she has to do with Clare Buchanan. If Clare was a whistleblower and she died as a result... now there's a story the British people would want to read about. And tell me more about this Thomas Holt.'

Chapter 4

Santiago, Chile
3 January, 2017

In the small hours Tom had found himself a bed in a hostel in Bellavista. Twenty thousand pesos per night in the height of the Chilean summer. Together with the laptop and his passport, he was in possession of a small amount of clothing, running kit, one toothbrush and a total of five hundred dollars' worth of local currency. From what Aksel had told him, he would need at least four thousand US to get him on to a ship to Panama.

He was awake by nine, sleep having eluded him, the faces of the Belosi brothers – as he was now calling them – still haunting his thoughts.

Sancho Belosi had been living in Uruguay. He had been instrumental in organising a power cut so that Tom and Anil had been able to get into the compound at *Aves de Las Colinas* to rob Sabina Cordero's safe. Belosi was a psychopath. It would make sense that he would have two sons who were similarly inclined. Had Belosi sent his sons after him the moment he had left Buenos Aires? How had they traced him to Pucón? Did they know he had been in Bariloche, and that he had sent two parcels from there? The lawyer, Denham, had put him in touch with Belosi, now Denham was dead.

He changed into his running kit. He was staying at the foot of San Cristóbal Hill. A statue of the Virgin Mary was at the top and accessible by foot. He needed time to think, consider his next move.

Capricorn wanted him dead, that much was clear.

Anton, Capricorn's attack dog, and the man who had almost killed him back in Buenos Aires, would have ordered Belosi after him the moment Anton realised he was no longer in possession of the laptop.

And what of Becca? Half-way through his run up San Cristóbal Hill, where the track turned to road, he came to a halt, sweat pouring off his neck and chest. He bent over double and pictured her face.

Had Anton killed her? Had they murdered her for lying? She knew he had watched Clare's video statement on the laptop. She knew what was at stake. Yet she had lied about it to Anton's face. He still couldn't work out why, so unlikely that the red-headed thief would want to protect him, leading Anton straight to them in their hotel room in Buenos Aires.

On the hill, he spat on the pavement in disgust. He despised himself for thinking about her, for ever having fallen for her games. He pushed on to the top, witnessing a brilliant blue sky marred only by layer of yellow polluted haze that eclipsed the majestic snow-covered caps of the Andes. He knew he had to get to Valparaíso on the coast, and get out of Chile as soon as possible.

First, he needed money.

Second, he needed to contact Diane Cambridge in London.

Back in Bellavista, Tom gave himself a clean shave and

trimmed his hair. He asked the receptionist to direct him to a shopping mall and took a walk across town to the Costanera Center, one of the few skyscrapers in the country's capital, cap pulled low on his brow. He was surrounded by people with dark features, making two burly Argentines hard to spot. He purchased a late lunch and two international calling cards for use in a public payphone, of which Chile, at least, still seemed to still be a fan. He continued on foot, overly warm in the summer heat, before descending into Tobalaba metro station, the concourse below street level dank and dingy and heaving with people, but it was an area where he could make a call without being noticed. He had two phone numbers written down in his pocket, courtesy of the receptionist being more than happy to allow him to carry out two simple internet searches using her smartphone.

He punched in the digits on the international calling card, followed by the first phone number. He pressed the handset closer to his ear, struggling to hear over the roar of background noise, the movement of trains below him rushing through the station. There was a crackling sound before the phone started to ring.

'Good afternoon, Bentley Atherton estate agents, how may I help you?' a plummy voice answered at the other end.

Tom cupped the receiver. 'Hi. I need to speak to Christian Holt, please,' he said.

'I'm afraid Mr Holt is with a client at the moment. Can I take a message and he'll call you right back?'

'Actually this is a little urgent. Can you tell him Tom is on the line?'

'I, uh—' the girl began. 'It's not possible to call you back?'

'Like I said, urgent. Can you get him?'

'*Umm*, you said your name was Tom?'

'He knows who I am.'

There was a series of bleeps as she put him on hold. Tom waited, glancing around at blank faces inside the concourse, shifting his weight.

'Tom?' a cheerful voice came over the line. 'Ah, Tom, let me go into an office and we can talk privately.'

He didn't have a chance to respond, the beeping sound of being placed on hold returning.

Moments later, he heard the sound of a different handset being picked up and his brother Christian's voice back on the line, the professional tone dropped for one that he actually recognised.

'Nice of you to drop in, you complete motherfucking waste of space. I am talking to a *client*.'

'I need your help.'

'Help? Guess what, big brother? I have no interest in giving you any help. Where are you? Where the *fuck* have you been the last six months?'

He had to stop his voice from cracking. 'I can't tell you that, I'm sorry.'

He pictured his brother in a tailored pinstripe suit and tie, standing in a cordoned-off booth of a bland estate agent's office – the place where they usher clients to talk the money and the mortgages – all shop-bought framed landscapes, grey walls and matching carpet tiles.

'Do you have any idea what you've put us through? You *disappeared. Off the grid.* Our mother is worried sick. Let me paint a picture for you. Christmas at her house, she laid a place for you at the table, so convinced you would walk through the door at the last minute. And guess what, you couldn't even be fucking bothered to call and let us know you weren't dying in a ditch somewhere.'

'Chris, I don't have long. I need money.'

'What?'

'I need three thousand dollars. I can pay you back, I swear. I need to get to Panama.'

'Panama? Oh now we're talking. You're with Dad, is that it? You've both gambled everything away?'

'It's complicated to explain, but I swear one day I will. I'm not with Dad but I need to find him. Can you wire me some money?'

'It doesn't cost anyone three thousand dollars to get to Panama in cattle class.'

'It does when you need a fake passport.'

Christian went silent. Tom pressed the receiver hard against his ear, so he could hear his brother's laboured breathing. 'What have you got into? I should hang up right now.'

'Chris. You're all I have. You may save my life.'

'Where are you?'

'Santiago. In Chile. There's a Western Union on Avenida Providencia. I need the money there for tomorrow.'

Quiet again. He pictured his little brother twisting the phone cord in between his fingers. Of the three brothers, which included Jake, Christian had always been the nicer one of the three of them; the baby everybody thought was a sweetheart. But as a kid he used to get anxiety, one of the side effects of your parents divorcing when you were only nine years old. They had been close once.

'You promise me I'm not paying off a gambling debt?'

'I swear it.'

Another silence. 'When are you coming back?'

'Not yet. There's something important I have to do. I can't tell you about it now.'

More silence. When he spoke again, the voice coming down the line was the one he recognised from their teenage years. 'I'll do it first thing in the morning,' Christian said. 'Three thousand in dollars. I don't think I have much more than that. Can you call me here for the details?'

Tom closed his eyes. 'Yes,' he whispered into the handset. 'Thank you. I need one more thing.'

'What?'

'I need Dad's address in Panama.'

'I haven't spoken to him in years. I don't even know if he's still there. It's an office address, I think.'

'Whatever you've got. I'll call you tomorrow at noon, London time.'

He hung up. The conversation had gone a fraction better than he had anticipated. He thought about his mother, a wave of guilt washing over him. He should have called her from Uruguay.

He glanced over his shoulder, moving to the next payphone, and pulled a second international calling card from his pocket. He entered the pin code, then dialled the number on the piece of paper. His call was picked up by an automated answering system, asking him to dial the extension of the person he was calling, or to press zero to speak to an operator.

He did the latter, watching the passing faces out of the corner of his eye, pulling his cap down and sinking further back into the shadows, back to the wall.

He waited through the hold music until the phone was answered by a female voice. 'Good afternoon, you're through to Insight News International, how may I direct your call?'

'I need to speak to Diane Cambridge, please. It's very important.'

'I can put you through to her assistant.'

He opened his mouth to object but it was too late. Seconds later, an older female voice answered.

'I need to speak to Diane Cambridge, please,' Tom said again, 'It's urgent.'

'Who shall I say is calling?'

'Tom Holt.'

'I'll put you through to her voicemail,' the woman clipped.

Tom felt his shoulders slump. *You are through to the voicemail of Diane Cambridge. Please leave your message after the tone and press the hash key when finished.*

There sounded a long *beeeep*. He didn't speak, just gripped the receiver and realised he hadn't thought through exactly what he wanted to say, or not say.

'My name is Tom Holt,' he said. 'I need to talk to you about Clare Buchanan.' He read out the number printed at the top right hand corner of the payphone, ensuring that he included a +56, the international dialling code for Chile. He finished by saying, 'I'll wait by this number for thirty minutes.'

He hung up, then picked up the receiver and redialled the number for Insight News International. He followed the same steps, arriving back at Diane's receptionist. Once she'd finished speaking, he said, 'It's Tom Holt. I've left a voicemail. Whatever she is doing, you might want to pull her out of it. Tell her she's got half an hour to respond.'

He slammed the handset back into its cradle, hand moving instinctively to his left wrist to check the time on his watch, only his fingers brushed up against bare flesh. He grimaced. She had taken it in Argentina. The night they had made love and he'd woken to find Anton sat in their hotel room pointing a gun in his face; Becca fully dressed and robotically unresponsive stood by Anton's side like his faithful lap-dog. The two of them had already left the hotel by the time he'd discovered his watch was missing.

And now *she* had it.

Waiting by the bank of phones, he considered his next move. Tobalaba metro concourse was busy with the lunch-time rush, unfamiliar Chilean faces all blending into one. The sight made him nervous. He took note of the time on the wall clock inside the ticket office. Diane had thirty minutes.

When the phone started ringing seconds later he didn't believe it. He lifted the handset, hearing voices at the other end.

'Hello?' a woman's voice said. 'Mr Holt? You're speaking to Diane Cambridge. With me is journalist Nashaly Akinyemi. You're on conference call. How are you?'

It was some moments before he spoke. 'I've been better,' he said. 'Yesterday two men tried to kill me. I don't know who they were but I know they're connected to Charlie Ebdon somehow.'

'You think he ordered them after you?'

'Yes, I believe so.'

A different voice came on the line. He tried to remember her name. Nashaly. 'Are you alright?'

'Yes. You've seen the video?'

'Yes,' the same voice confirmed. 'We've seen it.'

A sense of relief washed over him. That he was no longer alone in this. 'When I sent it to you I also sent it to DCI Neil Rawlins at the Met Police. I was expecting a statement, a re-opening of Clare Buchanan's case, but there's been nothing.'

The voices went silent. 'We've seen nothing to that effect. You think the police have buried it?'

'Rawlins, he asked me to send the package to his personal address. It's possible.'

'Tom,' Nashaly said. 'We've been in touch with Sabina Cordero. I leave for Montevideo tomorrow. Can you tell us your connection to her? How did you get hold of the video?'

'Did she tell you what happened to her?'

'No. She won't talk over the phone.'

'I signed a gag order. When you speak to her, you'll understand.'

'Where are you now?'

'I'm in Santiago in Chile. My plan is to move on to Panama. Try and get information on Ebdon's finances. Track down the money trail.'

'We combed the Panama Papers,' Diane said. 'Searching for Ebdon's hidden wealth. We found nothing.'

'He uses a different name. Solomon Capricorn.'

'How do you know that?'

Tom glanced around the concourse, wiping the sweat from the back of his neck. He didn't want to drag Becca into this. 'I can't tell you that right now.'

'What else can you tell us about the video?' Nashaly asked.

'Clare says she was being followed. I can have a stab at who was following her. His name is Anton. I don't know a surname, I met him only once. Forty-odd, tall, with dark hair parted in the middle. He's got a rugby player's nose, heavy brow. When I met him he was carrying a gun; sooner kill you than look at you. He had an odd accent, he didn't sound entirely English. He works for Capricorn, I think. Does his dirty work, maybe. I don't know where he is, or where he's based.'

'Do you think this man could have murdered Clare Buchanan?'

'If he knew she was planning to give information about Capricorn to the police, then yes I believe he's capable of killing her. That or Capricorn ordered him to.'

Nashaly spoke again. 'Tom, forgive me for asking, but who are you? How did you get tied up in all this?'

He fell silent. Admitting his identity made it all seem tangible. That he had picked a side, chosen his fight. That he had chosen to expose Capricorn, and reveal to the world what happened to Clare, whilst risking his life in the process. He thought about Anil, how he would never see his young daughter grow up. Capricorn might not have pulled the trigger, but he was the man ultimately responsible for Anil's death.

'I was security consultant. Before that in the Army. I was sacked from a firm called Vlok Petersen in South Africa. Look it up. I was offered a job I can't tell you about by a lawyer named Albert Denham. Albert Denham is dead, assaulted in South London. I believe a targeted assault.'

More mutterings, then Diane Cambridge's voice. 'How can we contact you?'

'You can't. I'll call you. Be careful who you talk to. Do not be seen with Sabina Cordero. Consider me your confidential source.'

Nashaly was still firing questions when he hung up the receiver, fingertips tingling. It was all real.

He steadied his breathing then took the stairs to ground level, taking a different route back to Bellavista. At the hostel, he put his head down, tried to sleep, waking in time for dinner at a local bistro: a bowl of ceviche and some grilled sea bass, washed down with a couple of artisanal brands of beer. The following day, he would call Christian, who all being well would have wired him some cash.

Now a couple of journalists in London were investigating Charlie Ebdon, aka Solomon Capricorn.

He would keep picturing the man's face, and telling him, *I'm coming for you.*

Chapter 5

Montevideo, Uruguay
5 January, 2017

The flight from London Heathrow to Montevideo, via Madrid, took over sixteen hours. Taking into account the two-hour delay in the Spanish capital, and including check-in times and transfers, they had been travelling for close to twenty-two hours. Nash stood by Miles Ferretti's side in a deserted baggage hall at Carrasco International Airport, the walls a shade of bright orange, waiting for a motionless carousel to spit out their suitcases from the baggage abyss.

'This place is a bit like the arse end of nowhere, don't you think?' Ferretti said, hands in his pockets.

Nash didn't reply. Conversation for the duration of the journey had been anodyne. She had updated him in the briefest of terms. Next to Miles, she felt tense, her mouth dry and her body grimy.

He'd arrived at Heathrow wearing a pair of black ill-fitting jeans paired with scrappy trainers, dark hair sticking up and his jawline bristling with stubble; Ferretti was renowned in the Insight offices for his scruffy, low-key appearance. His leather satchel had seen better days. He'd changed his glasses since their last meeting, or at least the tortoiseshell frames she remembered had been folded on the nightstand the morning after. Nash wrinkled her nose at the memory. If the wheels of the Insight gossip wagon had travelled as far as her mother's door, then her mother was keeping silent.

'I need coffee,' he muttered.

Her mother had favoured Miles Ferretti since he had somehow managed to muscle his way into the Consortium of Investigative Journalists at the tender age of twenty-seven, prior to the Panama Papers bombshell, becoming an overnight sensation in the Insight offices.

Ferretti wanted another stab at Charlie Ebdon, or so her mother said.

Keeping her eyes on the carousel, Nash recalled a balmy August night six months prior, the taste of his lips, the way he'd pressed his inexperienced hands into the small of her back, and the ugly smirks that had come her way in the office the following afternoon.

The baggage carousel whirred into action, bringing her back to her senses.

In the arrivals hall they were greeted by Feliciano Ledesma. Sabina Cordero's husband was a tall, slender man, with a triangular-shaped face, long fingers, elegantly coiffed hair and a closely cropped beard, not quite the dark-skinned Argentine she had envisaged. He wore tight-fitting jeans, leather shoes, an open-collared shirt and jacket, like something lifted out of a men's magazine.

'Welcome to Uruguay,' Feliciano greeted them, in English, shaking Miles by the hand and kissing her on the cheek, throwing her off guard.

When Nash had finally contacted Sabina Cordero, via her husband, a surgeon at the British Hospital in Montevideo, the woman had answered in pitch-perfect English with a syrupy Spanish accent. 'If you can come to Uruguay,' she'd said, 'then I will tell you everything.'

On the plane she and Ferretti had discussed a list of key questions, based around Clare Buchanan's video statement and what she had gleaned from Tom Holt's phone call. Other than that, it felt like they were walking in blind.

'How was your flight?' Feliciano asked, taking control of her suitcase.

Nash offered him a polite smile. 'Only one of us likes to fly.'

She watched as Ledesma glanced towards a pale-looking Miles. 'Oh. That's too bad.'

Ledesma drove a white Honda CRV with not a scratch on it. It was twenty-six degrees out, Ferretti tugging at his jacket the moment they stepped out into the car park under a cloudless sky. Ledesma explained that the house his family lived in was only a short drive away.

'I should probably tell you,' he said as they drove along a dual carriageway, overtaking a car whose bonnet was held in place by a piece of rope tied to the side door handles, 'my wife is not at her best. Her brother, Nico, passed away in hospital in Buenos Aires soon after Christmas. He was in a coma and never regained consciousness.'

'What happened to him?' Nash asked in surprise. In the back seat Miles leaned forward.

'Back in November he was attacked after dark. The police said there were no witnesses. Nothing was stolen, not even

44

his wallet. But he suffered a head wound. My wife believes it is all connected.'

'Connected to what?' Nash asked.

He let out a laugh, as though surprised she didn't know. 'To the robbery.'

For a moment, a fog cleared. 'You were robbed.'

'I thought you knew that.'

She glanced back at Miles. They exchanged looks. Was that the job Holt had been talking about? 'We really don't know much at all.'

'It seems the timing would fit her theory. The robbery took place back in November whilst we were at the hospital in Argentina. I am less convinced than my wife. Buenos Aires is a dangerous city these days and Nico was no saint. It's why we came to Uruguay in the first place.'

'You think she'll be willing to talk about it?'

'The police here in Montevideo, they have done nothing about the break-in. Since we received your phone call, Sabi has been desperate to speak with you.'

Her head was pounding. Dehydration most likely, Nash considered, as she stared from the window at passing cars sporting some more interesting modifications: a back window replaced with a bin bag and some badly applied sticky tape. They had turned off the dual carriageway. A sign had read *Aves de Las Colinas*, a photograph of a family out playing some golf with a large blue house in the background. She remembered the name. She looked out at the trees lining the road, tall and spindly with silver bark. The car plunged downwards into another pothole.

'Sorry,' Ledesma apologised. 'These roads used to be dirt

tracks. Then they paved them over but they didn't do a good job. They can't cope with all the construction vehicles for all the new housing.'

'Is it all gated communities out here?' Miles asked from the back.

'Yes, three or four of them. Montevideo, like Buenos Aires, can still be a dangerous place. Out here you think you'll be safe but it seems your house can still be broken into.'

They passed a row of shops, rustic looking, two of the larger housing communities on the left, all surrounded by an electrified security fence. Nash took note of the large houses, glamorous-looking, some painted white with flat roofs, light and airy, the sort of house that would look completely out of place in England, their style more Californian. At the front gate to *Las Colinas*, they were asked to show their passports. Feliciano opened the boot of the car. A security guard gave a cursory glance inside. On entry, the road was smooth. They were driving through a golf course, people driving around in buggies, houses visible in the distance. After a roundabout Feliciano came to a halt on the road, seemingly for no reason. Nash craned her neck. A tarantula, brown and furry, was creeping its way across the concrete.

Ledesma parked the car outside a modern, sprawling property, spread out over a double plot. It was larger than its immediate neighbours, situated well away from the perimeter fence, in the middle of the compound, though it was hard to tell the size of the housing complex surrounded by green fairways. Sabina Cordero emerged from the front door whilst they were still in the car. She looked older than the picture they had located on the internet, yet stylish with a glowing complexion, her skin dark and tanned against the light shade of her clothes. Her eyes were tired. Nash got out of the car to meet her.

'Mrs Cordero,' she said with a smile, holding out her hand. 'My name is Nash.'

Sabina ignored her hand, instead clasping her fingers around Nash's upper arms, giving them a squeeze and planting a firm kiss on her right cheek. Her skin was tinged with expensive perfume. '*Hola, buen día*,' she said, in her lilting tone, 'Please, you must call me Sabi.'

She ushered them both inside, their luggage remaining in the boot of the car. The interior of the house was equally impressive, open high-beamed ceilings, a split level leading down to an open kitchen and living area, glass windows on almost every side and a separate door to an upstairs area. A sizeable bull mastiff lay docile on the grass in the back garden, which had its own pool and view of the fairway. Sabina had laid out breakfast on a large dining table: a fruit platter, cereals, fresh juice and sweet croissants accompanied by gooey caramel, what Sabina called *dulce de leche*. Nash tucked in hungrily as Ledesma bid them farewell and left for work in a different 4x4. Nash got the impression that Sabina Cordero wasn't much for eating, judging by the size of her waist.

Sabi made fresh coffee. Miles slurped his, wiping his mouth with the back of his hand, causing Nash to give him a look. She watched him reach into his bag and pull out a notebook, the one they had used to brainstorm on the plane.

Nash took out her phone, setting it to voice record.

'Would you be happy if we start before we go to our hotel?' she asked. 'I'd like to record this if you don't mind.'

Sabi lowered herself into the chair opposite, for a moment wearing a troubled expression. She grasped her hair into a ponytail, twisting it at the nape of her neck. On release, the hair unravelled down her back. 'Of course,' she half-smiled. 'I've kept silent long enough. It is time.'

Nash exchanged looks with Miles, beginning the recording. 'Perhaps you could start in November, the time of the robbery.'

Sabina took a breath, wiping stray tears. 'I apologise,' she said. 'It's been an emotional few months.'

'Take your time,' Nash said.

She relaxed her shoulders. 'I was in Buenos Aires. My brother, Nicolás, he was in hospital in a coma. Whilst I was there I received a call from the alarm company here in Montevideo. I set the alarm every time I go out and again at night. The company noticed that the alarm had been unset for three days, from the early hours of eleventh of November and that it hadn't been set since. I called the guardhouse here at the compound. They sent someone over. They confirmed that the back door was damaged and that there was some small evidence of a break in.'

'What do you mean by small evidence?' Nash said.

'Feliciano flew back from Buenos Aires the next day. It wasn't until he got to the house that he confirmed someone had got into our safe. But apart from that back door behind you, there were no other signs of forced entry.'

Nash and Miles had turned around in their seats, looking

over at the back door leading to the garden. It was surrounded by white PVC with a long glass pane.

'Did the robbers break into the compound? Or were they already here?'

She offered him a shrug. 'Shortly after midnight, on the eleventh of November, there was a series of power cuts. The authorities believe the robbers used that time, when the compound was in darkness, to get inside. They believe they may have come through a water pipe, which has since been blocked up.'

'And where is your safe?' Nash asked.

Sabi pointed. 'Through that door. A door which was locked when I left for Buenos Aires and still locked when my husband returned. And only I, and my brother Nico in Buenos Aires, had the key.'

Miles raised an eyebrow. 'And what about the safe?' Nash asked her.

Sabi gave a shrug. 'It had been opened and closed. They had the code. The safe was emptied out completely. They took everything they found in there.'

'Who knew the code?'

She seemed to laugh, threw her hands up in the air. 'We were stupid. I thought having that door would give me an extra layer of protection. And only I and my husband knew the code. But the code to the safe was the same as the intruder alarm. This is why the police here, they claim the whole thing was an inside job.'

'How so?' Miles asked, scribbling a few notes in his notepad.

'Until just after the robbery I employed a maid. Her name

was Manuela. She was from Paraguay. I left our dog with her when we travelled to Buenos Aires to see Nico. On our return, she had vanished. Left the dog with her neighbour. Gone. When I asked, I was told she and her daughter and her grandchildren had returned to Asunción. She never even said goodbye. The police think she gave somebody the code, that she could have easily seen me punch the numbers into the alarm keypad.'

'But that wouldn't explain the key to the security door,' Nash commented, helping herself to some strawberries and glancing over at Miles, 'would it?'

'It would have been impossible for Manuela to copy this key,' Sabina said, pulling out a chain link necklace from beneath her top, on which hung a sizeable key, bronze in colour with a black top. 'I wear it all the time; I don't take it off, even for the shower. The only time I take it off is at night when Manu has already taken the shuttle bus and gone home. She could never have got her hands on this key.'

Miles held out his hand. 'Do you mind?' he asked, and she looped the chain over her head.

Miles got up, walked over to the door. Nash followed. It was heftier looking than the others. Miles was studying it, taking note of its thickness, of the bolts, the lock mechanism, sliding his fingers down the side, looking for signs that another implement could have been used to pry it open. She wondered if Tom Holt had been here, if he was the man responsible.

'This is a purpose-built security door,' Miles muttered, more to himself. He sniffed. 'There is no getting through this bad boy without the key'.

Nash turned and looked to Sabi, who had wandered over.

'Sabi, if you don't mind me asking,' Nash began, making eye contact. 'Why would you install a door like this in your house? Why did you wear the key? Why were you so determined to protect yourself?' She paused. 'What was in the safe?'

She watched her. Sabina's entire body language had altered. She was no longer the relaxed female who had greeted Nash at the front door, neither was she the shaken, emotional woman who had sat down at the table to give her side of the story. This was another side to her. She was angry now, pacing. She hugged her waist.

'When the police came, I told them there was eighty thousand US dollars in the safe. That much was true. I didn't tell them about the other two items.'

'The video made by Clare Buchanan,' Nash said.

She turned. 'You know about it? How?'

'Someone sent us a copy,' Nash confirmed. 'It's why we're here. We went through all the records of Clare Buchanan's disappearance. Your name is not mentioned once. We want you to tell us how you know Clare, and why you had that video in your safe.'

Sabi's eyes glistened. She tried to smile, but it evaporated as her bottom lip began to quiver. 'I never met her,' she said. She took a moment to compose herself. 'Not once. But I knew who she was. I knew her by her reputation.'

Nash noted the steely determination in her gaze. 'For you to fully understand,' Sabina sighed, 'I need to start from the beginning.'

Chapter 6

Montevideo, Uruguay
5 January, 2017

Nash yawned, padding barefoot down the corridor at the Hotel Cottage in Montevideo, knocking on Miles's door. She wore jeans and a cropped cotton vest. In one hand she carried her phone, in the other a bottle of Uruguayan Tannat from Sabi and Feliciano's wine collection. It was 8 p.m., 11 p.m. in the UK. On arrival at the hotel in the afternoon, they had crashed out. Jetlag had made her mind fuggy.

She caught his look as he opened the door, the base of his neck flushing crimson, pushing the black frames of his glasses up his nose. Nash resisted the urge to roll her eyes. On that August night she'd found herself going back to his flat in Hoxton, he'd asked about the death of her father, of all things, as though curious as to why Diane Cambridge would have been attracted to a hulking Nigerian dude.

'Don't tell me you weren't the teensiest bit surprised when you discovered the daughter of Diane Cambridge wasn't whiter than white,' Nash had quipped.

'I knew she had fallen pregnant at a young age,' had been his self-conscious response. 'But she married him, didn't she? Your father.'

'Yes, Miles. She married my dad, the colossal black man.'

In the hotel room, it didn't go unnoticed that Miles looked to the floor as she entered, as though unwilling to acknowledge their shared history, however brief. She felt relieved, handing him the bottle of wine. She walked to the window, staring out into inky blackness of the River Plate Delta, two small lights from ships blinking out on the horizon, the sand at the top of Carrasco beach visible under the lights of the coastal road which Sabina told her was called *La Rambla*.

'So what did you think?' she asked.

'I think she has no reason to lie,' Miles said. 'What about you?'

'I didn't expect to feel sorry for her,' Nash shrugged.

Miles was opening the wine.

The Panama Papers had been released in April 2016. Ferretti had worked long nights and weekends, pouring over reams and reams of data that might implicate Charlie Ebdon and his company Elate International in corrupt practices, in tax evasion, in dodgy dealings along with all the other celebrities, shady businessmen and world leaders who had been swept up in the leak. Yet it had all come to nothing. No one had managed to unearth a connection to Charlie Ebdon, or Elate, and there wasn't single shred of evidence to money tied up in Central America or the Caribbean. Either the money wasn't there, or Ebdon had gone to great lengths to cover it up.

Yet they now knew from Tom Holt that Ebdon had been using another identity: Solomon Capricorn, a name that screamed alias if ever there was one.

Her mother said that the story had recaptured Miles's

interest. That he possessed a combination of hunger, ambition and determination that could aid her investigation. Looking across at him struggling to open the wine bottle, the memory of his pale white body over hers still lingering, Nash remained unconvinced.

'I was twenty-four years old when I finished my studies in Buenos Aires,' Sabi began, nestled in her white sofa, as Nash pushed her phone a few inches closer across the surface of the table. 'I decided I wanted to study in London. I had enough English to get by. I was accepted to study at the London School of Economics.'

'What year was this?' Nash asked.

'Two thousand and two,' Sabi replied. 'The September. In the October, a man came to the university to give a lecture. He was introduced as Charles Ebdon. Everyone knew who he was, everyone except me, of course. My friend told me at the time he was a businessman, an entrepreneur, he had a large company, Elate International. She was… impressed by him. She insisted we go and talk to him after the lecture. We introduced ourselves, he barely looked at me and I thought that was it. We went home. Two days later a man came to my door. He said he was a lawyer. He told me that Mr Ebdon had been impressed with me and wanted to talk to me about Argentina, and would I be willing to talk to him. So I gave the lawyer my phone number.'

Nash and Miles exchanged a look. 'The lawyer,' Miles asked. 'Do you remember his name?'

'Of course,' Sabi replied. 'It was the first of several visits. His name was Albert Denham.'

Miles's eyes shot up to meet Nash's stare. She felt her heartbeat quicken. 'Sabi, Albert Denham was beaten to death on a London street back in November. Not long after your house was broken into.'

Sabi closed her eyes, shaking her head, expression incredulous.

'Please, continue,' Nash continued. 'What happened with Charles Ebdon?'

'The first time we met, alone, the two of us, we were in a London pub. It was in Chelsea, I don't remember the name. I felt awkward. He was *significantly* older than me. My friend told me he was married with two kids, but I told her it was strictly business.'

'But it wasn't,' Nash said.

Sabi's lips twisted. 'For a few minutes, maybe. He made his intentions very clear from the beginning.'

'So you had an affair.'

Sabi averted her eyes, face clouding over. In her expression there was contempt. 'He was charming. I had no money. He bought me gifts. I was twenty-four. I'd had one boyfriend back in Argentina. I had no experience of men. At first I tried to resist, but… I was flattered. He was persistent in his pursuit of me. I told nobody. The first night I spent with him was in a flat near Victoria Station, about a month after we first met. After that he gave me the money to rent a place in Mayfair, which I did. And by that time… I was in love with him.'

'And a couple of years later you got pregnant.'

Sabi's eyes flashed. 'You saw the birth certificate?'

'The person who sent us the video told us. So the birth certificate was in your safe.'

'Where is it now?'

'We don't know.'

'Is this the person who robbed my house?' Sabi spat.

'We don't know that either. We're trying to put the pieces together.'

'Those two things. I kept them in my safe. Because I knew I would never be able to escape.'

Miles looked up. 'What went wrong between you and Ebdon? Why did things come to an end? Was it because of the pregnancy?'

'No. It was before that. About six months into the affair, I picked up my first shadow.'

Nash checked the recording on her phone. 'What do you mean, shadow?'

'A figure would follow me. Every time I left the house, everywhere I went. Charlie told me it was for my own protection. It drove me crazy. He was obsessed with the idea that I somehow wasn't safe alone.'

'Did you ever speak to the man? Who was he?'

'I never spoke to him. He was always *there*. In the background. But never close enough to talk to.'

'What did he look like?'

'He was tall. Black hair. He had this habit of wearing a long black overcoat. He had a big nose, squashed into his face. It looked like it had been broken.'

Nash exchanged another look with Miles. 'Did you ever find out his name? Was it Anton?'

Sabi's eyes narrowed. 'No. But that does sound familiar.'

'How old was he?'

She shrugged. 'He was about my age, I think. If I rode on

the London Underground, he would be in the same carriage. If I went to a party he would wait outside on the street. And yet now, nothing has changed.'

Miles. 'How so?'

She looked flustered. 'Wait. Let me finish. About a year after I met Charles, I told him that I'd had enough. We argued too much about the man he insisted follow me. I ended the relationship, flew back to Buenos Aires. I thought he would accept my decision. For a while, things were quiet. I tried to start again, but I was weak. Cried for about a month. Then the phone calls started coming. The emails. He begged me to go back to London.'

Nash cleared her throat. 'So you went back.'

'Not straight away. But yes, in 2004, I went back. I was offered a teaching job. This time there was no shadow. I didn't see that man again. Things were good between us, or so I thought. I got pregnant, by accident. The same year as his wife was expecting their third child.'

'Was he angry?'

'Very. He made it clear to me he thought I should get rid of it.'

'And when was your daughter born?'

'The day after Christmas Day. 2004.'

Miles wrote down the date. 'The same day as the earthquake,' he said under his breath.

Sabi's eyes glistened. 'Yes.'

Nash frowned.

'The Indian Ocean earthquake and tsunami,' Miles reminded her. 'The disaster that Clare Buchanan was raising money for. Clare went missing two months later in February 2005.'

Nash paused the voice recording, started a new one, the breath catching in her throat. 'Sabi, can you tell us what you know about Clare Buchanan?'

They sat on Miles's hotel room bed, feet dangling off the edge, sipping wine.

'So Sabina Cordero knew who Clare Buchanan was, she just didn't *know* her,' Miles surmised as they listened back to the voice recording. 'They never met in person because no one knew Sabi even existed as Ebdon's mistress, apart from Ebdon and the shadow slash henchman who may or may not be Anton X.'

Nash shared the last dregs of wine between their two glasses, eyelids drooping. 'She overhears a conversation between Charlie Ebdon and another unidentified male about Clare's intentions to blow the whistle about where the funds were really going. She takes a USB stick from his briefcase as collateral and the next day flees on a flight back to Buenos Aires with their baby daughter and the original birth certificate in tow.'

'Six days before Clare Buchanan goes missing from the number forty-three bus.'

'In Buenos Aires she's disowned by her strict Catholic parents and years later meets Feliciano Ledesma,' Nash continued. 'The two get married, move to Uruguay for a better life, but then Sabi picks up a second "shadow". I'm not convinced she wasn't paranoid by this point.'

'But you think her emails to Ebdon triggered the break-in at her house?'

'If what she says is true, that she has some kind of stalker,

58

her emails threatening him were probably driven out of madness.'

'But in South America? You think Ebdon can have that kind of reach?'

'Maybe he wants her to know that he's keeping tabs on her. Plus her eldest is still his child.'

Miles yawned. 'His design to intimidate her backfired.'

They sat in silence for a moment.

'She's never heard the name Solomon Capricorn.'

Miles gave a second shrug. 'Neither have any of us. That's why we're merely scratching the surface.'

'I need sleep,' Nash said.

'Me too,' Miles seconded.

'Breakfast at eight?' she asked, hauling herself up, tossing the empty wine bottle in the bin.

It took her several attempts to get back into her room, the effects of the wine leaving her lightheaded. Nash stumbled through the door, tossing her phone on the bed. She had left the bedside lamp switched on. Turning on the bathroom light, she squinted into the mirror, then had a job focussing in order to get the toothpaste onto the bristles of the toothbrush.

She glanced up.

The shock ran to the end of every capillary, jolting her consciousness. The reflection of a man's grizzled face stared back from behind her in the doorway. She stiffened in fear, dread exploding in her chest, fingers clamping down on the tube of toothpaste sending a long string of the creamy substance spurting forth over the Formica surface. She opened her mouth to scream but in reply a gargantuan hand came crashing into the back of her head, twisting it and slamming into the mirror, sending her entire frame sprawling forward. His other hand clamped over her mouth and she felt herself being lifted off the ground, coming crashing down again onto the scented linen on the bed. Nash felt the weight of him, the sheer size of him bearing down on her clavicle, pinning her legs against the mattress. Amidst her panic, looking up at him, her first thought was of Blackbeard the Pirate. Shaggy hair in ringlets framed his face, falling down around his ears. In the dim light, his eyes were almost black. Nash reached out with her arms, grappling for anything within reach. She felt her phone underneath her, pressing into her spine. There was nothing else. She grabbed at fresh white linen.

'Your name,' the man demanded, and she felt flecks of his spittle rain down on her cheeks. He had a dense Spanish accent. 'Tell me your name.'

He removed his hand from her mouth. She gasped breath. 'Natalie Cambridge,' she said.

'That's not the name in your passport,' he growled, squeezing her cheeks together.

'Please,' Nash stammered. 'If it's money you want—'

'Your name!'

She obeyed. 'Nashaly Akinyemi,' she confirmed out of fear. 'I am Nashaly Akinyemi.'

His fingers were at her throat, still bearing down on her, sweaty. 'What do you do?'

She dug her nails into the hairy flesh on the back of his hand. He teased them off one by one, pinned both her wrists above her head, bringing his face so unbearably close. There were morsels of food still in his teeth. 'What is your job?' he spat.

Tears stung her eyes. 'I'm a journalist,' she breathed.

'And why are you in Uruguay?'

He didn't pronounce it the way she expected. There was an '*oo*' sound at the beginning. In response to her silence, she felt the hot sensation of the back of his hand slamming into her cheek. Her shoulders came up in pain.

There was a knocking at the door.

Miles voice came from the other side. 'Nash?'

The man's head snapped round, following the sound. Nash tried to scream. His palm stifled the sound.

'Nash?'

Without warning, Blackbeard the Pirate let go of her, thrusting her back against the mattress. He whirled around and opened the door, leaving her with the blurred image of him pushing past Miles.

'Hey!' she heard Miles say and she lifted her head, trying to warn him off. 'Nash!'

The next thing she knew he was floating above her, touching her face, asking if she was alright. He went back to the door, looked out into the corridor.

'Miles, stop,' she managed.

She pulled herself up into a sitting position, clutching her neck and cheek.

He came to her. 'God, are you alright? You're trembling.'

'I'm OK,' she croaked.

'Who was that?'

'He was in my room.' She glanced down. There was toothpaste covering her top.

'We need to call the police,' Miles said, leaning over towards the hotel phone.

Her hand clamped down over his forearm. She gasped breath. 'Don't. He knew who I was. He knew the name in my passport.'

'What did he want?' Miles breathed, eyes pleading. 'Jesus, look what he's done to you. You need ice.'

'He'd been in my room. I told him what I did.'

'That you were a writer?'

'He *knew*,' she said, thinking out loud. 'He knew what I was doing here but he asked anyway. I've fucked up. I could have told him anything. He wanted to hear Cordero's name. I think that was him.'

The shock registered across Miles's features.

'I think that man was Sabi's second shadow. Ebdon's man, who watches over her here in Montevideo. You know what this means?'

He did. She knew it by the look in his eyes.

'It means they'll know we're looking into them,' he said. The look he gave her was serious, with no visible evidence of the fear. She wondered if he was feeling the same on the inside. 'First thing tomorrow,' he said, 'we need to leave.'

Chapter 7

Chile
5 January, 2017

Tom perched on a circular wall surrounding a palm tree at Plaza Echaurren in the port city of Valparaíso eating a sandwich, away from a fountain where local Chileans gathered to bask in the summer's warm rays. He sipped on *Mote con Huesillos*, a sugary drink made with peaches, from a local vendor. He wore a cap and sunglasses. Yards away, a pensioner hobbled across the square feeding a flock of pigeons, babbling to himself. Here, away from the tourist district of Cerro Alegre, his white skin, no matter how tanned, made him stand out.

Tom had parked Aksel's bike between two other vehicles. It was hard not to flinch at any large black 4x4 passing by, or shake the idea that someone could have been watching his every move since he'd left Santiago. He focussed instead on the address that Aksel had written down for him, the contents of which he had memorised some time ago, which appeared to be situated above a small convenience store. At the main entrance, he watched who came and went.

In the space of an hour, the same man came in and out. Small and balding, with a healthy-sized belly, half-moon spectacles, waistcoat and grey trousers, he made two trips to other destinations across the plaza. On his third trip, Tom waited until his return before discarding his sandwich and following him inside the two-storey building and on to the stairs.

'Are you Panchito?' Tom called out in Spanish on the off chance.

Up ahead the man stopped dead. He turned, cautious. 'Who wants to know?' the Chilean replied, looking up from the set of papers he was holding over the rim of his glasses.

'Aksel sent me.'

The man removed his glasses, putting the end of the frame in his mouth. 'From Sweden, no? Not seen him in years.'

Tom couldn't help but smile. 'That's the one.'

'Little shit owes me money,' the man said, carrying on up the stairs.

'How much?' Tom said.

'Come up. We'll talk,' Panchito called back.

Tom almost bounced up the stairs. At the top, in an office of sorts, two obese minders sat behind a pair of desks, wearing tracksuits and digging into takeaway boxes of ceviche. The room was painted the shade of tangerines, paint on the dilapidated walls chipped and crumbling, the window open, an ancient rotary fan blowing out air. On the desks, paperwork was piled high and held down with various articles used as paperweights. The two heavies eyed Tom as he entered.

'Where are you from?' Panchito asked, ignoring their presence.

'London,' Tom said.

'Are you looking to get back to London?' Panchito said, switching into English. 'Because if you are, my friend, this isn't the place.'

'I need to go north. To Panama.'

Panchito sucked air through gritted teeth. 'Ship leaves two weeks tomorrow. Valpo to Colón in the north of Panama. Doesn't leave me with much time. Plus it's fully staffed already. Not much by way of positions left.'

'I can do anything, whatever you have.'

Panchito put his hands on his hips. 'You sure 'bout that? Aksel still owes me seven hundred dollars. You want to travel on a Chilean passport, I can do it for six thousand.'

Tom winced. His brother had wired him three thousand pounds to the Western Union in Santiago.

'Things have changed since I last saw Aksel,' Panchito said, noting Tom's look. 'Inflation, no?' He let out a laugh. 'What do you have?'

He could feel his chest rising and falling. It would leave him nothing for Panama, nothing for onward travel. He would have to rely on his brother for money, or to track down their father in Central America on his behalf. It would have to do.

'I can offer you three thousand and Aksel's motorbike.'

Panchito's shoulders trembled with more laughter. 'What kind of a bike is it?'

'Turn of the century vintage Suzuki. One of a kind. You could sell it, at least make back the money he owed you.'

Panchito laughed out loud again. Even the heavies had been stirred enough to let out a snort. 'I still can't do it.'

He would have to call Christian back. It wasn't what

he wanted to do. He could get on a plane, using his own passport, in his own name, lead them right to him. He would probably be dead within a week.

Panchito looked like he was contemplating something. 'You wanted by police?'

'Police aren't my problem right now.'

'And your Spanish is decent.' He said it as a statement rather than a question. 'Come back here tomorrow morning at nine. I'll see what I can do. Bring me your real passport if you have it. I'll take the bike then too. What's your name?'

'Thomas Holt,' he replied.

Panchito was reaching up, tugging a roll-down white screen suspended from the crumbling ceiling, signalling to a position on the tiled floor where Tom should plant his feet. Tom did as he was instructed as Panchito reached into his desk drawer for a small hand-held digital camera. He took Tom's photograph before reaching out and gripping his shoulder.

'*Bueno*,' the Chilean said, fingers digging firmly into Tom's flesh. 'Tomorrow, Thomas Holt, I make you a citizen of this great nation of Chile.'

Chapter 8

West India Quay, London
12 January, 2017

Rum & Sugar. The bar was filled with a horde of bodies. It was low lit with a wood-beamed ceiling. Nash froze in the doorway, seeing her attacker everywhere. Swallowing her emotions, she inched her way through the crush, rubbing shoulders with stockbrokers and the City boys and girls letting their hair down, craning her neck to locate Miles in the crowd. When she spied him, he was coming her way.

'Where have you been?' he asked. 'I sent a ton of messages. Gus is waiting.'

Nash held up her phone. 'No battery,' she lied. 'I was on a train.'

He grabbed her hand, leading her to a table.

'Nash, meet Gus Fendy. Gus, meet Nash.'

Nash put down her bag and phone, forced a smile, held out her hand. Gus Fendy had freakishly long fingers, a square-shaped chin and dimples, skin like sandpaper despite him being under forty. A vape pen stuck out of his jacket pocket and on the table in front of him were a dog-eared broadsheet and a hardback biography of Stalin. She'd had her doubts about him the moment Miles had mentioned his name.

'Miles told me all about you,' Fendy said.

'Right.'

'You're Diane Cambridge's daughter. He knows which side of his bread is buttered.'

Miles had said Fendy verged on the side of cocky. Nash decided that she would have gone further than that. Fendy flashed a grin.

'I'll get us another round in,' Miles said as they took their seats.

She watched him go to the bar. Fendy leaned closer. 'Miles says you're going after Charles Ebdon.'

A kind of prickly heat rose up from the base of her neck. 'We're investigating what happened to Clare Buchanan. And if Charlie Ebdon was a part of that.'

Fendy smirked, running his finger around the glass rim of his drink. 'You'll never get to him.'

'Miles said you got nowhere with the biography.'

The look on his face altered, telling her she'd hit a nerve on the first go. A journalist by trade, Fendy was a sometime writer of non-fiction, including a string of unauthorised biographies of well-known public figures. Ten years earlier he had tried to write a book about Charles Ebdon: philanthropist, socialite, businessman, entrepreneur.

'So why didn't it work out?'

He gritted his teeth, checking his watch and drumming his fingertips on the surface of the table. 'First I got a cease and desist letter, which I ignored. Then I got a visit from a lawyer to my house. The threats I could live with. Made me want to write the damn thing more. Then I went north, to the place where Ebdon's family is originally from. South of Hexham in Northumberland. It's called Ketteridge, a small village community in the northern Pennines.'

'What did you find there?'

Sticking his fingers in his drink he picked out an ice cube and started crunching on it, recalling the memory with some amusement. 'Soon as people there got a whiff of what I was doing, researching his family tree, they wanted me gone. Up there Ebdon is a hero; they don't have a bad word to say about him.'

'So you decided to throw in the towel?'

'Nope. Still didn't stop me. I carried on. Until a man broke into my house one night and threatened to murder me and my then girlfriend.'

Nash felt her chest tighten. 'What man?'

Gus shifted in his seat, gave a shrug. 'Police never caught him. He was tall. Kind of broad. Physically fit.'

'Was his nose broken?'

'He wore a balaclava and gloves. I only saw his eyes. Darkest brown.'

'Were you scared?'

Gus leaned back in his chair, didn't make eye contact. Instead looked over at the bar, checking on Miles's progress. 'It was a long time ago,' he said with a half-smile.

'What happened? Did you call the police?'

'Of course. I told them about the biography I was writing. About what had happened up north.'

'And?'

'And they advised me to stop writing it. Don't say I didn't warn you.'

There it was again. The grin. Underneath the table, Nash found herself digging the heel of her boot into the floor. 'Did you ever look into what happened to Clare Buchanan?'

'Didn't get half a chance. Ebdon was too busy funding a search campaign for her, stumping up a cash reward. I'll tell you right now, not one person out there thought Ebdon was involved in her disappearance.'

'Except you.'

'I didn't say that.'

He was looking over at Miles again, finally getting his drinks order in at the bar.

'You know, he told me what went on between you two. Why didn't you return his calls?'

Nash forced another smile, tight-lipped. 'I don't know what you mean.'

'Miles said every message, every call he made to you afterwards went unanswered.'

Nash felt her throat constrict.

'Not your type maybe. That's what I heard.'

'Right. You're done here. You can go now.'

'What?'

'Thanks for the insight. You really don't have to stay for another drink.'

'Look I've got no problem with it, but you have to admit, you strung Miles along there—'

Miles came back over, carrying three drinks. 'OK then…'

'Gus was just leaving, weren't you, Gus?'

Fendy got to his feet, collecting his newspaper and book.

'You're leaving already?' Miles asked in a stunned voice.

She watched Gus shake Miles by the hand, smack him hard on the back, wish him luck. He then gave her a courteous nod and left.

'What did you say to him?' Miles asked.

'I might ask you the same thing.'

She marched across the North Dock footbridge, away from Rum & Sugar's bustling crowd, Miles on her tail, pulling on his coat. Since Uruguay, the darkness set her teeth on edge, causing her to search in the shadows for something not there.

Miles caught up with her. 'I don't understand, what did he say?'

Nash whirled around, jabbed her finger in his chest. 'You told him! You told him we'd slept together!'

Miles's jaw bobbed open. 'He's a friend. I happened to mention it. I'm sorry. It wasn't like no one else knew.'

Nash looked him in the face, a rush of guilt sweeping though her chest for the many messages she hadn't returned.

'*Uhm*. How did it go with the dead lawyer's secretary today?' he asked after a silence, changing the subject.

Nash swallowed, relieved again. 'Her name's Orla Drake. She worked for Albert Denham for more than twenty years. She said despite that there were some days when she felt like she didn't know him at all. That he was a completely private person. Did you know he was married three times?'

'That's not unusual for any London City lawyer.'

'Not in itself, no. Orla Drake said that when she first started working for him in the nineties he got married to a woman named Belinda. That before that, there were some police charges for a sexual assault, but she said the charges were dropped. I couldn't find anything online. Denham and Belinda were married for about six years before divorcing, according to Orla because they couldn't have any kids.'

'What does that have to do with anything?'

'After they separated, she said Denham went completely off the rails. He shut down his business for two months; Orla thought she was out of a job. She thought drinking would be the death of him. Then Denham met someone. Not long after, Denham got married to this woman and they went to Italy for their extended honeymoon. Some years after, the woman killed herself by taking an overdose of pills in their flat. Almost a month to the day after Clare Buchanan disappeared in 2005.'

'Who was this woman?'

'That's the twist. I looked it up. Her name was Amy Ebdon.'

Chapter 9

Baku, USSR
8 November, 1979

'Show me your hands.'

He raised grubby, scrawny fingers. The man looming above him grabbed them, turning them over. It had been a while since anyone had cut his nails and he refused to bite the longer, chipped ones. There was plenty of dirt embedded underneath them.

The walls were a pale shade of green, strip lighting buzzed overhead. The bars on the window were painted magnolia white, a triangle at one corner of the pane where glass used to be, winter wind howling through the hole that was left. At the back of the room was a hospital bed, in front of it a cheap brown desk and plastic chair. Though he had lived his every memory in the building, he could not recall ever having been in this particular room before.

The man before him let go of his hands and straightened. He felt fingers wipe the top of his head. 'Are you Anton Moroshkin?' the man asked, speaking in Russian.

He nodded, kept his eyes on the dappled tile flooring, toes poking out at the bottom of his pyjamas. *Baba* Levchenko had woken him. It was dark outside. He didn't know what time it was. She was standing in front of the desk, her arms

73

crossed, holes in her tights, hair tucked inside a blue head scarf.

'This boy is filthy,' the man complained to her.

Anton turned to see her give a shrug. She was the oldest, fattest of all the *Babushkas* at the home for abandoned boys. His friends had often heard her refer to him as *polukrovka*. Half-breed.

'They get one bath a week,' she stated. 'It is the best we can do.'

The man shook his head, Anton snatched another look. The man's hair had some kind of grease in it. It was cut in a dead straight line against a bulging forehead.

'Does he have any possessions?'

Baba Levchenko let out a snort. 'He is six. He has nothing.'

'He doesn't have shoes?'

She took a couple of steps forward. Anton flinched at the sting of her fingertips flicking his earlobe. 'Run. Get your clothes and shoes. Go.'

He felt relieved to make a dash for it, back up the two flights of stairs to the dorm where twelve other boys – all aged between four and fifteen – were sleeping soundly. Moonlight reflected in a mottled mirror above a disused fireplace, allowing him to see into the shadows underneath his bed where his tracksuit was piled in a discarded heap.

The sign above the door read:

BOYS OF THE BLACK BLOOD
BOXING ACADEMY

'Can you read?' the man asked.

Anton had started shivering in the back of the car. Now the shakes were almost uncontrollable. He gave a shrug, hardly hearing the question.

'I suppose we shall have to get you a coat,' the man added. The driver's side door creaked on its hinges as he slammed it shut. The man jangled a set of keys in the darkness of the Baku winter. Anton shuffled behind him, following him inside a door in a wall made of wood, on which hung the crooked sign. Inside, the man pressed down light switches on a panel. One by one they clicked on, a corresponding sound echoing from the far end of the academy floor as each of six boxing rings was illuminated with a corresponding *boom*. The man turned, looking down at Anton whose breath emerged as vapour.

'My name is Dimitry Voronin. A man who works for your father gave me money to get you out of that place, Anton. Do you know who your father is?'

Anton shook his head.

'It does not matter. You shall probably never get to meet him. But he has plans for you. You should consider yourself lucky. Tomorrow, the man who works for your father will come here. In the morning, we will give you a bath, make you look presentable. You need a haircut too. I keep high standards here. I will teach you three things: how to box, how to fight, and most important, how to survive.'

London
6 January, 2017

Morality is for the faithful, for the flock.
When you live in the corners of shadows, there is no morality.
Right and wrong do not exist.
Let he with the glass jaw fight on the front foot.

Had he been a different kind of man, he might have considered it wrong, he thought, screwing the dead lawyer Denham's wife barely a month after the funeral. She was Tatiana, the Polish trophy bride, the woman Capricorn had asked Denham to marry. The fool had said yes, too. Denham's body wasn't even cold the night Tatiana had messaged him with the first photograph. Nothing explicit; only teasing. Explicit had come later. Videos: naked, arched, fingering herself, crying out his name. She knew he had received them, not that he had replied. Before that day there had been no formal communication between them. Yet she knew who he was, what he did for a living. She had his number. So when he'd turned up at the house in Streatham Hill on Christmas Eve it had been out of boredom, knowing she would submit. The sex on Denham's black leather sofa had been animalistic, over as swiftly as it had begun, without exchange of sentiments. He had got dressed and left soon after.

Anton had not expected it to continue, but with Denham gone Tatiana was a lost kitten. She had followed him back to his flat. Now she would be the one who would arrive unannounced, and not for conversation, leaving when he commanded her to. She was lonely, and he didn't care for loneliness. Dimitry had called his 'a life of extraordinary solitude', and it was all the life he had ever known.

He kept her out of the bedroom. Females thought of bedrooms as intimate places. So he kept the door closed, kept her in the living area. Only this time she had stripped off her clothes in the kitchen, spread her legs, so as he stood there bulldozing into her warmth from behind, it caused the dirty dishes to jangle together in the sink. His scarred fingers groped her hips, one hand splayed flat on her back, jeans around his knees as Tatiana moaned like a banshee. A mug fell and bounced on the linoleum floor as he felt the familiar rushing sensation, the sound ripping from his throat not unlike the igniting of a diesel engine.

He remained still, caught his breath, allowing the blood pumping in his ears to subside. He stood back and fixed himself, tugged his jeans up and left the room.

The line coming in and out of the City and Blackfriars railway station came right past his windows. All day he listened to the shriek of wheels against tracks, the vibrations humming in the walls. London's Elephant and Castle: the biggest dump south of the Thames. He'd been there too long, yet he didn't know how he would live without those sounds. The tremors especially were of strange comfort.

Tatiana emerged from the kitchen clutching her clothes in a bundle, hair in disarray.

'Will you let me use your bathroom?' she asked.

He nodded her towards the corridor, watched her naked ass jiggle out of the doorway. She wore too much makeup; had made herself too available too quickly. Yet she kept on coming back.

He heard the click of the door lock slide across. Feeling a sting of relief, he returned his attention to the window.

Tom Holt had evaded him for some weeks, gone to ground, the trail dead. But they had caught up with him. Dante and Rolo Belosi had been hunting him since the incident in Buenos Aires. They had found him in a quiet corner of Chile. Yet they had failed in their task and now Holt was on the move again. Dante and Rolo, the brothers who carried far too much weight between them, were trying to track him down. These were the kind of bozos he had to rely on. Holt, running, in possession of far too much knowledge: yet another mistake in a catalogue of errors. He had offered to go and finish the job himself, something Capricorn had ordered him not to do.

It still irked Anton that he hadn't known exactly what had happened in Buenos Aires in the November. He'd managed to reclaim the laptop containing Buchanan's statement before he and Becca had been ambushed at the airport en route to London. Somehow, he now knew, Holt had reclaimed the laptop and sent a copy of Clare Buchanan's video to the Met Police. Thanks to his contact, the video had been retrieved. The useless prick Rawlins had turned out to be not such a useless prick after all.

A soft tap at the door caused him to glance up, muscles stiffening. Apart from Tatiana, no one ever came to his home. His neighbours knew better than to disturb him. He slipped out into the corridor, pressed one eye up against the peep hole to find it black. Instinctively, he reached up high to the ledge and the knife that lay dormant against the wooden frame. He put the chain on, opened the door a fraction, knife behind his back, only to find himself looking down at a shock of red hair. He relaxed his shoulders, removed the chain and opened the door.

Becca removed her finger from the peep hole.

'Anton,' she breathed with a half-smile, sauntering in. 'You know your building has very poor security.'

He shut the door, returning the knife to its resting place. 'Where do you think you are?'

She eyed the knife, clocked its location. 'Made you nervous enough though, didn't I?'

He watched her yank off her coat; walk through to the living room. Recalled the first time he'd set eyes on her: standing in her school uniform, one white sock pulled up, the other slouched around her ankle, hem of her pleated green skirt stopping above her white bony knees, around ten years old. She was still as lithe as she had been back then, as talented as he always knew she would turn out to be. Yet since she had come back from South America, she was altered in one way or another. He could see it in the way she now looked at him.

He followed her inside. 'I don't remember the last time you came here,' he said.

She looked around. 'Well it hasn't changed, I'll say that much.'

'Where's Richie?' he said, asking after her brother.

She gave a shrug. 'Since he got out of prison he's gone back to his nocturnal habits.'

In that moment there was the sound of a toilet flushing from behind the bathroom door. Becca looked surprised. 'Who's here?'

He didn't have time to react. The door opened and Tatiana emerged, fully dressed in jeans and a low-cut top, lipstick on, blonde hair scraped back. Tatiana's face fell the moment she saw Becca.

Becca flashed him a look of accusation. 'What's she doing here?' It was more of a statement than a question.

A muscle pulsated in Anton's jaw. Tatiana awaited his response. The two women knew each other. He had gone with Becca to the registry office for Tatiana's wedding to the lawyer, Al Denham, simply to make up numbers.

'That's a new low, even for you,' Becca hissed, and he knew the words were meant for him, despite the fact she was looking the other woman up and down.

He looked to Tatiana, regretting ever responding her advances. 'Get out of here,' he clipped.

Tatiana looked stunned. '*Kretyn*,' she muttered in her native Polish, grabbing her handbag and pushing past Becca. He waited in silence until the door slammed behind her.

'What are you doing?' Becca snapped.

'It's nothing,' he responded.

'Why would you even go there?'

'She came to me.'

'What have you told her?'

'We don't talk, we fuck. She knows nothing.' He was tired of talking about Tatiana. 'Why are you here?'

Her stance shifted. She was oddly upbeat. 'I want to help. I'm bored of sitting in the flat all day. What is happening with Holt?'

Holt's name was on her lips, casually throwing it into conversation. He felt an irrational stab of envy. He hadn't worked it out yet, whether she genuinely disliked Tom Holt or whether there had been a connection between the two. Whether Holt had been the one to cause a ground shift in her. She had claimed not, that it was being in another country that had awakened her sense of adventure.

'There is nothing you can do to help,' Anton said. 'Unless you can take a life, and you are not one for killing.'

Her shoulders went back. 'I could be. You've never let me.'

'Then your first kill should not be someone you already know. It's easier that way, there's no complication. It's cleaner.'

'Was your first kill someone you knew?'

He didn't answer. He had stamped out the memory. In the other room, his phone was ringing.

'Wait there,' he said to Becca, stalking to the bedroom and closing the door. He kept four different phones and it took him a moment to work out which one was making the racket. He snatched the right one out of the door of the bedside cabinet. The screen read 'SB'. The letters stood for Sancho Belosi.

'Sancho,' he said into the handset. The line to South America crackled. '*Cómo les va?*'

'She has new friends,' the voice hissed back, coarse words spoken in English with a grating Spanish accent. 'One man, one woman. They are not from here. But she's been talking to them.'

Anton stiffened. He looked down at his unmade bed. When it came to Sabina Cordero, Sancho Belosi knew everything. He knew this because when she had been a young woman in London, Cordero had been *his* charge, the woman *he* had spent hours and hours of his time following around. At the time she'd been Capricorn's mistress. Now the job of following her belonged to Sancho.

'What people? Who? Did you get names?'

'You know my nephew had to have surgery?'

Anton closed his eyes. When Sancho had, days earlier, informed him that Holt had escaped Sancho's nephews in Chile – Dante and his twin brother Rolo – he had been more concerned that Holt had put a knife in Rolo's belly. Anton had underestimated Holt. So had Denham. Rolo, on the other hand, had enough belly blubber to protect him from any lasting damage.

'No I didn't know that. How is he?'

'In recovery. We got him back across the border to Mendoza in time. He'll live.'

'I'm happy to hear that. Who are the people talking to Cordero?'

'The surgery cost twenty thousand US. We had to get a specialist.'

Anton gritted his teeth. 'Again, I'm sorry to hear that.'

'Holt did this. I want him dead. I want my twenty thousand back.'

'I can't authorise that kind of money.'

Belosi was hissing down the line. 'Then speak to your fucking boss, you fucking lap-dog. I want my money. When I have it you can have the names of the *periodistas* she's been talking to.'

Anton felt every fibre in his body tense. *Periodista* was the Spanish word for a journalist.

Sabina Cordero had gone to the press.

Sancho Belosi had hung up.

Anton lowered the phone from his ear, absorbed the Argentine's words. A split second later, he hurled the handset against his bedroom wall, the screen shattering on impact.

Throwing open his bedroom door, his eyes landed on Becca. He had forgotten she was waiting for him. The lack of control was killing him. He paced, fists squeezed so tight the dry skin on his knuckles began to pull.

'Who was that?'

Anton let out a snarl. He couldn't stop moving.

'Anton!' Becca chided him. 'Tell me.'

She offered him a gentle, pleading look, one that would disarm a different kind of man.

'Cordero's gone to the press.'

Becca seemed to open her mouth to speak, but no sounds came out.

'Because of the robbery. Either that or they went to her because Holt alerted them to Cordero's existence and to the contents of the laptop,' Anton continued.

Again, Becca said nothing.

'Belosi wants twenty thousand US to cover the costs of his nephew's surgery before he gives up the names.'

'Did he say they were definitely journalists?'

'That's what he's saying.'

'Let me help you.'

That pleading look again.

She had rarely let him down. Always followed his every instruction, and even when he'd chastised her for failure, she'd gone away and come back stronger. He had no reason to doubt her.

'Let me go after Holt,' she said in a low voice. 'I know him. I know how he thinks.'

'Fine. Do everything in your power to track him down. I can send bodies to finish the job.'

'What about Mexico?' she asked.

'Mexico can wait. Once I have Holt, I'll go there myself. Destroy everything.'

She nodded, almost standing to attention, sure of herself. 'So what will you do?'

Orders issued, he had already blocked her out. His mind was already ticking. Tonight he would see Capricorn and they would discuss who else needed to die.

Baku, USSR
9 November, 1979

'Anton. This man is Gearhart Keller. Mr Keller works for your father. Stand up straight.'

Anton did as he was told, shoulders back, arms by his sides, gaze fixed on the chipped paintwork of the opposing wall.

Dimitry had taken him to the market that morning after a bath. He stood at one stall whilst Dimitry had measured two sweatshirts up against him. 'You are too scrawny,' he had grumbled before purchasing Anton a brand new pair of trainers.

He was standing in the centre of Dimitry's kitchen,

situated above the entrance to the academy. The room – which contained a large stone fireplace, above which was suspended a copper pot – was filled with the delicious aromas of savoury *qutab*, cinnamon and fennel. After the market square, they had moved on to the bazaar to buy a dozen jars of Beluga caviar for the man Dimitry now called Keller.

Dimitry had told him that he would never be going back to the home for boys, the only home he had ever known. Even now, as Keller grabbed Anton's chin between his slender fingers, forcing his mouth open in order to inspect his teeth, Anton did not understand the reasons for the stranger's visit. No one had ever told him the identity of his father, even his first name, or why it was that his father had shown a sudden interest in him.

'Thankfully, he has the mother's looks,' Keller said in Russian but with an accent Anton didn't recognise. Dimitry was sitting at the table, mouth full of *qutab*, bits of lamb falling down onto his plate. Anton felt his mouth beginning to water.

Keller let him go. The stranger had a square frame, a long face and high cheek bones. The remaining strands of white hair on his head were slicked back.

'Teach him English,' Keller said, looking to Dimitry. 'I expect fluency. A lesson a day, along with everything we discussed. And feed him up.'

He turned and walked over to a leather bag, zipping it open. He reached inside, pulling out a cardboard box. He held it up for Anton to see.

'You know what this is, boy?' Keller asked.

Anton shook his head.

Keller moved closer, opening the box. 'This is a gift from

your father.' From the box he pulled a second box-like item, this one made of plastic, with buttons. Keller then unwound an odd looking wire with two pieces of orange sponge connected by a curved metal strip.

'This is called a *Walkman*. It's a new thing. You put cassette tapes into it and you can listen to music through these.'

Anton felt himself tense as Keller placed the two pieces of sponge over his ears. Keller pressed a button on the plastic box. The beat began. Anton's eyes widened. He had heard the song on the radio before. His face broke into a smile.

In his seat, Dimitry started laughing. 'I think the kid likes it.'

Keller's face was impassive. 'There are five cassettes in all. Michael Jackson, Scorpions, Frank Duval, two others. You have permission to buy more.'

Anton let the pulse of the beat consume him. Eyes closed, he felt a bony finger prod his chest. When he opened his eyes again, the air flashed white. Keller had taken his photograph with a Polaroid camera. He then replaced the camera back in his bag. Anton couldn't hear the exchange between the two men, only watch as Dimitry got to his feet and shook Keller by the hand. Keller glanced back at him one last time before he was gone.

Anton felt his new guardian's fingertip brush against his scalp as the device was removed from his possession. The music kept playing until Dimitry clicked a button and they were left in silence. He held up the box that Keller had called the Walkman.

'I don't know what you did. I suspect you did nothing. But someone thinks you are important. This you can have back when you've done something to earn it.'

Chapter 10

London, England
13 January, 2017

Becca Wylde stood guard in the shadow of an alcove that was overgrown with ivy, her brother making quick work of picking a front door lock. Tom Holt's London flat was on the first floor, and it was likely there would be another door to get through on the inside.

They had taken a night bus to Crouch End before finishing their journey to the Turnpike Lane area on foot, stopping for kebabs along the way. The light from the nearest street lamp grazed the ornate wrought iron of the front gate. She had worn a woolly hat, red hair concealed underneath. She knew they had to be careful; the area they were in was hot on Neighbourhood Watch schemes. It was after 3 a.m., the street in darkness.

In the night air, Richie hissed and she snapped to attention. He held out his hand, offering her the chance to go in first. She felt uncharacteristically nervous. The door, which was heavy painted wood with a stained glass window, typical of the types of red brick houses lining the surrounding roads – Victorian or Edwardian, one or the other – proved difficult to open. She used the weight of her shoulder to give it a shove, wedging her booted foot inside at floor level. Her body relaxed at the sight of the piles of post covering a tiled floor, blocking the way. No one had been through this door in months; the ground floor flat must have been empty. She took a large step forward over envelopes, jarring the door open, relieved at the sight of junk mail snaking around the inside of the foyer. Richie followed then pressed the door closed behind him. Becca picked up a few of the envelopes, held them up in the dim light. A few were addressed to 'Thomas Holt Esq.': bank statements, bills and the like, some handwritten envelopes that looked like Christmas cards, one marked 'FINAL NOTICE' in red lettering. She ignored the quickening of her heartbeat at the sight of his name. They were faced with two inner doors, marked 'A' and 'B'.

'B,' she said, remembering how she'd signed her note to him with her initial, telling him that she was sorry, that she had done what she'd had to.

Richie placed his palm flat against the door, painted magnolia white. It felt good to see him out in his natural habitat.

There was a Yale lock at the top of the door, a mortise at the bottom. Richie removed a small torch from his pocket.

'Think you can do it?' Becca whispered.

'Yeah,' he muttered, keeping his voice low. 'Mortise isn't on. If there's a burglar alarm we're gonna have to scarper, and quick.'

'There's no sign of one on the outside,' she confirmed, still distracted by all the letters.

Richie went to work again on the Yale with his lock-picking tool. 'You gonna tell me why we're here?' he asked.

She didn't answer. She had returned from Argentina two

months earlier, in the November. Richie had been released from Wandsworth – courtesy of some strings pulled by their uncle Charlie – not long after. It had been her condition for going to South America in the first place: part of the deal that she had made with the dead lawyer, Denham. *I go to South America and Capricorn gets my brother out of jail.* Uncle Charlie had kept to his word.

Yet something was altered. South America had changed her. The job had changed her. The robbery – planned and executed along with Tom Holt, Anil Choudhury and Ray Caulder – had caused her world, and everything she thought she had believed in, to shift on some kind of invisible axis, making her question her position in life. Anil was dead – shot in the head by Ray – and Ray had gone to ground, fleeing back to London with the contents of the safe. She and Tom had escaped to Argentina, with the laptop containing a copy of the safe contents. She had betrayed Tom Holt, bringing Anton right to his door and stealing the laptop. She swallowed, a bitter taste filling her mouth. She had been loyal to Anton and Capricorn for as long as she could recall. Yet, in Argentina, Tom Holt had been the one to save her life.

She blinked, Richie sliding down the handle to ease the door open. He opened it wide, revealing a carpeted staircase. There was no sound, no alarm. Becca stepped forward. Light from an upstairs window filtered through to a wall at the top. She took a step up, the sole of her foot sinking into the fabric of the carpet.

'We're good,' Richie whispered, nudging her forward. 'Go.'

Something held her back. It felt like another betrayal. She

had promised Anton that she would help track him down. So Anton could send his thugs to take Tom's life. The emotions swirling in her chest confused her. She wanted to prove to Anton that she was worthy of this. She badly wanted to see Tom Holt again in the flesh. *To do what? Say what?*

She moved up the stairs, clinging to the wall. Richie followed, clicking the door shut. On the landing she turned to face a living room, Venetian blinds closed but light from the street lamp streaking through. The air felt musty. There was a second staircase leading to more space upstairs.

'What are we looking for?' Richie whispered. 'Come *on*, Bec.'

She shook her head. 'Sorry.'

'Tell me what I'm looking for.'

'Anything that could indicate how we might track him down. We need a starting point.'

'So ransack the joint?'

She pulled a face. 'See what you can find.'

'What's this dude's name again?'

'Tom. Thomas Holt.'

'And why's he so important?'

'Because Anton wants him dead. Because he knows too much.'

'What about you? Do you want him dead?'

'I've had enough of scraping by picking pockets,' she said and walked forward towards the stairs. 'I'll check the bedroom, you check the living room.'

Richie puffed out his cheeks. She had sensed his growing frustration over Christmas. Her silence, her unwillingness to talk about what had happened in South America had somehow offended him. They had always been a good team. Her little brother with his mousy hair, boyish looks and permanent layer of too-lazy-to-shave stubble. He had always been a night-crawler. Yet she saw it in the way Richie looked at her following his stint in Wandsworth Prison. That she wasn't the only one altered after time away; that Richie now suspected his big sister had broken away and was functioning as a separate entity, no longer the *yin* to his *yang*.

He was right. She didn't quite know herself anymore.

She climbed the second staircase. In the roof space was a bedroom, left tidy by someone who knew they might not be home for a while, the bed made. She took one step inside. Wondered what he'd say to the intrusion. Keeping the lights off, she started with the wardrobe, opening the doors to find a row of smart suits and shirts, shoes lined up in pairs underneath. She ran her fingers across soft fabrics. It was impossible to picture the man she knew wearing a tie. The image didn't fit. She checked drawers, rifling through pairs of clean underwear. There were no photographs in frames, not even pictures on the wall. She moved to the bed, tossing back navy blue covers. A crumpled T-shirt lay in a heap on the sheet. She paused, fingertips hovering over it. Closed her eyes for a moment, immersed herself in a fleeting memory of his body, before swearing out loud, shaking her head, carrying on the search. She found books, magazines, pairs of cufflinks, two watches still in their boxes, each item ending up discarded on the floor. She went back to his underwear drawer, emptying the contents before her fingers came into contact with cold metal. She picked up the item and pulled it out from the shadows, staring at the iPhone cradled in her palm.

She heard Richie on the stairs. He entered the room, glancing around.

'Anything?' she asked.

Richie held up a photograph in a frame. 'Which one is he?'

Becca took it. In the darkness she could make out three male figures. Tom was in the middle, grinning, arms around the two other men who bore a striking resemblance to their sibling.

'Middle,' she said. 'Those must be his brothers.'

'Found this in the kitchen,' Richie said, handing her a crumpled business card.

Abandoning the phone, Becca ran her fingers over the surface of the paper, and the name embossed on the card. A vague smile touched her lips. Unhooking the catches from the back of the frame, she kept hold of the business card and deftly removed the photograph, tossing the remaining parts of the frame on the bed, satisfied with the night's graft.

Barnes, London
18 January, 2017

Becca felt the butt of her flick knife digging into the flesh of her left calf muscle, tucked securely inside the zip of her knee-high leather boot. She had dressed for the occasion: pencil skirt, smart blouse, overcoat and fifteen denier tights. She wore a long blonde wig, glasses with false plastic lenses. The money to purchase the outfit had come two days before from a woman's handbag in a Marylebone sandwich bar, the female in question oblivious to Becca's quick fingers, too busy yakking to her friends to notice she was being robbed.

Steam crawled up the windows inside the branch of Bentley Atherton Estate Agents in London, due to the continuous rainfall London had been receiving since before dawn. The business card Richie had found had been an old one, belonging to a different company, but it had taken one internet search to track down his current office. Over the phone to estate agent Christian Holt she had given her name as Arabella Blunt, two names picked at random from one of the free newspapers handed out at Tube stations. She had made the viewing appointment for the Tuesday at 11 a.m.

Capricorn was spitting blood. Sabina Cordero was speaking to journalists. Sancho Belosi wasn't talking, holding the information for ransom. Her uncle had threatened to send Anton down to South America to wring the names from Belosi's throat, demanding that he show *loyalty*. Taking the information from Sabina Cordero's safe and murdering her brother Nico had had the opposite effect than the one Capricorn had intended. Rather than being frightened into submission, Sabina had grown *stronger*. The idea made Becca smile on the inside. If there was anything her uncle despised, it was defiance. Anton had been right all along about robbing the safe. The can was now well and truly open, and worms were going everywhere.

Though now no longer the priority, the orders regarding Tom Holt were still clear.

Find him, eradicate him.

In the estate agent's office, a plump woman in a suit approached her. 'I'm so sorry, Ms Blunt, Christian has been delayed at another appointment. But someone is available now and can drive you to the viewing instead.'

Becca turned the diamond on her ring finger, the one that Tom Holt had given her in Uruguay when they had been faking it as fiancées. She produced a wan smile. 'I'm happy to wait for Christian. I'm in no hurry.'

Becca lowered her head to the magazine in her lap, unable to see the appeal of working in a conventional office and forced into being *oh so pleasant* to everyone. Sliding her finger inside her boot, she teased the handle of the flick knife a little to the right and continued to pretend to be reading.

Her stomach performed a flip when twenty minutes later, Christian Holt entered the office. He was smaller than his brother by a fraction, the hair light brown as opposed to dark blond, a wider jaw, but there was no mistaking his looks. In another life, she and Christian could have been acquaintances. Friends even. Brother- and sister-in-law. She looked down, frustrated by her own lack of focus, her instincts going against everything Anton had ever taught her.

Leave your emotions at home.

He bounded up, thrust out his hand, all smiles.

'Hello, sorry I'm late, I'm Christian.'

They shook. He had a firm grip like his brother. 'It's no problem. Nice to meet you.'

'Shall we go?'

He led her outside to his car, a silver Toyota Avalon. Christian Holt held the passenger door open and she lowered herself into the seat. He was chatty, overly so. She chewed the inside of her cheek, pulled the seatbelt over her chest.

Hearing his voice reminded her of emotions she wished she'd never felt.

'You're getting married, I see,' Christian said, making eyes at her ring.

'Yes,' she replied, failing to muster any warmth. 'My fiancé is… abroad.'

Conversation seemed pointless. She reminded herself to go through the motions. Get him away from his office so he couldn't throw a hissy fit in front of his colleagues and fling her out on the street.

'Obviously it's not that special on the outside,' he said as they parked at the end of a cul-de-sac off Barnes High Street near the river, yanking up the handbrake. She gave a cursory glance towards the red brick block of flats with individual balconies. She had chosen the property at random on the internet. She had already scoped it out. 'This one was built in the fifties, so the rooms are of a decent size.'

On a standard day, if she was looking at a house or flat it was with a view to breaking in and robbing the place. It felt oddly uncomfortable to be shown around a flat with a view to purchasing it. Her uncle had provided the flat she lived in with her brother in Wapping. Thieves and pickpockets did not get mortgages as far as she knew.

Christian Holt was still droning on about the local area. Becca followed him through the secure metal door inside the stairwell, climbing to the second floor. He was going through a set of keys. She lingered behind him, waiting for him to open the door.

Inside, he gave her some more estate agency blurb: something about genuine marble surfaces, faux fireplace, a *bijou* balcony. Becca feigned interest, moving from room to room, resisting her magpie urge to pocket a set of three pearl bracelets from a vanity chest. Had Anton been inside, he would have already tugged on a black leather pair of gloves and squeezed the man's windpipe until the information came spewing out of him like vomit.

Christian had come to rest in the living room, politely standing beside the doors to the balcony. Becca cleared her throat. He had run out of things to say.

'Is there anything else you'd like to see?' he asked.

'No,' she said. 'I'm all done.'

'Well then. Shall we…?'

'I need to know one thing,' she deadpanned, and he stopped in his tracks. 'I need to know the whereabouts of your brother.'

Christian said nothing at first, a look of confusion flickering across his features. 'I'm sorry, what?'

'Your elder brother. Thomas Holt. I need to know where he is.'

Christian Holt took a step backward, held up one hand. 'I'm here to show you a flat.'

Becca took a step forward. 'I'm not interested in this flat. Let me give you a nudge. Your brother was last seen in South America, in Chile. I need to know where he's gone.'

She watched his face for the reaction. Gone was the uber-friendly, salesman act. He was frowning at her now, the nature of her questions sinking in. He stood his ground, a muscle ticking in his square jawline. 'I've not seen my brother in over a year. I have another appointment to get to. I have to ask you to leave.'

She held up her hands in submission. 'Tell me where he is and I'm gone.'

His expression darkened, his voice dipping a notch. 'I don't know who you are. I know nothing. Now get out of this flat before I call the police.'

She felt pleasantly surprised to find that Christian Holt was indeed in possession of a backbone.

'I said get out,' he repeated.

'Have you heard from him?'

'I'm not answering any of your questions.'

'Has he called you?'

He turned then, making tracks towards the front door. Becca bent down, lifting the knife from her boot. She followed, her pace quicker than his. Turning her shoulder, she pushed the full force of her body into his back, sending him crashing into the front door. Sinking her fingers into the cotton fabric of his shirt collar, she yanked him around, only to have him knee her in the stomach, sending her sprawling backwards into a photograph frame on the wall. He yanked open the front door, moving out into the stairwell and on to the stairs. Becca went after him, leaping over the bannister, and – stymied by the tight fabric of her pencil skirt – came crashing down on top of him, sending the two of them tumbling half-way down the concrete steps. Becca clambered atop his chest, flicked out the knife, lifting it underneath his chin, drawing a thin line of blood. His breath came out in rasps.

'Tell me where he is,' she ordered.

'I spoke to him, he was in Chile.'

She pressed the knife harder. 'Where in Chile? When?'

He was holding out hands in horizontal surrender. She looked to his eyes. Sweat had pooled on his upper lip. There were two or three flecks on blood on his collar, his tie shunted out of place.

Be like Anton, she thought. *Gouge his throat.*

'He didn't say. He didn't say where he was going.'

'But you spoke to him.'

Christian Holt managed a nod. She wondered if Anton got a kick from their fear, the people he went after, a rush of adrenaline.

'When was this?'

'About a week ago.'

Downstairs, the metal security door opened with a low squeak. Becca glanced down through metal railings to witness a man entering with some shopping bags, humming to himself. Straightening, she wiped the blade of the knife with two fingers, folding it away and tucking the article back into her boot. With one further glance at Christian, she hit the stairs at a run. Pushing past the man with the bags, she was out of the door and on to the road within a matter of seconds.

Chapter 11

London, England
18 January, 2017

Anton reverse parked the battered silver Citroën Xsara into its space, a ten-minute walk from Elephant and Castle. He kept the engine running, yanking up the handbrake, allowing his gaze to rest on an ageing steering wheel. Dry heat rattled through the vents. The interior smelled fusty, the view through the windscreen soon obscured by drizzle. The drive back to London had taken more than two hours, in which time he had thought about precisely nothing.

Anton remained seated. He knew he should get going. His flat, which he had pictured in his head on many occasions, would be frigid and empty. The dishes would still be balanced precariously in the sink, dried food encrusted on the ceramic surfaces and splashed on to the linoleum floor. Outside the window, train wheels would shriek against the tracks until midnight. He questioned whether he would find himself alone in the darkness again, sat on the sofa, unable to sleep despite emptying his mind of all other thoughts. It was at these inconsolable moments he would allow himself one brief flash of the white sand underfoot, a calm flat ocean, a palm tree and a hammock. In a split second the picture would be gone again.

He reached across to the glove box for his phone inside. Switched on the handset, which, after a few moments, registered a missed call from Becca. He called her back.

'Did you get anything?' he asked when she picked up.

'Holt's brother has spoken to him. Says he is still in Chile,' she said.

Anton straightened in the driving seat. 'You got a precise location?'

'Not yet. I couldn't get any further. We were disturbed.'

'You want my help? I'll talk to Belosi.'

'Give me some more time. Did Belosi give you the name of those journalists?'

'One of them. He doesn't know the other.'

There was a silence. All business transactions complete, he realised their conversations didn't flow as easily as they had done before she went away.

'How's Richie?' he asked, in his best attempt at small talk. 'Boss was asking.'

'He was still asleep when I left this morning. I think he's enjoying his old routine after prison regs. He's all right.'

'Tell him I said hello.'

'I will.'

She hung up. He stared at the screen on his phone. She hadn't asked about his trip to see Capricorn. Usually it would be one of the things she would ask about, given that she saw her uncle rarely. He killed the engine, frustrated by his own paranoia.

The rendezvous point had been a wooded clearing on the western edges of the New Forest beside a burned-out tree. They had met there once before. He parked his car a mile north, making the rest of the journey on foot over coarse, wet terrain. It felt good to be out of the city, with spongy moss and brambles underfoot, Anton more used to the soles of his shoes pounding grimy concrete. The dew on the ground lingered out in the countryside, an early morning layer of mist that the sun hadn't yet been able to shift. When he reached it, what was left of the deciduous tree was in the shape of a V, dead and ugly on one side, the bark on the other still thriving. Soggy brown leaves surrounded the base.

Anton pulled his overcoat around him, only the sound of the cawing crows for company. There was no road to the clearing, only a dirt track that stopped two hundred metres away, yet he knew to expect the imposing shiny black Mercedes-Benz GLS Class any minute. It would be driven by Haaziq, an orphan from Tower Hamlets who'd spent his childhood in and out of foster homes. Anton didn't know Haaziq's full story: that had been Denham's domain. It didn't matter to him. What mattered to him was that so far, the young driver had proved reliable.

Minutes later, as expected, Haaziq stopped the Mercedes 4x4 a few metres from where Anton was standing. The driver got out, opening up the back door fully, allowing Solomon Capricorn's feet to touch the grass.

Anton straightened. It had been a while since they had extended the courtesy of shaking hands. Since their disagreement over whether to extract the contents of Sabina Cordero's safe and Capricorn's decision to have Denham organise a robbery, cutting him out completely, relations had still not thawed. Standing in the mist, Anton felt they were as cold as the air that surrounded them. Haaziq got back into the car and reversed it to a safe distance, the look on the driver's face one of relief that he didn't have to linger outside. Behind the windscreen he blew air into his hands cupping his mouth.

'Thank you for driving down to meet me, Anton,' Capricorn said. 'I had meetings last night and this morning in Cornwall. This seemed like the most logical place.'

Anton gave another nod, looked his boss over. He was wearing a suit, with an overcoat and cashmere scarf. He knew where Becca got her looks from; though it was Capricorn's late father who had possessed the red hair she had inherited. Richie had turned out more like his father, the hippy. Capricorn glanced at his watch. Anton took note of his pallid-looking skin. He lacked his usual finesse, looking like he hadn't slept.

'Can't linger, Anton, come on. Spit it out.'

Anton repeated the information that Sancho Belosi had told him over the phone from Uruguay. 'The name in her passport is Nashaly Akinyemi. She's a journalist who goes professionally by the name Natalie Cambridge. Her mother is Diane Cambridge, the newspaper editor. She works out of the Insight News International building—'

'It's in West India Quay. I know it. I've met Diane Cambridge before.'

Capricorn was pacing over the wet leaves in his brogues. Anton looked down. The shoes were picking up mud and grass at the edges of the soles. He reminded himself to tell Capricorn to wipe his shoes before he got back into his car.

'And the other one?' Capricorn asked.

'Belosi didn't know his name. Male, black hair and glasses. I'm trying to get that information.'

There was a silence.

'Why do I feel like your standards are slipping? In the past you would have had that information for me by now.'

Anton looked up, Capricorn's glare burning a hole through his ribcage.

'Belosi refused to speak to me until the funds had reached the account.'

Capricorn gave a snort. 'Twenty thousand for the identity of one pathetic little girl. I would that his nephew had died a horrible bloody death at the hands of Thomas fucking Holt.'

'I need a few days and I will know who the other journalist is.'

'Make it quick.'

He was looking him up and down. It reminded Anton of the first time they had set eyes upon one another. They had been young in those days. Capricorn had been sizing him up back then, asking himself whether Anton was a man worthy of the task ahead.

'Do we know what they discussed with Sabi?'

Anton gave a light shrug. 'The robbery, most likely. The contents of the safe. Her brother's death in Argentina.'

Capricorn's face was lined with tension. Anton knew that the only reason Capricorn hadn't ordered Sabina Cordero dead years ago was because he was still obsessing over her, whether or not she still cared for him, which in Anton's view was not possible. If she had held any regard towards him then why would she now decide to talk to the press? Because she was no longer in possession of her collateral? It didn't matter to Sabina Cordero that she was mother to Capricorn's illegitimate child. But it mattered to Capricorn. As it turned out, there were some lines even he was unwilling to cross.

'Do you think she contacted the press herself?'

'Either she contacted them, or Holt sent another copy of Clare Buchanan's statement elsewhere. He could have sent it to Diane Cambridge like he did Neil Rawlins.'

Capricorn was pacing. Anton noted the fleeting, yet twisted flinch at the mention of Buchanan's name.

'I need to know exactly what was said,' Capricorn snapped, almost as though reading Anton's mind. 'I want transcripts of the interviews. We don't have anyone inside Insight News?'

'I'm working on it.'

'Work harder. Apply some pressure.'

Anton gave a nod.

'What about Holt? Can we have at least one Belosi nephew go after him? The *uninjured* one?'

'Dante. Rolo is the injured one.'

'I don't fucking care which is which.'

'Holt could still be somewhere in Chile. Becca is tracking down Holt's younger brother as we speak.'

'Becca?'

He gave a shrug. 'With Denham gone—'

Capricorn looked away. The breeze rustled the branches overhead. Anton questioned whether Capricorn regretted getting rid of the lawyer now that journalists were involved.

Capricorn was looking at his watch. 'Fine. Keep Belosi in check. Not another cent until they find Holt, understood? A bonus if they can slit his throat. You follow the newspaper trail, find out what they know. I'll look for a replacement for Denham.'

Anton stood motionless. 'Anything else?'

'That's all.'

'You have mud on your shoes.'

'What?'

'Mud. Wipe it off before you get back to London.' Capricorn's wife had a habit of asking questions. 'I'll be in touch regarding the journalists.'

Anton raised his hand, signalling to Haaziq to bring the car over. He was out in a flash and opening the back door. Anton watched as Capricorn got into the back. His arm reappeared, muddy set of brogues hanging from his fingers. Haaziq took them, expression unsure.

'Wipe them over there, on that patch of moss,' Anton said, pointing.

Haaziq did as he was directed before getting back into the driver's seat.

As the car reversed away, Anton raised his hand to Haaziq. Twenty minutes after he had arrived, soles of his own shoes sliding over a squelchy landscape, he returned to his car. He sat with the heater on for bursts of five minutes at a time for an hour, ensuring Capricorn was long gone, before making his way back to London.

At Elephant and Castle he walked from his parked car through fine drizzle, reflecting on his conversation with Becca. He knew how he would have handled Holt's younger brother, so now he would have been in no doubt of Holt's exact location. He gritted his teeth, reminding himself that Becca deserved a free rein, and that she would have had her own way of doing things. He owed her that much. He was used to her picking pockets. She'd never expressed an interest in anything outside of that realm before, and, other than perhaps her brother Richie, she was the finest pickpocket he knew.

Becca was reliable. She could be trusted. Yet she was still finding that she had to prove herself to Capricorn.

Something niggled in a dark corner of his mind. He told himself it didn't matter that Becca had seemed so keen to find Tom Holt again. That she was driven by loyalty to her family.

He was still thinking about Becca as he entered his building. He emerged from the lift to find a figure crouched outside his front door. Anton tensed. She was back.

When she raised her head, he could see her eyes were raw and puffy. The last thing he needed inside his flat, along with dishes piled high in the sink, was an emotional, needy female.

'What are you doing here?' he growled, putting the key in the lock and proceeding inside, wishing she would vanish.

Tatiana struggled to her feet. He allowed her to enter before slamming the door shut.

'You come here and I'm not here, you don't wait,' he reminded her. 'I've told you that. Don't ever wait outside this place again.'

A fresh wave of tears spilled over to her cheeks. She was wearing a denim jacket lined with a layer of white fluffy material; hair scraped back off her face and piled high in a top knot and too much make up. She was knocking her knuckles together.

'I heard from a solicitor today about Al's will.'

Anton pulled up short. He looked back at her, eye makeup smudged, shoulders hunched and tears streaming, causing him to question why he had ever bothered taking advantage of her in the first place.

'He's left me the house in Streatham. Everything else… he left to her.'

Anton took a moment to absorb her words. A small explosion detonated in the pit of his stomach.

'What do you mean?'

'Denham's first wife. She gets everything else.'

Anton squeezed his eyes shut, ran fingers through still wet hair. His head began to throb. He should have seen it coming.

'What did Capricorn tell you when you married him?' Anton hissed.

More tears leaked onto his carpet. 'Sh- show him love.'

'Show him love. And now he's left everything to his ex-fucking wife.'

Tatiana crumpled. 'But I did not love him! I never did!'

Anton stared down at her. 'It doesn't matter. It wasn't what you were supposed to do. Do you know the trouble Capricorn went to, to get you here? You are an ungrateful little bitch.'

'He's left her a house in Miami.'

It took him another moment to decipher what she had said through all the sobbing. 'What house in Miami?'

Snot was oozing from her nose. 'There was a house in Miami.'

He raised his voice. 'What house?'

'I didn't know anything about it. He never mentioned it.'

Anton massaged the uneven bridge of his broken nose. A lot of the nerves had died, the sensation numbed. Tatiana was wiping her face and nose on her sleeve. He hadn't known anything about Denham owning a house in Florida. The idea worried him. He had always suspected Denham of concealing things from Capricorn. What could Denham have concealed, away from Streatham on foreign soil? And why had he left everything to his first wife?

He closed his eyes. 'The first wife. Remind me of her name.'

Tatiana wiped her cheeks, got to her feet. 'Belinda Channing. She was at the funeral.'

'Where does she live, do you know?'

She shook her head: no. 'Anton? Will you... hold me, please?'

Fresh tears, more than he could deal with. 'Get out,' he hissed as Tatiana's expression collapsed into another bout of unadulterated sobbing. 'Get out.'

He grabbed a portion of her collar, yanking her roughly towards the door. Shoving her outside in the corridor, he listened to the sound of her crying echoing for several minutes after he had slammed the door in her face.

Part Two

Chapter 12

Panama
11 February, 2017

Tom stepped off the gangway, soles of his shoes landing on Central American concrete. For eight hours the previous afternoon, the vessel had traversed the Panama Canal. On any other day, it would have been a sight to behold, had he not been so impatient to get his body back on dry land. The ship had docked in the northern Port of Colón, on the Caribbean coastline, the passengers all disembarking the previous afternoon. Tom snatched a breath, slung his bag over his shoulder, sticking to his plan to slip away the moment the crew were granted permission to leave.

There had been a breeze up on deck, not so on the ground. Hot air hit him like a wall. According to the stewards it was dry season in Panama, temperatures hovering around thirty-one degrees during main daylight hours. Under his jeans he was already starting to perspire. Clouds were non-existent.

After immigration, a short line of yellow cabs lined up waiting outside the main cruise terminal, each vehicle more banged up than the next. The driver at the front put up a hand. Tom squeezed his frame into the rear of the car, the chassis creaking under the additional weight, asking in Spanish to be driven to the local bus terminal.

'*Tres dólares*,' the driver grunted, pulling away, Tom giving him a nod in acknowledgement.

The radio was on, audible over the whirr of the air conditioning vents.

It was a catchy tune, upbeat and sexy, a gentle throb to it. He didn't know the song, but the lyrics gave him something to focus on, the Spanish provocative, something about making a girl forget her last name. *Despacito. Slowly.* An image of Becca floated through his mind. He wondered what she was doing at that very moment.

He shook off a memory of her on a beach from months earlier. Through the cab window, the centre of Colón seemed like a series of ramshackle buildings and corrugated iron roofs, streets blighted by fly-tipping, chain-link fences and falling power lines. The stewards on the ship had warned him of the dangers of a gringo walking alone through the centre. Of the one hundred and twenty-five dollars he had remaining in his pocket, the short cab ride suddenly seemed worth every penny.

Back in Chile, Panchito had handed him a burgundy red-coloured passport with the words *República de Chile* emblazoned on the front in gold letters.

'Welcome Stefan Schneider,' he had said, looking over his glasses. 'You were born in 1979 in Santiago. Your father's name was Kurt, your mother's, Agnes. You are of German descent, as were your parents. You speak any German?'

'*Ein bisschen*,' Tom had replied, looking down at the passport and turning it in his fingers.

'Good thing we speak Spanish here in Chile, no?'

The document was an impressive fake. Inside had his

scanned picture, taken one day prior. It had a one-week-old issue date.

'Thank you,' Tom had breathed, handing over the keys to Aksel's Suzuki. 'So you managed to get me on the boat?'

'Yes, yes, of course. You are part of the crew now, with years of experience travelling on cruise liners. It will get you to Panama as requested. Your salary will be paid into a bank account which belongs to my associates.'

Tom stopped short. Panchito pulled an apologetic face, held up his palms. '*Perdón, mi amigo*. Passage only. You can keep any tips that you make.'

Tom frowned. 'What am I getting tipped for?'

'You'll be working the casino. As… I don't know how you say in English. *El Crupier*. You know much about gambling?'

The frown had dissolved into a gentle smile. He hadn't bothered explaining to Panchito how he had come to be in South America in the first place. How gambling away his previous boss's company money at a Cape Town casino had caused him to accept a job offer from a lawyer named Albert Denham, in order to pay off a debt. So yes, he knew a thing or two about being a croupier. As it had turned out, of the nine hundred US he'd made in tips on the cruise, most of the money had been divvied up amongst the crew, the chefs and stewards.

There had been a lot of time to think on the cruise ship. Too much time in between shifts. The casino ran two shift patterns: the early, from 11 a.m. to 7 p.m., and the late, from 7 p.m. to 3 a.m. Tom preferred the latter, when the more serious gamblers would emerge from the woodwork and the tips grew larger with every cocktail the punters could consume. They came from a variety of backgrounds: rich Latinos, richer Europeans and Americans looking for a change from the Caribbean Sea routes. When the late shift finished he would down a couple of rum and Cokes before crashing into bed, waking at noon the following morning. The early shift meant killing an evening in his matchbox-sized cabin, yet no matter how often he tried to focus on getting to Panama and finding his father, his thoughts would invariably turn to her: the red-headed thief.

Becca wasn't his usual type. She was skinny with small, flat breasts, no meat on her, but with striking ginger hair. She wasn't even personable. That she was still inside his head after a three-month absence was irritating.

The cab pulled up outside the bus terminal. At the ticket office Tom asked for the cheapest fare to Panama City and was duly directed to a *diablo rojo*, a 'red devil' bus: a gas-guzzling graffiti-covered, flamboyant neon monstrosity that in any other territory would have been banned for crimes against the environment, had it not still been tearing up the roads in Central America. Her name – the bus's name – was Maria Guadalupe, and on her grime-splattered rear, complete with reflective mud flaps, was the flamboyant image of a busty, winking, Latina female with full lips, an ample chest and a cinched-in waist. He purchased a ticket, sat near the back on a moth-eaten seat next to an open window. The driver gave him a backwards glance, the sight of a six-foot-two gringo not going entirely unnoticed. The vehicle stopped every seven or eight minutes at the start of the journey, picking up and dropping off curvy women with generous buttocks and tight denim cut-offs, hot pink vest tops, cheap material caught up between voluptuous rolls, dark-skinned grubby toddlers in tow, little girls with frizzy hair tied up like the top of a pineapple. They peered at him in fascination over the back of the seat with innocent eyes, white-toothed coy smiles. Sometimes he waved and smiled back, all the time wondering how he'd managed to get himself into this position, foolish enough to have ever let Albert Denham into his London flat.

A jolt brought him back to reality: the bus plummeting in and out of a large pothole. He flinched, rubbed his stubble. On each side of the motorway was dense jungle, a blur of flora, banana leaves and tropical palms: a lush sea of green. The high-rise skyline of Panama City crept into view before lunch, the bus having covered barely thirty miles.

Tom got out at the main bus terminus, asking the driver to direct him to the nearest subway station. He had researched the journey on the cruise ship inside the staff quarters, knowing he had to get to *Iglesia del Carmen* station on the subway and continue on foot to an area known as Bella Vista and the location of his father's office. He thought about what Oliver Holt would look like these days, and if he would choose to welcome his long-lost middle son back into his life. He highly doubted it.

At the subway station he purchased a travel card from an automated machine. It was a short journey – only four stops – to *Iglesia del Carmen*. He was the only non-Latino male in the carriage, garnering a few stares from shaven-headed *hombres* with tattoos. The ride was a lot smoother than the London Underground, only four carriages per train. As he climbed the stairs back up to the surface, Tom pulled out a hand-drawn map to his father's office from the back pocket of his jeans. At street level he was met with a chorus of engines, a horde of traffic lining up at the lights beside a magnificently ornate white church with twin spires. *Iglesia del Carmen* certainly had more majesty than he had expected. Glancing down at the sketch map, he tried to work out his north from his south, asking a passer-by for the way to Bella Vista.

Within minutes the back of his neck felt grimy. He turned off the main drag, descending down a slope into an area that seemed to be filled with hostels, casinos and places to exchange cash. There was a smell of refuse in the air, the pavements rocky and uneven, a couple of dark-skinned vagrants. Walking downhill, his gaze was hooked by a woman in a floating sun-yellow dress, cut too low, with spaghetti straps that barely supported her breasts. She had bright red lips, skyscraper wedged shoes. Averting his eyes, he reminded himself that he wasn't in Chile anymore. Checking his map for a second time, he managed to locate the Lebanese restaurant at the corner of a T-junction, and knew he must be close. Panama City was diminutive in comparison to most other capitals. He used his rolled-up shirt sleeve to wipe the sweat from his brow, feeling the heat rising amongst the traffic fumes. Cars were bumper to bumper. It was half past eleven. Walking fifty metres further, when he had managed to find the supposed location of his father's office – the address Christian had given him over the phone in Santiago – he looked on in disbelief. A chain-link fence surrounded a would-be car park, the entire area lined with the remnants of concrete debris, left over from where an entire building had obviously been brought down months, or years, earlier. Squinting at the map, he checked he was looking in the right place.

His palms were sweaty, heart banging. He found himself turning in circles, looking for answers. There was a Marriott hotel across the road, clearly marked on the map. His father's building was on the map. *It was on the damn map.*

Heat from the sun prickled his skin, his tongue sticking to the roof of his mouth, the back of his neck already starting to tingle with the prelude to burning. He didn't have a phone, only a change of clothes and a pile of creased-up dollar bills. He pictured his father on a beach somewhere, rotund, pale skin lobster red, bare feet up on a sunbed under a parasol, sipping on a bottle of local beer and wearing a hat. Was he in Panama, or had he moved on to Costa Rica or Mexico, anywhere safe enough for an old man to live out his days in peace? In his haste to escape Chile, Tom had not ruminated on the idea of what he would do were he unable to locate his father. Panama could still hold the information he was looking for on Capricorn, but he would have no way of accessing or, more pertinently, *paying* for any of it.

He chewed his lip. There was a breeze whipping up. Nearby was a coffee stand, under an awning lined by a bamboo fence. Grateful to be in the shade, he collapsed into a seat. Without his father, he would have nowhere to go. A hundred and twenty dollars was not going to stretch much beyond a couple of nights in a shitty hostel. He ordered a coffee, wished it could have been a cold beer.

He sat for a while, contemplating what to do. He could ask Christian to wire him some more cash, though his younger brother would likely refuse. His older brother Jacob probably wouldn't even pick up the phone to him. He thought about contacting the journalist, Nash.

After an hour spent in balmy shade, he got up and walked in a direction away from the subway, what he guessed to be south. Within a few minutes he was in a financial district, all steel and glass, within another few minutes finding himself looking over a calm Pacific Ocean, the tide out, back to where he had been before the ship had traversed the canal. Yet in that two-day period he had made zero progress.

He took a left, kept walking for several minutes against the traffic flow, sweat pouring off his hairline. He managed to locate a couple of payphones in the shadow of a giant concrete overpass. Inside a small department store he persuaded a female cashier to exchange dollar bills for coins, twenty of them, shiny with the word 'balboa' minted on them.

Back outside under the shop's awning, allowing some respite from the relentless tropical sun, Tom fed the unit with enough coins to make an international call. When Christian answered, he heard background noise, as though his brother was in the pub somewhere. The payphone beeped, alerting him that it required more change. Tom fed coins and spoke at the same time.

'It's me,' he said, raising his voice above the grind of the traffic.

'Shit, wait, I need to go outside.' There were some rustling noises. 'Where are you?' Christian asked when he came back on to the line.

'I'm in Panama City.'

'Thank God. I told a woman you were in Chile.'

'What woman?'

'A woman, she pretended to be a client interested in a flat viewing. A week ago. She attacked me. Held a fucking knife to my throat.'

Tom froze. The traffic snarl reverberated off the overpass. 'Did she have red hair?'

'No, sort of blonde.'

'Could it have been a wig?'

'I don't know. Maybe.'

'What was her name?'

'Arabella Blunt. About thirty-odd.'

'Did she have kind of a pointy nose? Kind of moody?'

'Yes.'

'She's dangerous, don't let her near you. Did you tell the police?'

'No. I told work I'd fallen on some stairs. Should I have?'

Tom faltered. 'No.'

'Are you going to tell me what's going on? Did you find Dad's office?'

'It's rubble. Nothing there but a car park. You got any other addresses for him?'

'Shit. Not that I know of.'

'Chris, I'm running out of options here.'

'I've got some old papers in a box at home. Might be something there. I'd need to check. It's been years—'

'Can you do it now?'

'Right this minute? I'm out with work.'

'Tell them something came up. I'm on a payphone, I'll give you the number. I'll wait here until you can call me back.'

'I might be a few hours.'

'I can wait. And, Chris… watch your back.'

The security guard tried to move him on twice, but he kept on coming back, eager to escape the heat, to wait on the tiled floor beside the phone so as not to miss Christian's call. Hours later, the sky had turned a shade of coral, temperature dipping to something wholly more bearable, pleasant even. Under the awning there was a breeze on his cheeks. The level of traffic under the overpass had trebled, the sound of horns rising from the streets in unison like the world's worst orchestra tuning up.

He was weary, in need of a shower. At the shrill echo of the ringer, Tom lurched to his feet, grabbing the handset.

'Chris?'

'I looked through every single box of crap I still own,' he heard his younger brother say, Tom's heart sinking. 'I think I may have something.'

A much-needed gush of adrenaline hit his veins. Tom straightened. 'Tell me.'

'I don't know whether it's right, but it says Apartment 7B, Camino Real. Somewhere called Punta Paitilla.'

His sinking heart sat up and sang for its supper. He forgave his brother's non-Spanish pronunciation, instead committing the words to memory.

'Look, this was yonks ago, I don't know if he'll still be there,' Christian continued. 'It's on the back of a postcard from 2002. He must have sent it after I left college.'

'I can try.'

'Let me know if you find him, yeah?'

'I owe you.'

'You're telling *me*.'

'I'll make it up to you I swear.'

'I remembered something about the woman. She said she was engaged. Wore a diamond ring.'

Tom couldn't think about Becca at that moment. 'OK. Cheers, Chris. Look after yourself. I'll be in touch.'

He hung up, repeated the address in his head. Turned and went back inside the department store to find that the sour-faced shop assistant who had exchanged some coin change for him was still on duty. As he reappeared at her checkout, she looked up, expression unmoved.

'*Disculpe*,' Tom said politely, asking in Spanish where he could find his father's building.

She raised one hand, making gestures towards the back of the shop and beyond. '*Esta zona es Punta Paitilla*,' she mumbled, indicating that he was in the right place. She shrugged at the name of the building.

An American behind him in the queue pointed him in the right direction. Paitilla was up a hill, apartment blocks crammed in one next to the other like a giant rabbit run. Camino Real itself was one of the smaller blocks and, despite its prime position with views of the ocean, compared to some of the surrounding edifices looked squat and outmoded.

The building was a soft shade of peach, a large canopy protruding over the front entrance with its name across it in black lettering. The street lights were coming on as Tom approached a guard, sitting inside a booth beside the entrance to the parking garage. He explained that he was looking for the gentleman living in apartment 7B.

The guard looked blank. Tom repeated the name: *Señor Holt.* He watched the guard's slender fingers move some things about on the desk in front of him that were covering a pile of papers. Without showing Tom, he glanced through it then shook his head.

'*Nadie en ese nombre vive aquí,*' he said. No one of that name lives here.

Tom massaged his eyeballs. '*Estás seguro?*' Are you sure?

'*Si si, señor.*'

Tom asked to speak to the person currently living in 7B.

Gingerly, the guard raised a white handset. Speaking to the person at the other end, he asked if he could bring up a visitor.

Tom was escorted upstairs in an old lift. On the seventh floor the lights were dim, an odd scent coming from underneath one of the two doors leading to apartments A and B.

The guard rang the bell to the apartment, Tom hanging back. The door opened a fraction; at floor level two cats were making a seemingly desperate escape. Inside, there was little light, the atmosphere hazy, a stench of tobacco hit his nostrils. An old woman poked her head out, her face a myriad of wrinkles, hair grey and curling, eyelids droopy. She brought a half-smoked cigarette to her mouth, taking a long drag, exhaling smoke out behind her. Tom heard the squawking of parrots.

The guard stammered that Tom was looking for someone named Oliver Holt.

At the mention of the name, the woman's eyes narrowed yet more. Tom wondered when it was she had last ventured outside. When she opened her mouth to speak, the sound that emerged was mechanised, gravelly, as though her vocal chords were too loose or had been damaged by years of nicotine abuse.

'*Casco Viejo*,' she said, and closed the door.

He sat in the corner of a rum bar called Pedro Mandinga, a place that distilled its own spirit. Ceiling fans rotated overhead, the evening pleasantly warm, the décor a shout out to the days before anyone had even considered the challenge of building a canal through the isthmus, heavy on the wood panelling and muted tropical motifs. He had tried their house rum, followed by a different brand called *Abuelo*, and was starting to feel his brain floating around inside his skull, as though disassociated from the remainder of his body. He was contemplating sleeping on a bench, or perhaps finding a cheap hostel that would let him shower and get his head down. Tomorrow he would have to start knocking on doors.

Panama's old town was, geographically at least, reasonably petite, in a Spanish colonial style, what he imagined Old Havana could look like with a greater financial investment. Not to say that Panama's old town was not dilapidated, only that the investment had clearly been made in some parts and not others. Little cobbled streets were lined with boutique balconied apartments, neat pavements, bars and restaurants, not a skyscraper in sight. It was stylish, yet quaint.

He knocked back the last of the *Abuelo* rum, signalling to a curvy waitress for the bill. He gave her a healthy tip, despite the knowledge that he needed to retain as much money as he could. She reminded him of the carefree Chilean girls out on the lake.

His thoughts settled on Becca. He grimaced. She had a habit of creeping up on him when he least expected it. Christian had said the woman who had attacked him had been wearing an engagement ring. Becca had a talent for pretending to be something she wasn't; he had seen it first-hand in Argentina. She excelled at faking anything she turned her hand to, intimacy included, if it was of some benefit to her, or more pertinently, her employers. Had Anton tasked her to go after Christian? He hauled himself to his feet, swaying, picking up his backpack, resolving not to dwell on her, knowing he would probably never see her again.

The room slanted and for a few seconds he was transported back to the cruise ship. In front of him, the barman was concocting three separate rum cocktails. Tom's fingers gripped the lip of the polished bar surface.

'I'm looking for an Englishman who lives around here,' Tom slurred in his native tongue. 'Name is Oliver Holt.'

The barman looked up before continuing on with what he was doing. Squeezing a lime over a glass, he said, 'Stay on this road, there's a French bistro on the left. Keep walking, he lives in the building on the corner of the next block.'

Tom blinked, gripped the bar tighter, reeling. The barman was signalling to the waitress to fetch the drinks he had finished making. Tom mumbled in gratitude, turned, veering out into the street, letting the wind rush through him. Since Chile, he had felt like a hollow form of himself, a paper cut-out. He started walking, through drunken eyes the streetlights pulsating in anticipation. The barman's comment had been almost throwaway. *He lives in the building on the corner of the next block*. Tom quickened his pace, finding it hard to walk in a straight line, keeping to the pavement as the traffic crawled by.

The French bistro looked warm and inviting. He was hungry, but kept on. Didn't know an apartment number, which meant he would have to choose at random.

At the door, his finger collided with one of the ten or so doorbells. A voice came through the intercom.

'*Buscando a* Oliver Holt,' Tom spat into the speaker, tongue too thick in his mouth.

The voice on the other end spoke perfect American-English. 'Try number three.'

Whoever it was had hung up before he could offer thanks. Tom squinted in the dark at the key pad. The ink behind the number three button had faded. He pressed it. After no reaction, he pressed it for a second time, this time holding his finger down for some time before releasing it.

'*Si?*' a voice said.

Tom moved closer to the intercom speaker. '*Hola, buenos noches. Estoy buscando a mi padre, Oliver Holt.*'

There was a silence, before he detected the crash of the phone handset being dropped. Moments later, coming from the inside, he heard a door creak open and the thump of footsteps, followed by the crack of a lock. The main door opened a fraction, a face peering out. The man, who was Hispanic in appearance with dark skin, regarded Tom with a dubious expression. Without warning, he grabbed Tom by the bicep, yanking him inside. The floor was tiled with a navy and white variation on fleur-de-lis.

'*Ven rápido!*' the man barked at him, Tom allowing himself to be towed up the staircase, clutching the wrought-iron banister, not quite aware of what was going on.

At the top of the stairs they entered an apartment, the number 3 hanging at a crooked angle. Inside the man hammered on a closed door along a corridor. 'Oliver! Holt! *Abre esta puerta!*'

There was no response. 'Oliver, stop!' the man then continued in English. 'Please! Your son is here!'

Tom straightened, a hit of adrenaline bringing him back to life.

'He's in there,' the man breathed. 'Please, you have to be quick.'

'Dad?' Tom said out loud, running his fingers against the roughly painted surface of the door. 'Dad, it's me.'

He twisted, dropped his bag, bringing his shoulder into contact with the wood. It wasn't enough. He took a step back, tried it again, shoulder slamming up against the surface, pain shooting through his tendons. He used his foot. On the fourth try, the lock broke and the door flew open.

It took a moment for his eyes to adjust in the dim light. Lying on the bed was the unmistakable figure of his father, the man he remembered, only older, fatter, wearing shorts and a shirt, one leg hanging off the side of the mattress, a full head of shock white hair sticking up in all directions on the pillow. His eyes were closed; face puffy, shirt unbuttoned almost to his belly button. The window was open, curtain whipped up in the breeze.

Tom's eyes dropped to the nightstand. Next to his father's head was an empty glass on its side, a bottle of *Abuelo* rum with two fingers left inside, and a loaded gun.

Chapter 13

In the early hours, Oliver Holt opened his eyes. They were bright blue and bloodshot. Tom spent the night on a wooden chair beside the bed, drifting in and out of sleep, watching his father's chest rise and fall.

'Is that really you?' Oliver managed.

'Hi Dad,' was Tom's reply.

His father struggled to raise his head. As he did so, a shaft of light from the window illuminated the full head of white hair, still in Einstein levels of disarray. 'Are you a dream?'

A smile touched Tom's lips. To prove it, he reached out and gave his father's forearm a squeeze. 'It's really me.'

'You look tanned.'

'I've been in Chile. Working on a lake.'

'South America? I thought South Africa.'

'Things changed.'

His father sunk back against the pillows. 'You look like your mother,' he muttered, his eyes gently closing again.

'Can I get you anything?'

Oliver didn't reply. Tom watched him sleep. He had lost track of the years, the last time he had seen the old man in the flesh. Now he would be seventy-three. His skin was deep brown, leathery, in stark contrast to the white hair on his head that curled in a matted layer on his arms and legs.

On his face was a white moustache, neatly trimmed, his nose showing signs of alcohol dependency.

Tom dragged his gaze away. The sunlight now streaming into the room was the first time he had been able to take in his surroundings. The room – no, the entire apartment – was threadbare, signs of damp where the ceiling met the walls, a wonky shelf containing a few paperbacks, presumably no more because they would start to slide off. One was a dog-eared copy of Dumas' *The Count of Monte Cristo*, the other a doorstop-sized Proust. Tom's gaze settled on the gun, a snub-nosed revolver, a Smith & Wesson Model 36, two bullets in the chamber. Earlier in the night, he had moved it out of his father's reach to the other side of the wooden cupboard with missing doors that doubled as a nightstand. He wondered, had he not ended up at the rum bar the previous evening and discovered his location, whether his father would ever have summoned the courage to pull the trigger.

He heard a soft knock. Miguel Navarro Garcia – the Latino who had introduced himself to Tom the previous evening – poked his head around the door. He was Panamanian; a friend of his father's.

'Good morning,' Miguel said in heavily accented English, eyes glancing to Oliver and lowering his voice. 'I thought you and I could take a walk. Maybe fetch coffee.'

Tom heaved himself to his feet, stretching up to the ceiling. He badly needed a shower. 'Will he be alright?'

'He'll sleep it off.'

Tom leaned forward, lifting the revolver and the bottle containing the last dregs of rum. 'Can we find a home for these?'

Miguel took them. 'Leave it to me.'

Minutes later they were walking down cobbles, sun on their backs and a breeze in the air. Tom followed Miguel without the first clue where he was going. The older man was a head shorter than him, wearing jeans, a crisp white short-sleeved shirt, leather loafers without socks and his hair slicked back.

'How do you know my father?' Tom asked.

Miguel put his hands in his pockets, puffed out his cheeks. 'I was his client once upon a time. In the days when your father first came to Panama; '93 I think it was.'

'That was two years after he walked out on my family.'

'He has nothing but good things to say about your mother.'

Tom swallowed. 'Tell me. Why does my father want to kill himself?'

Miguel held out his hand, signalling that they should turn to the right down a small street with buildings only to one side. On the other side was a set of blue railings, below them a rocky beach, further out a road raised by vast concrete stilts in the Pacific Ocean.

'Out there is the Amador Causeway,' Miguel said proudly, pointing. 'Built in part with earth and rock removed from the area that is now the canal. The rainbow building you see in the far distance is the Museum of Biodiversity.'

Tom stopped, shielding his eyes. The tide was out and the leftover rocky seabed held little appeal. He looked to the sky.

'What are the birds?'

Miguel answered him without a look. 'Vultures circle in the skies above Panama City. All year round. Sometimes they land on the sidewalks and take a more human form.'

Tom squinted. They looked like black hawks. He had seen hundreds of them the previous day. Watching them circle above the low tide, it felt like a bad omen.

'Your father knows that if he doesn't kill himself, then they are going to kill him,' Miguel said.

'Who are *they*?'

Miguel smacked his lips, clasping his hands behind his back. 'That, my friend, requires an explanation, one that I will tell you over coffee.'

Tom sipped his Americano in a café with a low ceiling and black-and-white Dutch checkerboard flooring, situated adjacent to a white-pillared edifice that Miguel reliably informed him was the French Embassy. He could detect a hint of his own stench rising up from underneath his shirt. The coffee and aroma of sweet pastries masked the smell. Miguel sat on the other side of the table with his back to the wall, a frothy latte in front of him. Tom felt the urge to go and find his father, to check that he hadn't managed to locate another gun in order to blow his brains out.

'Tell me everything,' Tom said.

Miguel sipped his coffee, wiping the leftover froth from his lips with the back of his hand. He took a breath and spoke matter-of-factly. 'The short answer is that your father owes a large amount of money to a man named Juan Carlos Aguinaldo. He's a wealthy *Panameño*, who, together with his brother, owns a large amount of property all around the city. The Aguinaldo family was in up to their necks with Martinelli but no one can find enough evidence against either brother to prosecute them, or rather nobody wants to because *La*

Familia Aguinaldo have the most corrupt ties you can think of; they grease the palms of the highest levels of government and nobody, not even the lawmakers, wants to go up against them.'

'Martinelli,' Tom repeated. 'He was the former president? Deeply corrupt.'

'Right now he's laying low in Miami.'

Tom nodded once. 'Tell me more about Juan Carlos Aguinaldo.'

'The family owns entire buildings in the city built on laundered money, shining steel and glass structures with not a single soul working inside. And on the flip side, they are slum landlords in Chorillo and Curundú, but rent is cheap to keep the poorer occupants happy. Juan Carlos is the younger of two brothers. The elder brother is Oscar. Nobody has yet worked out who is the more dangerous of the two men, though Juan Carlos is said to be the more ambitious. They no longer communicate. Their business continues through intermediaries.'

'Why don't they communicate?'

'A few years ago Juan Carlos married Oscar's former wife, a woman he was screwing whilst she was still married to his brother. Blood was shed when Oscar found out about it.'

'Whose blood?'

'Jesus Vasquez. A man who worked for Oscar and who knew exactly what was going on and helped facilitate the meetings between Juan Carlos and Oscar's bride. The rest of the family is now split down the middle. I heard only the mother managed to maintain neutrality, only because she's an eighty-year-old woman with poor hearing and almost no eyesight. His enemies call Juan Carlos *El Rey*, the King.'

'His enemies call him that?'

'It's an insult. There's supermarket chain here by the same name, the implication being, that Juan Carlos went to the supermarket and didn't stop until he'd eaten all the food.'

'What does he want with my father?'

Miguel let out a sigh, put down his coffee. 'In short? He wants his money back.'

'How much?'

'More than your father can ever afford to pay. Money he invested on Juan Carlos's behalf before your father's business crumbled. Apart from an ageing Chevrolet Camaro, that apartment over there is all your father has left.'

When Tom entered the apartment he saw no sign of his father. Immediately checking the bedroom, he saw him still in the bed; relief flooded his chest.

'I'll show you the spare room,' Miguel said, nodding down the hall. 'You can shower there.'

The door clicked and groaned as he entered. Tom crossed the threshold with a sense of foreboding. He had focussed so hard on finding his father that it was hard to adjust to the reality of what he had found.

'I'll fetch you a towel,' Miguel said. 'Bathroom is behind that door.'

Tom thanked him, sinking down onto the mattress of the double bed. For a moment he blinked, then once more absorbed his surroundings. The room was painted a dirty yellow, though the paint had faded so much it was possible to see patches of the previous white wall underneath. There was a wooden wardrobe to one side. Large cracks travelled down one wall from the ceiling, diverging mid-route. It reminded him of a crumbling property in Montevideo, where he and his team had stayed when they had first arrived in the capital of Uruguay. At least there was no water coming in through the ceiling.

Fatigue hit him in waves. In the bathroom, Tom removed his clothes, skin tacky from a perma-layer of salty sweat. He glanced at his reflection in the mirror. Switching on the tap, the water, summoned from ancient pipes, came dribbling through the showerhead with the force of a whisper. Three cockroaches and a dried-up scorpion had met their final resting place in the base of the shower. He wondered when his father had last had visitors.

When he emerged into the kitchen, wearing his only remaining set of clean clothes, his father was sitting at the table, still in the same crumpled shirt, under the elevated ceiling and nursing a mug of steaming coffee. Tom stood still, watched his father rise from the chair, unsteady on his feet, the wrinkles on his face more pronounced in the light. Miguel hovered in the shadows.

'I didn't believe it was you,' his father said. 'Miguel tells me my eyes aren't deceiving me.'

Tom edged around the table. 'Do you believe your eyes now?'

His father stepped out from his chair. 'My son,' he said, tears in his eyes. Tom wrapped him in an embrace, buried his head in his shoulder, his father's scent setting off memories of his childhood in England. He held on tight, thankful he was still alive. Oliver was slapping him on the back. 'How did you find me?'

'A rum bar down the street,' Tom half-laughed, releasing his father. 'Are you alright?'

A look of shame passed across his father's features, his gaze travelling to the floor. It wasn't in keeping with the larger-than-life character Tom remembered as a nine-year-old.

'I'm glad you're here,' Oliver said. 'Sit. Would you like something to eat? I want to hear everything. How you've ended up in Panama.'

Tom lowered himself to the table. 'I came here for your help, Dad, but – now that I'm here, I can't help thinking that it's you who needs my help.'

'Help?' He waved his hand. '*Bah.* I don't need help. I need a bloody miracle, but that's another matter.'

As he'd said the words, his father had exchanged a look with Miguel, standing with his arms crossed beside the window. 'I told him about Juan Carlos,' the Panamanian confirmed.

'Why would you try and take your own life?' Tom said.

His father took a moment to respond. 'So they don't take it for me.'

Tom looked to Miguel. 'Is there a way to fix this?'

'There isn't,' Oliver interjected. 'And there won't be.'

'I wish I could help you,' Tom said. 'I've money but no access to it. Right now, I have next to nothing.'

'You said you were in Chile.'

'I had to move. I came here on a cruise ship on a false passport.'

His father's bushy brows drew sharply together. 'A false passport? Why?'

'It doesn't matter. There's a man in London who wants me dead. His influence stretches further than I thought. It's why I've come to Panama. I need help with a money trail. To expose him.'

'What do you mean? Wants you dead? What money trail?'

'You know who Charles Ebdon is?'

'The business mogul?'

'The same. He's running money through shell corporations. He's stolen millions in charitable donations for personal profit. I have no idea how deep it goes. He uses a fake name. I'm in touch with a journalist who's investigating.'

'Have they tried the Panama Papers? You know yesterday they arrested both Mossack and Fonseca; threw them in jail.'

'That's part of it. But I need to get to the heart. I need to find out who's involved and how deep it goes.'

'Why would *you* need to do that?'

Tom took a breath. 'To save my own skin. To avenge the death of a friend. And to finish what a woman named Clare Buchanan started.'

'I don't understand. Who is Clare Buchanan?'

'You wouldn't remember her. You'd left England by then. She disappeared when she stepped off a London bus in 2005. She worked for Charles Ebdon and I believed he had her murdered for what she knew.'

His father was shaking his head. 'How did you get into all of this mess? I thought you were in South Africa—'

'Long story. I got offered a job to break into a safe inside a secure compound in South America.'

'In Chile?'

'In Uruguay.'

'You were successful at this?' the Panamanian piped up, Tom detecting a change in his usual tone of voice.

Tom looked at Miguel and nodded. 'I didn't do it alone.'

'How were you not caught?'

'Because we spent months planning it.'

'But you yourself did this?'

'Like I said, I had help.'

They sat in silence. Tom pressed his palm to his forehead, allowed his eyes to drift closed. His facial hair was getting out of control and he needed a shave. Despite the open windows, the air inside the kitchen had grown stifling and sweat was once more trickling down from his hairline.

Miguel's expression was serious. He straightened, his body no longer lounging against the wall.

'I might know a way we can fix this,' he said, and Tom raised his head.

Chapter 14

London, England
9 February, 2017

Nash stared aghast at the email that she had received from Gus Fendy.

> I wanted to apologise for the way that I acted in the bar when we met. I can be a bit of a dick at times – ask Miles.
>
> I thought you should know that as part of my research for the ill-fated Ebdon biography, I did some digging into his family tree. I wanted you to see what I found – it might save you some grief. I've attached a PDF with a diagram but here are the highlights…

Nash took a swig of her cappuccino and grimaced. It was stone cold. She had commandeered a pokey meeting room at the Insight News International offices, with views over the North Dock at West India Quay, for the clandestine investigation into the disappearance of Clare Buchanan. In return she'd had to suffer the wrath of the Insight accounts team, who'd had to retire to the communal kitchen for any formal get-togethers, and who all also knew that any attempts to regain their turf would be rendered fruitless because Nash was the boss's daughter. In reaction to their unhappy glares, Nash had written a sign with a marker pen and stuck it on the inside of the window before yanking down the blind: '*Nepotism Rocks*'.

Miles had sent her a WhatsApp to say he was on his way. Nash discarded the rest of her coffee and kept reading.

Charles Ebdon's father was William 'Bill' Ebdon. He was born in 1905 and died in the eighties. He went to Oxford University and served in WW2. I never managed to get my hands on his military records. He was married twice and had five children, the second of whom died in infancy. Charlie Ebdon was the second child from his father's second marriage, when Bill Ebdon was already fifty-one. Charlie had an older sister, Ione, and a younger sister, Amy, who famously killed herself back in 2001. Ione is also dead, having died in a car crash a few years before that.

I didn't get much further. If you've got any questions, let me know.

Best wishes,

Gus

Nash opened the PDF.

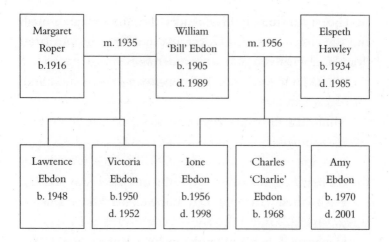

| Margaret Roper b.1916 | | William 'Bill' Ebdon b. 1905 d. 1989 | | Elspeth Hawley b. 1934 d. 1985 |
| m. 1935 | | | m. 1956 | |

| Lawrence Ebdon b. 1948 | Victoria Ebdon b.1950 d. 1952 | Ione Ebdon b.1956 d. 1998 | Charles 'Charlie' Ebdon b. 1968 | Amy Ebdon b. 1970 d. 2001 |

Miles burst through the door, causing the Venetian blinds to clatter. The tatty backpack he insisted on carrying around was slung over his shoulder. He was grasping a free newspaper in one hand, a takeaway coffee in the other, a London Oyster card was pressed between his lips. It occurred to her that he had probably been wearing his Guns N' Roses T-shirt in bed, judging by the faint odour. His glasses had partially steamed up and, as she was realising was standard for Miles, his hair was sticking out at right angles à la Sid Vicious. Nash watched as he kicked the door closed with his foot.

'Hi,' she said.

Miles dropped everything except the coffee onto the surface of the table, spitting out the Oyster card. He took off his glasses and wiped them on his shirt.

'Morning,' he replied. 'I have news, though it's not good.'

'OK, well I have good news. You first.'

'There is no record of anyone named Solomon Capricorn in the Panama Papers. *Nada*. Whoever Solomon Capricorn is, or whoever is running his finances, they did not go through the law firm Mossack Fonseca. We need to find out from Tom Holt where he got that name from.'

'I'll add it to the list of questions.'

'What's your news?'

'Your mate Gus Fendy emailed me.'

'To apologise?'

'He sent me through a rough family tree for Charles Ebdon based on his research. Turns out there was another sister who died, not only Amy Ebdon. And Ebdon's father was *proper* old.'

She turned her laptop around for him to see. Miles squinted at the image from Fendy. 'Looks promising.'

'And that's not even my exciting bit of news.'

'Oh?'

'This,' Nash said, swiping up an unsealed brown envelope from the surface of the table and pulling out a luminous USB flash drive, 'contains all the CCTV footage taken from the bus on the night Clare Buchanan disappeared. Wanna watch?'

'Of course I want to bloody watch. How did you get it?'

She tapped her nose with her index finger. 'I know a guy who can crack the Met Police storage cloud. He's done it before for me a couple of times.'

'Is his name James Maloney?'

Her face fell, unable to shield her disappointment. 'How did you know?'

Miles shrugged. 'Did some work for me last year. That guy will do anything for a backhander. You do know his nickname is Jimmy Cranks Baloney?'

Nash shook off her feelings of inadequacy and faked a laugh for Miles's benefit. 'Well Jimmy *whatever-his-name-is* did say something odd. He said all of the CCTV footage from the Clare Buchanan missing person's case had previously been available online in the hopes that it might lead to information from the public. There was an appeal in 2010 by Clare's sister. He said a few years ago it was all available on YouTube. I double-checked, of course. But it's not there anymore. The only footage available online is that taken when Clare was *off* the bus, and that's limited. There is no CCTV footage from inside the number 43 that Clare Buchanan took the night she went missing.'

'So, by that, you mean there's no longer any footage of the main person of interest in the case?'

'Nope. Other than the newspaper headlines, which have the still shots, none of the CCTV footage is available.'

Miles rubbed his hands together. 'But now we have it. Let's see what you got.'

They huddled round her laptop, Miles draining the last dregs of his coffee. His upper arm was pressed up against her own. Glancing to her right, she was close enough to him to trace the line of his stubble, the shape of his skin over his Adam's apple, the curve of his lips. Her mind flashed back to the night she had spent at his flat, her stomach performing a somersault. Realising she was staring, Nash shook her head, removed the lid to the flash drive and inserted it into the laptop's USB port. The video files were numbered and divided into the different views from each CCTV camera on the bus.

Nash clicked open the first file.

'Where is this?' Miles asked.

'This is where she got on, on the south side of London Bridge, near Elate International HQ.'

The footage was grainy, in colour but with no sound. It seemed faded somehow, the CCTV of eleven years prior showing its age. A time and date stamp was featured in the top right corner: 18:37 21/02/2005.

'That's her in the green coat,' Miles said as Clare's figure appeared at the main door, shuffling with all of the other commuters, tapping her Oyster card on the reader beside the driver. She was carrying a brown handbag over her shoulder and wearing a white pashmina, her coat noticeable for its vivid green colour, even on a washed-out CCTV recording. The coat was memorable from the press coverage at the time. The view of Clare left a lump in Nash's throat, recalling the video she had watched at her mother's and a hundred times since, which would have been recorded around the same time. Clare was doing what she thought was right.

They watched as Clare walked to the staircase, making her way to the upper deck. The section of footage came to an end. Nash double-clicked on the next file, which was thirty minutes long. She scrolled through to half way, to the moment Clare arrived on the upper deck. Their subject moved to the front, taking a free seat above where the driver was sitting.

'She looks nervous,' Nash commented. 'Look at her back, it's completely straight.'

Miles was rubbing his stubble, still watching. 'Wait for it. Here he is.'

Miles tapped the keyboard. The footage paused. Nash stared at the grainy image of a man in a dark overcoat emerging from the stairs. It was difficult to make out his individual features.

'The person of interest,' Miles said.

'Anton,' Nash breathed.

'Tom Holt said he had hair parted in the middle, nose like a rugby player. I know it's not much to go on but look at that profile.'

Nash brought her face closer to the screen. There was something menacing about the figure on the bus. The man's shoulders were hunched as he lolloped to his seat. 'He's not as big as I imagined.'

'Holt said he was forty-odd, so he would have been around thirty here. Is that a limp?' Miles asked.

'Could be,' Nash mused.

There was little movement over the next ten minutes, neither Clare nor the male figure moved from their seats. For a while, the seat next to Anton was the only one unoccupied on the upper deck, the image of him often obscured by another passenger sitting in front. After a few minutes, Nash watched as Clare reached for a mobile phone in her bag.

'That's her texting the boyfriend,' she said.

'What did it say?'

'Something banal. *On way, back soon, kiss.* That was it. Nothing about anyone following her.'

'What happened to the boyfriend?'

'He's got a kid now. Not married, I don't think.'

On the next video file, the upper deck had emptied out. Clare Buchanan glanced behind her, and without warning gripped her handbag straps and flew out of her seat, hurtling downstairs in a flash of emerald green.

'Look at that! Did you see that?' Nash blurted.

Miles was equally stunned. 'He edged out of his seat! Tried to follow then changed his mind.'

'Now he's texting someone because he's lost her.'

'Did the police get phone records for passengers on the bus?'

'It was unregistered. Burner phone. So was the number it texted. The driver said he thought he was using a day travelcard, which the footage seems to confirm, and they couldn't trace where it had been purchased.'

'Do we know what was said in the text?'

'It said "Angel", as in the place where she got off. It said, '"Heading north on the right side". Then something about her coat colour. The police report says there was no activity on either phone again that night, or ever. They had both disappeared from the network before seven fifteen that same evening.'

'So she *was* murdered,' Miles said.

'The police report never went that far. When it was challenged in the press the police said it was not a murder investigation. Yet. Twelve years on, it's never *been* a murder investigation.'

'DCI Neil Rawlins said that,' Miles corrected her. 'And he was potentially taking bribes from, or was being threatened via, Ebdon.'

'Or Anton.'

'Who was working for Ebdon.'

'We can't prove any of that yet. And we can't talk to Rawlins if that's the case.'

Miles sat back in his chair and puffed out his cheeks, resting his hands on top of his head, causing his top to rise above his belly button and reveal a sprinkling of hair. Nash swallowed, shifting her gaze. He was staring at the footage on screen.

'We need to find out who Anton really is,' he said. We need to positively ID him and for that we need a surname. The E-fit image the police produced in 2005 doesn't emphasise any broken nose because you can't see it properly on the CCTV.'

'So we run his first name against a passport or a driving licence database. But manually, comparing photographs. Let's say he's around thirty in this image. There can't be that many Antons born in the mid-seventies.'

'How do we know his name's not Antony?' Miles shot back at her. 'Or that Anton isn't even his real name? It could be anything. Holt said he had a trace of an accent meaning he probably wasn't even born here. He could be Eastern European. He could be here on an EU passport.'

Nash gritted her teeth, looked to the beige carpet. 'I'm throwing out ideas. We have one single detail that the police never managed. We have a first name.'

Miles chewed his lip.

'What about the lawyer, Denham?' Nash continued. 'His first wife. She might know something.'

Miles shook his head. Nash frowned. He appeared to be laughing at her.

'What?' she snapped.

'The lawyer's first wife has a direct line to Charlie Ebdon. They could have been best friends for all we know. We mosey on over, start asking her who Anton is, you don't think she might make a few calls?'

'What are you trying to say?'

Miles got to his feet. 'I'm trying to tell you to calm down and try not to put a target on your back.'

'Jesus, you sound like my mother.'

Miles ignored her comment. He was pacing, thinking about something, wringing his Guns N' Roses T-shirt. 'We could ask Jimmy for help with the ID. Might not get anywhere, but if he could give us direct access to a passport database—'

'Do it,' Nash interrupted.

When she glanced up, he was looking straight at her. Nash averted her eyes, pretending to massage her neck, admitting to herself that Miles had his uses.

Impatience gnawed away at her insides. As a rule she didn't like office spaces, with their stained beige carpets, ceiling tiles and straight lines. Her handwritten poster had not gone down well with the accounts team, and the looks they gave her as she walked past their banks of desks confirmed as much. Miles, on the other hand, was greeted with smiles and air kisses.

She continued her research into Ketteridge, the town where Charles Ebdon had spent his childhood. Gus Fendy's version of the family tree was helping her draw a picture of a wealthy family. Nash was eager to visit, to see what dirt they could dig up. When Miles left to meet a friend for a drink around five o'clock, she shut herself away and typed the name Belinda Channing – Albert Denham's first wife – into her computer. As a result, she spent a good couple of hours reading what seemed like the equivalent of the society pages.

As a girl, Belinda Bosen had grown up in Putney, the daughter of a barrister, and had attended private school at Cheltenham Ladies College. After divorcing Albert Denham, Belinda had seemingly gone on to marry an architect named Archibald Channing and had three sons. Nash felt a pang of sympathy for the dead lawyer, knowing from her conversation with his secretary that their childlessness was the main reason behind the split. She remained unconvinced that Belinda Channing had known her husband was working for Charlie Ebdon. Locating a Facebook page for Belinda, Nash looked it up on her phone. She selected the option to direct message. Her fingers hovered over the keyboard, knowing Miles would disagree with her actions. She told herself that it was her choice, that she was the lead for the investigation. Miles was an accessory, someone her mother had sent in to babysit. She opened up the phone app and typed out a short message:

> Hello. I am a journalist. I would like to speak to you about Albert Denham please. If you are willing, send me a message with a location and a time, somewhere discreet. Thanks.

She sent it, bit her lip, leaned back in her chair and realised her stomach was growling. Gathering up her things, Nash found parts of the office almost in darkness, save for the nighthawks at the other end of the floor plate.

At Canary Wharf Underground station, she clicked her tongue on discovering that the downward escalator to the Jubilee line platform wasn't in service. She joined the line of passengers taking the aluminium stairway on foot, worker ants returning to the nest, soles of their boots clattering against the hard metal stairs.

At the platform, the sound of the train was familiar, like a wind-up mouse running out of steam as it slowed to a halt. Inside, commuters were packed tight. It was eight stops to Bond Street where she would change to the Central line. She selected to stand in a small nook at one end of the carriage. She had picked up a copy of the *Evening Standard* en route and absorbed herself in the headlines. The stop-start, swaying rhythm of the Tube was more than familiar. Growing up it had become a way of life, the continuous high-pitched shriek of the Jubilee line trains that allowed her to escort her much younger, paler sisters to visit their mother when her office had moved to Canary Wharf.

Nash thought about Belinda Channing and how long she might have to wait for a reply.

The doors opened and shut. Bodies jostled in the fight to get on and off, every Londoner going his or her way with the common goal of arriving at their destination without delay, which only ever happened at a maximum seventy-five per cent of the time.

Minutes later, Nash glanced up out of the window, the train approaching the steel fortress that was London Bridge station.

It wasn't customary to look at people on the Tube. Direct eye contact was only for foreigners and those who foolishly decided to brave the Underground on weekends.

She could hear the sound of someone breathing, a man standing in front of her. She raised her eyes as far as his overcoat. It was woollen, black. He wore a pale blue shirt underneath it.

In, out, in, out, an autumn flurry gusting down a wind tunnel. She questioned how it was that a person could breathe so loudly. Nash shook her paper, shifted her feet. The breathing was so close as to be in her ear.

She raised her eyes in irritation. His face, inches from hers.

She noticed his crooked nose first, before the heavy brow. Her eyes flashed to his centre parting, like he had stepped out of the CCTV from twelve years earlier and into her world.

The eyes, drilling into hers.

Nash's lips parted as the train lurched to a halt. She stopped breathing.

The doors slid open and he shoved past her, disappearing up the enclosed platform.

Nash felt her legs go weak, rammed by moving bodies from all sides. She gripped the waxy yellow handrail, lungs on fire, tears stinging her eyes. Questioned whether it was him, whether her constant thoughts of him meant she was seeing things.

'Anton,' she wanted to plead with the other passengers, but they wouldn't know. His name would mean nothing to them.

Anton.

He was here. The look he had given her said he knew everything.

The doors about to close, Nash pushed past her fellow passengers onto the platform, jostled on all sides. She bent double, gripped her knees, gasped breaths.

She stood, raising her eyes to the sign on the platform as the train departed. On the navy blue sign surrounded by the familiar red circle, the words read 'London Bridge'.

London Bridge. The place where Clare Buchanan had started her bus journey.

Was that a coincidence? Nash whirled around, looking back at the passengers filing away from the platform. She started running. At the back of the line for the escalator, she craned her neck, hopping up and down, trying to catch a glimpse of the man she had seen.

She looked back. In the centre of the concourse, separating the two platforms, was a staircase, leading to the entrance to the Northern line.

He was there, leaning against the railings. Like he was waiting for her.

Then he was gone.

Nash thrust her way through the crowd, across the tiled floor, determined to get a better glimpse of the man she had been watching over and over on CCTV. Ducking low, she bounded up the stairs, impatient to get past all the commuters, ignoring the tutting and looks of disapproval coming her way. Leaving a steel metropolis that was the Jubilee line behind her, the walls became whiter, the ceilings lower and the air thicker. Emerging from a tunnel, she saw him up ahead, down a set of stairs wearing a dark coat. She heard her mother's voice, questioning whether she should follow.

Down the stairs, Nash turned towards the northbound platform, eyes scanning the crowd. Waiting passengers were two persons deep. She heard the rumble of an approaching train, the air whipping up a breeze through her hair.

She had lost him.

Backing away, she saw the southbound train enter the station. Racing to the platform, her eyes scanned the faces. Her breathing unsteady, she felt the beat of her heart pounding in her ears. The train ground to a halt, doors opening.

Nash turned around, her next move undecided. She wanted a glimpse. To know for sure that Anton had been delivering her a message.

As the doors closed as the train pulled away, Nash watched the windows.

Inside, she saw his face. Standing in the middle of a carriage, holding on to a rail, he was watching her on the platform. The train swept him away, and he was gone from view.

The words lingered, unspoken on her lips, the two red lights from the train disappearing into the tunnel as she watched it go.

I am not afraid of you.

Chapter 15

At 3.30 a.m., Richie Wylde checked his pockets: finding a pound coin and two shiny twenty-pence pieces, together with three crisp notes – two fives and a ten – stripped out of a wallet he had lifted in Whitechapel. The coins he liked to think of as his own. He bought a greasy bag of chips to last the journey on the D3 night bus. By the time he reached Wapping, he was already sucking his fingertips clean.

Three months after his release from Her Majesty's Prison, Wandsworth – courtesy of his uncle's under the table deal-making – Richie had slipped comfortably back into his nocturnal habits. Only now he appreciated the breeze on his cheeks, and the ability to walk in a straight line for more than thirty metres without hitting a concrete wall or turning right back into the dank misery of a shared cell, windows smashed out and mended with Sellotape and trampled on milk cartons to seal out the cold. The boredom he had experienced inside had been nothing like he had ever imagined. The prison grub had made him want to vomit, the lack of fast food – his personal favourite – quietly incinerating his reasons to live. And then Becca had stopped coming. She had been tasked with a job, the dead lawyer, Denham, had explained, on the only two occasions he'd bothered to visit; an ill-concealed look of disdain on his face at having to visit him at all.

He didn't know why he'd expected nothing to have changed once he'd got out. It was all he had thought about inside, pacing in his cell, him and Becca going back to their previous existence, pinching shit for kicks and laughing about it later. Small-time crook stuff; all he had known. There was nothing else for them to do between the more important jobs that Anton gave them. Neither he nor Becca had ever earned a salary, nor paid a penny in tax to the UK Government. They had scraped by, invisible to the wider world, making their living as thieves. Yet it was Becca's so-called job – the details were still sketchy but the one that involved her going to South America – that had tipped the balance. She was the same Becca she had always been; only she wasn't. There was a far-off look in her eye, like her mind was living elsewhere. Now the South America issue hung over them like a guilty secret, Richie having lost the ability to read her thoughts.

The boiler at Parry House had packed up, plunging the flat into bitter cold. Closing the front door behind him, Richie found his sister curled up shivering on the sofa, coat on, a duvet stretched out over her legs, vapour emerging from her mouth, half-awake, half-asleep.

'Why aren't you in bed?' he asked, placing the money he had stolen in the kitchen jar.

Becca stirred. 'It's warmer out here than in my room.'

It had been Denham's responsibility to sort the monthly bills. Now that task fell to Anton, when he remembered. After more than ten years of living there, there were still patches of chipped paint and damp crawling up the walls.

'Didn't you call the boiler people?'

'Do you have six hundred quid?' Becca retorted, her tone flat. 'Plus anything extra for replacement parts?'

'Six hundred? Are you serious?'

'If you want to feel the tips of your toes again.'

'Did you talk to Anton?'

'I'll call him in the morning.'

Richie hovered over her. 'Go on then, let me in.'

She stirred. He huddled up next to her, taking some of her duvet. Leaning his head on her shoulder, Becca pulled away, passing him a cushion instead.

'You smell like a kebab house,' she muttered.

He awoke to light peeking through the thinning curtains of the flat, the sound of mugs clattering together and Becca making coffee, duvet pulled up to his frosted nose. Turning his head, Richie looked over towards the kitchen. She was still in her coat, warming her hands over the electric hob.

'You alright?' he yawned.

She glanced up, catching his eye, puffing out her cheeks and ignoring his question. 'You planning on sleeping all day?'

'I don't have to.'

'Good. I thought we could take the bike out for a spin later today.'

The motorbike Anton had purchased for them a decade earlier was secured to a railing at the entrance to the building. 'What for?'

She went silent, focussed on coffee-making.

Richie grasped the opportunity. 'You know, one day you're going to have to talk to me about it.'

Becca said nothing.

'The guy,' Richie ploughed on. 'From the flat the other day. The one with the brothers.'

'What about him?'

'Do you like him, or what?'

'Of course not. Why would you think that?'

'You never talk about it. About what happened. You don't talk about him.'

'There's nothing to say. He needs to be found; he knows too much.'

'And if you find out where he is? What then?'

'We give up his location to Anton, of course.'

Richie killed the rusty Kawasaki's engine, Becca yanking off her helmet behind him. In Friday traffic the journey to Barnes in South West London had taken over an hour, Becca shouting directions in his ear whilst looking at Google Maps on her phone, Richie weaving the motorcycle in and out of cars across a congested Putney Bridge.

'Where the hell are we?' he asked, pulling off his own helmet.

'Barnes,' Becca confirmed. 'You should come here sometime. Money out this way.'

'Think I'd rather work somewhere I actually fit in. Why are we here?'

He took in his surroundings: tall, narrow red brick edifices with attractive shop fronts, pavements nicely swept. There were no ex-convicts here; not in this neck of the woods. Becca nodded across the road at the branch of Bentley Atherton Estate Agents. At close to five, the light was dwindling.

'That's the brother's office,' Becca said.

At the flat, she had talked him through the plan. On a Friday night, Christian Holt hit the pub with his colleagues. Becca had been watching him, or so she said. On each occasion they had walked to the Sun Inn, a five-minute stroll from the office. Tonight Becca planned on talking to him. On leaving the pub, Richie was to follow and find out where Christian lived.

'Take the bike,' she said. 'Buy yourself a drink and find a quiet corner with a good view. And keep an eye on your phone. They might move on somewhere else.'

'You're starting to sound like Anton.'

She looked irritated, like she did a lot these days. 'Maybe I'm tired of scraping by in a flat that's colder than Siberia. Maybe I want more from my life than nicking other people's shit. Maybe I look at Anton and see something worth becoming.'

Richie held up his hands, palms open. 'Wasn't a criticism. Personally I'm happy being outside of a cell.'

Becca winced. 'Sorry.'

She positioned herself with her back to the estate agent's office, flashing up one third of the now dog-eared photo that Richie had found in Tom Holt's flat, the part that featured the brother, Christian Holt's, face. 'Remember, this is him,' she continued, folding the photograph and pocketing it as quickly. Richie nodded.

Inside the Sun Inn, an upmarket pub with a countryside feel, he queued up at the bar and ordered himself a pint of cider, claiming a free table near the entrance door, the only one available, pretending to look at his phone as he sat down.

When he entered with two other men – part of a larger group – Christian Holt wore a black leather jacket over his office shirt with the tie removed, hair slicked back, talking animatedly. Richie watched him, careful not to stare, conscious of how out of place he already looked, alone at his table, like a manual labourer in a sea of wanker bankers. Holt had the curious remnants of a bruise on his right brow. It occurred to Richie that he was surrounded by the kind of people he enjoyed robbing blind, because he knew they were the ones who could afford the loss: well-heeled customers with trust funds and generous inheritances. For him, it was low-level guilt for maximum profit. Plus Richie could guarantee they were always holding a wad of cash.

Christian Holt and his friends moved towards the rear of the pub, to a covered area, out of sight. Richie sipped his pint over the din, waiting for Becca to show. It had come as a surprise, to know that she had been spending her time monitoring the movements of an estate agent. It was becoming clearer to him that her experiences in South America had shifted her perspective; made her want different things.

Becca slipped through the entrance twenty minutes later, hair pulled back off her face, wearing a coat he'd not seen before. She'd applied makeup, worn high-heeled boots, blending in seamlessly with those around her. Though she often argued with him that he had a more natural talent for theft, Richie had to admit his sister was a chameleon when it came to blending in with a crowd.

Richie was too curious not to follow. He knew Becca

would probably freak out about it afterwards if she saw, which was why he waited a few minutes before picking up the remnants of his cider and making his move to the rear. It wasn't like she could say anything in front of Holt. He knew Holt could recognise him if he followed later on, but he was prepared to take the risk, if only for a glimpse into the world his sister seemed to want to shut him out of.

He lingered by a step, back to them, close enough to earwig on the conversation. Becca had pulled Christian Holt aside, her back to Richie. Holt's face was marred by a deep frown, unconvinced with whatever she was saying to him.

'You don't look so confident now, without the wig. You've lost your swagger,' Holt was saying, arms crossed over his chest.

'I have something for you,' Ritchie heard her say, reaching into her pocket. Richie leaned his head to one side. The metal strap of a watch caught his eye before she brought it out into the open, cradled it in her palm. It wasn't an object he had seen before.

'Do you recognise this?' she asked, handing it over.

Christian Holt took it, turning it in his fingers, silver watch face flashing.

'What is this meant to prove?' Christian said. 'It proves nothing. That you've been in contact with my brother, that's all. How do I even know this is his?'

Becca shifted her stance. Richie realised he wasn't used to seeing her interact with others. 'It has the engraving on the back,' she was saying. 'Your brother gave this watch to me. He gave it to me because he trusts me. But he's in hiding. I need to find him and I know you can help.'

Holt went to laugh, swallowing more of his pint, the look he then gave her filled with raw malice.

'He asked me if the woman who attacked me had red hair. Stupidly, I told him you were a blonde. But he said I should stay away from you. Warned me that you were dangerous.'

Becca took a step back. Richie held his ground, looked to the floor. There was softness in her tone when she replied. 'You spoke to him?'

Holt leaned close to her. 'I'm not telling you a thing. Where he is; or where he's gone. You fucking come near me again and I will sound every alarm there is.'

Richie witnessed a muscle flex in Becca's jaw.

'Don't forget your watch,' Holt said, thrusting it back into her hand and moving back towards his colleagues.

Richie put his head down, shrinking away from the wall, leaving Becca looking deflated. When he was back at the bar he witnessed her bolt from the pub, swearing that he saw tears in her eyes.

The wait was tedious, made worse by staying off the hard stuff and drinking Diet Coke when he preferred Pepsi. Prison had taught him to appreciate simple things, like the sensation a fizzy drink made against his tongue. Richie stifled another yawn, waiting for the moment the barman would call last orders. He had positioned himself so that he had both a view of Holt and of the exit. Christian Holt drank pints of ale, joking with his colleagues, seemingly unfazed by his earlier visit from Becca.

When Holt rolled out of the bar before 11 p.m., Richie downed the remainder of his drink, counting to forty before rising from his seat to follow. He hung back as Holt swayed his way along a dimly lit Station Road, past imposing houses that distracted Richie with their pebbled driveways and loft extensions. The houses turned to greenery, Station Road narrowing, darkening. Richie hung back in the shadows, keeping to the other side of the street, watching Holt veering forward with his head down, hands thrust into his pockets, breath turning to vapour in the night air.

At Barnes station, Christian Holt boarded a Kingston-bound train, carriage lights accentuating his general state of inebriation, Richie boarding at the last moment when the warning signal rang out that the sliding doors were to close. He took an immediate left, having pinpointed the position of Holt's seat on the interior from the outside. Crowds filled the carriage, streaming out of central London, the floor littered with discarded McDonald's wrappers. Richie felt his mouth water.

Back in Wapping by half past midnight, Richie found Becca curled up on the sofa, under a blanket and several layers of hooded clothing, the temperature inside the flat having dropped another couple of degrees on the night before. She stared vacantly at the TV. Richie tossed his keys on the table, stifling another yawn.

'I left the bike in Barnes. I'll have to pick it up tomorrow.'

'Did you find out where he lives?' she asked.

'We got any food?'

'Yes or no?'

'You know, if I wanted bossing about, I would have asked Anton for something to do. Seems like you're taking on his role these days.'

'This *is* a job for Anton. I offered to go after Tom Holt, and that's what we're doing.'

'Then why do I get the feeling you have your own agenda?'

Becca threw her head back, gave an exasperated sigh.

'What was that you showed the brother? The watch.'

'You were *spying* on me?'

'Why do you have Tom Holt's watch?'

'Because he gave it to me. We got separated before I could return it. I used it as leverage, that's all.'

'Does Anton know you have it?'

She swallowed, eyes flitting to the TV screen. 'It makes no difference whether I have it or not.'

He looked at her, feeling like he didn't recognise her anymore. That the world he had expected to find on his release from prison had all but disappeared.

'It's a ground floor flat, Cedar Grove in Richmond, 32A,' he stated.

'Thank you,' she breathed.

'I'll help you, you know I will. I'd do anything for you, Bec. But the day you start going up against Anton…'

He didn't have the heart to finish his sentence. He went to his room, closed the door. Though he hadn't witnessed it for himself, he knew what both his uncle and Anton were capable of.

Chapter 16

Panama City, Panama
22 February, 2017

He waited beside Miguel in the lobby of Hotel El Panama in a louche district of the city known as El Cangrejo: The Crab. Miguel had instructed him to wear a suit. He wore sunglasses, no tie, a new pair of leather shoes. A dance convention was taking place at the hotel, young Latin girls in black leotards and too much makeup bustled past them in excitable groups.

'Juan Carlos speaks almost no English, so speak solely in Spanish,' Miguel said. 'It's a sore point because his brother speaks perfect English. Don't bring it up. Don't speak to me in English. Don't talk unless you have to. We only have one shot at this. If he tells you what he wants you to do, let him talk. Don't try and act like you know everything already.'

Tom nodded once, wiped the perspiration from his top lip despite standing in an air-conditioned atrium. He had expected an upmarket hotel in a more salubrious part of town. El Panama wasn't exactly run-of-the-mill, nor was it swanky either. As hotels went, it was average.

Another dance troupe passed them by, a cluster of pre-pubescent girls with glitter swiped up their cheekbones like war paint, greased-back hair and the word *Colombia* emblazoned across black and yellow outfits.

'Why here?' Tom asked.

Miguel looked at his watch. 'He keeps a suite here. I heard he likes the pool area. There're Russians here; he does regular business within that community. One of Juan Carlos's main houses is in the San Francisco area of the city, it's low-rise. He wanted to knock over his neighbour's house to build a bigger pool. His neighbour refused to sell. A few days later two masked men entered a café in Punta Pacifica and shot his neighbour in the leg during his morning coffee run.'

'So what happened?'

'Now, Juan Carlos has a really big pool outside of his house.'

At the end of the lobby a set of glass sliding doors parted and a man wearing a red basketball vest with baggy jeans emerged. He gave a nod in Miguel's direction.

'They're ready for us,' Miguel said.

The pool area at El Panama was sizeable, hardly five star. The hotel building was overlooked, all white. Tom followed Miguel through a covered, shaded walkway, conscious that he was about to beg for his father's life in return for a job he didn't know if he could pull off.

Juan Carlos Aguinaldo relaxed on a plastic sunbed with his feet up, balancing a cocktail on his knee under a parasol. He was flanked by two men in sunglasses and black zipped-up jackets. The third man in the basketball vest hung back. Aguinaldo was the size of a small walrus, wearing a gargantuan short-sleeved military-style shirt stretched across his belly. He had dark skin, a wide nose, a double-chin dappled with acne scars, a head of thick, coarse hair.

Miguel bent down, shook Juan Carlos by the hand, and introduced Tom.

'*Mucho gusto,*' Tom said, speaking Spanish, following Miguel's lead.

There was no shade where they were sitting. Sweat ran down the sides of Juan Carlos's rounded face, despite the parasol. The two men behind him were like statues. The man in the basketball vest pulled up two white plastic chairs for them to both sit on; asked if they wanted something to drink. Tom asked for some water, tugging at his collar.

'This is *Señor* Holt's son,' Miguel said, also in Spanish.

Tom raised his eyes. Kept them steady on Juan Carlos's face whilst the Panamanian looked him over.

'Your father owes me a lot of money,' Juan Carlos said.

Tom cleared his throat, back of his neck already starting to burn. 'I understand there's a way I can help pay off the debt.'

'The people in Panama City,' Juan Carlos mused, 'they're afraid of me. They're afraid of my brother. Get too close to me; you've made an enemy of my brother. Get too close to him…' His voice trailed off. He pushed out his bottom lip. It made him look like Marlon Brando.

'I'm not from here,' Tom said. 'If you're offering me a chance to save my father's life, then I'll take it.'

'No one wants this job.' Juan Carlos squinted. He sounded irritated. 'Nobody wants to fucking volunteer. Nobody wants a price on their head. So I ask myself, why not you?'

Tom cocked his head, unsure whether he was being asked a question.

'Miguel told you about the job?' Juan Carlos continued.

'I have told him what he would need to do,' Miguel confirmed.

'The copy of the painting. It's good, I've seen it, but it is incomplete.'

'We'll talk to her,' Miguel said.

Tom's gaze shifted from Miguel to Juan Carlos and back again. He knew he had nothing to lose.

'If I do this for you,' Tom said, looking directly at Juan Carlos yet feeling the heat of Miguel's warning stare, 'then other than clearing my father's debt I would like to ask one more thing of you.'

Juan Carlos straightened in the sunbed. When his hefty body shifted, the statues behind him moved in subtle unison.

'First, tell me how you're in a position of asking things of me,' Juan Carlos stated in a low tone.

'Call it a gesture of good will. If I am successful in doing what you ask of me, then you grant my father immunity from his debt, and you provide me with some information.'

'What information?'

'A man in your position must have links to every established law firm in this city, correct?'

'That you have to ask is a demonstration of your own ignorance.'

Tom nodded. 'I want information on a potential client. A British client.'

Juan Carlos unwound into the sun bed, patches of sweat visible under his arms, the two statues at his back relaxing a notch.

'Do this job for me,' Juan Carlos said with a dismissive

wave of his hand, swallowing the rest of his cocktail before smacking his lips. 'I can get you whatever you want. Send over the details.'

Miguel got to his feet, a sign the meeting was over.

Tom pressed down his shirt, damp with perspiration. He stood, held out his hand to Juan Carlos Aguinaldo. The fat Panamanian didn't take it, instead holding up his empty glass to the man in the basketball shirt. Tom felt Miguel's fingers grip his bicep, signalling that the time had come for them both to vacate the area.

'You and your father, you both know how to walk a thin line,' Miguel muttered in the hotel lobby, walking ahead of him, back to speaking English. 'You don't mess with these people.'

'It's a start,' Tom countered, thankful for the stay of execution. 'It's bought us some time.'

His father wasn't home.

'Come,' Miguel said. 'I'll buy you lunch. Show you a corner of the real Panama.'

They walked through charming cobbled streets, opening out into a square past the Pedro Mandinga rum bar. Miguel pointed out a majestic four-storey white-washed colonial building to one side of Plaza Herrera, the American Trade Hotel. Cutting through back lanes, the landscape changed abruptly to virtual slums, crumbling buildings on the verge of collapse, the sounds of reggaeton seeping through barred windows. They emerged into another square, the streets bursting to life, humming with activity, Miguel walking him past the church of Santa Ana, the area dominated by

Panameños. There were no foreigners here. They walked past shops selling cheap Chinese-manufactured bric-a-brac, a butcher hammering a chicken carcass with a meat cleaver, mongrel dogs lounging under the awnings, avoiding the scorched concrete. Wherever he went, Tom felt his back drenched in sweat, a constant thirst on the tip of his tongue. Miguel ducked into a dingy-looking café with rotary fans suspended on the walls, a flat screen TV mounted on the wall and curved wooden-backed chairs around tables. To one side was a metal counter with a variety of buffet-style foods, a whirring, clapped-out fridge lined with bottles of cola.

'They call this a *fonda,*' Miguel explained, ordering two plates of *Arroz Frito con Pollo.* 'They serve traditional Panamanian food for the price of a half latte in Starbucks five minutes' drive down Cinta Costera. You won't find one of these amongst the shiny office buildings.'

'So this is a city of the have and the have-nots.'

'Look at where your father lives. Twenty-five years ago Casco was a mess, the badlands, as a gringo you couldn't come down this way without risking your life. *El Chorillo* ruled. Now Chorillo and Curundu are the last remaining slums in the city. The dollars flooded in, legal and illegal, the tap for Colombian drug money. Now it's all 4x4s, steel, glass. Even Donald Trump bought himself a tower.'

'Yet you still like to eat in a *fonda.*'

Miguel held up one finger, gave a half-smile. 'The people around here, they are the ones who haven't been bought. No one gave them the offer.' They took their seats as a man of Asian origin brought over their plates of food. 'Panama is an easy place to make money, according to those with the means to.'

Tom loosened his collar, tucked into his food, which at a price of two dollars seventy-five he counted as one of the best meals he had eaten in a long time.

When their plates were scraped clean, he said, 'Tell me more about this painting.'

Miguel sipped on a bottle of cola, wiping perspiration from his brow. 'It was painted by Francisco José de Goya. You know who that is?'

'I don't know much about art history, no.'

'Eighteenth and nineteenth century Spaniard. He painted *The Third of May, 1808* about the Spanish resistance to Napoleon. Then later, *Saturn Devouring his Son*, you know the one? It hangs in the Prado in Madrid.'

Tom didn't, but resolved to look it up. 'Right.'

'He also painted *La Maja Desnuda* and, about five years later, *La Maja Vestida*. In between that time, Goya completed a study for *La Maja Vestida*, a small painting which he gifted to a physician who helped treat him for tinnitus. That physician's name was Domingo Berganza. Berganza's grandson, whose name was Aguinaldo, inherited the painting and brought it to Panama at the end of the nineteenth century. It's been passed down the male line in the Aguinaldo family ever since. As the elder son, Oscar Aguinaldo inherited it.'

'But Juan Carlos wants this painting for himself.'

'The original is held in Oscar's house on the island of Contadora, on the Pacific side. Part of the Pearl Islands. Juan Carlos wanted to try to steal the painting. His associates talked him out of it. Too much bloodshed, they said, plus politically his brother has more sway, which is important, here in Panama. So he came up with a plan to replace the painting with a forgery, so that Oscar wouldn't even know he'd been robbed. Even hired his forger right here in Casco Viejo. About three months ago he hired an El Salvadoran thief who promised Juan Carlos he could deliver. But the guy wanted a half payment up front. Juan Carlos eventually agreed, but the dude took the money and ran all the way back to the slums of San Salvador, where Juan Carlos's men are still trying to track him down. Juan Carlos heard rumours of Oscar's plan to gift the painting to his son at his upcoming wedding and he doesn't have anyone he trusts anymore to complete the job.'

'He can't force someone? Put a gun to their head?'

'They're a complicated family. Everybody knows what happened to Jesus Vasquez, the man who helped Juan Carlos steal Oscar's wife. They found his body parts spread all over the city, including in the canal.'

Tom grimaced. 'That painting must be worth millions.'

'Nobody even knows if Goya painted it anymore, or a student of Goya. That's not the point. Nowadays it's all about ownership. Juan Carlos is like a man possessed.'

'Who's the forger?'

'A woman named Camila Corazon, a talented artist from Caracas. Her mother and father brought her and her brother across to Panama to escape the Chávez regime. But when it was clear the job wouldn't happen, she stopped painting it.'

'Does she still have it? The incomplete copy?'

'I'll put in the call.'

Miguel puffed out his cheeks. In all the conversation Tom had forgotten his new companion was a man of advancing years. 'Where do you fit into all of this?' he asked.

Miguel looked away, focussed his gaze over Tom's shoulder on to the flat screen TV. 'I'm the one who recommended your father to Juan Carlos, as someone experienced at investing money.'

'So does that mean you have a target on your back, too?'

Miguel gave a shrug. 'The only difference between me and your father is that I'm not a gringo. I worked for Juan Carlos and Oscar's father, God rest his soul. They respect the work I did for him. It is the only reason I'm still walking the earth.'

'What about me? I'm a gringo.'

Miguel brought his eyes back, sharply focussed on Tom's face. 'It means that, like your father, Juan Carlos will have no qualms about killing you, should you not give him what he wants.'

Chapter 17

London, England
1 March, 2017

Nash pressed the buzzer beside the door to the house and waited, taking one last glance over her shoulder.

She hadn't seen Anton again. Hadn't mentioned the incident on the Tube to Miles or her mother. She knew it was idiotic, keeping silent. She didn't need to see the CCTV footage from the Tube train. He had been close enough that she could smell the food on his breath. He was the same man on the bus in the footage from 2005: the same man who had followed Clare Buchanan. Now she knew how Sabi Cordero had felt in London all those years ago.

Anton knew what she was doing. His masters knew. She raised her chin, refusing to be intimidated.

Impatient, she rang the buzzer again. It was raining in Wimbledon. After a moment, the door clicked open a fraction, chain on, and half of Belinda Channing's face appeared in the narrow gap. The door closed again and she removed the chain, ushering Nash inside.

Nash stood dripping in the hallway on a well-trodden brown coir mat covered in unopened envelopes. On the mat was written the words *Proceed with Caution*.

'Nashaly?' Belinda said.

She held out her hand and Belinda took it. 'My friends call me Nash.'

'It's good to meet you.'

Belinda led the way upstairs. Nash put her age at mid-fifties. Albert Denham's ex-wife looked like the kind of woman who had at one time retained her looks, even into middle age. Now she looked tired, face tanned but minus any glow, pale blue eyes puffy. Her hair, with extensive roots showing, had been scraped back off her forehead and tied in a bun at the back. She wore a designer watch but no other jewellery, and gave off an expensive scent.

'Whose place is this?' Nash asked on the stairs.

Belinda opened another door to a flat on the floor above. 'This belongs to my stepson. He's a web developer, works on Oxford Street. I'm sorry for the mess; I've only been here ten minutes.'

Nash crossed the threshold, glanced around at the scattered piles of laundry on the sofas, ceramic bowls containing the remnants of some cereal, milk pooling and left to dry out at the bottom. Whoever he was, Nash noted, he had the habits of a student and a female companion with slutty underwear.

'I would offer you a tea but there're no teabags,' Belinda said, wringing her palms together. 'Or milk for that matter.'

'I'm fine, really,' Nash said.

'How did you find me?'

'I spoke to Albert Denham's former secretary. Orla.'

Nash thought she saw tears in the woman's eyes. 'What is it you want to ask me about?'

Nash took out her phone. 'Would you mind if I record this?'

Belinda was quick to respond. 'Actually, yes, I do mind.'

Nash faltered, pocketed the handset. 'No problem. Do you mind if we sit?'

Belinda darted to the sofa, scooped up piles of miscellaneous clothing, clearing a space on a stained light-grey three-seater, looking around and transferring the pile to the dining table. 'Of course. Please.'

'I'm investigating the disappearance of a woman named Clare Buchanan twelve years ago,' Nash said, sitting and delving into her bag for a tattered notepad and pen. 'Do you know who that is?'

Belinda's face clouded over. 'Yes.'

'I wanted to ask you about your former husband. I have reason to believe he worked for Charles Ebdon, CEO of Elate International.'

She watched Belinda grapple with her emotions, eyes darting to the closed Venetian blinds, the stained carpet, anywhere other than on Nash, mascara smeared down her cheeks. She didn't stay seated long. She darted to her feet, taking other pieces of laundry and folding each garment with experienced motherly precision.

'I'm sorry,' she breathed, wiping tears. 'These have been the hardest few months of my life.'

'Albert was attacked back in November, is that right?'

'He was murdered. Simple as that.'

'Murdered? By who?'

'It doesn't matter, they were faceless, hired thugs. All part of Charles Ebdon's underworld. Whoever carried out the attack was acting on his orders, and was paid by him.'

'How do you know that?'

Belinda twisted a T-shirt between her fingers. 'I don't. I mean, I have no proof. But I know because Al all but told me. It was around August, over six months ago. We were sleeping together; we would meet in hotels. I hadn't seen him for a while; we met in Holborn. It was the second to last time I saw him before he... He made a point of giving me a copy of his will, and a letter to open should anything—' Belinda stopped short, took a moment to compose herself. 'He knew his time was up.'

'You were back in a relationship with your husband?'

'He wasn't my husband. He was that Polish woman's husband. Tatiana. She was there at the hospital. They looked to her to identify the body, not me. As if that woman really knew him. She looked almost bored to be there, as if the whole ordeal was one big inconvenience for her. I had to convince the hospital orderlies to allow me to bid him farewell.'

Nash scribbled down the Polish wife's name. 'Did Tatiana know you were sleeping together?'

'Of course not.'

'Tell me about the letter.'

'I haven't opened it.'

Nash raised an eyebrow. 'You haven't? Why not?'

Belinda continued folding, shook her head. Rain splattered against the window pane. 'I can't.'

She sniffed, swallowed a deep gulp of breath. 'In his will he left me a house. It's in Miami. I didn't even know he owned a second house, let alone one in another country. It makes me wonder if I ever really knew him. I'm frightened that the letter contains some kind of confession.'

Nash felt a pang of impatience, taking notes. 'A confession of what?'

'His guilt.'

In the silence that followed, Nash found herself fantasising about a series of newspaper articles, expanding the scope of the piece beyond the disappearance of Clare Buchanan, and the look on her mother's face when she discovered how deep the conspiracy went. It was the biggest story she had ever chased. It could be the one that made her. What were the things Albert Denham had done for Charlie Ebdon? And had he confessed them all to his former wife?

'Forgive me, Belinda, but I would really like it if you could open that letter.'

She felt the woman's hard stare. For a long moment, Denham's former wife didn't speak.

'Are you married?' Belinda asked.

'No.'

'Is there someone… in your life? A boyfriend?'

'No.'

'Have you ever been in love?'

'Once.'

'What happened to him?'

'Her, actually.'

'Did she break your heart?'

'I think it was the other way around.'

Belinda turned her back again, finished her folding. 'Then you don't know. How can you possibly know?'

Nash looked to her feet. Talk of love and relationships made her queasy. Had she ever had one big love? No. Her mother would say she was too in love with herself to make room for anyone else, and she was probably right.

'Orla said the pair of you divorced because you couldn't have children.'

Belinda's shoulders stiffened. Her tone remained resolute. 'Do you know the history? Of what happened, before we were even married? You know, I don't think you can even access it now. The search engines have been wiped. I don't know how but they were.'

Nash frowned. 'I don't understand.'

Belinda seemed not to hear her. 'I knew he was doing bad things. I sometimes wondered what portion of his soul he'd had to sell to get himself off the hook. He would disappear sometimes, come back in the dead of night and say nothing of where he'd been. That, along with my desperation for a child of my own, drove me to leave. I never stopped loving him. But he was no longer the man I fell in love with. I had to separate myself from him for my own sanity.'

Nash wiped perspiration from her top lip, vowing to herself to dig deeper into Albert Denham's history. 'These others. The ones pulling the strings. Does the name Anton mean anything to you?'

Nash studied the look on Belinda Channing's face. If she was already pale, she was now a shade paler.

'Say that again,' Belinda whispered.

'Anton. He has black hair. A nose that's possibly been broken a few times and never fixed.'

Her eyes had gone glassy. 'I've not heard that name in years. Al used to call him the gatekeeper.'

'The gatekeeper? Gatekeeper to what?'

'Al said he lived in the shadows… he was the one who organised all the… work.'

Nash leaned forward, the nib of her pen pressed hard in anticipation on the surface of her notebook. 'What more do you know about him?'

'He's Russian, I think.'

Nash felt her fingers tingle with the rush of adrenaline. 'Your husband told you that? Did he ever tell you his surname?'

Belinda shook her head, seemingly in a half-daze. Nash wanted to get out of her seat and shake the information from her.

'Marevski, something like that. I don't remember. Not English. Al said very little about him.'

Nash scribbled the word down on her notepad with her biro, asked Belinda how she thought it was spelt. Her stomach carried out a somersault at the thought of knowing Anton's true identity.

'Did you ever meet him?'

'I saw him. Once. He came to our flat in Clapham.'

'When was this?'

Belinda shrugged. 'Over twenty years ago.'

Nash held her tongue, unwilling to break it to Belinda that Anton was alive and well and still stalking young women on the London Underground. 'Do you mind if I run some other names past you?'

'Of course.'

'Sabina Cordero.'

A shrug. 'No idea.'

'What about Thomas Holt? Or Tom Holt?'

Belinda shook her head, *no*.

'Thank you,' Nash said. She decided she liked Belinda Channing, the more steely side of the older woman revealing itself in flashes. She toyed with the idea of asking her to open her husband's letter again. 'Do you think your ex-husband could have had anything to do with Clare Buchanan's disappearance?'

Belinda's eyes were wet again. 'If he was, he wasn't given a choice.'

Nash burst through the door, wet from the rain, a half-eaten packet sandwich dangling from her fingers, satchel sliding down her bicep.

Miles shot to his feet. Nash kicked the door closed, tossing her bag on the table. She was out of breath.

'Where the hell have you been?' Miles shot at her. Dark circles surrounded his eyes. 'Your mother is freaking out. She's riled.'

'Anton Marevski. He's Russian,' Nash blurted with her mouth full, ignoring the puppy dog look of concern on her colleague's face. She was getting the job done. She didn't have to be in phone contact twenty-four seven.

'*Russian*?' Miles repeated. 'How—?'

'Surname is unconfirmed but similar. Possibly born in the old Sov Bloc. Not clear exactly. Should narrow the field of candidates significantly though for Jimmy to search the database.'

'This comes from where?'

'Never mind that, let's get him searching the database.'

'Nash. Your source.'

She felt heat pricking the base of her neck. 'I saw Belinda Denham.'

Miles gave an exaggerated roll of the eyes. 'Jesus! Whilst you're at it, why don't you paint a bullseye on our backs? They know we're coming for them. Hell, she's probably talking to them right now.'

'She's not. We were discreet. She didn't have a single good thing to say about Charlie Ebdon. She believes Albert Denham was murdered by Ebdon's thugs.'

'You're an idiot.'

Her arms flew up in the air. 'Miles, I don't know where you learned to be a journalist, but clearly it wasn't somewhere where they told you to get out there and sniff out a story! Maybe you should go and write op-ed pieces for the weekly periodicals if you're not prepared to get your nose dirty.'

He rolled his eyes. 'Hundreds of people your age are writing shit-pieces for local websites, blogging their arses off for literally no money, trying to catch that break, but no, not Nashaly Akinyemi. You caught your break the day you were born. It's skewed your view. You've never had to put in the legwork and it's made you reckless.'

'Jesus, Miles, enough with the abuse! I can't help who my bloody mother is! Plenty of people *my age* are way more successful than me.'

She noted the vein pumping away in his temple. 'When they pull you out of the ground, you won't see me telling people that you didn't see it coming.'

'Don't be such a baby.'

He had a tick in his eye when he got angry. 'Have you forgotten the intruder in Uruguay? The man in your room who almost strangled you to death? *They know what we are doing.*'

'Exactly why we should push on. The longer we drag it out the more dangerous it becomes. We expose Ebdon soon, before it's too late.'

Miles took a step back, wiping his palms down his face, jittery. 'I have to go,' he muttered, grabbing his coat from the back of his chair.

'Come on, you've come this far. Where is it you need to be?'

'You don't get it, do you? I care about you, Nash!'

He'd flushed bright red. The words hung in the air, unable to be retracted.

'It's one-sided, I get that,' he stammered, when she said nothing. 'I get you're not interested. You… you have tunnel vision. You're ruthless, you care about number one, but you're not checking your wing mirrors, Nash.'

The silence that followed went on for longer than she anticipated.

Her throat dry, she said, 'I'm sorry I didn't reply to any of your messages. I—' She didn't finish, instead gave a shrug.

Miles shook his head, running his fingers through his hair, and left.

She let him go then flipped open her laptop and started typing up her notes from the meeting with Belinda Denham, furious fingertips slamming against plastic keys, refusing to relive the moment Miles had admitted he cared for her.

He'd always been attentive – perhaps because she was the boss's daughter. He had emailed one afternoon, inviting her out on a date. She'd said no on account of him not asking her face to face. At a bar in Canary Wharf, she'd drunk too much, her judgment clouded by vodka.

It was dark by the time she finished the copy. She paid for a cab instead of taking the Underground, arriving outside her mother's place in torrential rain, splashing through puddles to the front door on Lansdowne Road.

There was a light on in the kitchen, a single beam spilling on to the worktop from underneath a cabinet. No sounds came from upstairs.

'Pete? Mum?' she said out loud, closing the door, peering up the stairs.

She meandered into the kitchen. A handwritten note was waiting for her on the work surface from her stepfather:

> *N,*
> *We are out tonight.*
> *There are some pie leftovers in the fridge.*
> *A parcel was delivered for you.*
> *P.*

The parcel in question was on the side. It was rectangular – the size of two shoeboxes, one on top of the other, covered on the outside in white plastic accompanied by the name of a courier company she didn't recognise. Her name had been written in bold letters using a marker pen. The address was also handwritten, no sender's address present. She turned the box over in her hands. There sounded a dull thud of objects moving around on the inside.

Nash paused. Leftovers no longer sounded appealing.

She pulled a knife from the worktop drawer and slashed a hole big enough for her to slide her fingertips inside the plastic.

When it was discarded, her first thought was to the smell. Nash wrinkled her nose, slowed her movements, retreating from the worktop. It was a box that had been used before, dented and scratched with an old layer of Sellotape. It was unsealed. Her heart began to thud. She reached out to the box, flicking one of the cardboard flaps open. Drawing it an inch closer, the rancid odour grew in strength: the stench of uncooked meat left out all day in the sun, a sweaty, fleshy, bloody aroma permeating her nostrils. Nash covered her mouth, took one step closer, and opened the second flap with the edge of her fingernail.

She took a final step forward, hovering over the cardboard rim. Her stomach heaved at the sight.

Inside the box, lined with clear blue cellophane, were the corpses of five rats, heads decapitated and interspersed with the lifeless, mutilated bodies. Mouths open, lips curled back over bared teeth as though they had suffered as they had perished, tails now entwined. In horror, she realised the tails too had been sliced off. Nash glimpsed a slip of paper, visible right at the bottom. Using the discarded plastic to shield her fingers, she reached in, picked it up in a pincer movement, fingers trembling, before holding the handwritten note up to the light.

She closed her eyes at the sight of her name, stained with the blood of the dead vermin.

Nashaly Akinyemi.

Chapter 18

Baku, Azerbaijan
23 February, 1993

Anton caught the look of disdain on his uncle's face as he tore off the red and white sparring headguard, tossing it towards the boy whose job it was to fetch and offer water. The boy caught it in both hands. He lobbed his saliva-covered mouth guard up towards the warehouse academy ceiling, not caring where it came to land. Anton slid between the ropes, dropping to floor level.

'Hey!' his uncle shouted after him. 'Get back here. Where are you going?'

Anton grabbed his towel, soaking up stinking sweat from his face, turned to see Dimitry Voronin bracing the top rope.

'Out,' Anton stated.

He turned his back on his uncle again, no interest in providing him with further details. He'd had enough of being punched in the head.

'I need someone to spar! You're not finished here today!'

His uncle liked doling out orders. Anton raised his head, flipped him the finger, throwing Dimitry a look that said *I'm done*.

Four years earlier, the son of one of Dimitry's customers – a boy of fifteen named Elnur Huseynov – had challenged him, following an argument amongst adolescent boys, to a bare-knuckle brawl outside at the back, on a patch of concrete where the metal dumpsters were stored. Anton had accepted the challenge without his uncle's knowledge, and came out of the experience with a badly broken nose. His uncle barely flinched at the sight. Elnur's father was paying a fat load of *manats* to learn how to box at the academy in the 3rd Microdistrict. Anton's role back then: to douse the client's face with water in between sparring sessions, offer them the chance to sip fluids. At sixteen, having trained him from the age of six, his uncle decided to put Anton in the ring with fully grown men. Most of Dimitry's wealthier clients didn't even bother asking his name, yet his nose had ended up broken twice more.

Anton threw the remainder of his things into a tatty sports bag, ignoring the ripened stench of his boxing boots. He wanted to shower before he left. Slinging his bag over his shoulder he took a few steps before sensing his uncle's presence at his back.

'You're going to Badamdar, aren't you?'

Anton stopped in his tracks.

'You think I'm blind?' his uncle continued. 'You think I don't watch you skulk around here? I know what you've been doing.'

Anton turned on him. 'I'm leaving in two months. You're sending me away! Keller is sending me away. This may be my only chance.'

When he spoke, Dimitry softened his tone. 'If you go there… it will lead to only pain, I promise you. It's everything I've taught you not to be. You do not want to go to Badamdar.'

Anton recalled the day his uncle had first introduced him

to the man he knew as Keller. The day Dimitry had told him that his father – whom he had never met and who lived in a different country – had plans for him. Plans Dimitry Voronin was tasked with carrying out.

'You kept silent about it all these years,' Anton said.

'I should have told you sooner, yes. I am sorry for that, Anton.'

'Find someone else to be your guinea pig,' Anton growled, tired of having the same conversation with a man who wasn't even his real uncle.

London, England
28 February, 2017

He had used humane traps, spiked with marshmallows to lure the rodents in. There was no shortage of vermin south of the river. Six traps in total, placed underneath one of the wheeled bins in the office car park next to his building. One rat was so fat it got its backside caught in the trap opening and was stuck there early the following morning, half in, half out, its thick tail still twitching. Anton had loaded them all into a shoebox at dawn, taking the fire escape stairs and transporting them back up to his flat. He knew he could have used poison. Yet he wanted the satisfaction of having them alive when he sliced off their heads.

In the kitchen, Anton set out a chopping board and a sharpened meat cleaver: his guillotine, he the executioner. He wore two pairs of blue medical gloves, his method involving holding a black plastic tube upright so that the creature fell to the bottom end. He would then open the top lid of the trap and fix his middle and index fingers over the entrance. Once the trap was horizontal, the rat, or mouse, would then attempt a scurrying escape. He would open his fingers a fraction, allow the rat to push through, enough so that its entire head was out of the trap, its upper body trapped between his fingers. With his other hand, he would bring the cleaver crashing down. Then he would drain most of the blood from the leftover body and head out over the sink.

It was not the first time he had sent a box of dismembered vermin to an individual as a warning to desist and it likely wouldn't be the last. He had confirmed a physical description with Belosi in Uruguay. The girl on the Tube had been the right one. Nashaly Akinyemi. Journalist. Dark skin, corkscrew curly afro hair, younger than he had anticipated. The daughter of a Nigerian mercenary who was stabbed in Lagos before Nashaly had seen her seventh birthday, according to her mother's online bio. Holt had sent her Clare Buchanan's tape to investigate. There was no other explanation.

In the bed, Tatiana stirred. Her feet were sticking out of the sheets, the shade of her red nail varnish chipped on her toenails. Anton had called her to ask that she find out the address of the Miami house, instructing her to turn out all of Denham's papers in his office with the purpose of finding it. It was only the second time he had initiated a phone call with her.

She had turned up at his door again unannounced, only this time she had handed him a fat envelope before turning and walking away down the corridor.

'You're not coming in?' he'd asked after her.

186

'No.'

'Come,' he'd said to her back, not sure why. 'Come inside with me.'

She had come to a halt in the passageway. She wore skinny jeans and a black bomber jacket, more akin to Becca's style of dress.

'I have to go.'

He said nothing; let the words hang in the air. When she turned around again, there was a sullen look on her face.

'Everything Al had is in the envelope, and I found nothing about a house in Miami,' she continued, followed by some garbled Polish that he was pretty sure amounted to an insult.

'I might have questions.'

She rolled her eyes, came back down the corridor.

He let the door slam behind her, turned and looked her over. Tatiana hadn't made as much effort with her appearance as she normally did. He'd realised then that he preferred her in her more natural state. Her face might have been paler, cheeks more drawn, but standing there, she no longer looked like a slut, or the wife of a dead lawyer. She looked like a lost girl from Poznań, like the first time he'd seen her, before the other Polish immigrants had introduced her to the excesses of living in the United Kingdom.

He tore open the envelope she had brought, casting a brief eye over the contents, cursing Denham for being so good at hiding his secrets. He resealed it, vowing to look at it later, before returning his attention to Tatiana.

'I wasn't so nice to you, last time you were here,' he said. 'This time I thought I could give you a key, so you never have to wait outside again.'

She refused to make eye contact.

Anton took a few steps closer. Reached into his pocket, pushing a key into her reluctant palm. 'Thank you. I know you tried.'

At the sight of the key she looked like she might weep again. Gone was the confidence of the harlot sending him videos of herself mid-climax. 'You never tell me anything,' she said. 'You're like the lawyer.'

Anton moved closer still. 'You know why.'

'I don't know why, no.'

'Because of Capricorn.'

She was silent for a moment. 'How did you come to be here?'

He gave a shrug. 'I was a gift.'

'A gift to Capricorn?'

'To him and his family. I was trained to serve them. It's what my father wanted. I prepared for this all my young life.'

'Would you ever go home?'

It was the most honest conversation he'd ever had with her. With any female other than Becca.

'I'll never go back to where I came from.'

'To Russia?'

'To Azerbaijan. Baku, on the Caspian Sea.'

She raised her eyes to his. 'Did your parents send you away?'

'I never met my parents.'

He'd had enough talk. Her eyes dipped back down. He stepped forward so that he was inches from her face. Tatiana appeared to flinch.

'Do you ever get lonely?' she whispered.

Reaching down, he wrapped his fingers around her wrists. Waited for her to lift her cheeks again.

'I take strength from within myself.'

His fingers let go of her wrist and went to Tatiana's chin, compelling her to lift it. Her eyes were wet. He looked at her face, noticing the fine lines around her eyelids. Lowering his head, he crushed his lips to hers, forcing them to part, to accept him. Tatiana gave way, pushing the length of her body into him. He yanked the bomber jacket down her arms, peeling off her ribbed sweater. She wasn't wearing a bra.

For the first time he let her in the bedroom. Fucked her face to face on the bed, her back on tangled sheets, him bearing down on her. She wrapped her legs around his middle, her body welcoming. Feeling himself nearing completion, Anton slowed his movements. Tatiana opened her eyes and moaned, sending a jolt through him, an unfamiliar sensation he revelled in for a moment before an unfamiliar vulnerability began to creep into his chest.

He closed his eyes, picturing red hair.

Tatiana shifted, causing him to roll back on the mattress. When she straddled him, he felt emotions getting tied up, Becca's face still blurring with Tatiana's. Her question about whether he ever felt lonely throbbed in his brain, overtaken by the urgent need to release.

'Faster,' he muttered through gritted teeth and Tatiana bucked her hips, his climax causing little spasms to spread down his arms.

'I have thought about it,' he said, out of breath. 'Being alone.'

Tatiana collapsed onto him then, showering his lips with kisses.

He must have fallen asleep again. When he opened his eyes, she was standing on the carpet, pulling one of his grey T-shirts over her still naked body.

'I'm hungry,' Tatiana said. 'Do you have food?'

Anton relaxed his head against the pillow. He wasn't sure what time it was, only that lunch had come and gone.

'Try the fridge,' he muttered.

She gave him a shy smile. 'It's nice to see your bedroom for a change.'

She padded back outside towards the kitchen and he found himself wishing her gone.

A thought occurred to him too late. The next sound he heard was that of Tatiana's scream.

The rat – the one that was too engorged for its own good – had, as it turned out, thicker skin than all the other vermin. He had hacked at it, but it had proved problematic to slice off its head. Dropping the headless, drained bodies of the other rats into the package lined with plastic, he had tossed the turgid rodent towards the bin, its blood splattering all over the floor. He had successfully delivered the package to Holland Park, disguised as a courier, and come back to clean the board and the meat cleaver. In his exhausted state, the kitchen floor, the blood-drenched cabinets and the fat rat's severed head were another story.

Baku, Azerbaijan
5 March, 1993

He waited in the corner of the Badamdar café, back to the wall. The name scrawled on the shred of paper in front of him read 'Igor Ziyali'. The man he knew to be Ziyali was lounging outside the café wearing a thick winter overcoat and smoking a shisha pipe with three of his comrades. Ziyali was swarthy, with a patchy beard and double chins, the tallest man Anton had ever seen. Ethnically, Ziyali looked more Arab than Azeri.

Anton had long finished his drink, waiting for Ziyali to settle up and make a move. Some feet away, a woman ten years his senior sat nearest the door making eyes at him, crossing and uncrossing her legs, licking her lips under the arid warmth of the blow heater, the small unit mounted on a shelf, as though warmth was a commodity to be exulted. Her hair was scraped back off her forehead and she wore an overly thick layer of makeup. This part of town, he now knew, was notorious for prostitutes soliciting their clients in downmarket establishments such as this one. He felt the urge to shout out across the café that he didn't have enough change even for a *lavash*, let alone a quick fuck, and that despite appearances he was only nineteen years old.

Outside, Ziyali got to his feet, stretching his arms above his head and curving his spine. Anton lurched forward, afraid to lose sight of him. Ziyali bid farewell to his comrades. Anton waved his hand for the bill and rooted around in his pocket for his pile of remaining *manats*.

He followed Ziyali on a deserted back alley littered with

discarded office furniture. The sky above was a lead shade of grey, clouds indiscernible, the smell of shisha still tinged on the air. The man lumbered at a steady pace, smoking a cigarette.

Anton followed as he emerged on to another street, reaching into his pocket for a set of keys to a nondescript door at the bottom of a sandy-beige building with very few windows.

'Are you Ziyali?' Anton said, catching up to him.

Igor didn't bother turning around, sliding his key inside the lock. 'Fuck do you want?'

'This is your brothel. I'm looking for a woman. Valentina Moroshkin.'

'Valentina, uh? Tell me, what does a boy fresh out of school want with Valentina?'

'She's my mother.'

He stopped in his tracks, turned and gave Anton a hard stare, one eye squinting. Anton felt water from puddles seeping through the hole in his baseball-style canvas shoes, the cold entering his bones. The café seemed like a haven in comparison.

Ziyali started laughing.

'Why do you laugh?'

Anton could see Ziyali's shoulders trembling. 'That's impossible. You've got the wrong whore.'

'It was a long time ago. Before she started working for you.'

'You're wrong, boy. Now fuck off.'

'Valentina Agnieszka Moroshkina. Born in April, nineteen fifty-seven. You took her from one of the clubs in Nasimi around '86.'

Ziyali left his key dangling in the lock, turning to face Anton. Anton leaned back, Ziyali the more gargantuan the closer a person got. 'She kept her looks pretty good for someone who would be turning forty next month,' he sneered.

Anton's chest rose and fell in the wind. His entire body was cold, to the tips of his fingers.

'Kid, your mother is dead. Knifed in the throat by a client eight weeks ago. Motherfucker fled to Istanbul. It was in the papers, didn't you see? We had to close down. Six years in the slammer I'd have got if I didn't pay up.'

Ziyali turned his back, twisted the key in the lock and stepped inside. 'Liudmila!' he bellowed as he entered.

An older woman appeared at his side. Anton peered through the doorway at her leathery skin.

'Get this boy some spirits and send him on his way.'

Ziyali disappeared. The woman's thick frame filled the doorway. 'What are you here for, boy? Come to pop your cherry?'

Anton had already started to pace, clenching his teeth, burying his hands deep in the coarse fabric of his jacket. Inside, he still carried the Walkman that Keller had given him as a child.

'I'm not here to speak to you, you old cunt. I want to talk to Ziyali.'

He didn't see it coming. A sucker punch: her balled fist with gold rings catching the bridge of his nose, the cartilage already twisted and broken from the previous blows. Pain burned up into his brain and eyes. He stumbled backwards, clutching his face, eyes watering. When he withdrew them, blood trickled over his fingers.

Anton cursed her, charging at the door, hitting her squarely in the chest. Liudmila shrieked, losing her footing. He barged past her into the whore house, ascertaining that Ziyali had turned left, away from the main staircase.

He found him in the kitchen, standing on red tiles and putting a filled copper pitcher onto a lit stove.

'Get the fuck out!' the beast of a man roared.

Anton didn't give him a chance to react. Leaping over the kitchen table, he wrenched the jagged commando knife from his pocket, slamming into Ziyali's chest, sending the man sprawling to the tiles.

He stabbed the blade into Ziyali's throat three times in swift succession, the knife grasped between agile fingers.

'For not protecting my mother,' he said in a low voice, yanking out the blade for a final time and hovering above the man's chest, straddling the body, his breathing ragged. Anton watched as below him the beast bled out onto cold tiles, choking on the tide of his own blood, the light already faded from glazed-over eyes, and felt nothing.

Chapter 19

Panama City, Panama
28 February, 2017

Tom ducked as a paintbrush the size of a hammer flew out of the door, ricocheted off the wall, whistling past his ear. At the top of the staircase, inside the loft, a lovers' tiff had escalated into a full-blown war of vulgar Spanish insults. The woman accused the man of being a lowlife cheat; he in turn charged her with whoring herself out to his office colleagues. Moments later, the male, a slimline Latino with hyper-smooth coffee skin and slicked-back hair, burst out of the doorway, suit and tie in disarray. Tom felt himself being elbowed out of the way, the Latino briefly registering his presence as he careered down the flight of stairs.

Continuing forward, Tom reached the top level. Inside, he glimpsed the woman pacing back and forth, cradling her face in her hands, still sobbing and cursing the air. Luxurious coal-black hair was piled into a high ponytail. She wore a tight white cropped vest under a baggy pair of dungarees; neon-coloured toenails peeped out at the bottom and a tattoo of Frida Kahlo's face was on her forearm. On her wrist, more than fifty silver bangles jangled together.

Tom tapped on the doorframe, gave a polite cough. The woman removed her hands, eyes flashing in his direction.

'*Buenas,*' he said in greeting before switching to English. 'You must be Camila. I seem to have come at a bad time.'

She wiped her face, smearing makeup under her eyelids. 'You're *Señor* Holt. No, no, you haven't. Miguel said morning. Please. Come in.'

He moved inside. Camila Corazon turned her back, composed herself before turning again to face him, revitalised. Even with tear-streaked cheeks, flecks of paint dappling her skin and fingers, she was something quite exquisite to behold: liquorice pupils accentuating the whites of her eyes, a petite, straight nose, distinct cheekbones and a pout that could stop traffic.

'I'm sorry about that. Another no good *muchacho* on his way out. Can I get you a drink?'

'Sure.'

She cocked her head to one side. 'You're Oliver's son, right?'

Tom gave a smile, took a step forward across the threshold. He held out his hand and she shook it. 'Tom. You know my father?'

'He bought a painting from me once. Had to sell it again when his business went under. I'm not sure where it ended up.'

As she went to the kitchen off to one side, Tom took in his surroundings. He was inside the loft space of a three-storey building in the Plaza de la Independencia, adjacent to some kind of cathedral, the façade covered in scaffolding. Inside there was a low ceiling, the walls a shade of golden yellow with chipped paint, floorboards smeared with splatters of colour, the vigorous odour of turps in the air. Various easels, some occupied with half-finished canvases, were scattered around the room.

'What do you paint?'

'I do a few things,' she responded from the kitchen. 'Acrylics. Some sculpture. I like to paint people. Women, mainly. I teach too, sometimes life drawing.'

She reappeared with two glasses, handing him one.

'*Salud*,' she said, touching her glass to his, the healthy dose of rum and cola warming the back of his throat.

'Where did you learn English?' he asked, because her Spanish accent was treacle.

'At the Colegio Internacional de Caracas,' she said.

'And where did you learn to paint?'

She sipped her drink, cheeks flushing. 'My grandmother. Then my father sent me to classes in an art school in Miranda, a neighbourhood in Caracas. Then in '99, after Chávez founded the movement and came to power, we left, first to Colombia, then to Panama.'

'Where are your parents now?'

'Miami. My father is a plastic surgeon. I can paint you a new nose and he can be the one to build it for you.'

'Do I need a new nose?'

She was laughing again. 'Relax. It was a joke; your nose is fine.'

He liked her. She was an antidote to Becca. Camila was blessed with Latin curves, voluminous hair and caramel skin, breasts the size of pomegranates that were buoyant enough to be judged not quite genuine.

'Did Miguel tell you why I'm here?' he asked.

Camila's expression darkened. She moved past him, closing the door to the loft then locking it.

'It's in the bedroom. Come with me.'

Tom followed her across the studio. Camila ushered him inside, once more closing the door behind her, pushing her hair from her eyes, body language suggesting a certain unreleased tension. The walls were painted a crimson red, the bed linen a matching shade. The bed itself was in disarray, Camila gathering up a set of lace underwear. She straightened out the quilt and closed the curtains before diving underneath the bed and bringing out a sealed wooden box. On the wall, an air conditioner blasted out an icy breeze.

'It's unfinished,' she said, perhaps nervous to display her talents. 'This was my fourth try. It still requires some work.'

Tom had studied the picture of *La Maja Vestida* by Francisco Goya, or at least the one available on the internet. He had no clue as to how the study owned by Oscar Aguinaldo differentiated from the original.

'What did you copy it from?' he asked.

Camila opened the box and took out the diminutive painting on a 20 x 20 centimetre canvas, unfurling it from what looked like muslin. She held it up, handing him a printed sheet of paper containing the original in colour, surrounded by a gilded frame, and two similar photographs.

'This is the one that's hanging on the wall in Contadora.'

Tom looked from the print out to the photograph. 'The colours are…'

'A shade too light, I know. When it's done it will be glazed and varnished. It will be a shade darker.'

His eyes flicked back and forth. So far so good. 'You have excellent craftsmanship.'

A flicker of a smile crossed her features. She snatched back the piece of paper and photographs. 'I'm not the first artist to fake a Goya. I'm sure I won't be the last.'

'Do you think the one in Contadora is the real thing?'

She sighed, letting her shoulders drop. 'It's not about that anymore, it's about…'

'Ownership.' They said the word in unison. Tom offered her a smile.

'You've been talking to Miguel,' she said, rewrapping the painting in the muslin.

'How soon can you get it finished?'

She chewed her lips. 'If I work hard, a week, maybe. Then it requires some time to dry under ultraviolet light.'

'Why is that?'

'The light speeds up the drying process. I've already used a… I don't know how you say in English. *Secante*. Is there some kind of hurry?'

'My father's life depends on this job. And possibly mine. I may not have long.'

She blew air from her bottom lip, dispersing the loose hair framing her face, looking worried.

'How authentic does this thing need to be? You never want Oscar Aguinaldo to find out about this, right? I mean the forgery.'

'So long as Juan Carlos gets the original, seems no one cares how long it takes his brother to work it out. And I'll be long gone.'

She shook her head, expression registering frustration. 'I'll see what I can do. I'll paint you your painting, but I'm not ready to die for this.'

'I'm hoping nobody has to die doing this.'

'You're going to do this yourself?'

She looked at him like he was insane, like he was a too decent looking man to get involved in a robbery. Yet she had no clue as to his past, his motives, and what was at stake.

'What do you know about Contadora?' he asked.

'Contadora? It's the most beautiful island that the world never talks about. Not where you come from, anyway. A hidden paradise. In the time of the conquistadors they used to take inventory of the pearls there before sending them onward to Spain.'

'I need someone to show me around.'

She tilted her head to one side. 'So ask Miguel.'

'Don't get me wrong, Miguel is perfectly nice, but… Miguel doesn't have your smile, or much of a sense of humour. And I doubt he looks that good in a bikini.'

A smile was tugging at her lips again. 'You want this painting or not?'

'Twenty-four hours.'

She bit her bottom lip. He waited for her to make up her mind.

'When do we leave?'

'The moment Miguel finds me a boat.'

His father had given him the keys to his vehicle, a 1999 black Chevrolet Camaro, left idle inside a vacant plot of land that had been converted to a makeshift car park and cornered off by sheets of graffiti-covered corrugated iron. Miguel had purchased him a phone with a local SIM card unlocked for international calls. In the driver's seat, Tom started the engine. It spluttered before roaring to life. He gave it some revs; she sounded healthy enough. The petrol gauge showed half a tank. He switched on the handset, watching the screen spring to life. Waiting for the phone to register on a network, he dialled the number for the Insight News central offices in London, as he had done in Santiago, asking to speak to Nashaly Akinyemi. When asked, he gave his first name only. Moments later, he found himself put through.

'Tom?' a familiar voice came on the line. 'It's Nash. How are you? Where are you?'

'In Panama City.'

'You made it. Did you find your father?'

'I did.'

'Can he help us?'

'Not exactly. But I'm working on it. My father's in a bit of hot water. I may need to save his life at the same time. How about you?'

'I need to know how you discovered the connection between Charlie Ebdon and Capricorn.'

She said it bluntly, no niceties. He held on to the phone, sweat at his temples. He knew the answer, and Nash deserved to know the truth. Yet the truth had come from Becca. So far, he had managed keep her out of the equation.

'Tom? Are you there?'

'I'm here.'

'How did you know he was using the name Capricorn?'

'I was told by someone who works for him.'

'And who was that?'

'Nash, I have to go, can you see this number?'

'No, read it out to me.'

He fumbled around, locating his number, read it back to her.

'Can I call you soon?' she asked.

'Call whenever you like,' he said, and hung up.

Switching off the engine, Tom stared though the windscreen at a cloudless blue sky, swirling with vultures; unsure as to why he was protecting Becca Wylde anymore.

Chapter 20

Tom stood in the blistering heat at the metal gate to the Isla Flamenco Marina at the tip of the Amador Causeway and the Pacific entrance to the canal, waiting for his father to arrange access to the vessel known as *La Señorita*. Glancing through his sunglasses at the number of polished yachts and majestic masts on show, he was beginning to think he had missed his calling in life.

Oliver Holt emerged from the marina's main building, putting on his sunglasses, wearing a short-sleeved white shirt paired with a Panama hat.

'We're all set, Mr Schneider,' he said with a fatherly nod, flashing his teeth and handing Tom back the false Chilean passport he had used to enter the country. 'Has our guest arrived yet? They'll need to see her ID.'

'Not yet,' Tom replied. 'I said 10 a.m.'

'Took you all of two days, I'm impressed. You must get it from me. Surely there must be trail of broken hearts around the world.'

Tom squinted in the sun. He thought of Eden Van de Vlok: his former fiancée and the boss's daughter, and those that had come before. Becca on the other hand... Becca didn't have a heart *to* break.

'You wait here, I'll get the booze,' his father continued.

Oliver Holt had a very distinct set of priorities, in ascending order: alcohol (rum, European Cabernet), cured meats (Spanish or Italian), fish (any variety, only fresh), casinos (slots or tables), and French novelists (Dumas, Flaubert, Proust, Balzac). Since his arrival, Tom had found himself asking after his father's whereabouts daily, only to find him dining at his favourite restaurant, *Finca del Mar* – hardly a man eating like there was no money left – or sat alone on a bench in the Plaza Simón Bolivar that backed on to the Casa Blanca Hotel, under his Panama hat, nose in a novel. Despite the threats to his life, a suicide attempt, and his middle son appearing out of the blue after twenty-odd years, his father had carried on as though nothing was amiss. He had spent the morning packing a heavy-duty American-style cooler for their trip, filled with wine, beer, cold cuts, fresh loaves and a bottle of *Abuelo* rum for good measure.

When his father returned, Camila was with him, laughing along at something Oliver had said. Tom removed his sunglasses and took a moment to admire the view. The flecks of paint were gone, everything else as he remembered, even the bangles and hooped earrings, though this time she was wearing a flimsy dress that did little to cover her most appealing assets. He felt a healthy desire surge downward and into his veins, a sensation he hadn't experienced in far too long.

'What's so funny?' he asked as she approached, taking her bag as they exchanged a chaste kiss on the cheek in greeting, her skin scented with white-spirit tinged perfume.

'Your father was telling me that as a young boy you never wanted to leave your mama's side, even when you were ten or eleven, and he used to worry that you'd never let her go. Then the next thing he knew, you'd gone and joined the military.'

He felt his cheeks grow warmer. 'That sounds about right.'

'I think your mama must be one lucky woman.'

She held his gaze for a moment longer than was necessary. She was good… maybe too good. Confidence and innocence did not make for exemplary bedfellows. For a moment he wished for his father's absence.

'Take the other side of this thing, will you?' said Oliver, slapping him on the shoulder and lifting one handle of the cooler.

Once Camila had shown her passport to the stewards, they were permitted access. Tom moved along the floating walkway parallel with his father, holding one side of the weighty cooler, Camila out in front, the curve of her ample rear bouncing up and down as she walked, the edge of her skirt flicking up.

'When you said a boat, I didn't think you meant a *boat*,' she grinned, as they arrived at the numbered mooring spot.

Tom set down the cooler on the walkway and removed his sunglasses, admiring the impressive vessel, waiting for Oliver to locate the keys. According to Miguel, the Predator 57 MK II was a thirty-six foot Sunseeker model owned by a moneyed *Panameño* known as Xavi Futuro. Futuro was a close *compadre* of Juan Carlos Aguinaldo and a former lawyer who had amassed his fortune in the nineties by making Colombian drug money look legitimate, enabling the continuous trafficking of cocaine going north. Looking at the Predator 57, it occurred to Tom that illicit drug-dealing somehow had its upside.

'Panoramic hull, nice touch,' his father said as they climbed aboard.

Along with his other passions, Oliver Holt knew a thing or two about boats. Except after the business collapse, he said the yacht he'd owned had ended up side-on in the waters off Amador, only the gunwale still visible, before being towed away by the Canal Authority. Stepping aboard *La Señorita*, Tom had never seen his father so contented.

With clearances, it took almost an hour to navigate out of the Flamenco marina. On exit, Camila took up position on the sun lounger front deck, Oliver picking up speed as he took charge in the saloon, pumping out Clapton's 'Layla' from the on-board speaker system. Tom removed his shirt, sat by the railing, hanging his legs over the side, watching the spray from the hull spew out over an endless, majestic Pacific. Despite the luxury of it all, there was an uneasy feeling in the pit of his stomach. He pictured Charlie Ebdon. Anton. Becca. Anil's smiling face before his slumped-over dead body. Clare Buchanan. After Panama, he would need to move on. He couldn't go home, not yet. For the threat to be removed he needed information. He needed the evidence to put Ebdon away.

'Come over here,' Camila shouted in her Venezuelan lilt over the wind. He turned to see that she'd stripped down to a mustard yellow bikini with loosely-tied spaghetti straps, a stunning hip to breast curve ratio, the definition of hourglass. She was holding out a bottle of sunscreen in invitation and he was more than glad for the interruption.

The Pearl Islands came into view around lunch-time, rising into blotchy green peaks on the horizon. Sailing onwards past Saboga, dense with trees, Tom glimpsed the merest hint of a beach and postage stamp of a jetty, craning his neck for a better view, one hand securely wrapped around Camila's waist on the sun deck, fingers brushing the still bare top of her thigh, the other around a can of beer. Below them the water was a translucent shade of turquoise. Contadora Island – according to his father – was one of the smaller landmasses in the Pearl group but the most popular for residents and tourists.

Camila pointed. 'This is the north side. Playas Executiva and Galeon, where the public ferry comes in.'

He witnessed small, clandestine white sand beaches, little pieces of paradise nestled amongst craggy outcrops of rocks, overgrown trees and untidy jungle, secluded enough that it could pass for Scaramanga's hideout. Oliver slowed their speed, water churning underneath them. A group of villas rose up on the east side of Galeon, wood shack domiciles planted into the rock on stilts and shaded by palm trees. As they rounded the corner – yet another cliff face – the boat turned starboard and began its trek south. A longer, wider white strip of sand came into view, the tide high, to one end what looked like a shipwrecked graffiti-covered vessel. Camila called it Playa Larga. In the backdrop was a group of gutted buildings, the ghostly remnants of a resort that once bordered the beach, but had clearly ceased to thrive, now in the final throes of a death caused by rust, abandonment and disrepair.

'Apparently it belonged to a Colombian drug lord, back

in the sixties,' Camila told him over the sound of the engine.

Oliver kept the boat on course. Camila explained, 'The next main beach, on the south side, is Cacique, the most popular beach on the islands, where most boats that come here drop anchor. All along the cliff edge are houses and residences, on both sides. Weekend residences, mainly. On the beach itself are a couple of boutique hotels. Oscar Aguinaldo's place is on the far right-hand side, with a set of stairs leading up the cliff edge from the sand. Not the biggest property but one of them. That's where the painting is kept.'

They were passing two smaller, empty beaches, inaccessible over the rocks, the sand littered with driftwood and detritus spat out by the sea. Tom glimpsed the start of a small runway. A road came to an end, turning to dirt track leading back around to Playa Larga. This was not Bermuda, or Barbados, or anything like those islands he had pictured. This was rural territory, overgrown, developed only in uneven patches, the rest of the island claimed by Mother Nature's wild and unpredictable evolution. This was not the home of the Hilton, or the Marriott. It was a bohemian hideaway, its former glory days a faded memory away, and yet an unpublicised utopia with clear turquoise waters.

The sight of Cacique caused him a sharp intake of breath. In contrast to Playa Larga's ramshackle, dilapidated buildings, grand houses lined the cliff faces bookending a stretch of white sand, nestled in a rocky kind of cove. His gaze went from house to house, settling on a cliff-top villa that had its own staircase leading up from the sand, protected by a gate.

His father killed the engine, the wind dropping. They were fifty metres from the shore; Oliver dropped the anchor between a sleek catamaran and a sailboat. Camila got to her feet, stretched out her back, then wandered forward to the bow.

'You coming in?' she invited him.

'Right now?' he asked with a smile.

'Now is as good a time as any,' she said, climbing over the railings in the bikini, diving in backwards.

He watched her, admiring the ease at which she conducted herself, as if nothing in the world mattered.

'It's beautiful!' she shouted, emerging from the surface.

He took a minute to glance back at Oscar Aguinaldo's house on the cliffs, etching the lines in his brain so that he could ask questions later. In the saloon, his father was taking some photographs on a digital SLR, as Tom had instructed him to. Glancing overboard to locate Camila, he found she had backstroked to the stern and was climbing back aboard via the hull-level platform.

He squinted in her direction, water cascading off supple skin, the triangles of the bikini now partially transparent.

'I thought we were swimming,' he said.

'You missed your chance,' she replied, as Oliver handed her a towel and she offered Tom a conciliatory wink.

He reminded himself why he had come to Isla Contadora, before realising he'd stopped listening to that part of his brain the moment she'd stepped onto the boat.

Movement around the island was by hired golf buggy. Tom sat on the rear-facing seat with Camila, legs dangling over the back, watching the road slip by from under their feet. Oliver went too fast, causing Camila to cling to his arm, digging her nails in, clothes and hair still damp with sea-water, lips parted, a fraction too close. The interior of Contadora was something of a ghost town, ageing vines hanging from frail trees, overgrown woods thick with jungle, concealing the paradise beaches that lay beyond. Apparently those with enough money to buy a weekend home would settle for nothing less than a sea view and a three-metre high security gate.

Miguel had secured them a property for the night, another reason to spend time on the island. Get a feel for the place, routes in and out. He asked his father to drive the full circuit, all of half an hour, taking the road past the Aguinaldo house, which led to a dead end beside the southern strip of the runway. It was impossible to see the property over the wall, a closed metal access gate for cars lined with metal spikes.

'Not much to see,' Camila commented drily.

Dinner was at Casa Tortuga, one of only a handful of restaurants on the island, and in his father and Miguel's view, the only one worth dining at. An open-air patio setting, partially covered by a tiled roof, Italian food served fresh. His father spent the entire evening regaling Camila with stories of Tom's early childhood, much to her delight.

'He's only telling you all this because it's all he can remember,' Tom told her, refilling her glass. 'He left my mother before my balls even dropped.'

Oliver shifted in his seat, downing the contents of his glass. Camila was looking his father's way. 'I had three sons,' Oliver offered up. 'It wasn't a highlight.'

'So nice then, that you're helping your father out now,' Camila smiled back at him, eyes sparkling in the moonlight.

'If we can't pull this off, then we might all be dead anyway.'

'What are you going to do?'

'I haven't worked that out yet. Somehow we break into that house and we replace the Goya with your fake.'

'You're going to start a war, you know that?'

He lifted his glass to his lips. 'I don't have the time or resources to do things differently. Juan Carlos wants that painting; it's what he's going to get. So long as my father lives and I get the information I want, I'm not here to worry about the repercussions of the theft of a single painting. My war is elsewhere. I couldn't care less what the *Panameños* do to each other.'

A smile tugged at her lips. As he downed the remainder of his wine, under the table her toes were gliding up the outside of his jeans.

He lay on his back in the darkness, Camila's naked body curled into his, fingers entwined in her hair.

Too much rum. Oliver had cracked open the bottle of *Abuelo*, whipping up three Cuba Libres over ice before the front door was even closed. The walls in the rented house were the shade of paella. Two hours later, at almost three o'clock in the morning, his father had finally fallen into a deep slumber, still clutching a highball glass in his lap, snoring like a bear in hibernation. Tom had turned his head, Camila already grinning at him. He'd taken the glass from her hand, placing it on the nearest table. She hadn't argued when he'd moved his hands from her waist to her behind, pulling her in closer.

'Christ, I thought he'd never stop reminiscing,' Tom said, lowering his head.

Her tongue tasted of rum and cola. Her fingers unfastened his shirt buttons in full view of his sleeping father. The moment Oliver Holt snorted in his sleep, Tom had got to his feet, pulling Camila behind him into the bedroom, thinking there was only so far you could go in front of a parent.

The sex had been frenetic, wordless yet intense, two people being as silent as they could be in the heat of the moment. He'd pushed away a memory of Becca back in Uruguay. Camila was open, inviting, sensual: everything the redhead wasn't. His first experience with a Latina female had left him sated and slick with sweat. That Becca was still on his mind when it was over left him feeling tetchy.

His phone was ringing at first light. Tom leaned over the bed to the floor, pulling the handset from his jeans pocket. The 'N' he saw on the screen stood for Nash. He answered, rolling on to his back where Camila was stirring.

'Hey.'

'Did I wake you?' Nash said.

'Yes,' Tom confirmed. 'It's alright though.'

'Where are you?'

Camila had turned, reaching down under the sheet. Tom tried to focus on his conversation. 'Did you want something?'

Nash went silent for a moment. 'Tell me,' he added, trying to sound less hostile.

'Look. I didn't mention something when we spoke yesterday. Anton tracked me down.'

Tom bolted upright, pushing Camila's hand away.

'What? Nash, you have to get out; you need to leave.'

'I'm not afraid of him.'

'You need to be. You—'

'I met with Albert Denham's first wife. She told me Anton is Russian. Anton Marevski, we think. We're trying to track down a passport. Soon we're going north, to where Ebdon grew up. See what we can dig up. I need more time. I feel like I'm missing something, something that links all of this together.'

Tom ran his fingers through his hair, screwing up his face. That Anton was a Russski came as no surprise; he'd hidden the accent well. 'If he knows about you, right now they will be moving all the chess pieces into place. You will end up like Clare Buchanan, Nash, I swear to you. You need to release Clare's statement publicly; you need to do it now. Let all the other journalists swarm over it after that; it will be in the hands of the police, the right police. There's nothing they can do if you splash it all over the internet.'

'Except come after me.'

'Except come after you. But by then it'll be too late.'

'You're saying it's too late for you?'

He stared at the blank wall. It took him a moment to realise their call was a bad idea. 'Nash, hang up. If they've got to you they can find me.'

He hung up, wiping the beads of sweat from his forehead. The room was moving.

'What was that all about?' Camila said.

He turned to her, searching her face. They needed to get back to the city. Right now, success depended on her.

'How soon can you finish that painting?' he asked.

Chapter 21

London, England
8 March, 2017

Becca had learned a thing or two in Buenos Aires, during her time with Tom and Anil. That sometimes, what was required of a job was perseverance. Patience. Patience was not a gift she had been blessed with. As a thief she had always been a chancer, an opportunist. Becca acknowledged she wasn't good at sitting around waiting.

If the job in Uruguay had taught her anything, it was that that planning was everything.

Christian Holt was not going to give up his brother easily. Telling that to Anton's face would be like an admission of failure; that she was not up to the task at hand. Send in Anton, and Christian Holt would be pissing information within minutes. That's how people were with Anton. Once Christian Holt was done leaking information, he would have been dispensed with.

In the two and a half weeks since her conversation with Christian at the Sun Inn, she had backed off, redirected her and Richie's efforts to the London streets. However things turned out, they were going to need cash, and plenty of it. An economy class, single flight to Chile was in the region of five hundred and sixty pounds at the cheapest. Richie had hit the jackpot in a restaurant on the King's Road, lifting a woman's purse containing three hundred in notes, together with a wad of euros. Some of the money she had used to buy clothes at a Chelsea charity shop, for what she hoped would be one of the final phases of her plan.

That plan had taken Richie by surprise. It had meant he'd had to get out of bed in the morning, get to work in daylight hours. Excited by the mission at first, she knew her silence – and the unanswered questions hanging over them both – was now beginning to piss him off.

Christian Holt had a management consultant girlfriend called Shelley Robbins. She worked freelance, mainly from home, from their ground floor flat on Cedar Grove in central Richmond. Their stakeout of the property every morning for two weeks, under various guises, showed that Robbins disappeared off to work in an office somewhere on Tuesday and Friday mornings, wearing a houndstooth blazer, high heels and carrying an oversized tote bag with a laptop inside.

On the Tuesday morning, Becca wore a beige trench coat, her own too-small pencil heels pinching her toes. She stepped over gaps in the paving tiles, talking to no one on the phone. She hung back as she watched the now familiar dark-haired female striding with purpose towards the train station, reacting as any innocent bystander would when a hooded youth slammed into her shoulder, sending Robbins sprawling to the ground, tote bag vomiting its contents over the pavement.

Becca rushed over.

'Oh my God, are you alright? The cheek of that guy!'

'I'm alright, thanks,' Robbins stammered, shaking her head. 'So rude.'

'You think you should say something, but then you don't know if he's carrying a knife. Are you sure you're OK? Did you hit your head?'

'I'm fine, really. Not hurt.'

'Let me help you up.'

Becca sent Shelley Robbins on her way, extending more sympathies, waiting until she turned the corner. Swivelled on her heel and walked back down Cedar Grove. Richie had removed the hoodie; now balled up in his arms. Before he joined her on her side of the road, he tucked it behind the wheel of a car parked up on the curb.

'We good?' he asked at her side.

Becca allowed Shelley Robbins's set of keys to slide down her sleeve, dropping into her palm. 'You doubting me now?'

'Never,' Richie grinned.

'If she realises once she gets to the station, we'll have about ten minutes on the inside. You take the bedrooms and bathrooms, I'll do the rest.'

'Done.'

Becca hit the steps at a pace, Richie close to her back. They couldn't linger in the doorway. The street was littered with old codgers with nothing better to do than to people watch.

They knew there would be no alarm, despite the yellow ADT box fixed under the roof awning of the house. A pungent scent from a reed diffuser filled the entrance hall. Becca closed the door. They pulled on surgical gloves, Richie off like a whippet. She kicked off the high heels, flexed her toes, started with a desk in the corner of the living room. On the surface, a photograph of Christian and Shelley grinned toothily back at her, dressed up for a black-tie event, arms encircling one another.

She rifled through paperwork, bank statements, loose photographs, old wedding invitations. No mention of Thomas Holt. She moved to the kitchen, checked the fridge for notes; found only a magnetic whiteboard containing shopping lists and birthday reminders.

Becca flinched at the sound of an ambulance in the near distance. On the side piled up with some magazines was a small white notepad. She ran her fingers over minute ridges in the surface, held it up to the light. Tore off the top three sheets and looked around for a pencil, coming up with a Bic biro with a chewed lid. Rubbing the nib gently over the paper, the words 'buy wine' appeared. Sweat crept on to her upper lip. She could hear Richie diligently working the bedroom. She kept rubbing, more illegible scrawl appearing under faint blue ink. Towards the middle of the page, she squinted, altered the angle of the paper. Three words were visible. The first: Paitilla. The second and third: Panama City.

'Check this out,' Richie said, appearing in the doorway holding up an iPad. 'It's a map point on Google. Camino Real, Punta Paitilla. Does that mean anything?'

Becca put down the biro, screwed up the sheets of paper and stuffed them inside her pocket.

'It's in Panama City.'

'How do you know that?'

'Put it back, let's go.'

'Are we done?'

Becca was already out in the hallway, pulling off the plastic gloves and squeezing her feet into the pair of stilettos. She looked forward to the moment she could toss them into the bin. 'We're done.'

'I'd do anything for you, you know that, right?'

Becca had wiped the keys of prints, dropped them on the hedge at the point at which Richie had knocked into Shelley Robbins. Richie joined her in the Cricketers Pub on Richmond Green, taking a different route to her from the flat.

'I know you would,' she said, twisting a glass of orange juice. 'But we can't stay together for ever.'

'Why do you need to do this so badly?'

'I need to give Tom something. Before Anton finds him first. I need to remedy some things.'

She sensed his frustration. 'What did he do to make him so important? So important that you can't be happy with what you got?'

She said nothing, hard to know where to begin. Her stomach growled. They had no money on them for lunch. Richie puffed out his cheeks. 'So that's where you'll go? Panama City?'

She nodded. She would have to, and she would have to do it soon.

'Take me with you.'

She tensed. 'You come with me and we go against Anton's orders for the first time in our adult lives.'

'And you're willing to do that?'

She nodded for a second time, feeling her chest swell.

'Then count me in.'

'Richie, you understand, don't you? Anton can never know. He can never know where we've gone.'

Chapter 22

Northumberland, England
14 March, 2017

The pub landlady at the Ketteridge Arms handed Nash a set of keys, eyeing her up and down. She had the skin of a smoker, a myriad of leathery lines. 'We shut up shop at midnight,' she clipped in a Geordie twang. 'If you're coming in late, use the key to the door at the back. Rooms are at the top of the stairs.'

'Thanks,' Miles replied on Nash's behalf, reaching over and lifting his own set of keys from the bar surface. Nash didn't appreciate the sour-faced cow's blatant visual appraisal, as though Afro curls were something of a rarity in a secluded northern country village. The landlady wore jeans and a bulky wool cardigan, ash blonde highlights in her badly cut hair.

'Breakfast is from seven,' the woman added, turning her back and getting on with the pint she was pulling.

'How do we get to Ketteridge Community Home from here?' Miles asked.

The landlady turned, didn't bother looking Nash in the face. 'Out of the pub, turn right. Down the bottom of the hill, take the road that forks right. You'll pass the gate about fifty metres along.'

The single mattress was lumpy, Nash sleeping feverishly, kicking off sheets, Anton Marevski and the box of dead rats floating in and out of her consciousness. Several times she had found herself on the verge of telling Miles, knowing the moment she did would incur more fears for her safety, more caution, more stalling. That Anton hadn't attacked her up to now meant that he was being held back by something. That the threats were just that; idle threats. At this stage, she considered going after Ebdon and Anton more important. In Holland Park, she had got rid of the evidence itself, emptying the contents and bloody plastic lining into her mother's neighbour's compost bin, tossing the battered box over the fence.

Breakfast was mediocre. Nash pushed rubbery scrambled eggs around her plate with the prongs of her fork. She was eager to get going.

The information on Ketteridge Community Home was available in the public record. It was a grand house and garden, having been in the Ebdon family for generations. Before they were Ebdons they were Haskills, the name changing via the marriage of Bill Ebdon's grandmother Victoria Haskill, an only child, to Martell Ebdon, a businessman. Nash had expanded on Gus Fendy's family tree, and Gus had confirmed the existence of a sole surviving domestic employee. Charlie Ebdon had donated the house and grounds to Northumberland NHS Trust in 1998, soon after the death of his older sister, Ione, to be used as a home for the elderly and infirm, heavily subsidised by money coming out of Charlie Ebdon's own pocket. No wonder he was considered a local hero.

The entrance to the Community Home stank of bleach, laced with a hint of lavender. Like the Ketteridge Arms, the heating appeared to be switched to maximum. Nash yanked off her coat and satchel. A male orderly dressed in blue mopped the tiled floor, behind him a carpeted staircase leading to a set of crosshatch windows. Miles propped himself up against the reception desk. His Sid Vicious hair had made a comeback. Somewhere in another room a TV was on too loudly, behind the door a clack of heels against marble.

The door groaned on its hinges. A woman in a charcoal suit appeared in the atrium, wearing thick bifocals and a high-necked blouse, a lightning streak of white in her shoulder-length black hair.

'Can I help you?' she asked.

Nash straightened. 'Nashaly Akinyemi and Miles Ferretti. We're here to speak to Constance Thurlow.'

'Visiting hours are from two o'clock.'

'I talked to someone in advance. They said we could spend time with Constance outside of normal hours.'

'Is that so? I've heard nothing of it.'

Nash felt herself inhale. 'It's very important we speak to her.'

For a second time, Nash found herself being visually appraised. 'Well you're *clearly* not family. Constance Thurlow is ninety-five. Visiting hours for a woman of her age and condition take their toll. Who was it who made this arrangement with you?'

Nash looked to Miles, who was already pulling a hard copy of the email from his satchel. Nash doubled checked the name. 'Valerie Stokes. Your receptionist.'

'Miss Stokes no longer works here.'

'Since when?' Miles blurted.

'She left her role last week.'

'Left or was pushed?' Nash snapped. 'Are you the manager here?'

'I am the supervisor, yes.'

Miles gave her a look.

'What is it you wish to ask Miss Thurlow?'

'We're here to ask her about her employment in this house.'

Something flashed across the woman's features. The orderly stopped moving, the mop handle hovering motionless in the air.

'Miss Thurlow has dementia. She has no recollection of last week, let alone last year. You are wasting your time. Now, if you will excuse me.'

At one fifty-five, amongst a handful of other visitors, Nash sat in a ground floor waiting room next to Miles, his knee jigging up and down, watching the seconds tick by on a cheap plastic wall-mounted clock. When the door opened, a nurse entered, ushering forth the group. Nash rose from her chair, the nurse nervously making eye contact.

'Miss Thurlow is asleep,' the nurse said. 'I'm sorry; you'll have to come back another time.'

'Fendy got exactly the same treatment,' Nash heard Miles say as she marched ahead of him down the gravelled driveway. 'They know she's been approached before.'

'So they're all in on it?' Nash questioned through gritted

teeth. 'I doubt they even know the nature of the secrets they're protecting.'

'Constance never married, had no children. She's unlikely to have many friends left who can get us access to her.'

Nash pulled her coat more snugly around her, refusing to believe that this was the end to any enquiry. They walked the rest of the route back to the pub in silence.

'Is that…?' she heard Miles murmur, when they were within view of the pub.

Nash followed his stare. Two small suitcases were piled up on the concrete pavement outside the entrance to the pub. She frowned. One of them was her own, her unzipped makeup bag teetering on the top of the pile.

Nash burst through the pub doors, striding over to the bar, Miles not far behind. The landlady was pouring two glasses of orange juice at the same time. She granted Nash the same look of indifference.

'What the hell are our suitcases doing out on the street?' Nash blurted.

'If you'd mentioned you were journalists in the first place, I would never have let you step over the threshold.' She turned, grabbing an envelope from the cash till and then it was hovering under Nash's nose. 'Two refunds, in full. Go find somewhere else to stay. Word of advice: not in Ketteridge. We know why you're here. Now get out; you're barred.'

Nash took the envelope. For a moment, the landlady didn't let go. Nash thrust out her chin. 'Does Charlie Ebdon pay for your silence? What does it take to keep a woman like you sweet?'

'Out!' the landlady spat back, throwing up her arm, dismissing them. 'Take your things and go.'

'Everything all right here, Debs?'

Nash felt Miles's fingers close around her bicep. The man behind 'Debs' was six foot four with a thick neck and eyes positioned too close together. Nash felt herself fall victim to his uneven gaze.

'All good, Leeroy. These two were leaving.'

Outside, Miles loaded the hire car. Fifteen minutes' drive down the road to the Beaumont Hotel in Hexham, Nash collapsed onto the bed, burying her face in the pillow.

She could tell her mother to run the story. Splash it on the front cover but keep the focus on Clare Buchanan's video statement and her final bus ride in 2005. It didn't answer the question of who killed her, or who was ultimately responsible for her death, and whether the order came from Charles Ebdon.

When she awoke it was dark and she was still in her coat, sweat gathered at her temples. Beside her, her phone was vibrating; the illuminated screen the only light in the room.

'Mum?' Nash answered.

'Where are you?' Diane Cambridge's voice said.

She pulled herself into a sitting position. It was after 8 p.m. 'In a hotel in Northumberland.'

'Is everything OK?'

'We had to get out of Ketteridge. We weren't exactly given a warm welcome.'

'Did something happen?'

'Nothing. More like slammed doors.'

'Well we've received an anonymous call. Someone wants to pass you some information. Have you got a pen?'

'Who?' Nash blurted, locating her bag and rifling around inside.

'Female. She's given instructions to wait in your car, on Stowell Street in Newcastle, outside the King Neptune restaurant, tomorrow morning at ten. You're to pick her up. She said she's a friend of Constance Thurlow.'

Nash scribbled down the details.

'Sweetheart… this case,' her mother continued. 'I'm happy if you want to run with what we have. Splash Clare Buchanan's video on the front page, let others pick up the scent—'

'Mum. Jesus. Why would you say something like that?'

'I want you to be safe, that's all. You are being careful?'

The tremor she heard in her mother's voice irritated her. Diane Cambridge was notorious for pushing those who worked for her to go after every detail of a story, no matter how minor. Unless you happened to be her direct offspring.

'Stop worrying about me. Thanks for the tip-off. I'll see you soon.'

She hung up, tossing the phone on the bed, walking over to the door and sliding the chain on.

Nash stopped still in the centre of the carpet, the memory of severed rats' heads still lingering, the stench of rotting rat flesh, wondering if she was holding on too tightly to a story that wasn't worth dying for.

Chapter 23

The English Channel
1 April, 1993

Anton sat outside on the upper passenger deck of the P&O ferry, wind and salt in his hair, wearing an ill-fitting overcoat over a yellow and black tracksuit, the former coming from Dimitry's contact in Turkey. Keller's gift of the Walkman was shielded by an inside pocket as he watched frothy white foam spray against the ship's bow.

Dimitry had smuggled him out. Whilst he doubted that there was a single soul mourning the death of Igor Ziyali, there had been a witness. Liudmila, from the whore house, could identify him in a line-up. Yet by the time the police would come knocking on the doors to his uncle's boxing academy, Dimitry had activated the plans in place to ensure Anton would be half-way to Istanbul, on his way to carry out the wishes of a father he had never met.

To start his new life.

You are a gift, Anton. This is your path in life.

His new passport gave his nationality as Czech. Taking in the approaching white cliffs, he thought of his uncle, to whom he had said a definitive goodbye from underneath the blanket in the boot of a red Soviet-era Lada in the dead of night. The journey through Europe had taken three weeks.

Some by train, some by car. First to Bulgaria, then Romania, then to the newly founded Czech Republic via an overnight stop in Vienna, before heading north and collecting the passport from the contact in Prague who had taken him to a sex show in Národní as some kind of congratulatory gesture. Three days later, he took a train to Dresden, all the while the same mix tape played in the Walkman on repeat, his new favourite song The Scorpions' 'Wind of Change'. At Calais he had been dumped at the ticket office to the cross-Channel ferry.

Dimitry had told him that the man meeting him in Dover, England, was a lawyer, by the name of Daniel Benedict. The lawyer in question was tall, gangly almost, with a sinewy neck, pushing sixty, wearing a suit and a thin scarf.

'Nobody checked my passport,' Anton grunted after they had exchanged initial greetings, pushing the Walkman further into his pocket.

'Don't worry about it,' the lawyer confirmed, frowning at the lingering bruises surrounding Anton's already crooked nose. 'What happened to your face?'

Anton's eyes shot up, meeting the lawyer's pointed stare. 'I went looking for someone I shouldn't have.'

'No one told us about this. Mr Capricorn needs someone who can blend in. Be invisible. You will do neither of those things. We have to get it fixed. You are arriving earlier than we were led to expect.'

Anton looked down the length of the gangway, wiping his crooked, dripping nose on his sleeve. He considered his new life in the damp, grey, windy country he had set foot in. There was an icy blast coming in from the

Channel. Reaching for his headphones, he placed them over his ears, the orange foam so worn it had split apart at the seams.

'So expect me,' he said to the lawyer.

He clicked the play button, following the line of concrete in the opposite direction to the ferry.

6 October, 1993. 11 p.m.

'What is that relic you're holding?'

He stood with his legs rigid, feet apart on spongy grass, facing a bench under a vast birch tree. He'd worn another tracksuit, using the cash Benedict had given him to buy clothes, on his feet a pair of Nike Air Max fresh out of the box. He had been in England for six months.

Benedict had set him up in a flat, instructing him to lay low; to spend his days getting to know the streets of London by name – by day and by night – until the time came that he would be introduced to his new employer. Anton had requested a punching bag on a stand with a pair of sparring gloves. Within days, the set had appeared.

On the day that Anton was to meet his new employer, Benedict informed him of the location to meet: in the centre of Lauderdale Road Private Gardens in north-west London's Maida Vale. Benedict had accompanied him, shown him the steps down to a private veranda, the loose brick in the wall where the key to the gate lay concealed, the next steep set of moss-covered stone steps leading down past the backs of some houses. Benedict had accompanied him most of the way but the moment the path turned to grass he hung back, allowing Anton to walk alone.

The man Benedict had talked to him about – known by two different names – sat on the bench under the birch tree, sucking on a cigarette. Now he was pointing to the Walkman – the so-called relic. The plastic on the headphones had recently snapped in two, cemented together again by a strip of tautly wound sports tape. Anton looked to his feet, saying nothing.

'What are you listening to?'

Solomon Capricorn – the name that Anton had grown up hearing – was looking him up and down, seemingly amused. He was tall, suave-looking, ten years younger than Anton had expected him to be, wearing a suit and overcoat.

'Beastie Boys,' Anton replied.

Capricorn nodded. 'How do you like London so far?'

'It rains a lot.'

'You'd better get used to it.'

After a silence, Capricorn said, 'Benedict thinks we should do something about your face. He warned me about your appearance. Thinks you don't blend in well enough with the crowd. He forgets that what I need is something between a bloodhound and a pit bull. From what they've told me, and from what I can see by looking at you, you fit that description very well. So let's all do ourselves a favour. Don't listen to the lawyer. Keep your nose as it is.'

Anton nodded once; didn't make eye contact.

'Your father and my father were comrades; did they tell you that?'

Anton shook his head: *no*.

'Regardless, the association between you and I, it ends there. You are your father's gift to my father's legacy. Therefore, my father being in the ground; you live to do as I tell you. You live in the shadows; you don't call me by my name. You have no idea who I am from the beginning, is that clear?'

Another nod.

Capricorn finished his cigarette, tossing the butt against the birch tree before it bounced into wet grass.

'What do you know about your father? Anything?'

Anton raised his eyes. Dimitry had shown him a single photograph – dirty sepia, on soft paper with creases – the size of his then adolescent palm. His father, in uniform, some kind of military man.

'Your father was a Nazi. He negotiated oil deals for Hitler in the Caucasus. Turns out he had a fondness for life beside the Caspian. It wasn't Germany he wanted to go back to in '77, it was Baku. He was sixty-three when they brought your mother to him as a birthday gift. So, you're half German, did you know that?'

He hadn't known it. He had always assumed his that father was Azeri. Dimitry had instructed him to never ask questions.

Capricorn continued. 'He's still alive, you know. Barely. Lives with his extended family in Argentina. The majority of his family are not aware you exist, and the ones that do know choose to ignore the facts. Your father wasn't willing to give up on you completely. Why do you think he had you hauled out of that children's home and gave you a purpose in life?'

A muscle flinched in Anton's jaw. 'I came here to work. So give me work.'

A smile crossed Solomon Capricorn's features. He looked to the other end of the garden, where Benedict still lingered on the pathway beside a hedge.

'What do you think of that other relic over there?'

Anton followed his stare. Daniel Benedict stood motionless in shadow.

'He means nothing to me.'

'Good. He's risk averse. I've found myself a new lawyer, someone who will actually do as I tell them. His name is Albert Denham. He's green, but he has a lot of potential. So make Benedict your first target. I want him gone. Prove your worth.'

'When?'

Capricorn laughed. 'Look at you, chomping at the bit. Soon. Within a week.'

Anton nodded once. 'I need to know where he lives.'

'You'll have that information,' Capricorn said, before adding, 'I want it clean. Make it look like he took his own life.'

Chapter 24

Northumberland, England
15 March, 2017

'You think this is a trap?'

Had they been instructed to come at midnight, Nash might have agreed with Miles. Yet Stowell Street was bustling with pedestrians, the odd car growling past. The street was in the heart of Chinatown, Newcastle upon Tyne. King Neptune advertised itself as a seafood and Peking restaurant. Glancing out of the window at the building painted purple on the outside, Nash's mouth began to water at the thought of some Kung Pao Prawns. At the hotel, the complimentary breakfast curling under warm lamps had held little appeal.

'If it's a trap then why aren't we parked down a badly lit country lane or an underground car park? This place seems too open.'

'You've watched too much TV. This could be anything. An ambush.'

Nash glanced around, suddenly uneasy. 'The caller said she was a friend of Constance.'

Miles, in the driver's seat, didn't look her way, instead staring into his rearview mirror. 'Or she was just the person forced into making the call to make us believe this is all copacetic,' he hummed.

Nash swallowed, watched the road. The car's radio said it was 10.02 a.m. Miles looked dishevelled, like he hadn't slept.

She considered asking him about his personal life when the sound of the back road-side passenger door opening made her jump. A young woman slid into the seat, slammed it closed. She wore a denim jacket over a hooded top, gold hooped-earrings, hair scraped back off her face.

Nash stared at her. Miles had turned in his seat. She was thirty, or thereabouts, with a swollen belly, somewhere in the middle of her second trimester.

'You gonna drive or what?' she said in Miles's direction.

Miles faced the windscreen, started the engine, yanking the car into gear, pulling away into the one-way street.

'Where am I driving to?' he asked.

'Anywhere, I don't care. Around in circles. Stay away from the A69.'

Nash reached back, held out her hand. 'I'm Nashaly. This is my colleague, Miles.'

The woman took her hand, shook it limply. Her local accent was stark. She kept one hand resting on her stomach. 'I'm Naomi Kelly.'

'You were the caller to Insight News?'

'Yeah, that were me. Heard you were at Ketteridge yesterday.'

'When they said you were a friend of Constance Thurlow, I thought you'd be older.'

'I thought if I didn't mention her, you wouldn't talk to me. I know who Constance is. I volunteer there, at Ketteridge. I go over now and then, to read and talk to the occupants, like. Have done ever since it were converted.'

235

'You mean when it became a community home.'

'When I were young, I went to school with a girl that lived in that house.'

'I don't understand. You're here to tell us about Constance?' Nash asked.

Naomi shook her head. 'Constance isn't exactly with it, these days. No, I thought, being journalists and all, you know, you could help me find out what happened to my friend. And I could tell you what I know about that house.'

Naomi glanced across at Miles. His eyes were on the road. She puffed out her cheeks, took out her phone and set it to record an interview, knowing the sound of the car reverberating would likely distort much of the audio.

'We're not some missing person's agency but I'll see what we can do. What can you tell us? Who's your friend?'

'She lived there with her parents. Her name were Rebecca Wylde. She had a little brother, Richard, everybody called him Richie. She had this red hair, sort of auburn, dead straight, like. For ages we did everything together. 'Til one day it all changed. Her parents, they died in a car crash. Then she were gone.'

'Do you remember her parents' names?'

'Yeah. Her dad's name were Blake. Blake Wylde. Her mam's name were Ione. They were posher than us, like.'

Nash straightened in her seat. 'Ione, as in Ione Ebdon?'

'That's right.'

'And they lived at the house in Ketteridge?'

'Yeah.'

'What year was this?'

Naomi's brows drew together. 'We were about eleven or

twelve. So it would have been around '97. She'd come round to mine and we'd dance to the Spice Girls in my living room wearing tankinis, like Mel C.'

'What changed?' Nash asked, at the same time checking Miles position on the road, suddenly feeling comforted that he was there. 'Did it change when the crash happened?'

'No, about two months before the crash. Becky told me her parents were adopting another child. Not a baby, like. This lad, she said he were sixteen, but I knew he were way older by looking at him.'

Nash felt an odd, rolling sensation in the pit of her stomach, and not because she was twisted around in her seat. 'Who was he?'

'He looked like a mean fella, you know. Really dark hair and like this nose that were squashed over, like one of them UFC guys.'

The car swerved without warning, the propulsion causing Nash's shoulder to collide with the car door, the phone sliding out of her fingers and down into the back seat footwell. Miles slammed on the breaks. Other cars flew past, horns blaring. Naomi had stopped herself from being thrown forward.

'Sorry,' Miles mumbled in apology. 'Lapse in concentration.'

Nash had tensed, not only because she'd narrowly avoided a traffic accident. Hauling herself up, she looked over the seat for her phone. Naomi leaned down, picked it up off the floor mat and passed it to her. Breathless, Nash took it, as Miles pulled off, rejoining the lane.

'This boy, do you remember if he had a name?'

'Yeah. I wouldn't forget it. It were Anton Merrick.'

'And, what, what…' Nash lost her train of thought, found herself stuttering. 'Tell me everything you can about him. What was he doing there? Where had he come from?'

'Becky introduced him one day. Said he were going to be staying with her family and that they were looking at adopting him.'

'Do you know where he was from?' Miles asked.

'They never said but he sounded kind of foreign. Said he were taking some English classes.'

'What was he like?' Nash said.

'Kind of sulky. He smoked cigarettes in the back garden at Ketteridge. Becky's dad were a bit far out, you know? He smoked a lot of weed so he didn't care. But I remember we scrounged a ciggie off Anton this one time, to try.'

'What was his accent like? Would you describe it as Russian?'

Naomi shrugged. 'Guess so. Never met a Russian.'

'Then what happened?'

Naomi screwed up her face. 'Then the car crash happened. Everybody were talking about it. Her parents were dead, killed outright. I read that her dad lost control at the wheel and they went into a tree. Her uncle, Charlie Ebdon, arrived and took custody of Becky and Richie. I weren't allowed to see them. A few days after the funeral they all disappeared. I never even got to say bye. Then months later, the house were donated over to the community. Her parents are buried up in Ketteridge, in the local cemetery. It all felt… kind of clinical like. One minute they were there… then they were gone.'

'You didn't try looking her up? Some kind of social media?'

She frowned at Nash. 'I were only eleven, like, there were no Facebook. But later I did. There were nothing, not that I could find. Until about this time last year, I saw an article in the *Daily Mail*. Richie Wylde went to jail for manslaughter. Some judge died after Richie had mugged him. There were no mention of Becky. I didn't see any pictures of her. No mention of his relationship to Charlie Ebdon. Not one paper picked up on it. But it were Richie alright.'

Nash found herself frowning, glancing across again at Miles, who appeared to be nodding his head.

'You remember that?' she asked him.

Miles indicated, took a right turn into a residential road. 'I remember the story. Made headlines at the time of the incident. Judge died following an assault. Trial was low key but he got something like fifteen years. Made out like he was some kind of delinquent, no family. And there was definitely no mention of Ebdon.'

'So he buried the details somehow. But what about people up here? They would have known who he was?'

'There were gossip about it in Ketteridge,' Naomi said. 'But that whole place is watertight. And Constance Thurlow couldn't have spoken out even if she'd have wanted to.'

'Is there anything else you can tell us?'

'That's it. Becky vanished. Seeing her brother in the paper gave me hope that she might be alive. I didn't know who to ask. But when I heard you came to Ketteridge yesterday—'

Nash gave her a wistful look. 'This is really helpful. But I'm not sure I can help you with your search for Becky. If you have a photo of her, you could email it to me.'

She handed Naomi Kelly a business card. 'I might have one or two,' Naomi said.

'Why do you want to find her?'

Naomi looked down at her fingers splayed out over her rounded abdomen, gave a shrug. 'We were close like. And then it felt like she were ripped away. No address, no contact. It were like the pair of them had died, along with their parents. 'Til last year, I hadn't thought about her much. But every now and then, I wonder if she's still walking the earth.'

Miles drove Naomi to her requested drop-off point, the car park at the Royal Victoria Infirmary. Nash said her goodbyes, remained silent as Miles then drove them half a mile away to park on another residential street. He killed the engine.

'Well?' she blurted. 'What do you think?'

'I think we're finally getting somewhere.'

'It doesn't bring us any closer to Clare Buchanan.'

'It demonstrates Ebdon has criminal links in his own family that he's managed to cover up. It confirms a concrete connection from Anton on the bus that night to Charlie Ebdon, again via his own family. What if Ebdon persuaded his own sister to adopt Anton, a young, murderous Russian thug, in order to cement his status in the UK?'

'And maybe the car accident wasn't an accident at all?'

She witnessed Miles's far-off stare. Of acceptance perhaps, that Clare Buchanan was the tip of the iceberg.

'What next?'

'We try and get Home Office records for Anton Merrick. See if we can get an address for him.'

Nash nodded. A smile was tugging at her lips. 'God, that moment when you braked. Thought we were going to have a delivery on our hands.'

Laughter filled the car.

Chapter 25

London, England
15 March, 2017

The last time she had been in Streatham Hill was for Denham's funeral. Now Becca was back in South London, standing outside his front door, except she knew that once she'd pressed the doorbell, the lawyer wouldn't be the one answering it. Behind the windows, the curtains were closed. Weeds crept from cracked paving slabs surrounding the front step. An eerie chill had washed over her on approach. Denham's death had occurred on this street, and she knew the men who had ordered him gone. She had questioned in recent weeks whether either Capricorn or Anton would think twice about handing down orders for her to meet a similar fate.

There was no answer to the bell. She tried twice, replacing both hands in her pockets after each ring, keeping a careful watch on her surroundings. Out of frustration she gave the door knocker one last thwack, only for the door to open a fraction and Tatiana's face to appear. She looked washed out, eyes puffy.

'Oh,' Tatiana said. 'It's you.'

'I need to ask you something,' Becca said in reply, dispensing with a hello.

'You cannot call first?'

'I don't have your number.'

'What do you want? You don't even like me.'

'That's not true,' Becca lied.

'I need a minute,' Tatiana said, closing the door.

Becca shifted her position, feeling exposed. She couldn't be seen here but Capricorn had eyes everywhere.

The door opened again and Becca hopped up the steps, pushing past Tatiana before the latter had time to invite her in.

Inside, she glanced around the entrance hall. Tatiana had removed some pictures from the walls, ones that presumably had belonged to her now dead husband and didn't suit her tastes. When Becca looked back at the door, she realised Tatiana was still in her dressing gown, and it was almost 11 a.m.

'Are you unwell?' Becca asked, removing her hands from her pockets. 'You look tired.'

'I have a cold or something,' Tatiana responded, her accent seemingly thick with sleep.

'I rang the bell twice; did you not hear it?'

'I was in the bathroom.'

Becca felt her eyes narrow. Something felt off.

'What is it you want to ask me?'

Becca straightened, tried to sound casual. 'I want to know if you have a key to Anton's place. The flat at Elephant and Castle.'

Tatiana looked away at the mention of Anton's name, pushing her hair behind her ears. 'He gave me one recently.'

'Can I have it? I need to get inside. He's given me

instructions for something but he's busy. I need to get in.'

'You can't wait for him?'

'Do you have a key or not?'

Tatiana appeared flustered, embarrassed maybe. Becca pushed her tongue into her cheek.

'I have it.'

'Then I can copy it, if you can give it to me. I need an hour, there's a key cutter on the high street.'

Tatiana blanched. Becca thought she might pass out. She lunged forward, ready to catch her, but Tatiana steadied herself, placing one hand on the wall, one on her stomach.

It hit Becca then. 'Jesus. Are you pregnant?'

'Please,' Tatiana whispered. 'You cannot tell Anton.'

Becca took a step back. The girl looked truly awful. 'Are you sick or is this… sickness? Because of the—'

'It is nausea,' Tatiana wailed. 'All the time. I am so tired.'

'You're sure?'

Tatiana nodded, tears in her eyes. 'He would kill me if he knew.'

'I'm not so sure of that.'

'You cannot tell him.'

Becca straightened. Never in a million years did she think she would be keeping secrets for Denham's former wife. 'I won't. If you say nothing to him about the key.'

'It is fine,' Tatiana said with a wave of her hand. 'I have to go to the bathroom.' She pushed past Becca to a small hallway table, opening a drawer. 'Here, you need both of these.'

Becca took the keys, pocketing them. 'I'll be back in an hour to check on you.'

'I am not going anywhere except to vomit.'

Becca bit her lip and looked down at Tatiana's stomach under the dressing gown. There was zero sign of any bump. She thought about asking when she was due.

Tatiana covered her mouth. Becca took a step back, not wishing to have the contents of the Pole's stomach sprayed all over her boots.

He was out of London, he'd said, which meant either he'd had a task from Capricorn, or he was seeing the man himself. Anton had asked her for an update. She'd fed him Christian Holt's home address, as something she'd managed to find. He had been unimpressed with her level of progress.

Becca took the 133 bus from Leigham Court Road direct to Elephant and Castle, hands still buried in her pockets, flashing a carefree smile to the security guard at the entrance to Anton's building. She'd never pictured Anton as anything other than a mechanical lone entity, not a human being capable of producing offspring. In the lift to his floor, she pondered on the idea of a Tatiana/Anton combination, what that child might look like, and for a fleeting moment felt oddly pleased for him. Moving down the corridor towards his front door, she heard the familiar screech of trains. Her heart was thumping. Entering his flat, taking what she needed, it was the end of the line. Once he knew, there would be no forgiveness. Her betrayal would be absolute. The thought gave her pause as she placed her ear against the surface of his front door, listening for movements inside, the freshly cut key still sharp to the touch hovering millimetres from the lock. The idea that she couldn't go through with what she needed to; those thoughts were the ones that she wrestled with the most. She had told herself 'no' on too many occasions; to do as she was instructed. Now the thought of facing Tom Holt again plagued her; the impossible made possible by her own change of direction, to hell with her uncle and Anton Merrick.

Inside, the flat smelled of stale sweat and festering food, as it always seemed to. Becca considered whether the prospect of a proper girlfriend and a baby could rid Anton of his staunch bachelor's habits. Shifting swiftly to the bedroom, she found an unmade bed, tangled sheets spilling over onto the floor, leftover coffee cups and clothing littering the carpet.

The item she had come for – an item that had inhabited her thoughts since before the New Year – was, she knew, kept hanging on a hook at the back of his rickety wardrobe. Rifling past some suits and shirts, she felt around the back panel, fingers closing around another set of keys. Unhooking them, she brought them out, staring down at them in her palm. There was nothing special about them. They were unlabelled, and if found, a stranger might consider them rather ordinary. Becca slid them into her pocket, planning on visiting her second locksmith in a day.

They were, in essence, the keys to everything. Copying them went against every belief she had ever held and using them would constitute the ultimate act of treachery. Becca stood for a moment in Anton's bedroom, allowing the last thought to roll around her stomach. She knew it wasn't too late to change her mind; that she still had the chance to walk away, to put a stop to her current trajectory. Her origins were with Anton and with Capricorn. And maybe she would end with them, right back where she started.

Becca caught a glimpse of her reflection in the mirror on Anton's wall. It felt like a different face staring back at her, to the one she had been used to looking at for so long. Behind her reflection, on a shelf, was a black ceramic skull with an intricate gold-painted design. It grinned. Anton had buried skulls in the ground, only those had been real, not like the one looking back at her, the one that came from the same place as the key. The place she needed to take Tom Holt. She contemplated her life if she simply replaced the keys back on the hook and walked away. Tom would be none the wiser. Nothing would change.

Inertia.

In her reflection, Becca placed the set of keys in her pocket, gave herself a curt nod of approval and left Anton's apartment.

On her return, she slid back through the door. The locksmith had been on Great Suffolk Street, a much further walk from Anton's flat than she had anticipated.

Inside, she glanced at the floor, the breath catching in her throat. A bag lay open at her feet. In the bathroom, the shower was on, the door only partially closed.

Anton was home.

Feeling her chest cavity crumple, Becca hotfooted it to the bedroom, returning Anton's original set of keys inside the wardrobe where she had found them, sliding them over the hook. Over the noise from the shower, Anton's phone was ringing. The shower was then switched off, Becca still hovering beside the unmade bed. Out of instinct, she ducked to the floor, ready to wiggle underneath the wood frame if she had to.

She couldn't see Anton, only heard the sound of his voice as he answered in the corridor.

'Gal,' she heard him say. Knew it was short for 'Galib', an individual Anton had mentioned a few times in passing.

She flattened herself against the floor, her heart pounding against the carpet, knowing that if he found her there, there would be no excuse for her presence. Anton's voice grew closer until she could see his still-wet hairy feet moving around on the other side of the bed. The towel dropped to the floor, followed by a sound of a drawer opening and Anton pulling on some fresh underwear.

'I just got back,' Anton was saying into the phone. 'But I need something. There's a guy, he's an estate agent, works in Barnes, it's in the south-west. Name is Christian Holt. My girl is working on it but she's not getting what I need. He knows the whereabouts of his brother, Tom Holt. I need those precise details and I'm running out of time. The address is 32A Cedar Grove, it's in Richmond. Once you have him in the house, call me. He tries to leave, keep him there. There's a girlfriend too. Don't let him see your faces. He resists, take it to the next level but do not fucking take him out.'

Becca swallowed. Next level, in Anton speak, meant tying a man to a chair and putting his balls in a clamp, or removing his fingernails with a rusty Stanley knife.

Anton was still talking on the phone yet he had left the room. A moment later she heard the clattering of plates in the kitchen. Becca willed her legs to move and she was on her feet, ducking down, movements lithe, body pressed against the wall, past a still-steaming bathroom and back towards the front door. She slipped out, eased the door half-closed without allowing it to click shut, not permitting herself a breath until she was inside the graffitied walls of the fire escape staircase. She bounded downwards, two stairs at a time, palms sweaty, trembling at the shock of Anton's return. On reaching the ground floor, Becca composed herself, slowed her pace, sliding out into the lobby and back out onto the craggy pavement before the security guard on the door had a chance to notice her repeat presence.

Anton was calling for backup and his reasons were clear. He was getting jittery, and Capricorn would be growing impatient. As she suspected, he wasn't the only one running out of time.

She started running. It was two o'clock. With any luck, Christian Holt would still be at work. Her plan could only hold successfully in place if he kept his trap shut. On reaching Waterloo station, Becca took an overground train out to Barnes.

Holt was on the phone as she stalked into the office of Bentley Atherton Estates. She ignored everyone around her but him. He looked up, witnessed her hurtling approach, cupping his hand over the receiver.

'Get out,' he hissed in her face as she leaned over his desk, some of his colleagues looking up in surprise. 'I'm calling the police.'

'Hang up the phone,' Becca said under her breath. 'You've picked up another trail and I might just save yours and your girlfriend's lives.'

He stared at her, aghast.

'I need five minutes of your time.'

Christian removed his hand. 'I'm going to have to call you back,' he mumbled into the receiver and hung up.

He got to his feet, straightened out his suit jacket. 'Right this way,' he said stiffly to her, holding out his hand and ushering her to one of the offices as though they were about to discuss in the politest of terms the conditions of a mortgage. Becca followed.

'What the fuck are you playing at?' he hissed the moment the door was closed behind a glass panel.

'The people I work for, they know your whereabouts. You need to leave London, you need to contact your girlfriend, and you need to do it *now*. You don't, and you are in a whole world of pain you can't even begin to comprehend.'

He stared at her, eyes flitting through the glass. There was a tremor in his breath, as though she'd hit a nerve.

'What kind of people?'

She threw him a look, as if this wasn't the right time to spell it out. 'You need to call Shelley and pull her out of whatever she's doing. Toss your phone. Drive north or to Wales or Scotland, I don't care. Take cash and do not go home. They will be waiting for you.'

'How do you know Shelley's name?'

'I know you don't believe me. I know your brother doesn't believe me. But I'm trying to tell you that I'm *on your side*. The people who want your brother dead are the same people that I work for and I know what they are capable of. Trust me when I say you need to go now. You don't want to, that's your choice. But if you want a future with Shelley I suggest you listen to me.'

His chest was rising and falling. 'Right now?'

'Right now.'

'How long for?'

'A few weeks, maybe more.'

'What do they want?'

'The same thing I want. Only this time, in exchange, they'll tear you limb from limb to get it.'

Richie was in front of the TV when she walked back through the door of their Parry House flat. A packed rucksack was at his feet. Becca's bones ached with going back and forth across the city.

'Anton called,' he said. 'He wanted to speak to you. Said you weren't picking up.'

'I know. What did you tell him?'

'That you were in bed with a bad case of the flu. I said you'd probably be out for a few days.'

'Did he believe you?'

Richie frowned, shifted in his seat. 'Doesn't sit well with me, you know. Why we have to lie to him.'

Becca looked to the moth-eaten carpet. 'I need to do this, Richie. Please. Stay with me.'

He returned his eyes to the TV, gave her a single nod. 'You should sleep. I booked a cab. We're leaving for the airport at 4 a.m.'

Chapter 26

Northumberland, England
15 March, 2017

At five o'clock, Nash walked under a black umbrella in the Northumberland drizzle, within view of Miles, the soles of her boots squelching in slippery mud. The churchyard was small with gravestones packed tight, all the way to the surrounding railings. The light was fading fast.

They had started at the back near a line of trees, where the headstones appeared to be newest. Nash had taken the graves on the left of the church, Miles starting off to the right. The rooftops of Ketteridge Community Nursing Home were visible in the near distance. Nash acknowledged that the bad weather had done them a favour, but it wouldn't be long before they were seen.

She raised the umbrella a fraction, checking on Miles. He was waving his hand in the air. When she reached him, he was pointing to the ground. 'This appears to be the Ebdon family plot.'

Nash surveyed the scene. Of the three graves beside the path, all in a row, two were for Charles Ebdon's sisters, both of whom had died young. Ione Wylde was buried in the middle, her husband Blake to her right, her sister Amy to her left. Amy's gravestone was smaller, as though perhaps she'd been cremated rather than buried. None of the headstones contained any information, other than their names and respective dates. Nash took out her phone from her pocket, taking a few shots in the bad light.

Behind them was a different matter. William 'Bill' Ebdon had a large stone, laid flat, with a long inscription, detailing his history as a veteran of war and his contribution to the local Ketteridge community. To his right was buried Elspeth Hawley, Charlie Ebdon's mother, who had died aged fifty-one. Ebdon's infant daughter, Victoria, was buried to his left, her mother's gravestone noticeably absent.

'Nash…'

She glanced back. Miles was making eyes at two figures approaching the entrance to the cemetery, hoods up in the rain.

'We should go.'

She was the first to move, Miles on her tail. Moving towards the gate, it dawned on her that one of the figures was exceptionally tall. The image in her mind was of Leeroy, the six-foot-four thug from the local pub.

'*Uhhm*, Nash?' Miles was saying.

She tilted her umbrella. 'Can we scale that fence over there?'

'I can if you can.'

'How far to the car?'

'Seventy metres? I have the key.'

She weighed up the options. 'On three. One, two, three.'

Nash bolted, her escape attempt thwarted by oozing mud, Miles sprinting ahead of her. Abandoning her umbrella, she scrambled to her feet, dirt covering her palms. When she glanced back, the two men were chasing. She witnessed Miles hop the railings, wishing she had his dexterity. Wedging her boot in between the iron rods, she heaved herself over, feeling sharp metal prongs poking into her ribs. One of them caught her coat and ripped it, sending Nash crashing to the wet concrete on her behind.

She could see Leeroy's face through the rain, his neck muscles straining and eyes bulging in fury. On her feet again, she looked back to see him leap over the fence.

It dawned on her that there was a chance she wouldn't make it.

Miles had raced ahead to the car. Once he was inside, she heard the splutter of the engine. Thighs pumping, Nash could hear Leeroy's rasping breaths at her back.

She watched Miles lean over, throw open the passenger side door. Swerving to her left, she willed her body forward, hurling herself inside, Leeroy catching her boot caked in mud. It flew off in his hand as Miles hit the accelerator, her car door wide open.

Nash screamed, grabbed it, yanked it closed, pain shooting into her shoulder. In her wing mirror, two figures became specks on the horizon.

Nash stood outside the door to Miles's room, in a service station hotel on the A1 near Doncaster. In one hand she held two empty glasses by their stems, picked up from the downstairs reception area bar, in the other an open bottle of Prosecco.

Moving the bottle to underneath her arm, she reached out and gave a knock on his door. The thought of Leeroy's face – the whites of his eyes, the way his lips had pulled tight, teeth bared as he ran to catch her – meant she didn't want to be alone.

As he opened his door, Miles was texting. He didn't bother looking up.

'Thought we could celebrate,' she said with a half-smile.

He closed the door behind her, still texting. Nash looked around for somewhere to sit.

'Sorry. I'm cancelling something. I was supposed to go and see a film tonight back in London.'

'Like on a date?' Nash joked.

'Something like that.'

His words took her by surprise. 'Oh, sorry I didn't – I didn't mean to pry.'

'Relax. She understood. She knows I'm with you. She works in the accounts team.'

'Oh. I see.'

'She knows that we—'

She watched his cheeks flush red again. Nash felt an irrational stab of envy: that maybe one of the calls she hadn't answered would have been Miles asking her to watch a film with him, or perhaps because he had a life away from his work that didn't involve her.

'Are we drinking, or what?' Miles said, recovering from the moment, rubbing his palms together.

Nash forced a smile and poured the drinks.

The Prosecco largely untouched, Nash had made her excuses. In the morning, following an early start, Miles dropped her off in the shadow of Billingsgate Market in East London, arranging to meet her at the office within a couple of hours. Wearing only one shoe, she had hobbled down the escalator into Canary Wharf shopping centre and purchased herself a new pair of boots.

At her mother's office, Nash yanked down the handle with such a force as to almost push the door from its hinges.

The visit up north had left her breathless, turbo-charged. So much had fallen into place in less than twenty-four hours. Inside, her mother was on the phone. On seeing Nash, Diane Cambridge muttered something and hung up.

'Where the hell have you been?' she yelled, rising from the far side of her desk.

Nash came to an abrupt halt, surprised by the explosion. 'We were on our way back from Northumberland,' she replied.

'They don't have phone reception up north?'

'I ran out of battery. What's the panic?'

'Last night your sisters went out with some friends. When they got back after midnight, a man in a balaclava had broken into their flat. He threatened them.'

Nash breath quivered as she exhaled. 'Oh, Jesus. Did you call the police?'

'Yes. He got away. That's not the worst of it. They were threatened *at knifepoint* I might add, because of *your* story. Whoever it was knew exactly what you were writing and they want you to stop.'

Diane came storming out from behind her desk. 'Who knows, Nashaly?' she bellowed. 'Who knows about the piece? Who knows about it besides you, myself and Miles and the people you've interviewed?'

Nash stared back at her. When they had found her father's body, it had dumped by the side of the road, sixteen knife wounds puncturing his back and sides. Nash had never been able to shake off what had happened in Lagos. They had been in England when the call came through, she and her mother. Her mother had flown to Africa the same day, attending the funeral alone in Nigeria when Nash was seven years old. The emotional distance between herself and her mother had begun the day of her father's slaughter.

'*They* know,' Nash said, raising her chin in defiance. 'They've known since we went to Uruguay to speak to Sabina Cordero.'

'Did Cordero tell Ebdon?'

'No. We were followed.'

Diane's eyes flashed. 'Why didn't you tell me this?'

'Because I knew you'd freak out about it.'

'What else? What else haven't you told me about this thing? Have they threatened you?'

Nash couldn't hold her gaze, her mother's angry stare penetrating her chest cavity. 'A couple of times,' she lied. 'I had a death threat, nothing of consequence.'

Her mother blanched. 'What kind of a death threat?'

'Some severed rats' heads in a box. With the bodies too.'

Her mother, gasping air. 'Severed rats? Christ. What? When? When did this happen?'

'About ten days ago now.'

'They sent something to this office?!'

Nash held her tongue. 'To the house,' she said.

Her mother's eyes widened in horror. Nash watched as she bolted back to her desk, grabbing her mobile phone. The call she put in was to Pete. He didn't answer.

'Darling, it's me,' her mother's voice trembled. 'I need you to pack a suitcase, tell the girls to do the same. We need to get out of the house for a few days. Call me, it's important.'

She hung up. Nash stared at her. Before she could speak, Diane was asking her for Miles's location.

'He went home to shower. He's coming back in. We've got a lot to be getting on with. That's what I came to tell you.'

'Call him. Tell him to pack a bag, get out of his flat.'

'Ma, I think you're overreacting.'

'To a box of severed rats' heads? What did you do with it?'

'The box? Tossed it, of course. I'm not going to be intimidated.'

Her mother, pacing, cheeks flushed. 'It doesn't mean they won't try. You've put yourself at risk.'

Nash held up her hands. 'I am not afraid of Charlie Ebdon. Nor his attack dog.'

'Don't you understand? Everything you've told me about this case, everything that has happened that has so far gone unreported. This man is surrounded by death. I believe he will stop at nothing to silence you, Nashaly, to silence *us*. In order to do that without suspicion, he must be protected at the highest levels.'

Nash felt the heat rising in her neck. 'If it was any other reporter standing here, you would be lauding that as some kind of accomplishment.'

Her mother's expression darkened. 'That is *not* true. No other reporter has dared lie to me as brazenly as you have. You put your sisters' lives at risk. Call Miles, book yourselves a hotel with decent security.'

'Ferretti, it's me. Pick up your phone.'

She paced inside their makeshift office, blinds drawn all the way down. Her mother had refused to let it go. Along with the disappearance of Clare Buchanan, Diane Cambridge had cited both the deaths of Ebdon's sisters – one by car accident, one by supposed suicide – as evidence of some kind of a cover-up. That, and a set of reports she had dug up of a driver who had previously worked for Elate International going missing twenty-three years earlier in 1994, along with his entire family from an isolated house in some Kent woods, yet no reporter at the time had been specific about drawing the connection. Clare Buchanan wasn't the only one, and in 2005, Ebdon had gone out of his way to offer rewards for information on his employee's disappearance. All the more reason to draw all the strings together and splash them on the front pages, surely, Nash reasoned, her fists balled up in frustration. It wasn't like her mother to get cold feet about a story with this many angles. Nash punched the air, knowing she had been gagged.

'I will not lose you along with your father,' her mother had argued. 'For now, we sit on this. Until we have solid evidence, we do nothing. Everything to this stage is conjecture and will get us sued, I don't care what Tom Holt says about what happened in Uruguay last year, or who we think this man Anton might be. Ebdon holds all the cards. He knows what he has to lose. Now, if you'll excuse me, I need to move my family to a hotel.'

Nash waited. Paced back and forth in the tiny space. Licked her wounds. Checked Twitter and her emails, twice over.

Opened up the blinds and watched a trickle of accounts department worker drones file out of the office to go to lunch. Miles hadn't shown. She left two more messages on his phone. WhatsApp put him last seen at 09.47.

On her way out she tried Ferretti again, the line ringing and ringing, her head down on the bridge over the Quay. She remembered the location from the morning she had fled his flat before he had even woken up: Fellows Court in Hoxton. Taking a Jubilee line train to Canada Water, she felt exposed, senses heightened, conscious of the scent of dried sweat on her own skin from their long car journey. As she changed to the East London line, the crowds seemed to press more closely into her, emotionless grey commuter faces each one blending into Anton's every time she glanced up, causing a kind of claustrophobia she'd never quite experienced before. The sounds of the rails underneath the train shrieked in her ears, sending her pulse quivering. He had gone after her sisters.

At Hoxton station, London E2, it took a moment to get her bearings. Finding herself in a familiar housing estate, she crossed the road in the rain, clouds a looming dark mass. She kept her head down, praying that Miles would open his door once she'd hammered on it. When he did, she promised to God she would knock his teeth out for making her hoof it across the city out of simple concern for his welfare.

The building was a red brick block, more akin to something out of Tower Hamlets, the keypad on the main door ripped away from the wall. Nash looked at it, puzzled, wondering if that could have been a recent development. She proceeded through the door and up the stairs, along the first floor walkway to his door, a sense of uneasiness seeping up from her toes. Ferretti lived in the last flat but one, the door painted navy blue. She swallowed bile, her throat constricting. The golden, scratched Yale lock was still in place, yet the keyhole itself had been tampered with, gone at with some kind of lock pick.

Nash nudged the gloss-painted wood with a single fingertip. It opened, rocking on its hinges. Breath shaky, she glanced around her.

Taking her chances, she pushed the door back, listening for any sign of life. Easing forward, she entered Miles's living room, the contents of his satchel spilled out over the floor.

A lightning bolt of panic felt like it had split Nash in two. On the carpet: a trail of blood.

Throat dry, pulse thumping, she raised her voice. 'Miles?'

When he came into view, her hands flew to her mouth, the phone in her hand dropping with a thud to the carpet. Slouched beside the door to his kitchen, his hands were in his lap, sticky, dark crimson fluid saturating the side of his face, neck and chest. She kneeled, reached out, his skin clammy to the touch. Miles stirred. Nash gasped, tears pooling in her eyes.

She saw his weak attempt at a smile. 'I held fast, Nash. I didn't tell them anything.'

His head rolled. She saw the full extent of the damage, one ear sliced completely off, now missing. She tasted bile. One hand covered her mouth, the other grabbing for her phone.

'Hold on, Miles,' she whispered, 'I'm going to get you help.'

Part Three

Chapter 27

Panama City, Panama
16 March 2017

Thursday evening, El Cangrejo. All over the city thoroughfares were gridlocked; horns blaring, the air sultry and impenetrable, sun dipping low. Miguel had taken a call from Juan Carlos Aguinaldo's people, with a direct summons to a party at El Panama, an order for Tom to come alone.

Tom wore jeans, a white shirt with an open collar. He'd driven his father's Camaro the length of Avenida Balboa before abandoning any hope of breaking free of the deadlock, leaving it parked in the Marbella area and completing the rest of his journey on foot. The sweat poured off him, damp fabric clinging to his spine. He moved north through the sweltering backstreets of Obarrio, the smell of rotting rubbish filling his nostrils, keeping one eye on the local faces, never quite at ease in his surroundings. It felt as though a target was still fixed on his back, the memory of the Belosi brothers and what they were capable of permanently raw.

Camila had completed the painting. For a fake, it was high quality, the varnish she'd used darkening the colours so that they were almost an exact match for the original, or at least the photograph they had of it. It was still at her apartment, under three high-voltage germicidal lamps to cement the drying process, the power required by the lights meaning Camila could use no other source of electricity simultaneously in her apartment without taking out supplies to an entire block.

His phone vibrated, flashing up an unidentified number. He didn't answer. Moments later, someone was calling again.

He withdrew from the street underneath an awning, outside a burger joint not far from the entrance to the Metro. When he answered, he listened, saying nothing.

'Tom?' he heard Nash's voice say.

He exhaled, the tension releasing from his chest. 'Jesus. Hey. Where are you?'

She sounded on the verge of tears. 'I'm in Madrid.'

He thought for a second he'd misheard her. 'You're where?'

'Madrid… in an airport hotel.'

On Via España, the snarl of the traffic made it impossible to hear. Tom tucked himself away closer to the wall, pushing one finger in his ear to filter out the background din, the uneasy feeling from earlier snaking its way back into his stomach. 'Why are you in Spain?'

'It's bad, Tom. Anton went to Miles's flat. They cut off his ear. His *ear*. They're trying to silence us. They wanted to know where you were. He didn't break, I swear it. He didn't give you up.'

Tom released an unsteady breath, running his fingers through his hair. 'Jesus. Is he alive? You're sure it was Anton?'

'Miles thinks so. He's alright. There were two of them. They wore balaclavas and gloves. We called the police. CCTV shows them outside the flat, both disguised. No way to positively identify them. Not a single fingerprint. Professional. They changed vehicles several times, they disappeared. Anton's threatened my sisters. I left the country. I had to.'

'Nash…'

She was talking too fast. 'I need to see you. I didn't want to fly directly to you. Please. My flight here was booked by Insight News, using a company card, an hour before I left for Heathrow. It was booked in my name but only one person knows I am out of the country and that's my mother. She made me leave, for my own safety. We're almost ready to go to print; I have a few holes I think you can fill in. Please. There's a direct flight out to Bogotá tomorrow arriving in the evening. I can take a connection to Panama. Let me come to you. Then I can move on as quickly, when we're done. We can take Ebdon down, Tom… and Anton with him.'

He went quiet for a moment. There was desperation in her tone, like she was barely holding it together.

'Can you buy a flight for cash?'

'Yes. I have enough US dollars. I would be there around half past midnight your time.'

Tom puffed out his cheeks. The idea he could help shape a front page news story had its appeal, despite the NDA he was supposedly bound by.

'Please,' she begged again. 'I swear it's not some kind of trick. I'm all alone.'

Tom relented, a fresh ripple of sweat breaking out over his forehead, dripping down his temples. 'Can you message me the flight numbers? I'll get my father to collect you from the airport. His name is Oliver Holt. Big guy, jolly-looking. Don't book any hotels; don't use your credit card for anything. Cash only. And watch your back at all times.'

Relief filled her tone. 'I will.'

'I'm sorry about Miles.'

'I should have listened to you.'

'See you tomorrow night.'

Tom walked up from Via Veneto; flash 4x4s rolled up in convoy outside the entrance to the hotel, men and women alighting in all their finery. Others were non-Hispanic; a swell of Russian voices audible as he climbed the stairs to the lobby entrance. Tom garnered a few disdainful looks as he dodged the staff at a table checking invites for the event, sidling past and heading in the direction of the pool.

Outside in the garden, the surge of voices continued. He kept his eyes low, walking the line of terracotta tiles leading to the far side of the pool. Without Miguel there to remind him, the only face he could recall was that of Juan Carlos Aguinaldo. He slowed his speed, glancing across at more partygoers, the pool itself empty. He stopped beside a white lamp, glancing around, waiting for someone to show.

At the far end of the garden, a man whom he then recognised appeared, wearing baggy jeans and a red basketball shirt. The man raised his double chin. He had wide lips, a buzz cut. Tom walked towards him and was led to a ground floor suite shielded from view by a cluster of palm trees.

'*Llega tarde, mano,*' the basketball shirt pouted. *You're late.*

'*Perdón, me entretuve,*' Tom responded, fastening the button on his suit jacket, straightening it out. *I got held up.*

Nervous, he ducked his head underneath an awning, the

door to the suite slightly ajar. Inside, the light was switched on. He was presented with the sight of Juan Carlos Aguinaldo lying face down on a massage table, white towel covering his rear, two females of possibly Thai origin rubbing their hands over his colossal back, the scent of incense in the air.

At the sound of the door closing, Juan Carlos turned his head.

Tom gave him a nod. '*Buenas noches, Señor Aguinaldo,*' he said, standing at ease, hands behind his back, as though he was back in the army.

The women kept moving. '*Sabes, esto se llama un masaje de cuatro manos,*' Juan Carlos crooned. *You know, they call this a four-hand massage.*

Tom nodded again, feeling uncomfortable at seeing such a large amount of slick flesh on display, the women with tiny yet powerful hands manipulating it away from his gargantuan frame like mounds of raw dough.

Juan Carlos clicked his tongue, continuing in Spanish. 'The painting, is it finished?'

'It's done. It's drying under some lamps.' He too spoke in Spanish, but was distracted by the two Thai women, working away diligently.

'There are some papers for you on the bed. What you were looking for.'

He turned in surprise. It was a bulky looking folder. Tom picked it up, opening it, eyes flitting over the contents. The first page showed the papers came from Quintero Bolívar, a Panama-based law firm and corporate service provider with an address in Marbella less than half a kilometre away from where he was standing. Albert Denham's name appeared repeatedly. There were certificates, email exchanges, lists of shareholders and trustees, addresses registered in the British Virgin Islands, the receipt of a transfer of funds in US dollars. Everything he could have hoped for. Tom was still absorbed in the papers when they were snatched from his grasp by the man in the basketball shirt.

'I get my painting, you can do what you like with those,' Aguinaldo said behind him in Spanish.

Tom gave him another nod, feeling a surge of exhilaration in his chest, followed by the crushing realisation that still he had no plan as to how he would be able to successfully break into Oscar Aguinaldo's house in Contadora.

'Diego, *dale la llave.*' *Give him the key.*

Diego, in the basketball shirt, reached into the pocket of his baggy jeans, pulling out a set of keys. Tom took them, turning them over in his fingers.

'*La casa de mi hermano tiene un tragaluz,*' Juan Carlos explained.

His brother's house had something, but Tom's Spanish didn't stretch to what.

'*No conozco esta palabra en español,*' Tom said. '*Tragaluz?*'

It was in that moment that Diego piped up, speaking in heavily accented English. 'There is a window, in the roof of his brother's house on Isla Contadora. Those keys will get you inside.'

'Does the house have an intruder alarm? CCTV?'

Diego consulted Juan Carlos. '*Hay una cámara en la puerta delantera,*' Juan Carlos responded, confirming that there was CCTV on the front gate. '*Solo eso.*'

'Can I guarantee they'll be no one patrolling the property who could blow my brains out?'

Diego translated and Juan Carlos started laughing, a wheeze emerging from his chest. He thrust away the hands of the two Thai girls. They held up their palms in surrender, stepping back, flinching, Tom realising then that they were both terrified of their present situation. Bile hit the back of his throat. He wanted nothing more than to get out of there.

'*En Contadora? Lárgate de aquí, maldito!*' Juan Carlos wheezed, his words reflecting Tom's thoughts perfectly. There would be no such patrols on Contadora.

'Then we have a deal,' Tom stated, switching back to Spanish.

Juan Carlos stopped laughing. After a moment he clicked his fingers and the Thai women resumed their torturous task.

'*No esperaré para siempre,*' Juan Carlos grunted. *I won't wait for ever.*

Diego cocked his head towards the door of the suite, signalling to Tom that it was time to leave.

'*Gracias, amigo,*' Tom said to Juan Carlos's henchman at the door, pocketing the keys he had been given.

'*Chinga tu madre,*' Diego muttered. *Go fuck yourself.*

He took a cab from Via España straight to Camila's loft. He made slow love to her on red sheets to the sultry strains of a brass band seeping in through the shutters from underneath the white pavilion in the heart of Independence Square. At the back of his mind was the sight of Albert Denham's name on the documents Juan Carlos had promised him, the name of the law firm. He needed to consult with his father and Miguel.

'What will you do?' Camila asked in the light coming from the street, her cheek resting against his chest, his fingers in her hair.

'I'll do what I have to,' was his response, to which he heard her sharp intake of breath. She got out of bed, the glow from the high-voltage lamps in her kitchen visible underneath the bedroom door. Outside, the band droned on. He followed her with his eyes, admiring the angle at which the light fell against her undressed stomach and thighs.

'Take me out. Tomorrow night,' she demanded from the end of the bed, hands on her hips. 'We'll go dancing.'

He laughed at that. 'I'm not really a dancer.'

'Then we'll go get drunk on *Ron Abuelo*.'

'Can't. Someone's coming here to meet me.'

'To Panama City? Who?'

'Nobody. She's a journalist.'

Camila cocked her head to one side. 'She?'

'It's not like that.' He glanced at his watch, still grinning. 'My father's collecting her from the airport tomorrow night.'

'Does she have something to do with saving your father's life?'

'It might be easier if she did. She's working on something important, something separate from that, but still connected.'

Camila gave him a look that said she didn't understand him anymore, held out her hand towards him. 'Come. I'll show you how to dance.'

17 March, 2017

The Teatro Amador Club was on the other side of Casco Viejo, taxis jostling for space with pedestrians in the narrow cobbled street; at 11 p.m. the inside of the club already pounding to energetic reggaeton beats, a live band playing at the rear. Tom paid the entry fee, having taken them both to dinner, the sweat dripping down his temples, the back of his shirt drenched once more. At the bar in the blue-purple light, he purchased a couple of rum cocktails, feeling Camila's arms at his waist, her lips kissing the back of his neck. Taking his hand, she led him upstairs to the balcony, the interior of the club bathed in a cobalt hue, the dance floor heaving with an enthusiastic crowd, the bald-headed DJ energising the crowd. Camila was up against the metal bars, his body pressed up against hers, lost in her, hands in her hair.

Moments later he raised his head, surveying the mob of bodies below. The lighting made individual features hard to make out.

Something he saw made his chest constrict. For a moment it was hard to breathe.

He blinked, questioning whether it was his imagination, whether it was the rum in his veins causing him to see things that weren't there.

Below him in the crowd, bodies writhed.

He'd seen a face. A woman's face, staring up at him, the only one not moving, eyes fixed on his and Camila's position.

His eyes searched the crowd, convinced he'd seen something, something rarely seen in a place like Panama City.

A flash of red hair.

Chapter 28

Tom's eyes scanned the crowd, leaning forward, gripping the metal barrier, palms sweaty. He caught sight of the back of a head, moving towards the main entrance, the hair a definite shade of auburn, tied back in a high ponytail. He couldn't see the face, but the body was her exact build. He heard Camila shout out his name as he left her behind, knowing he would have to move fast if he was to catch up with the female downstairs. Blood pounded in his ears. He needed visual confirmation to know he was mistaken. The last time he had seen her was in a field in Argentina, hood over her head, wrists tied, on her knees, as he reclaimed the laptop containing Clare Buchanan's video statement.

Outside on Avenida Central, the humidity hit him square in the face. The crowds had increased in volume, lingering aimlessly. He craned his neck, peering over their heads, left and right. He caught sight of the red hair on the other side of the road, outside the Strangers Club cocktail bar. She was walking away with a younger man in tow. He had brown hair, not dark like Anton's, his frame too lithe.

He chased after her in the darkness, dodging a couple of taxis, the tightness in his chest returning.

'Becca,' he called out when he was close enough, and the woman stopped dead.

When she turned, he was reminded of the first time he'd seen her face, sat on a red sofa in Buenos Aires, fearless expression collapsing into a frown the moment their eyes met. It was the same expression he was witnessing now. Her hair was scraped back off her face; she wore no makeup, a thin black zipped-up hoodie covering her arms and shoulders, skinny jeans.

'Holy shit,' he heard himself breathe.

He was met with stoic silence, her hands shoved in her pockets. The younger man she was with gave him a once-over. It occurred to him at the back of his mind that there was a resemblance between the two, yet he couldn't tear his eyes from her face.

'How did you find me?' he demanded, over the grumble of the late-night traffic.

Becca raised her chin a fraction. He resisted the urge to lay into her, commanding answers. 'Your brother's house in South London. Found an address scribbled on a notepad. An old woman over that way told us someone had been asking her the same questions, and sent us over here.'

She tipped her head towards Paitilla at the other end of the bay. He felt annoyed at his brother for leaving out his father's old address. Yet again Christian hadn't been prepared for what she was capable of.

'Is Anton here?'

'No.'

'Not in Panama?'

'No.'

'Does he know where I am? Did he send you here?'

'No. He doesn't know.'

He moved closer to her. 'You're sure of that?'

She seemed at a loss for words.

He raised his voice. 'Can he trace you?'

She shook her head, 'no'. Tom gritted his teeth, eyes flitting to the younger man's face. 'You must be the brother.'

The man said nothing, simply reached out and shook him by the hand. Her sibling was on the skinny side, expressionless, overdressed in jeans and a jacket, wardrobe ill-equipped for tropical weather, Becca's too.

'You're out of jail then.'

Richie Wylde nodded. Tom glanced back to find Camila approaching.

'What the hell?' she snapped. 'Where did you go?'

'I know them, they're from the UK,' he deadpanned, without introducing them.

'This is the girl you were expecting?'

He had forgotten about Nash's imminent arrival. 'No. Different girl.'

He took note of Becca's eyes, sweeping over each one of Camila's ample curves, the frown creeping back into her expression. In recent weeks, the rage he had felt towards Becca had softened to a dull indifference. Now, for a brief few seconds, it was as raw as it had been in the hotel room five months earlier in Buenos Aires. He composed himself. She wasn't worth the energy.

'I need to talk to you,' Becca stated, glancing at Camila with a look that said *not with her around*. 'That's why I'm here.'

'What makes you think I would be willing to listen to anything you had to say?'

She stepped forward, bringing her face close, her gaze

searching. 'I know you don't believe me. But we are here to help you and time is not on our side.'

He felt his chest rise and fall. His gut instinct said to turn and walk away; to leave her and her jailbird brother stranded on the pavement. He had trusted her before and it had ended badly.

Curiosity hummed in his ears. 'Swear to me, Anton's not waiting somewhere around here for your signal.'

'He's not. I swear it.'

At the entrance to his father's building he pulled Camila to one side, making his apologies. She wound her arms around his neck, kissing him with enough intensity to ensure Becca wouldn't miss the moment between them. In the shadows, it was impossible to see Becca's reaction, whether she'd turned her face away. There was some satisfaction there; inflicting damage on some level, revenge for all her lies and pretence.

He led the pair of them up the staircase and into his father's apartment. As he pushed the key into the lock he heard voices, his father back from the airport.

Nashaly was stood in the kitchen, his father handing her a bottle of local Balboa beer. Her face lit up when she saw him, getting to her feet. He offered her a smile, cocked his head and held out his hand. She batted it away, leaning up on her toes to embrace him. She was younger than he'd expected.

'It's good to meet you at last,' she said into his neck.

'Likewise,' he smiled, embracing her.

She pulled back. Her gaze travelled to the two individuals who had followed him into the kitchen, both now seemingly awkward, taking in their surroundings. His father took note of their presence, but said nothing.

Before he could introduce them, Nash said, 'You're Richie Wylde. Which would make you Becky Wylde.'

Tom frowned, not expecting her to know names. Richie's eyes shot to Becca's. Becca wasn't looking at him, instead directly at Nash.

'Who are you?' Becca replied sourly.

Tom noticed Nash's movements. She had tensed, looking from Becca back to her brother, jaw moving as if to speak, yet no sound had emerged.

'Becca, meet Nash,' Tom said.

The light went from Becca's eyes. She was the girl from the Buenos Aires' hotel room again, devoid of emotion, some kind of robotic entity. 'You're one of the journalists,' she said in Nash's direction.

'Does your uncle know you're here?' Nash shot back.

He thought he saw a wince cross Becca's features. Sensed the tightness in his chest returning. In the corner, his father had raised his eyebrows and was reaching for more beers.

'What are you talking about?' Tom said.

'You don't know?' Nash spat in his direction. 'This is Charles Ebdon's niece and nephew. You're looking at Capricorn's immediate family, right here.'

The words were a sucker punch to his stomach. He felt his jaw go slack, witnessed Becca's eyes slip closed at the revelation. Richie looked to the tiled floor, hands in his pockets. Tom stared at them, in that moment realising quite how much of an idiot he had been. How he'd never managed to connect the dots. How it made perfect sense. Why she'd know all about the client the entire time and those who worked for him. He took a step back; almost lost his footing, before coming into contact with the worktop.

Becca opened her eyes again. She looked as though she would speak, though no words came.

'How is it you know each other?' Nash questioned.

'The job in Uruguay,' Tom said. 'Becca was part of it.'

He could see from her expression Nash was trying to process everything, as he was.

'You called me Becky,' Becca said to Nash, Tom noticing the sweat pooling on her top lip. 'Who was it who told you about me?'

'Her name was Naomi Kelly. She said the pair of you used to dance around her bedroom to the Spice Girls when you were young.'

'Don't remember her.'

'You don't remember her? Perhaps only because you left. Or were you taken? After your parents *adopted* a son named Anton Merrick. I know he was on the bus the night Clare Buchanan died, the man the police completely failed to identify. The man who is the reason my colleague is in a hospital bed. What do you know about that?'

Tom watched Becca closely, thought he could see her throat constricting, her cheeks redden.

'We should go,' Richie said in a low tone behind her, brushing his fingers against her sleeve. It was the first time he had spoken in fifteen minutes.

Becca's eyes shot to her brother's.

'Tell me!' Nash ripped into Becca, lunging forward. Tom

grabbed her by the shoulders, tugged her back. 'He almost bled to death, did you know that?'

Becca's expression remained impassive. 'If Anton ever had the intention of killing him, believe me, your colleague would be dead by now.'

Nash shrugged off his hands. He could hear her rasping breaths, her face now inches from Becca's nose. Tom caught his father's warning glance.

'Step back,' Becca said.

He could hear the emotion in Nash's quivering tone. 'You take orders from Anton? Is that it?'

'I said… step the hell away from me.'

'Nash. You need to stop.' Tom raised his voice so that both women would look in his direction, diving over to where they were standing, manoeuvring himself between them.

He looked down at Becca. 'Tell me why you're here, then go.'

'Not in front of her.'

'Fine,' he said, grabbing her by her arm and leading her from the room, down the corridor before she had the chance to mouth off.

He thrust her into his bedroom, ants still crawling up the wall, kicked the door closed behind them. Kept his distance. Becca rubbed her bicep, took in her surroundings.

'Why are you even here?' Tom hissed the moment he'd turned around.

She was the Becca he remembered from the days she had first walked into his life. The hostile thief. She'd had the same dismissive tone from their first meeting in Buenos Aires.

'I had this plan to come here and grovel to you. Say how sorry I was, that I'd thought about nothing else. I guess the same can't be said for you. Clearly I didn't linger very long in *your* thoughts.'

'And you thought that you would? After that stunt you pulled in Argentina?'

Her eyebrows pulled together. 'I worked for Anton for half my life before I met you. He's not the sort of person you can walk away from. It takes some planning. Though I don't know why I bothered. Your reporter friend will lead him right to us.'

'You put a knife to my brother's throat!'

'To scare him! I would never have done him physical harm.'

'You drew blood the way he tells it.'

'Only enough to spur him into speaking the truth.'

'Anton teach you how to play that game, did he?'

Becca reached down into her jeans pocket, pulling out a set of keys, cradling them in her palm, holding them out for him to see. 'You can stand here and throw as many insults at me as you want. But what I came to tell you is more important. We don't have time for this. For any of this. We need to go to Mexico City. We need to go now. We don't and we might as well all be dead.'

He stared at her, incredulous. It was not what he had expected to hear from the niece of Charles Ebdon. 'What's in Mexico City?'

'A house. It's in the centre of Mexico City, a district called Polanco. Everything you need to expose Capricorn is inside that house in Mexico.'

He was frowning at her. 'You've been there? How do you know all this?'

'I've not been there in person, no. But I know the address and I have the keys to get us inside. Anton goes to Mexico once every three months. There are records stored there going back years. I know that they place a high amount of importance on that house. I'm not asking you to trust me, but I am asking you to trust what I am saying.'

He stepped back, unprepared for the onslaught of heady memories that came with being alone in the same room as her, running his fingers through his hair. 'I can't leave Panama. Not yet.'

'Why can't you leave?'

He looked down at the keys. 'You want me to trust you, then you have to do something for me first.'

There was a familiarity to Becca's stare, that steely, hungry glint in her eye when someone had offered her up a challenge. He'd seen the look before.

'Name it,' she said.

Chapter 29

Panama City, Panama
18 March, 2017

Nash yawned, following a restless night on Oliver Holt's sofa. The Tom Holt who sat half a metre from her in the front of the car didn't resemble the Tom Holt she had seen online. The photograph she had managed to locate – from the story concerning his sacking from Vlok Petersen and Associates from the *South African Times* a year earlier – showed an upstanding professional, a company photo, navy blue suit, neatly cropped hair, all smiles, the type of straight-up public-school white dude her half-sisters would lust after. Crawling along Panama's Cinta Costera, which bordered a flat Pacific Ocean, Tom Holt had one hand on the steering wheel. He was wearing an unironed shirt with the sleeves rolled up, dirty blonde hair in disarray, the beginnings of a beard, skin a shade darker than his company identikit photo. His face was thinner now. When he spoke it was like listening to an accountant or an estate agent, not someone who over four months earlier had been robbing Sabi Cordero of the contents of her safe.

The car rolled forward a few inches.

'Is traffic always this bad?' she asked.

He was staring from the window at the skyscrapers that

lined the inner highway. He said nothing, checked his wing mirror and, swinging the wheel one hundred and eighty degrees, turned into a car park opposite the rainbow-coloured Panama sign, boat masts forming a backdrop like TV antennas. Footbridges yawned over the Cinta in an S shape, allowing no one to get anywhere fast. It quickly became apparent why no Panamanian walked more than a hundred metres during the day. By the time they were approaching Rebecca Wylde's hostel on foot, Nash's skin felt slippery with sweat, her vest top mostly drenched.

'Do you trust her?' Nash asked Tom, referring to Becca, as they turned off the Cinta walking north into some kind of banking business district.

'I did once,' he replied.

'But do you now? How do we know she hasn't already picked up the phone and informed Anton of our exact location?'

'We don't.'

'Then how do you know she's telling the truth?'

'I don't. Right now my only choice is to believe her. I need what she can do, what she can get me. Her and her brother.'

He had explained his father's situation over their morning coffee. Why Becca Wylde could potentially be his only key to success. When Nash had asked why Becca had sought him out he had evaded the question.

'Was there something between the two of you?'

He didn't answer straight away. 'Like how?'

'I mean romantically. The way she was looking at you. It seemed like—'

'If there was, there isn't anymore,' was his clipped response.

It explained the tension from the night before. Nash saw the road curve ahead, a small white building coming into view, the words 'El Machico' hand-painted above the gate. Becca Wylde was waiting for them in a vest top and skinny jeans.

'I think she knows who killed Clare Buchanan.'

'Then if you're nice to her,' Tom said, out of Becca's earshot, 'you might find she can give you something you can use.'

Nash sat on the same side of the table as Holt, on the balcony of the Hilton Hotel overlooking the Cinta Costera and the Bay of Panama, traffic still congested, back in the direction of Casco Viejo. Moisture dripped down her temples and back of her neck. Opposite, a skinny-looking Becca Wylde had returned from the buffet with a plate piled high with pancakes, bacon, strawberries and an everything-omelette. She couldn't stomach it fast enough.

'When was the last time you ate?' Holt asked her.

'This time yesterday,' Becca explained, without looking Nash's way. 'We spent the last of our money in Starbucks at breakfast. We spent everything on the plane fare and paying for the hostel. Richie's going to be so pissed off he missed this.'

Nash watched her. She was a curious thing. She tried to imagine the redhead as a young girl, the first time Anton Merrick had entered her life. What had she expected from life after her parents' death?

'You should have said last night; I would have given you something.'

Holt said the words softly; Becca's eyes flitting up at him, cheeks fat as a hamster's. She didn't reply, but in her expression there was a glimmer of something; a certain warmth in his presence. Holt had seemed annoyed at her, but her behaviour seemed to be her attempt at making an effort. It hadn't escaped Nash's attention that Becca Wylde had kept her gaze on Holt and her plate the entire time, barely acknowledging Nash's presence.

'Out of interest, how did you pay for the plane fare?' Nash asked.

Becca finished another mouthful. 'We saved up.'

'What does that mean?'

'It means we went on a spree. You figure it out.'

'How long does that take?'

'As long as it takes. Swipe a Gucci handbag from under a table in a Mayfair hotel and you're all set.'

Nash pushed her tongue into her cheek. She watched as Becca put down her knife and fork, leaning back in her chair and rooting around in her jeans pocket. She pulled out a man's chunky silver watch and slid it across the table surface to Holt. Nash watched Holt's expression. He frowned, slowly reaching forward and picking it up, checking the back of the face for some reason before sliding it on to his wrist and fastening it. He averted his eyes, staring out across the bay. Becca swallowed her mouthful, picking up a glass of orange juice and downing the lot. When she finished, she put down the glass, wiping her mouth with the back of her hand, eyes twinkling, a smile touching her lips. Nash found herself warming to the girl's lack of social refinement.

'Did I miss some private joke?' Nash asked.

Nash waited for Becca to look her way, shoulders dropping, expression emblazoned with a severe frown.

'Something like that.'

'I see,' Nash replied.

There was a silence. Nash picked her moment. 'So tell me. How did your uncle get your brother out of jail anyway? A convicted criminal, thirteen years for manslaughter, *poof*, he's free and nobody in the system is apparently any the wiser. That's quite an accomplishment.'

Becca glanced back at the buffet as though she was ready for another helping. 'My uncle has a lot of reach.'

'Care to elaborate?'

'Not really. I didn't come all this way to give you an exposé.'

'Then why did you come all this way?'

Nash watched as this time it was Becca's turn to push her tongue inside her cheek. 'You like asking questions, don't you?'

'Not nearly as much as you like dodging them.'

'Go on then. Ask me a question. Anything.'

Nash didn't hesitate, leaning forward. 'Who killed Clare Buchanan? And by that I mean by whose hand did she perish?'

Becca gave a shrug. 'I don't know. Next question.'

'Was it Anton Merrick?'

'Told you. I don't know. Try another.'

'Were you there that night? In 2005, when she stepped off the bus. You would have been what, twenty-something?'

Becca stopped moving, lips together in a perfect scowl. Nash knew she'd hit a nerve, watching as Tom leaned his arms on the table surface, interested in whatever her answer might be.

When she eventually spoke, Becca pinched her bottom lip between her thumb and forefinger, eyes watching a blank space. 'I was nineteen,' she said.

'So you were there.'

Becca, still glancing at Tom. Nash remembered something her step-father had said to her when she was young, before the days when they knew the arrangement was going to be more permanent. A tigress hides in the grass, its black and orange stripes the perfect camouflage. It waits, unmoving, until it is ready to pounce on its prey. To really investigate, he'd said, you had to be prepared to lie in wait. Later, when she'd told him she wanted to be a journalist, he'd said, be a tigress. Know when to pounce. It occurred to Nash that maybe thieves thought the same way.

'Anton sent a text message when he was on the double decker with Clare,' Nash said. 'Were you the recipient of that message?'

A beat. 'I was,' Becca said.

'Tell me what happened.'

Becca raised her eyes, not in her direction, but again in Holt's. He said nothing, expression grim.

'I was waiting at Angel tube station that evening. She was wearing a green coat. I watched her cross Upper Street with the rest of the commuters. She stood out like a beacon. Made her an easy follow. She was wearing heels; I could tell she was struggling to walk fast. She kept looking over her shoulder.

I swiped her phone; it was too easy. She turned her head the other way; I snatched it right out of her pocket.'

'Then what?'

'Then nothing. I kept going. I tossed it in a hedge.'

'You didn't see her after that? You didn't see Anton?'

Nash watched her. Becca had started shuffling, moving articles unnecessarily around on the table, neatening her knife and fork.

'I'd told Anton before that night that I wanted to do more. He'd started training us about eight years earlier. His response was that I couldn't handle that kind of life.'

'What life?'

Becca's chest rose and fell. She was looking at Holt with pleading eyes but he was yet to return her gaze. 'To go down the road that he had. He didn't want that for me or Richie. What Anton does… what he is capable of doing… it's a whole different level. He taught me to steal and to break in, that's all. So, yes, I got rid of the phone in the hedge and I circled back round, because I knew the location of Clare's flat. Because I was curious back then; I wanted to see. I watched Clare Buchanan being pushed into the back of a car on a quiet street adjacent to where she lived.'

Nash straightened. 'Did he have help? Was it Anton? Who was there?'

Becca finally looked her in the eye. 'There was a driver. He was a lawyer; his name was Albert Denham. He's the man who sent us to Uruguay in the first place. He's dead.'

'So Denham was part of it?'

Becca snorted. 'Mostly Denham did as he was told. No, there was someone else pulling the strings that night.'

'Who?'

'He's the man who persuaded Capricorn that Clare Buchanan had to die. His name is Jonas Vázquez.'

Chapter 30

Becca remembered the torrential downpour in February of 2005; taking shelter inside the station as water cascaded over the circular Underground sign above her head, watching the florist across the street unsuccessfully try to protect his blooms by bringing them in their buckets under cover, the man shouting '*Standard*!' above the din, selling copies of the newspaper wearing a bright red poncho. She remembered the waiting, her back to a pillar at Angel tube station, wearing a pair of Converse One Star blue-suede lace-ups, faded skinny jeans, the tiled floor slippery with water and mud, surrounded by commuters also shielding from the rain. The Nokia handset Anton had given her that morning had been growing warm against her fingertips, insulated by the thin layer of polyester that lined her jacket pocket. She remembered butterflies in her stomach. Anton had shown her a photograph of Clare Buchanan so she had known who she was looking for.

By the time Anton's message arrived the rain had stopped falling. She remembered Clare's bright-green trench coat, fastened with a belt around her middle, the cream-coloured pashmina slung loosely around her shoulders, the woman stumbling in heels, glancing back, fear etched across exhausted features. Distracted, as though she was waiting for someone to appear. The Upper Street crowds around a visibly distressed female paid her no attention, unaware that a few days later it would be the same female's face on the front of the *Evening Standard* and all of the other newspapers, and only a handful of witnesses would be able to say for sure that they had seen her get off the number 43. Yet none would recall a red-headed female who had slipped by, and relieved Ms Buchanan of her phone with a sleight of hand that even the best magicians crave, and who disappeared into the night.

At the walled pool area at the El Machico hostel in Panama City, Becca sat on the corner of a dilapidated sun lounger, eyes on Tom Holt, listening, but with half a mind on Anton. When Clare Buchanan's phone had been located in a hedge on Liverpool Road, in Islington, six days after she had gone missing – the handset handed to the Metropolitan Police by a member of the public – Anton had turned up at Parry House, slapping a copy of the *Daily Mail* down on the table with the headline *'Where is Clare?'* in front of her, including a picture of the discarded phone.

'Next time, do a better job,' he'd stated.

'You said get rid of it,' Becca had argued back. 'You never said where or how.'

He'd launched himself at her then, dragged her across the flat with a fistful of her hair, smashing the side of her head down against the kitchen worktop. 'When I tell you to do things,' Anton had reiterated, so close that she could feel his chin stubble brush against her adolescent cheek, 'you do them in such a way that no one will ever find out about them. You do things in a way that are untraceable. Like I do. Do we understand one another?'

In response, she had nodded under the weight of his palm, the sting of tears burning her eyeballs. Richie had stood motionless in the background, watching in shock. She had murmured an apology. Until her return from South America eleven and a half years later, she'd never asked about Clare Buchanan again.

At the pool, Richie was opposite her, in baggy jeans and a T-shirt on another white plastic lounger, cramming food between his lips, the small amount that she had managed to smuggle back folded inside a napkin from the Hilton, paid for by the journalist, the only one of them who had any disposable cash. Richie was listening to Tom speak in hushed tones about the job he needed to do, details she should have been absorbing in full, except she couldn't concentrate on anything, her only comfort that when Anton learned of their absence he would not immediately know their whereabouts. Unless he caught up with Christian Holt – always a possibility – there would be no way of him knowing that they had got on a plane to Panama City via Amsterdam.

Richie had questioned her agreement to help Tom with his job. She could understand his doubts – it was the first time he had laid eyes on the man they had been chasing the few last months for reasons Becca had never quite fully explained.

'All our lives we've done the jobs we were told we *had* to do,' she had argued. 'This one I actually *want* to do. If we help him, he can leave Panama with us.'

'If you're so desperate to get to Mexico then why not go without him? You and I can go ahead; he can meet us there. Why do we have to put ourselves at risk for a man who Anton wants dead?'

She hadn't given Richie an answer. Since her return from South America, she had gone about actively making her own choices. It had felt good; exercising her independence. She had pleaded with Richie for his help, on her behalf, not Tom Holt's, and he had agreed, reluctantly.

At the pool, she tried again to listen to Tom, grappling to regain her lost focus. A group of three European students had entered the area and were now drinking beers and frolicking carefree in the water. On the lounger in front of Tom was the sketched map of an island, a short boat ride out into the Pacific. He called it 'Contadora', part of a group known as the Pearl Islands. Tom was pinpointing the location of a beachfront property where a painting was to be stolen, replaced with a fake that had been painted by the Latina princess he was now seeing. Watching his face, her throat constricted. At the Hilton he had barely looked at her. On returning his watch, he had said nothing. She had anticipated his resentment, hatred, anger, all of that. She had tried to mentally prepare for the contempt and the accusations that would inevitably fly in her face. Those were the things that had occupied her thoughts since November. It hadn't occurred to her that he might find a girlfriend along the way.

There was another distraction too, in the form of the journalist. Her presence irritated Becca. That Tom had invited Nashaly Akinyemi into his inner circle; trusted her, too, more than he did her at the present moment. She thought about Anton's reaction, knowing that she was in the presence of both Tom Holt and Nash-the-reporter. His instructions would have been clear. Give me their location, and keep them there. Or, if he could count on her to actually see it through, *kill them both*.

'Bec?'

Tom was looking at her. Being in Panama had tanned his skin, his hair a fraction blonder.

'Sorry, what?'

'I asked you what you thought.'

'About what?'

A look of irritation flashed across his features.

'It's fine,' Becca shrugged. 'Whatever you need me to do.'

'We only have one shot at this. We fuck this up, my father will die and I won't be long after him.'

'When was the last time you broke into a house, Becca?' the journalist interjected, a sardonic look on her face. Becca questioned why Tom had even brought her along.

In answering, Becca didn't return Nash's gaze, instead kept her eyes on Tom. 'I told you, Tom's brother's house, under a week ago.'

'Did Anton teach you how to break into houses?'

Becca ignored her and her constant fishing for titbits of information, kept her gaze levelled on Tom. His indifference was a hard pill to swallow, despite it being expected.

He ignored her, ploughing on. 'This house has a metal staircase leading up the cliff from the sand. It's secured at the bottom by a gate, but it should be easy enough to climb over the side. We should have free access to the house and the rooflight, to which we have the key. The painting is in a circular hallway directly below. From what I've been told, the challenge will be getting out again, because the ceiling is high, and it can't look as though anyone has been there.'

'Use a rope ladder?' Becca asked.

'But how to secure it?' Tom said.

'I might be able to hold Becca's weight,' Richie cut in. 'I'm not sure she can hold mine.'

'Which would make Becca the one to go inside the property.'

'Is there an intruder alarm?' Becca asked.

Tom shook his head. 'Yes, but with motion sensors only on the ground level. Only the downstairs doors are alarmed.'

'And what would I need to do? Switch the two paintings over?'

'Exactly. Camila is arranging the frame as we speak.'

Becca shrugged. 'Fine. Then I'll go in.'

She looked to Tom. He straightened, inhaled.

'Are there any dogs?' Richie asked

'No,' he replied.

'CCTV?'

'On the front gate only.'

'Security lights?'

'Two also over the front gate. Could be others, we don't know.'

'And where would we be coming from?'

Tom planted one finger on the map, out in the ocean on the south side.

'From a boat, here. You and Becca would have to swim to Cacique beach; about fifty metres, in darkness.'

A look passed between her and Tom, feeling a smile tugging at her lips. In Uruguay, Tom and Anil had worn wetsuits to break into Sabina Cordero's house in the complex known as Las Colinas, because they'd had to go through a body of water. It had become something of a running joke. Her smile faded when she remembered that Anil had perished wearing a wetsuit that very same night.

'Are there sharks in the water?' Becca asked.

'No sharks.'

'How soon?'

'Tomorrow night.'

Becca raised an eyebrow. Her gaze shifted to Richie. Tomorrow night. It was the kind of timeframe Anton would spring on her. *I need you to steal something for me… tomorrow night. I need you to follow somebody… tomorrow night.* Never with any choice. He had taught both Richie and her that failure would not be tolerated. She shuddered as she pictured his face, wondering if he knew yet that they were gone. That, despite all the orders he had given them to follow, in the end, they had been the ones to betray him.

She remembered the day she had first set eyes on him. Remembered the first time her mother had said his name.

'Becky, darling, come over here. I'd like you to meet somebody… this is Anton.'

Chapter 31

Northumberland, England
10 September, 1996

'Anton, this is my daughter Rebecca.'

Standing in the family garden, he had looked forward to the moment he would meet her in the flesh. For a month he'd been fingering a dog-eared photograph of her and her brother, arms around one another on a hillside, flock of sheep in the background. The boss had told her she liked to call herself Becky. Becky Wylde. Today she wore her school uniform, a white blouse and dark green skirt with pleats that stopped above her knees, one white sock pulled up, the other slouching around her ankle. The boss had said she would grow up to be an English rose, whatever that meant. She was skinny, with pale skin, freckles on her nose, white bony knees and braces on her teeth, distinct red hair scraped off her face. When she took his hand and smiled, he took note of her slender fingers. They would do nicely. She was around ten years old; the same age he had been when Dimitry had taken him to Nizami Street and taught him how to strip some of the merchants of their valuables as they chain-smoked illegal cigarettes. Already he could see Becky's potential.

'Anton is going to come and live with us for a while,' Becky's mother said.

Capricorn's sister was a good deal older. The boss said she had married a New Age caravan-dwelling type whom he couldn't stand. The sister wasn't interested in money, or making any. She wanted to raise her children in the old family pile. Capricorn had intended all along to ask his sister to support the family business by taking in a runaway he had come to be responsible for. She had agreed, only when pressed by her younger brother.

'Where are you from?' Becky asked him when they were left alone, head cocked to one side.

'Baku,' he replied.

'Where?' she asked, her voice shrill. 'Is that in England?'

He shook his head. 'It's further away than that.'

'Do you like the Spice Girls?' she then said. 'Which one's your favourite?'

He couldn't recall a time recently when he had caught himself smiling. 'The one with the red hair, like you have.'

Becky pulled a face, pointed to her own scalp. 'Everyone always thinks I'll like Ginger because of this. But I don't, I like Sporty.'

'Then maybe one day you can kick hard like her.'

'I can already, look.'

He took some degree of pleasure in watching Becky attempting her own childish brand of martial arts, kicking her feet so high that he caught a glimpse of her pink cotton underwear under the pleated skirt. She asked her mother then if she could go and see her friend, Naomi. As he watched her go, waving at him, grinning through her braces, he found comfort in the fact that he would be the one to train her. He hoped, over time, she would retain some of the wholesome qualities to which he had borne witness, even when her parents were long gone. Though he felt unfamiliar with the concept, he felt sure he could try to retain some level of innocence in her life, despite the things that she would now grow up to do.

London, England
17 March, 2017

Anton sat on his sofa in South London in the afternoon, showered and freshly shaven, staring at his main phone lying on the table. Two calls made to Tatiana the previous evening. Two more calls as he got out of bed. All unanswered.

He was short of manpower. Becca and Richie were both out of action, too lazy to get out of bed, infected with some kind of seasonal virus. There was still no trace of Tom Holt. Christian Holt, too, hadn't been seen in a couple of days, despite Anton ordering Gal and Selmani to split apart in order to keep tabs on Belinda Channing, as well as the estate agent. Galib Aganovic – Gal for short – was a Bosnian former child refugee who liked to hang with Rashit Selmani, a twenty-eight-year-old Kosovar Albanian who'd fled Pristina with his parents back in '98. The pair were reliable in the sense that they could do damage wherever it was required. Five months earlier, Anton had tasked them with the murder of Albert Denham on a dark South London street. They had come through in style. The newspapers had reported a violent mugging. Selmani was, on balance, the more psychopathic of the two, but Gal had a head for profit, appealing to Anton's sense of organisation and discretion. Galib also understood where their respective talents lay.

The attack on Miles Ferretti had made the headlines. Anton looked back on the incident with contempt. A fat lot of good slicing off his ear had done. The immigrant son of Italian parents – pasta peddlers – brought up in Isleworth, had stuck to the line that Holt was still in Chile.

Everything stalled.

Ferretti was still in hospital. Having called the police, Nashaly Akinyemi had gone to ground. Diane Cambridge had moved her entire family to a hotel.

Anton tapped his finger against the surface of the table, eyeing the inside of his front door. He was sure now that they were aware of his first name. Sabi Cordero could have easily given them that. He questioned whether they would know his full name by now, his legal British name which he had used since the lawyer Benedict had handed him his first passport back in '93. Still, there was nothing to connect the name Anton Merrick to a flat in Elephant and Castle. He had never ordered any mail; he had no internet or TV. The passport had been issued through one of Capricorn's contacts, to a false address. He had no bank account in the UK, the money he earned paid in cash and kept in a secure location in Mexico City. The flat itself was owned by a Swiss-based shell company; Anton paid the utility bills in cash to a bank clerk every month using a false signature. The council tax was registered to the same shell company and paid for on an annual basis, also in cash. He did not socialise.

The only people who knew where he lived were

Capricorn, Becca, Richie, Tatiana, and until his demise, the lawyer, Albert Denham. The guards on the reception desk knew his face, yet he had been careful not to make conversation for the entire time he had lived on the fifth floor.

He had to tread carefully. Things were threatening to spiral. Nashaly Akinyemi wasn't going to back down.

Gal had messaged Anton a video over WhatsApp, an uneven phone recording of a TV interview with a police officer in a high-vis vest about the attack. The officer described the main suspect as tall, of slim build, with an Eastern-European accent, who at the time of the attack was wearing black jeans, boots, a black sports jacket and a balaclava. Generic, but enough to set his nerves on edge. It would have spooked the girl, Akinyemi, though he still doubted it was enough to stop her from going to print with the evidence she had.

For a second time in a matter of weeks, Anton had warned Capricorn to prepare.

Dimitry had said: *You must be willing to die for them if it is required of you, because they have saved you from a life spent in the slums. Do not forget that, Anton.*

He questioned whether this was better than a life spent in the slums of the Caucasus.

Would he have been alone in a slum?

He kept his eyes on the back of the door, thoughts drifting back to Tatiana. He questioned what had caused her to lose interest. She had seemed keen enough. He had grown used to her presence, her expression permanently twisted in dissatisfaction.

He stood, walked through to his bedroom, blankets still

in disarray, the linen unchanged from when he and Tatiana had last had sex. He opened the wardrobe and searched through a pile of clothing he had used when he needed to blend into a crowd.

Half an hour later, he watched tiled rooftops merge into one from the smeared window of a Crystal Palace-bound Southern passenger train, wearing a Harlequins' rugby shirt with a coat, acid wash jeans and a battered cap pulled down close over his brow. The rugby shirt went a long way to explaining his crooked nose. Strangers stared at him for a fraction of the amount of time if they actually thought the injuries sustained to his nose were sports-related.

It was raining by the time he reached Denham's property in Streatham Hill. The blinds were all pulled down, seemingly no one home. Anton rang the doorbell, rapped on the door with his fist, stepped back and watched. Within seconds there was movement in the upstairs window.

Anton waited, motionless, head down. Tatiana didn't come to the door. He turned and walked away.

He carried on walking back down the length of Culverhouse Gardens. Denham's nearby neighbours, he knew, possessed a wrought iron gate which led to the gardens directly behind the row of houses. Whilst Denham's own garden was lined with hedges, his immediate neighbour's garden was not.

Anton glanced at his watch. It would be dark in three hours.

Two strong black coffees later, the rage Anton felt simmered inside his chest. He had chain-smoked a ten-pack of Marlboro on Streatham Common. For the first time in twenty-four years – since the moment Dimitry had shut him inside the boot of a car and smuggled him out of the Caucasus – he knew that he was *failing*. Since Holt had reclaimed the laptop in Argentina and with it smashing open new evidence behind the disappearance of Clare Buchanan, he had failed to stop the contagion, to suffocate those responsible for the leak. He considered that perhaps it had been a mistake to have had the lawyer killed, for it was he who had been the one to persuade Capricorn that Albert Denham was not up to the task. And now, he found himself desiring the company of the lawyer's wife. Failure was the malignancy; now weakness his cancer.

For his entire adult life, he had overlooked all emotions, even managing to suppress the most powerful feelings when they had increased in intensity, when starry-eyed thoughts of Becca Wylde had for a time clouded his judgment. As Dimitry had trained him. Though no one had ever said *for the rest of your life*, until the rest of his life had looked him in the face, then reached inside his chest and wrapped its lukewarm fingers around the place where his heart was supposed to be.

In English, they called it 'automaton'.

He walked back up the hill, passing scantily dressed revellers waving bottles of beer around. His memories at the boxing academy involved nights sat alone in a cramped room, masturbating over nude magazines having spent the evening cleaning down the surfaces of the ropes and rings.

Back at Culverhouse Gardens, he pulled on a pair of gloves, sliding from view, taking the neighbour's gate at speed, coming at it like Azeri high jumper Valeriy Sereda at the '84 Friendship Games, only head on, the tops of the railings scraping his ribcage as he flipped his body awkwardly over. He landed squarely on the concrete, retreating back into shadow. He used his upper arm strength to hoist himself over the wall of the neighbour's garden, the light in the kitchen on, yet the room vacated. The sound of breaking twigs and branches followed him as he scaled the hedge, Denham's too-long grass breaking his painful fall. He rolled on to his back, wincing, peering up at the stars. Light shone out from inside the house, upstairs a TV on.

He silently tested the back door. It was locked. Reaching into the depths of his pocket, he pulled from it an electric lock pick and his trusted slim tensioner wrench, having suspected there was every chance he would end up in this situation.

With a few pulses whilst jimmying the plastic handle, the door opened and Anton entered Tatiana's kitchen.

The room reeked of fried chicken. He re-pocketed his tools, closing the door behind him to the sounds of footsteps padding on the stairs.

Tatiana appeared in the doorway in a baggy T-shirt which skimmed her naked thighs, hair piled up on her head in a tousled top-knot and eating from a tub of ice cream. She saw him, shrieked, turning and lunging back up the stairs. Anton followed, grabbed her by the heel, forcing her to trip. Tatiana cried out. Anton grabbed her wrists, flipped her over on the stairs, compelling her to raise her chin.

'Please,' she breathed, turning her face away, 'do not hurt me.'

He let go of her, straightened, caught his breath. 'Why do you not return my calls?'

Tatiana sat up then, gesticulating wildly. 'I am sick! I don't return calls, you break into my house?! *Skurwielu*!'

He dodged the discarded ice cream carton as it flew towards his head, spilling pink melted dairy all over the carpet. When she tried to move he pinned her once more to the carpet.

'Let me go!'

'Are you hiding something?'

Tatiana was squirming furiously. 'No! Nothing!'

'Then you get bored, is that it?'

He brought his face close, watched the tears spill onto her cheeks. 'Go, please go. I don't want you here!'

'You find somebody else? Somebody new?'

'Let me go, let me go!'

He bounded past her on the stairs, grabbing hold of the hem at the top end of the T-shirt and yanked hard, exposing her breasts. She wasn't wearing any underwear. Tatiana's lithe frame bounced off each individual step.

'Stop, stop, I will tell you!'

He dropped her on the landing outside the bedroom. She frantically pulled at the material to protect her modesty.

'Tell me what?'

Tears in her eyes again. She stumbled to her feet. 'I didn't want... I was scared. You don't *hev* most calm personality.'

Anton steadied his breathing. She opened her mouth to speak.

In his pocket, Anton felt his phone vibrate. He pulled it out, Gal's name flashing up on the screen. He had to answer. 'What is it?'

Galib talked fast. 'She left the house with a big suitcase.

Loaded it into the back of a taxi. Looks like on the way to Heathrow possibly.'

Belinda Channing, Denham's ex-wife, was on the move.

'You're following?'

'Yes.'

'Don't lose her. She could be on a night flight. If she gets to the airport try and find out where she's going, if it's Miami.'

'Got it.'

He hung up. Tatiana had moved to the bed, hands folded neatly into her lap.

'I have to go,' Anton remarked. 'You don't have to tell me anything. You don't want to see me, I get it.'

Her face blanched. She was on her feet then, colliding with him, throwing her arms around his neck, fingers in his hair. 'No, no. *Jestem brzemienne*,' she whispered into his neck.

He stiffened. He didn't speak any Polish, but their languages outside of English had various similarities.

Tatiana let go. He searched her face for signs she might be lying but found only tears. She nodded.

'Say something,' she whispered.

It took him a moment to reply. 'I have to go.'

He turned his back on her and left.

Chapter 32

Panama City, Panama
18 March, 2017

In one hand, Camila held up the picture of the painting from Oscar Aguinaldo's Contadora property, in the other, the finished copy of the painting in a strikingly similar frame. Tom's gaze shifted from one to the other.

'Are you happy?' she asked.

A smile tugged at his lips. 'Come here and I'll show you how happy I am.'

She stepped forward, offered him a grin. He lowered his mouth to hers, at the same time wrapping his fingers around the frame and removing it from her grasp.

'It… needs… waterproofing…' Camila managed between kisses.

'What do you suggest?'

'Plastic sheet wrap, tomorrow afternoon. Followed by a double dry bag. I suggest you buy new ones today.'

'Done. Any idea where I can get some?'

'There's a dive shop in this area of town but it's closed on weekends. Try Albrook. It's a mall near the canal, across from the local airport.'

'OK. I'll take the Camaro.'

'Can I see you later?'

He kissed her again. 'I can't. Becca asked if she could buy me a drink.'

Camila took a step back. '*Chuleta!* The scrawny chick with the red hair? You're potentially leaving Panama in a matter of days and you'd rather spend time with her than with me?'

'It's not like that. She and I have... history.'

'You and I are about to have history, *mi fren*.'

Tom pulled her close; Camila thrust him away again. 'Forget you and your painting you piece of shit,' she spat. '*Sal de mi estudio!*' *Get out of my studio.*

At his father's apartment, Tom walked in on Nash sitting at the kitchen table, a Bic biro pressed between her lips, fingertips hammering the keys of her laptop, windows around all open, the breeze causing the old wood shutters to clatter against the window frame. Tom helped himself to an apple from the fruit bowl, biting hungrily into it.

'Are you done yet?' he asked from the opposite side of the table.

She didn't look up but spat out the pen. 'I emailed the copy to Miles ten minutes ago.'

'He still in hospital?'

'They're letting him go home soon. I'm not sure he wants to go. I'm not sure I would either.'

Tom watched her. He liked her single-mindedness, the dedication she had shown to the job. Yet she was young; younger than Becca even.

'Will you read it?' she asked.

'Of course.'

She stopped typing. 'The final piece of the puzzle is

those papers you pick up. We still won't know who killed Clare, but we'll have identified Anton as the prime suspect for a likely murder, demonstrated his connection to Charlie Ebdon and shown that Ebdon had motive to want her gone. And that Albert Denham was also involved in making Clare disappear. From what you've said, those papers will prove he was Ebdon's bagman. It should be enough for the police to arrest Anton and Ebdon. But I need you to do something for me.'

Tom tossed the remainder of the apple he was eating. He already knew what she was going to ask.

'This is about Becca, isn't it?'

'I want you to ask her two things.'

'No.'

'Hear me out. Firstly, I need you to ask her whether she'd be willing to go on record and say what she witnessed that night. Secondly—'

'I didn't agree to "firstly". Becca's not going to own up to anything by a simple admission of guilt. Forget it.'

'*Secondly*,' she emphasised. 'I need you to ask her about Anton's background. Where he comes from. How he came to be in England. Who his parents are. Where he lives. Why he works for Capricorn.'

'Did you see where my dad went?' Tom asked.

'Don't change the subject!'

He held up his hands in mock surrender. 'Jesus Christ, alright. I'll ask.'

Tom moved down the corridor, checking his father's bedroom, moving on to his own modest quarters. 'Can I borrow some money?' he shouted back.

Nash followed him into the room. When he glanced up, he noticed her skin was glistening. She crossed her arms over her chest. 'What for?'

'I need waterproof dry bags. For the painting. The kind divers and hikers use. Should be about twenty-five dollars for a large one and I need two, maybe three.'

'I'll give you a hundred on the condition you get me answers to all my questions tonight. If we're going to expose Anton as the prime suspect in Clare's disappearance, I want to be armed with as much information about him as I can be.'

She was holding out the dollar bills before he could offer her a response, the look in her eye steely. He reached out, swiped the notes from her fingers.

'What is it you want out of this?' he asked her. 'Is it a name for yourself?'

He watched her push out her bottom lip, give a tight shrug. 'When I first watched the video you sent my mother, I'd be lying if I said the thought hadn't crossed my mind. But that was months ago. Now I'm ready to bring these motherfuckers down, even if it means a part of me goes down with them.'

He left an agitated Nash at the apartment, pacing in the kitchen, waiting for her colleague to reply to her email. In his mind, everything depended on him retrieving a copy of the Quintero Bolívar papers from Juan Carlos Aguinaldo. Without it, the only ammunition Nash had was against Anton, who was very likely Clare Buchanan's killer. It meant the only evidence against Capricorn/Charlie Ebdon was

Clare's recorded statement, revelatory in its content, but not possibly containing enough evidence to secure an arrest. There was only one way to connect Capricorn to Anton, and that was through one of the people who apparently knew them best. Becca.

He thought back to their time in Uruguay and Argentina. They had planned for months to get inside Sabina Cordero's safe, until Denham had started pressuring them at the last minute to finish the job. Yet still, back then, he had known roughly what it was they had been walking into. The following night, on Contadora Island, they would be playing a guessing game at best. Even with the assistance of two seasoned thieves, he didn't like the uncertainty. Unlike the housing complex in Uruguay, Contadora outwardly had very little security, until they reached the house itself, key or no key. His concern was that they would be walking into something they couldn't get out of, or worse, never come back from.

He walked east past the tourist shops selling Panama hats and animal masks weaved by the country's indigenous tribes; located his father eating lobster at Finca del Mar, an open-air restaurant nestled under a crimson canopy, nose in a copy of Dumas' *The Countess of Charny*.

Tom pulled out a chair. 'I thought you had no money.'

'I don't,' was his father's reply, as he wiped his mouth with a white cloth napkin. 'I know the owner. He takes pity on an ageing fool like me.'

'He's the fool if he's giving away lobster. We need to talk.'

His father's face paled. He placed the book down on

the table surface, spine up. Tom knew that when it came to difficult conversations, Oliver Holt employed avoidance tactics like an old pro. Tom helped himself to a morsel of fresh lobster, leaned forward in his chair, kept his voice low.

'You gotta get ready, Dad. After tomorrow night… you need to leave Panama for good. Say your farewells to Miguel and get on a plane. If everything goes to plan, you'll be a free man. It's time to go back to England.'

'What about the apartment?'

'Leave it with Miguel. The car too. Whatever is left he can wire you the money. You'll never be safe here.'

His father sat back, wiped the sweat from his forehead, pushing the plate away. Tom gave him a look, pulled his plate towards him, tucking into the remains of the lobster.

'You think you'll be able to do it? Contadora?'

'I can't answer that.'

'Did you when you were in Uruguay?'

The image of Anil's bloody wound and slumped-over body launched itself into Tom's mind, causing him to wince. 'Clearly not, as I ended up on the run. Which is what we should all be planning to do if we can pull this off. Running.'

'Where will you go?'

'Becca wants me to go to Mexico City. Charlie Ebdon has a house there. She thinks it will unlock a lot of information.'

'And then what?'

'Depends on what we find there, I suppose.'

He finished the remnants of the lobster, wiping his fingers.

'You'd give what you find to Nash?'

'We can work to bring Ebdon down, but right now Nash has the voice. She's the one with the power to bring him down.'

Tom took his father's car, drove north to Albrook Mall and purchased three large dry bags, returning to the apartment to find Nash locked in a phone conversation about the initial *Insight* piece, focussing on the release of Clare Buchanan's video statement. Tom showered, watched his father pack a bag, bidding farewell to his beloved French novels and rum collection by sampling a taste from each bottle and deciding which ones were best to leave for Miguel.

In Panama it was dark by 6.30 p.m.. At eight, from the open air Tántalo rooftop bar, it was possible to see the pink lights of the Cinta Costera as it curved out into the ocean. Tom waited alone on a bar stool, sipping on a third bottle of Mexican-imported Corona. He had been waiting an hour. Becca was late. It was Jamaica night, the barmen all wearing Rasta hats with fake dreads, reggae pulsing over the speakers.

He finished his drink, signalling to the waiter for another. He was contemplating leaving when the lift opened and Becca stepped out, wearing cut-off denim shorts, a vest and flip-flops, taking in her surroundings.

'You're late,' he said when she approached.

'It's a longer walk than it looks,' she said, peeved, looking out over the bay, the lines of her collarbone glistening under the lights.

He glanced down at her plastic footwear, the straps having given her open blisters. 'You didn't take a cab?'

She shrugged and took a seat. 'The cab ride from the

airport was enough to make me never want to take a taxi in this country again.'

A waiter came over, speaking in a Spanish-tinged mock Jamaican accent, informing her that bottles of Red Stripe were on special offer. Becca agreed to one without smiling.

'Did you eat lunch?'

'Yes. We found twenty dollars and ate chicken wings.'

'Found it or stole it?'

She raised her eyes. The waiter delivered her beer.

'Would you believe me if I told you we actually found it?'

He took a slug of beer from the bottle. 'Not for a second.'

He glanced down. With one hand she was massaging the fingers of the other. He thought he saw a flash of disappointment cross her features. Becca said nothing. They sat in silence, a breeze flowing in from the ocean.

'If you're never going to trust me then why did you come?' she said at length.

'Believe me, I'm only here because I need your help. I need your talent, Becca, not your excuses.'

'I left you a note in Argentina.'

'I got it.'

'When?'

'At a launderette in Southern Chile. About four days after you let Anton into our hotel room.'

She screwed her face up. 'Excuse me for not having the time to write a detailed apology. I had no choice. My whole life, I've *never* had a choice.'

'You could have given me advanced warning. I was naked for god's sake.'

'Then we would both have ended up dead. I left you the

money. I lied for you. I did what I could. When it comes to Anton, you don't understand who you're dealing with.'

'Were you in contact with him the entire time we were in Montevideo?'

She was squirming in her seat. 'No. After we saw Denham in José Ignacio he called my phone. Told me he was close by. That's when I knew Denham had lost control of everything. It was Anton who ordered Ray to kill Anil. I only found that out later on, I swear it. I didn't know he was in contact with Ray, too, as well as me.'

He stared at her across the table, unsure if he could trust what she was telling him.

'Who is he?'

The eyes flashed up again. 'Who, Anton?'

'How did he come to work for your uncle? How did you come to work for him?'

'When I was young my uncle asked my parents to adopt him so he could remain in England. He was an orphan. He's Azeri... from Azerbaijan.'

'How does someone like that end up on English soil? Why didn't your uncle adopt him?'

'My parents were older; my uncle Charlie had got married. He's got a Portuguese wife. She's a little—' Becca put her finger to her temple and twirled it round in circles. 'Then my parents... they died. Everything changed. My uncle was given primary custody. And so we moved... and Anton taught me how to be—'

She glanced out towards the city skyline.

'How old were you?'

'I was ten when the crash happened. Richie was eight. I

wanted to tell you. I wanted to tell you who Capricorn was when we were together in Uruguay. I was in up to my neck in South America. If Anton tells me to do something, I have to do it.'

'Why? What's stopping you walking away from it all?'

She was silent for a moment. 'I went to Al Denham's funeral. And it made me realise that if they could do that to him, after everything he did for them, they can do it to me, they can do it to Richie. And I know, deep down, Al Denham hated them, but he never had the chance to walk away. So me being here with you now… this *is* me walking away. But it's not enough. Walking away means going up against them.'

She fixed his gaze. 'They'll come after you,' he said, absorbing the enormity of her decision.

'You and me both. I hope your brother got away in time.'

'You warned him?'

She nodded. 'I told him to start running.'

Tom puffed out his cheeks. 'Thank you,' he said.

Becca downed the remainder of her beer, wiping her mouth with the back of her hand. 'So you see; I'm a free agent.'

A free agent who would always be looking over her shoulder, it occurred to him.

'I'll talk you through tomorrow night,' he said, making a decision of his own. 'Then you can tell me about Mexico.'

Chapter 33

Panama City, Panama
18 March, 2017

At the open-air entrance foyer to the El Machico, Richie played a game of pool alone, listening to the sound of fireworks he couldn't see, sipping on watery local beer, back of his shirt wet with perspiration. Becca had gone to see Tom Holt, a meeting to which he hadn't been invited.

Richie's stomach clenched with hunger pangs. The only good thing about prison was that you were at least guaranteed a meal. Going back to the flat in Wapping he had been reminded how he and Becca scraped a living. In London, if he needed cash, he would simply take it where he saw the opportunity and blow it on a Burger King, or a madras with a keema naan. His mouth watered. He doubted they had a decent Indian restaurant in Panama City.

Panama City. He questioned the reality of their situation: lying to Anton so Becca could come and fawn all over her boyfriend from South America.

At his apartment in the old town, Becca had taken Tom Holt aside. Told him something. Something she said she hadn't wanted to say in front of the journalist, but Richie had sensed a reluctance from the beginning to reveal her entire plan. In London, she had kept money they had stolen aside.

Money she wouldn't even let them spend on food, until it had come to purchasing long-haul airline tickets. It was not how he had pictured his freedom.

It had been his one guarantee: that when he got out, Becca would be there. She would be waiting. Their future had always been set. They were a team. He had never considered that Becca would find someone she liked, because when it had come to the opposite sex, she'd never had anything positive to say. And now she was going to great lengths to save another man from being tracked down by Anton.

Underlying jealousy got caught in his throat.

If this was how it was going to be from now on, he was on his own.

And now Becca had signed them up for a job that didn't benefit them in any way, a job that hadn't come from Anton or their uncle.

Richie bent down, potting two balls with one strike. A couple of younger European girls in vest tops and mini-skirts emerged from inside. One of them he had seen at the pool earlier in the afternoon, in a microscopic bikini. Richie couldn't remember the last time he'd had sex. For a while before prison he'd had a thing with the neighbour's daughter. He'd never even had a proper girlfriend. It occurred to him that maybe that was what Becca was chasing: a bona fide relationship where there was no expectation of lying to or robbing the individual concerned.

Whichever way he looked at it, Becca's moving on still left him with the prospect of living alone in a London flat, no sister for company and no girlfriend to share his bed.

Around eleven he watched his sister step out of a taxi. Holt wasn't with her.

'How did it go?' he asked as she approached the hostel entrance, her movements fluid.

She nodded, looking down at the pool table. 'Good. It was good. Set 'em up then.'

Richie pulled out the rack, laying it flat on the table, positioning the balls inside. Becca helped herself to a cue.

'You can break,' Richie said.

Becca looked around for some chalk, not finding any. Richie thought back to a time in their twenties when they had spent hours in a pub near Limehouse, playing pool because they had nothing better to do. He watched his sister lean down, eyes fixed on the white, level with the line of scuffed blue felt, her position low. When she broke, the balls scattered, two of them smashing into corner pockets.

'Did you discuss tomorrow night? How we're going to do it?'

Becca kept her attention on the pool table. 'Tom thinks we don't need you. If there's a risk you can't support my weight then it would be best if he accompanied me instead. So, you can relax. Stay here and practise your pool game.'

When she took the shot, the white hit a green ball, sending the latter into a spin, as Richie gritted his teeth.

'You used to say I was a better intruder than you ever were,' he said.

The look that flashed across Becca's features said *Don't fight me on this.* 'I have to make it up to him, OK?' she said, stepping back from the table.

Richie bent at the waist, aiming his cue at the white ball,

planning to strike it as hard as he could. In his mind, the ball represented Tom Holt's head, and he wanted to crack it right open.

Chapter 34

Miami, USA
19 March, 2017

Miami. Palm trees, wide roads and balmy heat. Inside the house, the curtains were all closed, the burnt orange of the setting sun peeking through where the material didn't quite cover the French windows. Below the duct tape covering her eyes, ruby red lipstick was smeared up her cheek, visible outside the second strip of tape he'd forced over her mouth. He'd secured her wrists and ankles first, before hoisting her onto the bar stool beside the kitchen island, securing her to the frame under her ribcage with a roll of twine he'd located in a drawer. Belinda Channing hadn't fought. She'd been compliant with his demands throughout. She was lucid, afraid, yet not wailing through the gag. If she hadn't been trembling, he would have believed her calm, almost. Like she had half-expected him to come.

Anton left Belinda tied to the stool in the kitchen, content she couldn't move, and thinking even if she rocked herself hard enough from side to side so that the seat toppled, from that height she'd likely knock herself out. He took a moment to walk around the dead lawyer's Floridian pad. It was no fucking wonder Denham hadn't left the house to Tatiana. He hated to admit that it was a nice place. Chrome fittings,

Italian wood flooring, a floating staircase. Clean lines. As it turned out, Streatham had been a façade, Denham's very own Elephant and Castle. This was the real nest egg. His Polish bride would have hardly known what to do with herself. From the moment he had laid eyes on her years earlier, Anton had believed Tatiana's looks and personality were more suited to someone more downmarket. Someone like him: a man who'd come to England, penniless on a cross-Channel liner wearing another man's clothing, only a 1979 Sony Walkman to his name. Denham had known that, but Capricorn didn't hire Denham to get a difference of opinion, and so it was Denham whom Capricorn had asked to marry Tatiana.

Growing up, Dimitry had never talked to him about the opposite sex. The snippets Anton picked up were playground stuff. As a teenager he had experimented, schooled by the under-the-counter magazines some of the clients would bring in. Dimitry had only taught him how to steal and slaughter. Man or woman… that kind of detail was irrelevant. Flesh was flesh, bones were bones.

In Streatham Hill, from the moment Galib had put in the phone call, he had returned to Elephant and Castle, taking the bag from his wardrobe, the one that among other items contained his passport, a changes of clothes, and a wad of US dollars. He already had an ESTA. It was a while since he had last been in the States.

From the Heathrow hotel room, where Gal and Rashit were waiting, Anton waited whilst Gal booked him a ticket on the Miami flight, the only available seat the furthest possible from business class, next to the rear, the galley and the toilet.

He had seen Belinda once in person, during the nineties, in the days when she was still Belinda Denham. He had knocked on the door to their basement flat in Clapham to deliver a package, before Denham even knew Capricorn's identity. He questioned, if Belinda saw him on the flight, whether she would recognise him as the same person, knowing then that she was being followed. His hair had been longer then, hair mousse smeared through it. Anton pulled the hair clippers he kept in his bag, Selmani giving him a number three buzz cut on top, two on the sides. When he looked in the mirror, he was reminded of a seventeen-year-old Anton Moroshkin, sweaty on the ropes, blood and snot cascading from an already shattered nose. Laid out on the bed were a crumpled suit and shirt. Gal plugged in the iron from the back of the wardrobe.

'Give me your cap,' Anton said to Selmani, holding out his hand.

Having some prior experience of Miami airport, Anton knew the chances of him losing her were sky high. Gal had reported that Denham's former wife had loaded a suitcase into her taxi, which meant that if he lost her at immigration, he knew he would be able to catch her again at baggage reclaim. If she took a yellow cab, he would need to get into the car directly behind hers, all without spooking her, and be able to direct his own driver to stay on their tail. He doubted a woman like Belinda would take the train, but she could also have booked herself some form of private transport. She had always been the classiest of Denham's wives.

On the flight, before take-off, when the captain announced the showing of the safety video, Anton glanced across at an obviously pregnant female sat in the aisle seat, for the first time allowing himself to consider the words Tatiana had whispered to him in Streatham a few hours earlier.

He would be a father.

You will never marry, Dimitry had told him.

You will never have a family.

You must never emotionally connect yourself to anyone.

Dimitry was no uncle, simply the man paid by Gearhart Keller to train him from childhood, the funds exchanged in return going towards expanding the boxing academy. Anton knew that Dimitry would have forgotten about him the moment he closed the boot of the car and sent him on his escape across Europe.

Would Capricorn concern himself if he discovered Tatiana had given birth to his child? Anton pictured what the whimpering, shrivelled newborn might look like. Considered whether he would drown it at birth, as someone should have drowned him.

The flight landed on the Saturday at 2.35 p.m. Eastern Time. Anton filed from the plane, knowing she would already have disembarked. Head down, he dodged past his fellow passengers, striding across the carpet, first spying Belinda Channing queuing for the automated ESTA machines. The system having granted him a green light for entry, Anton followed in the direction he'd watched her go. An American immigration official with a bulbous forehead had the nerve to stare at his crooked nose, then down at the suit, pausing a fraction too long before the entry stamp went rudely into his passport.

In baggage reclaim Anton watched her, cap pulled down

to his eyes. Her attention wasn't on the carousel like the other passengers waiting for the bags to appear from the void. She was pacing near a wall, dialling a number into her phone. The call was brief, and then she hung up.

He had joined the taxi rank behind Belinda. She hadn't once looked back, instead she focussed on her own movements. Inside his own yellow cab, when the Hispanic-looking driver asked where he was going, Anton offered him three hundred dollars in cash to follow the cab in front. The driver had nodded in stunned comprehension.

A short drive later, Anton asked, 'What is this area?'

'Sir, this is Coconut Grove.'

'Do people with money live here?'

'You betcha.'

Belinda's cab came to a stop outside a vast white property, double garage, security fence. When Anton asked his driver to pull over, fifty or so metres further back up the street, he said, 'What road is this?'

'This is Oak Avenue.'

In the rear of the car, under the icy breeze of the air con, Anton craned his neck. Oak Avenue: a Neighbourhood Watch area. The Channing woman's driver was helping her unload her suitcase from the boot onto the pavement. Her bags secured, she paid the driver and he left.

'Is there a hotel close by?'

'There's the Mutiny.'

'Take me there.'

Half an hour later, Anton had checked into the Mutiny Hotel. The leggy receptionist appeared unnerved by both his physical appearance and lack of a prior reservation, yet battled her discomfort by smiling through straight white veneers. In his room he showered, masturbated to thoughts of Becca, stood on his balcony wearing only a towel, inhaling the early evening air. He glanced at his watch. Within the hour, he would have been delivered a hire car.

The lights dimmed in the Coconut Grove house, owned by Albert Denham, not long after 9.15 p.m. Belinda had shut and locked the gate. In the driver's seat of a nondescript Toyota that didn't possess enough legroom for his frame, Anton's eyelids dropped. He considered whether he could attempt a break-in; deciding against it, he returned to the Mutiny and collapsed chest down onto the bed sheets.

He was back outside the property by 7 a.m. on the Sunday with an Americano and a plain croissant, flaky pastry falling into his lap, wearing jeans and a black hooded top. Outside the window, a woman in a pink velour tracksuit and white shades power-walked along the pavement, chewing gum and talking on her phone.

The dead lawyer was haunting him. Beating him at his own game. Al Denham had been smart. Organised. The Miami mansion had been his planned retirement all along. Denham never planned on staying with Tatiana, that much was obvious now. The whole time, he'd been seeing his first wife.

Anton wiped his mouth, slurping the last of the coffee, convinced that Al Denham was also hiding something. At least Daniel Benedict had been rotten all the way to the core. He had practically admitted as much as Anton had watched the noose slowly drain the life from his grey, pallid cheeks. Not Al Denham. Denham had died still clinging to his fucking morals.

Anton thought about it. The lawyer would have never planned on dying, so there would have to be collateral somewhere along the line. Denham would have needed a big, fat bargaining chip to compensate for breaking free of Capricorn, followed by a move to Miami, a sunnier climate than Streatham Hill. Something to ensure his total emancipation. Anton's inkling was that whatever it was, it was inside the house he was now parked outside.

He sat up as one of the garages started to move. Belinda Channing emerged in the driver's seat of a barely used 4x4 SUV Jeep Cherokee, a shade of shiny cobalt. She stopped before the gates, Anton watching her tap something into her phone and attach the handset to the dashboard.

From the driver's seat Anton watched her crawl along the boulevards, not knowing where she was going, following two lanes over, cars behind him venting their frustration at his slow speed. To make her turning, Belinda almost hit another 4x4. The sign she followed said 'Pinecrest Gardens'. As they entered, it felt like more of the same, another leafy upper-middle-class Miami suburb.

She pulled up near to a farmer's market outside the titular gardens. Anton followed in the vehicle, parking the Toyota in the corner by a wall. Rolling down his window, from his side-view mirror he watched her take her time, moving from stall to stall. When it was looking like she was finishing up, he slid out of the car. Timing his approach, he positioned himself so that no one would see him put the knife to her ribs on her return, waiting until her vehicle was unlocked before he made his move. The knife had come from a drawer at the Mutiny: an ordinary breakfast knife, not that Denham's former wife could see that.

'Get in,' he hissed, feeling her frame tense in his grasp. Belinda Channing did as she was instructed. She didn't let out a scream, simply slipped into the driver's seat, grasping the wheel.

Anton reached for the door handle, ducking into the rear passenger seat behind hers, a new car scent filling his nostrils, pressing the metal tip to the nape of her neck through the gap underneath the headrest.

'Drive,' he told her.

She started the engine as two octogenarians wearing sun visors passed in front of the bonnet.

Anton sat back. 'Smile at them,' he told her.

He couldn't see if she had or not. Glancing left and right as they left the car park, it appeared that no one had paid them any attention.

'Do you know my name?' he asked, when they were on the road.

Belinda stayed in lane, silent for some moments. When she spoke, there was a faint yet audible tremor in her tone. 'I remember you. You came to our house years ago.'

'But do you know my name?'

It took her a moment to reply. Her eyes appeared in the rear-view mirror. 'Your name is Anton.'

Anton ran his scarred fingers over satin sheets, the kind that featured in society magazines. Upstairs, the bedroom was all white chic furnishings, mammoth-sized bed, slept in not made. A widescreen TV was mounted on the wall.

Belinda Channing knew his name. Anton stared at his reflection in the mirrored wardrobe and wondered what else she knew. He had monitored Denham for years. When the lawyer had married Tatiana, he saw no point in watching anymore. After Amy Ebdon's suicide, Denham had been a twice-broken man, fully under their control, his spirit deteriorated. Yet now Anton knew: under the charred remains, there had been flaming embers.

Anton's eye was drawn to a walk-in wardrobe, the door open.

He entered, running his fingers over a row of the lawyer's tailored suits hanging inside. Lighter shades than Anton had seen him wear, more suitable to a warmer climate, cut wide at the shoulders to fit the lawyer's expansive frame. He lowered his eyes.

At floor level, drilled into the tiles, was a small Yale-branded domestic safe.

Locked.

'The code for the safe, give it to me,' Anton hissed, back downstairs, ripping the tape from her mouth. Belinda let out a murmur; pressed her lips together to ease the burn.

'The code,' he repeated, grabbing a kitchen knife from the drawer.

Belinda flinched. 'One, zero, one, one,' she whispered as roughly he replaced the tape.

He took the floating staircase two at a time, rolling up his sleeves. He'd worn gloves the moment he'd entered her house. Back in the wardrobe, he punched in the code, heard the whirring of the secure bars slide open. A tugging sensation pulled at his insides, as though his guts were unravelling, spewing out of his body, as he yanked out the contents: a parcel with a letter. Anton brought them out into the bedroom, opening the contents of the parcel out onto the sheets. Inside were a set of women's clothes, all wrapped up in a see-through plastic bag. Anton knew instantly what they were. It had been years since he had seen them, since he had ordered their disposal. The sight of them weighed heavy on his shoulders. He opened out the letter, began absorbing the handwritten script in Albert Denham's distinguished hand:

My darling Belinda,

I never thought I would have to write such a letter to you. For so long I thought it would be you and I, together until the end. Though our lives veered off on different paths, I consider you my only love, my only constant. I hope you know that.

It is with a heavy heart that I write these words. Throughout our marriage, as you know, there were things I couldn't tell you. These are things that tore me up inside.

I enclose a copy of my last will and testament, which has been given to my London solicitor. My attorney in the US also holds a copy and all the appropriate paperwork has been completed should I cease to be. In it, you will see, I have left you the title deeds to a house in Miami's Coconut Grove that I bought not long after we were divorced. I hope you will love it. I had it decorated in your favourite style. I bought it with us in mind.

Inside the safe, you will find a package. Please do not open this package. It contains a set of clothes and jewellery which you will need to courier immediately to the Metropolitan Police in the UK, along with this letter.

The clothes belong to the woman named Clare Buchanan. I know you will remember her. She died wearing these clothes, on the night of 21 February 2005. I was told to destroy them by Anton Merrick. I know you know that name also. Rather than destroy them, I kept them, in the hopes that one day, they could help secure a conviction for her killer. The world needs to know that she is dead. She did not survive the night she went missing.

I do not know who was responsible for Clare's murder. The responsible man is one of three individuals: Anton Merrick, Charles Ebdon or one other, Jonas Vázquez. I was there, but I did not witness the act. I want you to know that.

I do not expect to survive these monsters. They have designs on my life. I have been monstrous with them, but unlike me, they have no remorse or shame. If you are reading this, then I am probably dead.

My greatest fear is that I will not be able to protect you. By leaving you the house, they may come looking for you. Please, lock your doors at night, my love. Stay vigilant, always.

You are, and will for ever be, my world, in life and in death.

I love you. Al.

Anton snarled, tore at the letter, scattering the pieces. Reading its contents left him pacing the carpet, shaking his head, a beast waiting to be uncaged. Kicking at the French doors until they were forced open, Anton burst out onto the balcony, over-looking Albert Denham's supremely manicured lawn and swimming pool. He gripped the wrought-iron bars, muscles straining in his neck and chest. He wished he could go back. To have taken Denham's life himself, to have squeezed his throat, watched his eyes bulging as the last breaths escaped his body like he had Benedict; to have cut him in two. With a cry he threw a chair over the railing, sending it crashing to the patio below, the hollow frame bouncing on the tiles until it landed in the pool, floating for a moment before sinking to its depths.

The lawyer's betrayal had been absolute. There was no ambiguity. He meant to drag them all down with him.

Anton drew breath through gritted teeth. Above everything, he despised being caught unawares. Dimitry had taught him to package up his emotions, leave them in a drawer. Leave them behind. Leave them wherever. He balled both his fists.

Drag me to hell and the love of your life will come too, Al Denham.

Your biggest fear is about to be realised.

He gathered up the pieces of torn paper, grabbing the bag of clothes, keeping the gloves firmly on. Later, he would burn it all. He checked nothing had been left behind. Looked in the mirror again. This time he saw Tatiana's face, pleading with him not to leave her apartment.

Back downstairs in the kitchen, Anton placed the items down on the edge of the kitchen island. Saw Belinda tense, flinching repeatedly, lifting her chin, trying to work out his position and distance from her, as though sniffing the air. Stretching out his neck muscles, he granted Belinda Channing the full weight of a thrusting uppercut to the chin, the move Dimitry had first taught him as a twelve-year-old, sending both her body and the chair she was sitting on crashing over onto the polished parquet flooring. The woman let out a cry of agony through the tape before her head walloped the ground. Anton didn't hold back, weighing in with numerous kicks to her sides and spine, until she was begging. She could die in a similar fashion to her husband for all he cared. He would kill her slowly.

The kitchen knife he had used to extract the safe code was abandoned beside the sink. Anton seized it, used it to detach Belinda from the chair. Her hands and feet were still tied, but she fought him, her calm level of compliance evaporated. He put the knife to her throat and held her tightly to him which stilled her. He mentally prepared himself to run it through.

The idea of Tatiana distracted him. Would he have killed her too, had she known what Denham knew? He tried to convince himself that he would have, before picturing her in full labour on a hospital bed, wailing in agony, a baby's head crowning between her legs. Would his child ever know what he was? If he had a son, would he end up like him? Would he ever get to meet him?

Belinda was crying through the duct table, snot oozing from her nose from the earlier slug to her face.

He loosened his grip, pulled up back into a standing position. Her legs went from underneath her.

'Stand up,' he barked.

She did as she was ordered, though her knees trembled. He went over to the kitchen table, dragged a chair across the floor. Pushed down on her shoulder so that she collapsed into it.

He pulled up a second chair and sat down, bringing his face close to hers. She flinched, ducking her head from left to right.

'Be still,' he said. 'I am not going to hurt you anymore.'

Belinda Channing stopped moving, sweat from her brow dripping down her temples, her nostrils flexing in and out and she steadied her breathing.

'Al Denham. Is there anything else he left for you inside or outside this house, other than what was inside the safe upstairs?'

She shook her head: no.

'Any other letters?'

Again, she was shaking her head.

'I am what you believe me to be, Mrs Channing, are we understood? You know what I will do to you if you discuss what you know with anyone, anyone at all, your family, your friends, what you have discovered in your ex-husband's letter to you. Are we clear?'

Some part of the calm, reasoned Belinda seemed to return to her body. She was motionless before her head bobbed once up and down.

'Today you will leave this house. I will give you some money, and you will disappear. You will not go back to England. If you go back to England, I will find you, and I will cut the throats of all your sons. I will make your life a living hell. You will remain here in America. You will speak to no

335

one about events here in Miami. If you go to the police, I will seek out your children. You'll wish I had mercy and killed you today. Are we understood?'

She nodded again.

'If you see my face again, it will be because you are looking at your last moments on this earth. Do you understand?'

A vehement nod, a sob emerging from under the tape.

Anton reached for the knife, cut her restraints.

After, he got to his feet, gathering up the fragments of Denham's letter to his love and the bag of Clare Buchanan's clothes, acknowledging that this was the first and only time he had failed to kill in order to protect Capricorn's interests, and the first and only time his own possible future had seemed something real, tangible, something possible. He knew he would protect his son, or daughter, from any ramifications of this decision. There was no one in the world that Capricorn could send to finish him, who could do what Anton knew he could do.

He burned them: Clare Buchanan's clothes. Under a palm tree after midnight on a far corner of Crandon Beach in northern Key Biscayne; the Miami skyline twinkling in the distance over a serene ocean. The last thing he had added to the pyre was the pieces of Denham's letter to his sweetheart, Belinda. They disintegrated into the flames, sending out tinder butterflies. When it was all gone, he buried the ashes deep in the sand, mixing them in with the grit and layers of wet gravel. No one would look for the remainder of Clare's possessions there. Save for Belinda Channing, no one would know of their existence.

336

Anton was walking back into the street beyond the parking lot towards his hire car when his phone started ringing. He glanced at the screen, not recognising the number.

He answered without saying a word, listened for sounds of the caller.

'Anton?'

It was Richie's voice. He sounded far away.

'What is this number?' Anton said.

The line crackled. The boy sounded wretched, sobbing. 'We've made a mistake.'

Anton stopped in his tracks. 'Tell me.'

'I want your p-promise that Becca and I are safe whatever happens. I need that as a guarantee. Then you can have him. I can tell you where he is.'

Anton's lungs felt like they had been clamped. 'Where are you calling from? Have who?'

The boy's voice still ragged. 'Tom Holt.'

A punch to the stomach. A realisation: Becca had gone after her man.

'Give me your location.'

'You give me your word, your guarantee. Becca and I, we're forgiven, we're safe. My uncle, he never has to know. Please—'

He paused. 'You have it. No harm will come to you. Give me your location.'

A moment, a hesitation. Anton's fingers squeezed the handset.

'We're in Panama City,' Richie said.

Deep inside his chest: detonation. 'I need an exact address.'

Chapter 35

Panama City, Panama
19 March, 2017

At 10 a.m., Nash opened the door for the redhead, immediately looking past her.

'Didn't bring your brother this time?'

Becca Wylde knocked shoulders with her as she shoved past, entering the apartment. 'I told him you'd be here so he decided to stay away.'

'Funny,' Nash said, closing the door and following her to the kitchen.

'Where's Tom?' Becca asked, turning to face her.

'With his other girlfriend,' Nash told her. 'The one you really wish he didn't have.'

'You like to think you know things, don't you?'

'It's my job to try and find things out, yes. Like how a nice little red-haired girl from a nice family gets roped into doing her uncle's dirty work for him, together with his hired thug. They sent me a box of dead rats with severed heads, did they tell you that? Or maybe you helped organise the package?'

Becca looked to the floor. 'They're scared of you. Of what you know. It's why they do the things they do.'

'Then why do you work for them?'

'I don't. Not anymore.'

Nash took a hesitant step forward. 'Look. I know you don't like me very much. But my story on your uncle and Anton. It has… holes.'

'Holes?'

'Anton-sized holes. I know he was on the bus with Clare Buchanan that night. I know he works for your uncle. I know he came into your life when you were a young girl and maybe, I don't know, he's trained you to become this elite machine… but I know nothing more about him. If the authorities are going to find him, or find out what happened to Clare, then they need to know where to start looking.'

Becca crossed her arms over her chest. 'And you want to be the one to tell them.'

'Frankly, yes.'

Becca took a step forward, closer than Nash expected. 'You don't care about Clare Buchanan any more than I do. You're driven by your own ambition to put your story on the front page of your mother's newspaper. I looked you up.'

'A week ago I would have agreed with you. But then your *associates* went too far.'

Becca looked away. Nash found herself grinding her teeth, staring at a stubborn female who wasn't going to give anything away. She had one final card to play. She had received an email that afternoon. Opening her mouth to begin speaking, Nash was interrupted by the sound of Tom returning to the apartment, carrying a black plastic bag.

He looked up as he entered, locking eyes with Becca. Becca seemed to stiffen, her back straightening. Whatever they had done to one another, it was still as raw and painful as an open wound.

'Your brother not here?' Tom asked.

'He's staying at the motel.'

'Is he cool with that?'

Nash watched as Becca's head bobbed up and down in confirmation.

'Is that the painting?' Becca asked.

Tom reached into the plastic bag, pulling out a black dry bag, bulky with the frame sealed inside. 'It's ready.'

Becca took it, checked the weight.

'Is Camila talking to you now?' Nash asked, raising an eyebrow.

She thought she saw Tom flush, Becca looking to the floor.

'We said our goodbyes,' Tom said. 'I told her that after tomorrow I'd be gone.'

'Or dead,' Nash added, regretting her choice of words the instant after they'd escaped her lips. She looked away. 'Sorry.'

Tom ignored her. He looked to Becca. 'My father's at the marina. Did you bring swimwear like I asked?'

Becca nodded. 'Then we leave within an hour. Did you book your flight?'

This time he was looking at Nash. 'KLM to Amsterdam,' she confirmed. 'It leaves at six fifty tomorrow night. Your dad's driving me.'

Tom looked perturbed. 'I've told him to get himself on the Copa flight to Miami with onward transit to London. Leaves around the same time.'

'You think he'll leave Panama?'

'Miguel's paying for the flight.'

'And what about you two? You gonna tell me where you're going to?'

Tom and Becca exchanged glances. Only one of them had the decency to look her in the eye.

'If we find anything, you'll be the first to know.'

It irritated Nash that Tom wouldn't give away their plans, as though the redhead had asked him to protect the information.

'Do you mind if I have five more minutes with Becca?' Nash asked. 'Alone?'

Becca looked at her, cocked her head to one side. Tom looked between them both, as though taken by surprise. He offered her a shrug. 'Of course not. Use a bedroom if you want.'

Nash went to the table, pulling out two printed sheets of paper from amongst her work pile. Tense, she led Becca down the corridor, into his father's bedroom. The room was sparse; the pictures no longer on the walls, a collection of empty rum bottles beside the open shutters, a pile of ragged novels on the desk, a packed suitcase lying open on the bed.

'Shut the door,' she said in Becca's direction. 'Maybe you should sit down.'

'I can stand,' Becca said, nudging the door closed with her shoulder. 'What's this about? If it's about that *Evening Standard* article—'

'What *Evening Standard* article?'

Becca looked away, gave a shrug. 'They ran a piece a year and a half ago about a 'sleight of hand' thief, a woman with red hair who'd been *terrorising* central London – Oxford Street, mainly, stealing money from unsuspecting old ladies.

There was a fuzzy CCTV image to go with it. But the Met couldn't identify her, or so they said. They claimed she wore different disguises.'

'And was that article about you?'

Becca crossed her arms over her chest. 'It wasn't just old ladies,' she muttered. 'I'm not completely coldblooded.'

Nash sobered, took a breath, resolved to look it up. 'Actually this was something else. After I spoke to your friend – Naomi Kelly – I approached a contact of mine about getting hold of a copy of a report for me from Northumberland Police. It was emailed to me this morning. The report I asked for was regarding your parents' car accident in 1996.'

Nash watched the reaction carefully. Becca Wylde didn't move. 'What about it?' she asked in a tone that was impassionate.

In her mind, Nash found herself fumbling around for the right words. 'The coroner recorded the deaths as accidental,' she said. 'The assumption was that your mother and father swerved on the country lane to avoid an animal before they ploughed into a tree.'

'So they told me. And?'

Nash held out the papers for Becca, fingers trembling slightly. 'The police at the time found a single cigarette butt in the back seat footwell. Apparently neither of your parents were smokers; at least not of traditional cigarettes. DNA samples were taken but police were unable to track down the young man whom Ione and Blake Wylde had supposedly recently adopted. There was no record of his existence with social services. The only thing they could find out from the locals was his name.'

Becca turned her eyes down. In the dim light she raised her hand, fingers hovering over the papers without taking them. Her voice returned to a murmur. 'Anton Merrick,' she said.

Nash watched as Becca grasped the papers. The redhead still didn't look.

'It's never crossed your mind?' Nash said, trying to sound sympathetic.

'What's never crossed my mind?'

Nash's throat had gone dry. 'That your uncle gave the order to Anton to… You were a girl. How could you have known? You thought they were protecting you.'

The papers hanging at her side, Nash watched Becca's chest rising and falling.

'What brand?' Becca said. 'What brand was the cigarette?'

Nash reclaimed the report, scanning the surface. 'It says somewhere. Here… Embassy Regal. Don't you want to read it?'

For the first time, Becca raised her eyes and Nash could picture her as a ten-year-old girl, hair scraped back, being told by her uncle that her parents were never coming back. There was a vacant quality to them, an emotional detachment that perhaps drove her to do the things that she did, with no apparent guilt.

'If you see my brother, please don't tell him about this,' Becca said, before she turned and left the room.

Chapter 36

Panama City, Panama
19 March, 2017

At 5 p.m., Tom glanced towards Becca in the back seat of the Camaro, Miguel at the wheel, as they departed Casco Viejo in silence, speeding past the Mercado de Mariscos up on to the Cinta Costera as it swept out over the ocean.

Fucking Nash, he thought. Couldn't have kept her mouth shut for one more day. Becca was peering through smeared glass towards the densely packed peaks of the city skyline on the other side of the bay, each one stretching for the clouds, the architecture of each structure a matrix of clean lines, sharp steel and glass angles glinting in the sun. She was contemplating, he knew, that Anton had been responsible for the death of her mother and father, her hair falling down in front of her face. Her entire world had shifted off its axis, now spinning out of control, the idea that it was no accident her parents were both dead. To Tom, the truth was unsurprising.

'Are you alright?' he asked her.

Her eyes flicked up for a split second before she returned her attention to outside of the window, teeth gritted, chin jutting out. For a while Tom had convinced himself that Anton was in Panama somewhere, waiting in the wings to take his revenge for events in Argentina. Come to put a bullet in his chest. Yet Nash had presented Becca with a scenario surrounding her childhood tragedy, that maybe her parents' deaths hadn't been accidental. That they had been part of Capricorn's plan all along. Now the rage that threatened to engulf her had reddened her cheeks and Tom felt sure that, had Anton been in the near vicinity, she would have gone after him.

'When this is over do you still want to go to Mexico?' he asked.

'I don't know,' was the eventual reply.

Undiluted fury threatening to spill out at any minute, ripping a hole through her chest, Tom selfishly hoped that she would be able to contain her emotions until the painting had been replaced and they had both feet back on the boat.

'Your uncle owns something like this, no?' Oliver Holt said to Becca as Tom helped his father with the bags into Xavi Futuro's Predator 57, moored at its same spot at the marina on Isla Flamenco, sparkling from a recent clean. 'Did he ever take you on one?'

His father thought Becca an odd kind of specimen. Too much brooding, he'd said, voicing his views, though he had at least tried to make conversation. Tom had confessed that Becca was the niece of Charlie Ebdon, and she happened to be a talented thief. Aloof, Becca stood on the floating walkway. When Tom had pointed out their vessel, it had been enough to stop her momentarily in her tracks.

'He owns a yacht in France, one in Portugal,' she murmured. 'But I've never seen them.'

Oliver looked at her, frowned. Held out his hand to help her step up onto the Predator. She took it.

'He has three daughters too; my cousins,' Becca added, somewhat out of the blue. 'I've never met them either. I don't think they know I exist.'

'Why would your uncle hide you away like that?' Tom asked.

'He's a manipulator. Like my grandfather was before him. I have more questions than you know.'

Something stirred in Tom's stomach, her indignant tone striking a nerve. He shoved the feeling away, found himself speculating over the brutality of her upbringing.

He sat on grey seats on the opposite side of the saloon to Becca, elbows resting on his knees as his father steered the Predator out of the marina into open waters. Out on the ocean, once they were free of the speed restriction zone, Oliver turned to Becca, asking her over the driving wind if she wanted to captain the boat. Possibly for the first time since their first meeting in Buenos Aires less than a year earlier, Tom witnessed trepidation in Becca's expression as his father guided her hands to the joystick control that powered both the bow and stern thrusters, and her look as under them, the hull lurched powerfully forward, cutting through the Pacific swell and taking them towards the Pearl Islands of Panama.

He had benefitted from Miguel's local knowledge of procedures at the marina. Goods taken out on to boats were not security scanned but the contents of bags and suitcases were often inspected by members of Panama's Fuerza Pública – Defense Forces – and formerly the National Guard, who wore military uniform despite their role as enforcers of public security. Miguel had warned that in Contadora, officers from the Fuerza Pública were on the lookout for narcotics, and excessive possession of alcohol during times of *La Ley Seca* – the Dry Law, or short-term prohibition – being imposed, such as national holidays, when, according to Miguel, Panamanian levels of liquor consumption verged on out of control. As a precaution, knowing they might be searched, Tom had concealed the dry bag containing the fake Goya at the back of a storage compartment under the bed. Their bags they had filled with ordinary clothes and toiletries. It was Becca who had suggested they pose as fiancés again, like they had in Uruguay, before she'd produced both rings he had bought her, the cheap one from the Montevideo-Buenos Aires ferry shop and the other, pricier edition from a jewellery shop outside Montevideo port market. Now both were planted firmly on her ring finger.

As the Pearl Islands crept up on the horizon as fuzzy grey mounds, the spray from the Pacific cooling his face and neck, he cast his mind back to the night he and Anil had broken into Sabina Cordero's house inside Aves de Las Colinas. There had been a sense of unease back then, as to what they might be walking into. Denham had rushed them into getting the job done, Capricorn unwilling to wait any longer to get his hands on Clare Buchanan's video statement. Becca had asked him that night if he had felt ready. He hadn't, yet looking back, he knew he had felt infinitely more prepared then than he did now. This job was bursting with unknowns, none of which he'd had time to prepare for. And for him, the stakes were higher. His father's life was on the line.

Further out, Oliver reduced both sets of thrusters, bringing the Predator's speed down to a steady ten knots, the waters around Contadora clear and calm. Around a hundred metres from Playa Galeon, the ocean floor was still visible through clear waters, tropical striped fish meandering over rocks, silt and reef. Becca was on her feet, arms crossed over her chest, chin up and neck strained, absorbing wide-eyed the jagged-edge cliffs and scraggy jungle, tucked-away pockets of sand and azure blue waters. For a moment, her rage had evaporated. When she glanced back at him, she shook her head like she didn't believe it. His father was grinning. Returning his gaze to Becca, a smile tugged at Tom's lips. Before it had been Camila smiling at his astonishment. Somehow Becca was now here, helping him achieve what before her arrival had seemed startlingly unachievable.

Oliver guided the boat around the north-eastern side of Contadora, Playa Larga rolling out ahead of them, the graffitied shipwreck and abandoned, old and rotten resort buildings adding to the mystery of the place.

'A rough diamond, no?' Oliver laughed in Becca's direction as she continued to marvel at an uninhabited pure white sand beach framed by palm trees. She had moved to the sun deck and was hugging her knees, taking it all in.

When he joined her, she said, 'I think I've changed my mind. I don't want to rob this place.'

His laugh was a nervous one, questioning in his mind if she was half-serious.

'I want to stay somewhere like this. For ever,' she added.

'There's nothing here. You'd go mad.'

He could tell that she saw it as somewhere she could hide away, the most remote place on earth, somewhere her uncle would never find her. 'Would I?'

'You haven't seen where the money lies yet. Come on. We need to be out of sight.'

'Are you ready?'

On the lower deck of *La Señorita*, he lowered the binoculars. Through the panoramic hull, gently bucking in the Pacific waters, a circular beam from a raised floodlight seeped over the sands of Cacique beach, fifty metres in the distance, in almost complete darkness. He had witnessed no movement for almost thirty minutes. The only other light was hanging from the sail of a nearby catamaran. His father thought the inhabitants had turned in an hour earlier.

At midnight, Tom and Becca had waited on the bed in silence, listening to the sounds coming from a boat further out – a sizeable yacht – as a group of shirtless Panamanians partied on deck, hurling themselves overboard into the dark sea, reggaeton blaring, bikinied women shrieking in delight. In Uruguay, breaking into Sabina Cordero's safe had been organised around a fixed set of timings. It irked Tom that on this night they were beholden to the actions of strangers: a setback, not an obstruction, but an irritant nonetheless.

'We're late.'

It was approaching 2 a.m. He had hoped to be on the move by now. On deck, he knew his father would now be wrestling to keep his eyelids open, despite being ordered off the rum for an entire weekend.

It was around a thirty metre diagonal swim to the shore, the tide at its lowest, water relatively warm. No need for wetsuits, unlike Uruguay, though they needed to watch their proximity to the rocks and being unwittingly swept up in the swell. He'd selected black rash guards to conceal the lightness of their skin in the dark ocean. They would be carrying a total of three dry bags: Becca carrying her change of clothes and a rope ladder; Tom carrying the painting in one bag, a low-beam torch and his change of clothes in the other. Like Uruguay, the key, this time, to the skylight at Oscar Aguinaldo's property, was secured around his neck.

'Are you ready?' she asked again, a touch of impatience entering her voice. 'We need to make a move.'

In the inky darkness, through the binoculars, it was possible to see the vague outline of the millionaires' mansions on the cliff tops overlooking Cacique. Tom shifted his eyes along the row, squinting to adjust to the dim shapes. The lights that were on appeared to be outside lights. It was impossible to tell if anyone was home. By Easter, the island would be full of rich locals taking their holidays before the start of the wet season.

'Tom,' Becca hissed.

He put down the binoculars, picked up his bags, securing them over his torso.

He had been mistaken; on the deck his father was wide awake.

'All quiet,' he whispered, as he held out his hand and gripped his son by the shoulder. 'I never said thank you. For saving my life.'

Tom shook his father by the hand. 'Save it for when we're back on dry land,' he said, taking a step towards the rear of the Predator and lowering himself into the sea.

Chapter 37

The salt hit Tom's senses first, stinging his corneas, rushing into his nasal passages, causing a sharp intake of breath. He checked for Becca behind him; glimpsed her momentarily, over-arching arms in a steady front crawl. It wasn't the silent swim he'd had to make in Uruguay; there had been no current back then. The gloom was the same, visions of predators lunging up from the depths sending the adrenaline surging out to the tips of each capillary, propelling him forward. The bags weighed him down. Forty metres from the shore he felt the first sensation of a blunt knife blade puncturing his body, slicing against his hamstring, then again and again until skin was on fire. He came to a halt, treading water, breath coming in gasps, body jerking with each unexpected onslaught. He looked back. Becca had felt them too and was writhing against the waves. He kicked hard, swam back, grabbing her by the hand, towing her forward, taking a more direct route to the shore.

'Jesus!' Becca hissed. 'What is it?'

Tom winced as the skin from his belly button to his sternum began to prickle painfully. Becca cried out as something caught her in the darkness.

'Jellyfish,' Tom responded, kicking harder, heading for the light on the shore, spitting out saltwater, the pain increasing in intensity, recognising that in the darkness there were potentially hundreds of invisible tentacles brushing up against their bodies, with no way of knowing if the venom therein was enough to trigger any kind of reaction.

Becca, still writhing, was beginning to panic, muted squeals escaping her lips. Tom could see the hulls from two separate vessels, near enough that their inhabitants could hear them in the water.

'Almost there, I've got you,' he said, swimming back behind her, guiding her forward, sensing an almost electric current between them as the jellyfish went on the attack.

Becca lurched forward, paddling hard with her arms towards the right-hand corner of the beach. Tom followed, watching as Becca collapsed into the spray and on to the sand. Eyes darting left to right, he knew they needed to move, and fast.

'It hurts, it hurts,' Becca breathed as Tom hauled himself breathless out of the ocean. 'It's everywhere.'

She had dropped the dry bags in the sand. Tom swiped them up, urging her onwards to the rear of the beach where the cliffs met the sand. 'Bec, we can't stop, we have to go.'

By the time they reached the shadows her body was trembling. He cradled her cheeks in his palms, soothing her as he would a child, his own fingers tingling with needle pricks. 'Breathe, breathe. It's a sting; it goes away.'

'Is it venom? Are they venomous?'

'No.'

'How would I know? What would happen?'

He put his arms around her, holding her tightly, felt her heart hammering against her ribcage. Brushed his lips against her temple. 'In another minute they'll be gone, I swear it.'

Her felt her arms encircle him, holding on. 'I've never swum in the ocean before.'

He drew back, searching her face in the dim light, fingers moving to her hair.

'I should have told you,' she whispered in what he took as an apology.

'We need to go,' he said. 'Are you in pain?'

'I'm OK,' Becca whispered, already starting to open the bags.

Tom looked over her shoulder. They had landed on the beach a good forty metres away from the bottom of the staircase where they needed to be. Out of wet clothes and hastily dressed in dry ones, he edged along the rough face of the cliff base, sand clogging between his toes, the sound of skittish geckoes fleeing into jagged corners, Becca at his back. Having her there gave him a sense of reassurance – of confidence – as cliff turned to wall and he began to move below the first of several elevated mansions.

Locating a sandy spot under what seemed to be a dilapidated wooden platform adjacent to the staircase, Tom unloaded the bags containing wet clothes. He couldn't see shit, feeling his way through withered palm leaves. Becca had the painting inside the dry bag still strapped to her back; Tom had taken the rope ladder. Keeping to the agreement to keep communication to a minimum, he reached for her hand. She gave it a reassuring squeeze and they were moving again, following the line of a wall to underneath a second platform, this one part of the steps leading Oscar Aguinaldo's property, the night blindness frustrating him, making him feel powerless.

They had agreed Becca would go first. She was up and out in a manner of seconds, a wisp of air brushing against his cheek, over the lowest part of the wall like a streamlined gymnast: at least that was the sound he could decipher from her movement. Then nothing. He followed, going for the front gate, using the upper slats for leverage until he had hauled himself over onto the steps. Up and up, without stopping, ducking low against the wall, a right-angled turn, the discernible glass wall of a private walled-off terrace. Tom looked down below, caught his breath. Out in the ocean, boat lights winked in darkness.

He mounted the glass panelling, landed on two feet. Becca was nowhere to be seen. A gentle whistle caused him to look up. As per his father's zoomed-in photographs of the property, Becca, the agile simian, had poked her head down from the circular roof of a concrete gazebo structure fixed to the balcony. He hadn't even seen her go up, the only method available bear-hugging one of the four pillars and shimmying up it as an island native mounts a coconut tree.

For a moment, he felt embarrassed, an amateur, questioning what the hell he was doing. Her brother would have proved a more nimble partner. She reached down and he passed her the dry bag. She clicked her fingers, pointed towards the railing, atop the surrounding glass panelling. He glanced over, back down into the gloom, the sound of the waves washing onto wet sand. Losing his balance would mean crashing over the panel, back down onto the steps below. It was a fifteen-foot drop at least, resulting either in a painful death or a broken neck or back. He wasn't sure how she'd managed it so quickly, but then that was what made her good.

Her fingers were snapping again, urging him to get a move on. The edge of an opened parasol, adjacent to the gazebo, was within reach. Using its taut canvas material for leverage, he held on, raised his leg to the top of the railing, pulling up, before grabbing Becca's hand. She pulled hard, he twisted, felt his world tip, catching sight of the steps below before he crashed down on top of her on a circular roof with slate tiles. She held on to him, breathing ragged. The last time they had been in that position, so close to one another, had been in the hotel room in Buenos Aires, a heated post-coital embrace. Except that time, there had been no clothes between them.

He raised his head, his damp cheek brushing against hers. She had placed her fingers against the back of his neck, as though holding him there. He rolled off her: there was little time for anything other than getting to the painting. Carefully getting to his knees, he peered in the darkness at the roof of the house. It was lined with terracotta ceramic tube tiles, the kind that slotted together. There was no rain gutter present, nothing to grip on to other than the tiles themselves. It was steeper than he would have liked.

'Ideas?' he whispered.

He watched as Becca got to her feet, took two steps forward before bounding upwards, landing on the edge of the roof with her foot and propelling herself upward, dry bag still attached to her back, demonstrating to him that it could be done without a rope support. She made it look too easy. Within a second she was far enough away that he could no longer see her expression.

He followed her motions, finding himself scrambling up the ceramic tiles on all fours to maintain some kind of grip without sliding back down and off the edge. Balanced, he pushed on up to the top, this time Becca following.

The rooflight was easy to locate, on the right side of the roof nestled between two ridges. Tom crouched down, took in their surroundings. By day they would have been exposed, sprawling houses to their left and right, a view of the front gate and garden, to the front of the house a panorama of boats littering the ocean. By night, the surrounding light dim and fuzzy, and under the slither of a moon, they were as safe from observation as they could have been for two thieves on the prowl.

Becca snapped her fingers again, impatient. He tugged out the key from under his clothes, sliding it into the rooflight lock shaft, turning it once. The surrounding edge he could feel was polycarbonate, the glass double glazed. He lifted the edges, the window opening to ten centimetres before coming to a halt on its hinges.

'Shit,' Becca hissed.

'It's OK,' he whispered, reaching inside. 'Manual hinge. We need to keep twisting.'

He located the bottom of the long screw shaft, feeling a circular hook. Opening would usually require a pole, but they could do it without; it would take time. Tom grasped the bottom end, the grooves of the screw cutting into his skin as he turned the metal, the window pane rising. They took turns, Becca taking over, manually twisting until they were both out of breath with red raw fingers and palms. Even fully opened, it was questionable whether Becca would be able to fit between the less-than-ninety-degree angle of the gap between glass and frame.

Becca had pulled open the toggle for the larger of the dry bags, reaching for the rope ladder and torch. She waited until the top half of her body was through the gap before switching on a low beam. It stayed on for a few seconds before she wiggled back out again.

'It's about a three to four metre drop,' she said. 'I can see the painting on the right side mounted on the wall, which is red.'

'Can you reach the painting from the floor?'

'Yes.'

Tom nodded, held her look for a moment. Becca was waiting for his signal. This was it.

Under blinking stars he reached for the dry bag containing the rope ladder, unravelling the opening and yanking it out. Keeping hold of one end, he unravelled the remainder down through the raised window pane of the rooflight. He knew Becca would have to go in feet first. Taking the dry bag containing the painting, he attached it to the rope, attaching the buckle over one of the straps, lowering it down. Then he backed away a fraction, allowing Becca to shift into position, turning over onto all fours before sliding the soles of her shoes through the gap. He watched her ease herself down, sitting on the top end of the ladder to weight it down, until only her head remained above the parapet.

Without warning, he heard the crack of a door being kicked open, followed by loud braying laughter.

Company. *Shit*.

He ducked down, eyes flitting to the source of the noise, keeping the ladder underneath him.

A couple had come out onto their balcony, less than thirty metres away, but very much in view.

He looked back at Becca.

'Let me fall,' she whispered.

He hesitated for a moment. This was their only chance.

He rolled off, releasing the ladder, grabbing the second dry bag, twisting his body towards the shadows, over the arched ridge of the roof and out of sight.

Seconds later, there came a distant thump from inside the house, as Becca plummeted to the floor.

Chapter 38

'Let me fall.'

In the same moment the words escaped her lips, Becca shifted her left hand from the rope ladder to the safety of the polycarbonate frame. She saw Tom's face disappear, and with her right hand, she yanked down hard on the ladder, feeling it give way from under her feet. She tensed her upper arm, holding on whilst she watched the entire object spiral to the floor below. Reaching her right hand up to the frame, she gripped on, knowing that her next action could mean the difference between making it out undetected or being Medevaced off a tropical island in the middle of nowhere. Anton had given her a lesson once, on how to fall correctly. *Go limp*, he had instructed. Becca held on, wincing, forcing her body into submission and to swing freely. The frame of the rooflight cut into her flesh. Loosening her grip for the briefest of instants, she felt herself suspended in mid-air before plunging onto a semi-soft surface. In an attempt to roll, she felt the ligaments in her ankle stretch and give way, sending a sharp stab of pain into her leg and her brain into alarm. Becca's mouth flew open in a silent scream. Gritting her teeth, she blinked, stared up at the outline of the rooflight as it came in and out of focus. In the far distance she could hear noises, a couple laughing, a woman shrieking.

She had told Tom to let her go. Now she couldn't move.

She tried to raise her head. The pain in her ankle came in waves, bombarding her body with a pricking sensation, not unlike the jellyfish.

Her lungs tightened before she remembered to exhale. She wiggled her fingers, one hand at a time, checking for any other pain source. Waiting for the pain to subside, she attempted to wiggle her toes too, inside her still-damp shoes, and found she could. She felt around her, realising she had crash landed onto a rug. Her next thought was for Richie, wishing now that he had accompanied them. He would have known what to do. He would have fallen with elegance, would have been up and about replacing the painting by now.

She could see the outline of the dry bag, at the bottom of the pile of rope ladder. Her eyes adjusting to the light, at floor level, out of the corner of her eye was a stuffed black bird, like the vultures that swooped above Panama City, glass eyes twinkling. She flinched, turning her neck, knowing now that it was something she could do. Fear pulsed through her for a second time, along with adrenaline. She raised one arm, then another, easing herself upright, her entire lumbar area still tingling. After another minute, she was back on two feet, unable to bear weight on her ankle. She collapsed back down.

She listened. Outside there was chattering – a couple nearby, possibly on a roof terrace. She wondered where Tom had positioned himself; how far he would've had to move back. Retrieving the dry bag from underneath rope ladder, she unfastened it, clicking open the belt buckle, rolling it open. She repeated the process with the second dry bag, before working to extract the painting from its layer of plastic protection. Laying it flat on the floor, she got to her feet, grasping the frame from the existing painting, seeing how easily it might come away from the wall.

The real Goya lifted off in her hands. Bending, Becca placed the two pictures together on the floor, sliding them underneath the rooflight for better sight of the pair side by side.

She swallowed, her heart rate beginning to pick up momentum. Tom's Latina chick had done a decent job of copying the painting. The frame, on the other hand, was a dead giveaway. Gilded, Tom had called it, in Becca's eyes a kind of garish gold. The weight and size were a close fit, yet she suspected it wouldn't take an art dealer to spot the difference. Right kind of garish; wrong shade of gold.

Glancing up at the window, she could still hear voices. She guessed that the couple might be outside for a while, so turned over the copy of the painting. On the back, there was a layer of wood, taped into place. Cradling the original, Becca lifted it, glancing underneath. In the gloom she could see dark wood, four flat wooden pegs holding the wood frame in place, plus a thinner strap of wood. The size of the two paintings was the same.

She got to work. The tape came off easily from the copy, allowing Becca to nudge the canvas from its frame. The original was trickier, the pegs, held by screws driven into the back of the main frame decidedly rusty. She could twist all but one of them, in theory allowing the painting to slide out of its ancient bindings. Applying gentle pressure from the front, she could lift the canvas enough that the wood backing could be released.

Outside, the woman was shrieking with drunken laughter. Becca questioned whether they had been joined by more people. Working quickly, she slid the original painting out of its frame. In the dim light, she held it up to see. A woman lay provocatively on a bed in an ankle length dress, mustard yellow sleeves, smiling like she knew something no one else did, and whatever thought she was having satisfied her greatly. It occurred to Becca that the item she was holding in her hands was the most expensive thing she'd had the audacity to steal. She turned the light canvas in her fingers, thinking about Richie, thinking that she would apologise for forcing him come all the way to Panama only to be made to feel useless.

Becca got to work on reframing the fake. The canvas was a tight fit – a good thing, she decided, as she slid the pegs back into place, pressing down hard to allow the thin layer of wood to fall into place. The last peg took some manoeuvring and Becca gave up trying for a perfect replacement, rehanging the painting, ensuring it was straight and flush to the wall, as it had been before. The fake woman's portrait still had a knowing smile, probably with the knowledge that her ankle-length dress wasn't worth the price of the canvas it had been painted on.

Becca paused. Above her: silence. Then, within a few seconds, Tom was back at the rooflight.

'Bec?' he whispered.

She looked up, the beam of the torch blinding her. 'What the hell are you doing?' he added.

'I had to reframe the entire thing. I'm done, give me a second.'

'Come on.'

Becca wrapped the original Goya into the plastic, loading it into one dry bag before sealing it inside the second, along with the faulty frame. Gathering up the rope ladder, she tried to stand, tossing one end of it up to Tom.

From behind her, she heard a sound.

In the darkness, her head whipped around.

She went still, listened, fear pounding in her ears.

The second time she wasn't mistaken. A man coughed, a too-many-cigarettes cough. It was behind a door, but close enough to send panic through her veins.

She wasn't alone in the house.

Tom had heard it too. Becca started scrambling, wrapping the strap of the bag around her torso, taking the ladder in her hands, hopping on one foot onto the first rung. The rope ladder swung forward with her weight.

Underneath a door, a light went on, the protruding shafts causing the red walls to glow and the eyes on the stuffed vulture to twinkle. The man, whoever he was, was hacking his guts up now, the sounds closer.

Becca attempted to climb, yet with the pain in her ankle it proved impossible. She shook her head frantically at him. Tom pulled the ladder, taking her weight, dragging her up. When she reached for Tom's fingers they were warm and welcoming. He yanked hard. Becca bent low, scrambling out of the rooflight, catching a clump of her hair on the thick screw they'd had to turn to get in.

'Go, go,' she hissed, using her arms to push herself out, rolling out of the way, watching as Tom began the achingly slow task of winding the rooflight to a closed position.

Inside, a toilet flushed. Tom paused. Moments later, the light from inside the house went off.

Becca glanced down, holding her breath. Her ankle throbbed. Over the side of the roof on the north side of the house, she could glimpse the top of a lofty boundary wall, painted white, separating Oscar Aguinaldo's front garden from his neighbour's, the line leading all the way to the front gate and to the island road. It would get them swiftly off the roof, and whilst they would be exposed, they could be away from the property in less than a minute.

She crouched low, waited, her breaths unsteady.

The rooflight closed, she yanked Tom by the sleeve, wordlessly raising her chin towards the wall. He saw what she meant. Replacing the rope ladder in the last dry bag, Tom slung it unfastened over his shoulder. They were on their feet, Tom quickly realising the limitations on her speed. Becca sat back down, dragged herself over rough tube tiles, onto the surface of the wall. Tom helped her up, Becca glancing down, placing one foot in front of the other, edges lined with broken glass for security, the central line uneven and crumbling in parts as she moved towards the road. Progress was slow. A short length of barbed wire was twisted between two exterior walls. Becca leaned forward, took in the height of the drop. She estimated over three metres to the rough-hewn edge of the cracked tarmac. She wouldn't make it. Crouching down, she attempted to decipher ways to circumvent the wire, feeling Tom at her back. There was nothing for it but to step their way through. It wouldn't be long before the sun was hailing a new day. Tom skirted around her, going first, dropping down onto the road. Gingerly, Becca raised one foot, easing it back down through brittle, twisted metal, taking a few nicks to the flesh, wincing as she did so. Tom motioned her down.

'I've got you,' he said, and she lowered herself down.

Tom took her weight as she walked, allowing Becca to lean into him, arm across his back, limping her way to the point where the road became a dirt track, the path disappearing into darkness beside a row of bulrushes. They kept silent – the only sound the distant waves and their laboured breathing. Becca felt keen to see the boat again, to escape the paradise island. As they turned a corner, the rotten shells of buildings came into view, eerie silhouettes on a roughly hewn landscape, remnants of a place forgotten; the orange sun peaking on a champagne pink horizon creating an unnerving set of shadows. On the beach was the ship that had run aground, rusted metal spray painted with layers of graffiti. Tom lowered her onto the sand. His father would be coming soon, Playa Larga their back-up location if they had to abandon the Cacique route. The only hints remaining that a robbery had taken place were the abandoned sets of swimwear on the sand, which she hoped would be swallowed by the sea in the morning tide.

Tom crouched near her. From his expression, she knew he still felt exposed. There were no celebrations, not even muted ones. He wasn't done yet.

'Thank you,' he said at length.

'You're welcome,' she smiled back, wanting to reach out. In London she'd pictured them sharing a sunrise. Those images seemed immature now.

'I regret not involving Richie.'

'He'll forgive you.'

'He would have done a better job than me.'

'I don't believe that. You changed the frame on the painting. You bought us time, which is not on our side. I couldn't have done this without you, Bec.'

His praise washed over her, when she knew it shouldn't have done. She'd craved Tom Holt's approval for months, and now she had it, she felt guilty. She fingered the tender swelling around her ankle and winced. In the distance, on a flat ocean, the Predator was rounding the corner from Playa Cacique. It was almost light. Allowing Tom to help her up, she vowed to bring Richie back on side, and never to abandon him again.

Chapter 39

Panama City, Panama
20 February, 2017

'The lawyers are content,' her mother said over the phone. 'Ebdon has no grounds for defamation based on testimonial evidence. Clare Buchanan's statement is also date stamped. Everything is ready.'

Nash chewed her nails. It was half past midnight. She had taken to drinking rum and colas, using up Oliver Holt's seemingly endless stash of liquor. She'd even found half-empty bottles under the sink, three more open in the freezer. She paced, staring out of the kitchen through the darkness and into the window opposite, wondering what Tom and Becca were doing at that very moment. They had agreed that had they not returned by 10.30 a.m. the following morning, she was to pack up and head straight for the airport.

'I never thought when we got to this point that I'd be in another country,' Nash sighed.

'Having seen what they did to Miles, I couldn't be happier that you are in another country,' Di responded. 'What's Panama like?'

'Hot. I haven't seen much of it. Tell me the order of play.'

It was 6.30 a.m. in the UK. Di was in a hotel suite in

Marylebone with a security detail paid for by Insight News. 'One a.m. tomorrow we will alert the Met Police and provide a copy of the video statement. I'm waiting on confirmation of who it will go to exactly; we're still working on that. At the same time, I'm putting a personal call in to Clare Buchanan's mother; and I've got her sister's number as a back-up. I'll brief them as to what's going on. Two a.m. tomorrow we post the video, plus your copy and by-line, and we alert across the network, first to Reuters. It'll be our lead story on Tuesday when no one else will have it on the front page. We're expecting the morning news channels to lead with it, so we'll have a crew on standby near Ebdon's Mayfair property from the moment we tell the Met. I'm expecting broadcast trucks. He's in London; we've had two contractors on him this past week, my best guys. Right now, very few people are in the loop.'

Nash had checked. A Monday evening flight from Panama City on Copa Airlines would take off before the story would break in the UK. By the time she landed in Amsterdam it would be headline news. Her mother would be the one to handle the inevitable press. She would miss her big moment. She felt the familiar pangs of disappointment stir in the depths of her stomach; considered asking her mother to delay for twenty-four hours.

'Are you happy?' she heard her mother say.

Nash found herself forcing a grin, as she would have had her mother been physically present in the room. 'More than,' she replied. 'Have you seen Miles?'

'He's alright. I've got him redrafting some of the follow-ups.'

'Redrafting? What was wrong with my copy?'

'Don't get defensive. You have a habit of being too subjective in your approach. Admirable quality, but not impartial. But it's wonderful work. This story, once it breaks, is going to be huge.'

'What about the stuff on Anton Merrick? Will it fly?'

'Miles has tracked down a copy of his passport. Until we have proof, we can't name him as Clare Buchanan's killer. After Clare's video statement has been released, we'll follow-up with the video feed from the bus from the night she disappeared. We can name him, at least, which is more than the police could ever do. They'll have their prime suspect.'

'He won't be as easy to find as Ebdon. He lives in the shadows.'

'But we will have given the Met the tools to track him down. And if our source can get us the information you think he can…'

Nash swallowed the lump in her throat.

Her mother had carried on talking. 'What about the red-headed niece? Would she agree to speak on record?'

'Off the record, maybe, at a push. She's evasive.'

'What if we named her?'

'As what? An accomplice? She told me what she saw. She says she doesn't know who killed Clare.'

'And you believe her?'

At 7 a.m. Nash woke to the sound of keys in the front door lock, tongue stuck to the roof of her mouth. She lifted her head, blinking away sleep, realising she'd drifted off with her head in her arms on the surface of the kitchen table, fully dressed. Oliver Holt came in first carrying a backpack, followed by Tom carrying Becca Wylde in his arms. Nash got to her feet, the awkward angle of her sleeping position having caused her bones to seize up. Shaking off pins and needles in her arms, she followed the group down the corridor.

'What happened?' she blurted, looking to Oliver Holt. 'Did they manage to switch the paintings?'

Tom Holt's father gave a knowing smile, holding up the backpack.

'Are you serious?' Nash asked, drawing breath. 'Can I see it?'

Holt was calling her from the bedroom. He was lowering Becca down onto the mattress. Her arms were wrapped around his neck, yet another scowl on her face.

'It's done,' he said. 'I need you to take care of Becca's ankle. Get some ice on it. I need to call Miguel and deliver the painting to Aguinaldo, collect what's owed. When I return, we need to get the fuck out of Panama, all five of us.'

He was helping to prop Becca up against the pillows, cracks in the paintwork emerging from behind the headboard like lightning bolts. Becca's hair was matted and tangled. Nash glanced down at her swollen ankle, the skin taut and purplish.

'Is it broken?' she asked.

Becca glanced up, expression tense. 'Doesn't seem to be.'

'Does it hurt?'

'Like hell.'

'Then it's probably sprained.'

'What makes you the expert?'

'I'll get some ice to put on it.'

Nash followed Holt from the room, watching him pick up his phone and dial Miguel, his Panamanian contact who would enable the last pieces of the puzzle to fall into place. By the following morning, it would be common knowledge that Charlie Ebdon had fleeced thousands of Britons out of their hard-earned cash, keeping the money for his own profit, and that a woman who hadn't been seen for twelve years had risked everything on revealing his secret to the world. Nash wished she could have told Clare face to face that her efforts hadn't been for nothing at last. But it would never happen. Clare's blood was on Charlie Ebdon's hands.

In the kitchen she opened the freezer, removing an entire bag of ice that Oliver Holt kept for when he decided not to drink rum neat from the bottle and instead pour himself a glass. She listened to Tom's mumbled cryptic conversation that he was having over the phone, half in Spanish, half in English, arranging a meeting at a place called El Panama. At the same time she arranged a pile of ice on a cotton towel, wrapping it up and replacing the bag in the freezer.

Tom hung up.

'Are you good?' she asked.

He was fidgety, unable to look her in the eye. She noticed the traces of sand in his hairline.

'I'll be an hour, two tops. Pack your bag; when I get back we can make a move.'

'You think Aguinaldo is going to have the documents ready to hand over?'

He nodded once. 'Miguel seems to think so. Then they'll be all yours.'

Nash glanced down the corridor, sidled close to him,

lowering her voice. 'What's it gonna take for your girl to spill the beans on Anton Merrick?'

Tom followed her gaze. 'Number one, she's not my girl. Try talking to her. She's not the machine you seem to think she is. And let her brother in when he arrives. Number two, how about a thank you for a change?'

Nash pursed her lips. The words were there, but they didn't come.

'Where are you going to go with them?'

A smile tugged at his lips. 'I'll tell you when I get there. I'm getting a shower.'

Nash sat on the edge of the bed, feet curled under her, resting the towel on the side of Becca's foot, holding the now soggy material up against her inflamed ankle. She could see the beginnings of grey bruising underneath the skin. The bed sheets were wet from several rounds of melting ice, the rotary fan letting out a clicking sound as it circulated humid air around the room. Becca and her brother sat in silence, Becca pulling a face every time Nash moved the ice covered in the towel even a fraction. Richie Wylde had sloped into the apartment as Tom and Miguel were departing for Hotel El Panama, Oliver Holt muttering something about taking a nap, having spent an uncomfortable night trying to sleep upright on the deck of a boat.

'I looked up that *Evening Standard* article you mentioned,' Nash said, determined to warm them both up to even the bare minimum of conversation. Richie Wylde had looked like he wanted to cry from the moment he'd walked through the door. 'You didn't mention that your estimated haul over the years was almost half a million pounds in stolen cash and goods. That's not bad for a sleight of hand thief the Met Police can't identify.'

Becca was looking morose. Nash questioned whether their earlier conversation had struck a nerve.

'My total was nowhere close to Richie's.'

'Oh?' She looked to the boy. His neck flushed red under her stare.

'Becca never went to jail,' Richie shrugged. 'I guess that makes me the loser.'

'What did you do with all that money? I mean, you must have bought some fancy stuff, right? Gone to some nice places?'

There was a silence. The pair looked at her as though she'd spoken in a foreign tongue. Then Becca turned her head, embarrassed somehow.

'It all goes to our uncle,' Richie said. 'He's our only family.'

'Wouldn't you prefer to live a normal life? Not skulking around?'

'He took us out of school. Gave us to Anton to train,' Becca snapped. 'What else do you want to know?'

'I want to know where Anton came from. Where he fits into all this. Who is he?'

'He's originally from Azerbaijan. His mother was an Azeri prostitute.'

As Becca began speaking, Nash saw Richie shoot to his feet.

'And how did he end up in England?'

'Our uncle brought him. His father was a Nazi who fled Germany at the end of World War Two.'

'What Nazi? Do you have a name?'

Becca ignored her, 'Anton was trained when he was young. Under his father's orders, he was given to the Ebdon family as a gift. As someone they could use for their own ends.'

'Bec—' Richie began.

Becca shook her head at her brother. 'I'm not doing it anymore. Anton was in the car when mum and dad died.'

Nash watched them.

'Wait… what?' he murmured.

'I never even considered it,' Becca said to her brother, who lowered himself to the bed again. Becca reached for his hand. 'It makes perfect sense. They never understood the choices he made. All that money… they objected to all of it.'

Nash felt the urge to reach for her notebook in the satchel at her feet, throat constricting with an unfamiliar rush of guilt. When she looked to Becca, there were tears flooding the redhead's cheeks. Richie Wylde looked as though he might crumple.

'Bec—' he whispered again.

Nash got to her feet, feeling she ought to leave the pair of them alone. Becca had leaned over, wrapping Richie in an embrace, eyes squeezed shut.

Only a second later, the same eyes shot open, Becca's head tilting towards the bedroom door. Nash was reminded of a nature documentary, a fierce little ermine picking up on the scent of its prey.

Becca moved back from Richie, pressed a solitary finger against her lips.

Nash heard it then, a soft clicking sound coming from

the corridor, coming from behind the entrance door to the apartment.

'Get in the wardrobe,' Becca hissed at Nash after a moment, getting to her knees on the bed and pointing, in her expression an urgency that had obliterated any other emotion. 'Move. Don't make a sound.'

Fear crushed Nash's chest before a surge of adrenaline battered her heart into an explosive reaction. She lunged for the wardrobe, doing as she was ordered, darting into the narrow right-side compartment, ducking under the clothes rail, stumbling over some pairs of old shoes as she turned, her fingers catching between the door and the frame as she concealed herself inside, the gap left behind barely a couple of millimetres in width.

Nash found herself in darkness, Becca having disappeared from view. She could see only Richie hovering at the end of the bed, and questioned the frightened look on his face. Within seconds the room exploded, raised voices all talking at once, a pair of boots pounding against wood panelling, Becca's shrill tones drowned out by a deep Russian-sounding dialect. Nash found herself in darkness, Becca having disappeared from view. Still Richie hovered.

Anton.

Yet Richie Wylde didn't get to express a word before Nash witnessed a thin blade pierce his chest at the speed of an arrow, landing with a *whump*, a knife which she knew had to have been propelled from close range, a sleek, silver handle protruding from his chest at a perfect ninety-degree angle. Richie Wylde only had a fraction of a second to glance down, to witness blood gushing onto his T-shirt from the space between his ribs, before his eyes rolled back into his head and his legs went from under him, collapsing out of Nash's view, the thud of his soulless corpse hitting the floor. The elimination had taken all of three seconds.

Blood pounded in Nash's ears. Out of her thin field of vision, Becca's resulting scream was one of pain, the pain of loss, the same sound that had emerged from her heartbroken mother's throat on receiving the phone call from the British Embassy in Lagos confirming the killing of Ayo Akinyemi. She recognised that wail.

The screech that followed was different, a cry of physical pain, a howl. Nash could hear walloping footsteps that faded a fraction, Nash guessing towards the kitchen, perhaps Becca being dragged on a faulty ankle, unable to walk due to injury. Nash felt herself being engulfed by panic, biting her lip to prevent a vocal reaction, palms raised to cover her mouth. The shock sent a jolt up her back, almost causing her to lose her footing.

The voice she could hear sounded like it was speaking Russian, combined with a sprinkling of English, interspersed with Becca shouting for her release. In the kitchen, bottles were being smashed, plates thrown, landing against the cupboards. Then the screams were abruptly stifled and what followed was eerie quiet.

Nash felt tears sting her eyes. Once Becca was dead, Anton would surely find her and Oliver next.

She waited, her body refusing to move. Heard voices, Anton speaking in muffled tones.

Minutes later, when the wardrobe door twitched, Nash stiffened, a pair of eyes appearing wild in the narrow gap.

Oliver Holt's head loomed large outside the door, hair scruffy from a deep slumber. He eased the door open with his left hand. Nash stared aghast at Tom Holt's father, shirt hanging open, armed with an old revolver.

Keeping his gaze fixed out towards the kitchen, he backed up, placing a single finger against his lips before beckoning her out.

Nash shook her head. Becca Wylde and her brother weren't the only ones Anton was looking for.

Oliver held out a hand. Heart still thumping against her ribs, she stepped from the wardrobe down to the floor. Bending double, with smooth motions she lifted her satchel with its contents from the floor, allowing herself a glance down to the foot of the bed where Richie Wylde had fallen. Her face span away. His eyes had been still open, his T-shirt a sticky mass of blood, the blade emerging from his chest as though it were territorial marker. Wordlessly, Oliver took her hand, leading her with padded footsteps to the front door of the apartment. Nash's heart was somersaulting as she neared the kitchen. She could hear Anton speaking in low tones.

A chair scraped back across the floor up ahead. Nash tensed, grabbed Oliver's bicep through his shirt as he eased the latch open. They were sliding out of the front door together as she caught the sound of Becca's muffled cry, a scream trapped inside her throat.

Chapter 40

Panama City, Panama
20 March, 2017

From the passenger side window, Tom watched up ahead across the bay, palm trees lining the Cinta Costera merging into a green brown blur, contemplating how long it was going to take Oscar Aguinaldo to discover that the Francisco Goya hanging in his Isla Contadora holiday house was an abject fake. At the Hotel El Panama, Oscar's brother and rival had taken the original in between his palms and kissed it – actually placing his slobbering fat lips against the priceless canvas, calling on his heavies to get out and purchase crates of champagne, beer and rum, to round up some *mamacitas*, for there was a *fiesta* to be had. He had invited Tom and Miguel along, Tom turning him down in the most genial way possible, claiming he had to be on a plane out of Tocumen later that afternoon. He said nothing about his destination of Mexico City. Juan Carlos had shaken him by the hand, snapped his fingers for the file of information to be brought and handed over. Tom asked for confirmation that Oliver Holt had paid his debt. The Panamanian had shrugged, nodded once, as though nothing further would be mentioned on the topic. Miguel, wearing a pressed short-sleeved shirt, had remained quiet throughout, on departure Juan Carlos congratulating him for saving his own skin. As they left the hotel back towards El Cangrejo, Miguel said he thought that the business with the painting would spill over into a violent turf war.

'What about Camila? Is she safe?' Tom had asked.

Miguel had thrown him a puzzled look. 'You mean she didn't tell you?'

'Tell me what?'

'Juan Carlos Aguinaldo bankrolls her entire outfit. As an artist she makes next to nothing. Sure, she teaches, but it's not enough for her to scrape by financially. He's obsessed with her beauty, with her Venezuelan heritage. He pays for her studio in Casco and in return, she services his needs every now and then. So yes, she's safe, she has his protection. I'd say from now on she's going to need it.'

Miguel was in the driving seat, gliding between heaving lanes of traffic in the Camaro. Tom let his mind drift, picturing Camila with Juan Carlos, the idea almost making him gag. She had said nothing about her wealthy patron. Still, the thought made it easier to settle on a goodbye.

He felt his mobile phone vibrating in his pocket. Nash's initial flashed up. He wiped the sweat from his brow. The woman was impatient. He had the folder inside an envelope in his lap. He was keeping it sealed so they could open it together. She deserved to be the one to view the full contents, the additional information that would help bring Capricorn down. To bring Clare Buchanan some justice.

He swiped the screen to answer. Didn't even get to say a hello before he heard the sound of her rasping breaths. She was on the move, her tone frightened.

'He's here,' she said.

An explosion went off deep inside his gut. He didn't have to ask who she meant.

'How? Where?' Tom blurted, making eyes towards Miguel to drive faster. Miguel put his foot down, taking the corner towards Casco too quickly and narrowly missing two local women at a pedestrian crossing.

'He came to the apartment. Richie Wylde is… Your father got me out.'

'Where's Becca?' Tom demanded.

'She's still in there with him. He's torturing her, I know he is.'

Tom couldn't think straight, his vision blurry, questioning how Anton had managed to locate them.

'Do I call the police?' Nash said.

Police. It seemed like the logical thing to do. Yet police meant a lot of questions. He was in the country on a fake passport. Together with Becca, he had committed theft against one of the most powerful figures in Panama. He had to get Nash and his father out.

'No police. Not yet. I'll make that call. It's me he wants.'

'That's suicidal.'

'Where are you now?'

'We're moving… we're out on the street. I don't know where. I'm with your father.'

'Tell him to meet me in the lobby of the American Trade Hotel.'

'The American Trade. OK, he's nodding, we're going there now.'

'I'll be there in five minutes. Do you have your passport with you?'

'Yes, my passport, my laptop, my notes. I left everything else behind.'

'It's all you need to get home.'

He hung up. Miguel's shoulders were hunched. The car lurched to one side as it tackled the cobbled corners leading up to Casco Viejo at speed.

'Remember there are government guards here,' Miguel said, referring to the uniformed soldiers who manned the roads outside the Presidential Palace of the Herons.

'Miguel. Promise me one thing. That no matter what happens you will make sure my father leaves Panama.'

Miguel nodded once. 'It is done. What about you?'

He swallowed the tight knot in his throat. 'There's a chance I might not be leaving Panama at all.'

Miguel pulled up on the corner of Calle 9a Este and Avenida Central, causing three yellow taxis behind them to wildly blast their horns. Slamming the door, Tom made his way to the pavement, midday traffic snarling. The American Trade was one of the most attractive buildings in Panama City, an old colonial style white edifice with regal balconies and a terracotta roof; on the inside, art deco-inspired floor tiles with tropical leaves and macramé wall hangings. Tom entered the hotel on the restaurant side. He had agreed that Miguel would take the car back to the lot and meet him near the entrance to his father's building.

It was lunch-time and only a few tables were occupied. Tom kept his head down, clutching the papers given to him by Aguinaldo. He spotted Nash on the lower ground, near the reception desk, hugging her waist and staring from the floor-to-ceiling windows. His father, balanced on the edge of an art deco rocking chair, saw him first, giving him a nod.

'What happened?' he asked on approach.

His father shot up. He could tell Nash was trying to contain her distress, eyeing passers-by distrustfully as they went out of the door leading to Plaza Herrera.

'I was asleep,' Oliver said. 'Woke up with the commotion. I'm not sure how he got in.'

'We were in the bedroom,' Nash blurted, keep her voice as low as she could under the circumstances. She huddled closer. 'Becca told me to get inside the wardrobe, so I did. Tom, Richie Wylde, he's… Anton put a knife in his chest. He's dead.'

Tom reeled. 'What?'

Nash shook her head in disbelief. 'He's gone.'

'I recommend calling the police,' his father said. 'There is no choice. Where is Miguel?'

'Parking the car. He's going to meet me.'

Nash again. 'You're not seriously thinking about going back in there?'

'I have to go back. For Becca. It's me Anton wants. I can't leave her there alone with him.'

'He will kill you,' Nash hissed.

It was too late for them to try and change his mind. From the moment Becca had turned up in Panama, he had mentally equipped himself to see Anton again, as though the meeting had been preordained. He looked down at the Manila envelope in his arms, then back up at his father's weathered face. For a split second wondered if he would ever see that age.

He had done what he needed to. *You stand or you fall*, Anil Choudhury had once said to him, the same night he died. He realised it was a motto he was starting to live by.

'Take this,' he said to Nash, passing her the papers contained within the envelope. 'I hope it contains everything you need to blow a hole in Capricorn's armour.'

Nash took it, looked down at it, eyes brimming.

'You need to go. Go now, both of you. Dad, you need to leave. Get in a cab, go to the airport, get on a plane. Don't look back.'

'What are you going to do?'

'I'm going to go and get Becca; then I'll think about coming with you.'

It was a lie.

'What about Anton?' Nash asked.

'Let me handle, Anton. The moment you get back to London, take that to a safe place. Protect yourself. You will have a target on your back.'

'I already do,' she whispered.

Tom wrapped her in an embrace. He felt one arm go around to his back, the other pressing against his chest, clinging to the envelope.

'I need to give you something,' Oliver said.

Tom let go of Nash. 'What is it?'

'Not here.'

Oliver made eyes towards the door. Tom followed with Nash. Outside, his father moved close to the side of the building, working his way around to an alleyway which cut through from Plaza Herrera back towards Avenida Central. From the waistline of his trousers, concealed by the length of his shirt, he pulled the snub-nosed revolver. Tom glanced left and right, taking the weapon, checking the hammer wasn't cocked and there were bullets inside all the cylinder chambers. It wasn't the most practical of weapons to have thrust down your jeans, but given the choice of that or facing Anton unarmed, he knew what his preference would be. Backing himself closer to the wall, he slid the nickel barrel into his waistline, pulling down his shirt to conceal the grip.

'We can wait.' His father was nodding, grasping him by the shoulders.

Tom shook his head, the antidote to his father's optimistic suggestions. He needed to get moving.

'You need to go, Dad. I want you to be on that plane. Go back to London. Escort Nash as far as she needs.'

His father looked to the ground. 'You don't have to do this.'

Tom hugged his father, grateful that he'd had the opportunity to spend some time with the old man after all the absent years. Hoped that his brothers would get to do the same.

'I'll be alright,' he said, giving Nash's hand a squeeze. 'Good luck,' he said to her, slapping his father on the back. He turned and walked back out onto the flat red bricks that lined the roads of Plaza Herrera, back towards his father's apartment.

Back towards Becca.

Back towards Anton Merrick.

Back towards the unknown.

Chapter 41

Tom looked back at his father and Nash, watching him walking away. He refused to think about whether or not he might see either of them again.

For them, he would be all smiles. But the fire had been lit. Crossing Plaza Herrera – passing the bronze statue of General Tomas Herrera mounted on his stallion – the rage he felt surged up from his stomach, flooding his chest. He questioned whether Anton was alone, whether he had brought company in the form of two burly Argentines like the ones who had come after him in Chile. He considered how long Anton had known his location and whether Becca had unwittingly led him straight to them. Yet if Nash was right, the fact that Richie Wylde was now dead suggested that Becca had been telling the truth all along. She was the only thing Anton knew had the ability to lure him back. There would have been no point killing Becca without him present, because, without her, Anton would know that he would have bolted. There was no way Anton could have known about the exchange of information on Capricorn in exchange for robbing the Goya painting. Unless Becca had told him.

He winced, hating that he still had his doubts about her.

Was it all a trap, an elaborate plan to entice him in? Was Richie Wylde really dead?

Or had it been Nash? Had Anton followed her trail? If his father could get her to the airport, she would be safe, at least for the time being. Her mother was about to release Clare Buchanan's video into the public domain. Capricorn would have nowhere to hide. And soon, neither would Anton.

He passed Pedro Mandinga, the rum bar where he'd first discovered the location of his father, and thought about how hollow he had felt back then. Further down the Avenida he saw Miguel, lingering in the doorway to a coffee shop near his father's building, hands in his pockets.

'No one has come out,' Miguel said. 'Only the *empleada* who works on the floor above. She looked like everything was normal.'

Tom looked up. He could see the open kitchen window, a breeze whipping through the part of the closed curtain that had escaped outside. He hadn't asked his father how he and Nash had managed to escape.

'Do you want my help?' Miguel asked.

Tom didn't doubt that even as an older man, Miguel could handle himself. 'It's alright, I'll go alone.'

'Who is this man?'

Tom took a moment to compose himself. He didn't know what would greet him upstairs. 'Somebody you never want to meet.'

In the stairwell, outside the apartment door, he pulled the gun from his waistband and cocked it. He entered fast, jamming the key in the lock and twisting his body inside, weapon arm outstretched, swiping the key out of its slot again. He glanced left and right down the corridor. In his bedroom, he could see a pair of legs lying motionless on the floor, a pool of blood seeping out from underneath.

Richie Wylde's body.

His heart felt like it plummeted, like he should have sprinted back the moment he stepped out of the car. But he would have been unarmed. Tom edged towards the kitchen. Downstairs, traffic snarled down the narrow Avenida as the sense of fear pulsated in his ears. Through the doorway, the end of the kitchen table came into sight. Anton had pulled the curtains, the light dimmed. Becca sat alone, her right eye swollen, dried blood going crusty at her temple from a cut at her hairline, a strip of duct tape placed roughly over her mouth. Her cheeks were glistening wet, lifeless eyes staring forward. Her right arm had been placed flat on the surface of the table, one of his father's kitchen towels bundled around her hand. It, too, was covered in blood.

Tom's eyes shifted to the table surface. Next to the corner of the towel were placed two slender, curled-up fingers.

Human fingers. Becca's fingers.

Jesus.

Tom moved his weapon arm to the left, knowing there was only one other place in the room that Anton could be waiting.

When he saw him, Tom let out an unsteady breath. The Azeri was seated in one of his father's chairs, in front of him a kitchen knife, blood-covered and upright, piercing the surface of the wooden table. His hands were in his lap. He looked different than he had done in Argentina, though perhaps a fraction less menacing. His hair was cropped short. He wore black jeans and a fitted long-sleeved black polo shirt.

Tom stepped over the threshold, turned himself so he was stood opposite Anton.

'Guess I'm the one with a weapon this time,' Tom said.

Anton began a slow nod of acceptance.

'Becca?' Tom said, without looking at her.

He glanced right. Becca sat motionless, as though in a trance. He looked down at the two severed fingers; seemingly just the start of Anton's punishment.

'Are you alright?'

There was no answer. Tom kept the barrel of the revolver levelled on the Azeri. 'What have you given her?'

Anton took a moment to respond. 'She is in shock. Her brother is dead. She knows that I was the person responsible for taking her parents' lives.'

Tom swallowed. 'How did you find us?'

Anton withheld his reply.

'How?' Tom reiterated.

'Richie called me last night. I don't think he liked the attention she was giving to you.'

The gun had dipped. Tom raised it again, aiming it at Anton's crooked nose. 'How did you get here so quickly?'

'I was in Miami,' he said.

'What's in Miami?'

'None of your fucking business.'

He had expected a violent confrontation, not a cosy chat about the past around his father's kitchen table.

'Why kill her brother and not her?'

Anton stared at him. He had the heavy brow of a boxer. For a split second Tom found himself wondering at the type of upbringing the Azeri had had to turn him into a merciless killer.

'Before you came along she never questioned anything,' Anton said.

Tom cocked his head, weapon still raised. Had that been *jealousy* in the man's voice?

'You can't kill her because you care about her. That's right, isn't it? So you sliced off two fingers instead. It's a punishment she will be reminded of for the rest of her life. It'll remind her of you. That's what you want.'

He glanced over at Becca again, her gaze, fixed, and realised she was likely suffering from trauma. The slaughter of her brother followed by the agony of having two of her fingers sawn off with a blunt blade and without any form of anaesthesia had sent her over the edge. He knew he needed to bring her back, to have her present in the room. Behind the empty stare, she had retreated into survival mode.

Anton rose to his feet.

Tom didn't hesitate. 'Sit down.'

Anton held out his hands, palms up. The knife sticking out of the table was within reach.

'I said,' Tom repeated, placing two hands on the grip, 'sit down.'

'This ends one of two ways, Mr Holt,' Anton said. 'Either I walk out of here alive, or you do.'

Tom took a step forward. 'Do you like to gamble? I do, always have. And my *bet* is on the person with the firearm making out of here alive.'

Anton stood his ground.

'Didn't have anyone in Panama to organise you a gun, did you? Now sit the fuck back down in your chair.'

Tom counted to five in his head, his chest rising and falling. Neither flinched.

Tom glanced down at Becca's towel-covered hand. The amount of blood had increased, seeping through the now dark red material. His refocus, he realised, was enough to give Anton the advantage. Within a millisecond, Tom's opponent had ripped the knife tip from its resting place. Tom fired the Smith & Wesson revolver at Anton's chest, but the sound he heard was a different kind of explosion, not the deafening gunshot he had expected to hear. His father's gun had malfunctioned in his hand, pieces of hot shrapnel singeing his flesh. Tom swore in agony, tossing the weapon as Anton launched himself at him across the table, armed with the blade. Tom jumped back, allowing him a fraction of a second's grace, to plant a swift kick in Anton's torso. The Azeri brought down the knife, Tom blocking him, twisting his assailant's arm outward whilst at the same time launching his knee into his solar plexus. The knife flipped to the floor. Anton snarled, doubling down, landing a perfectly executed right uppercut into Tom's chin. His lip split, Tom felt the impact from his opponent's fist firing through his jaw, sending little lightning bolts into each of his individual teeth, his head thwacking back against the kitchen wall.

He saw spots, vision blurry. When Anton came at him again, it was messy; Tom going for the jugular, grabbing hard at Anton's throat, grappling with his other hand to gain control of the situation. Anton thrust back, fighting equally to gain the upper hand. Tom stamped down, bringing the power through to the ball of his foot, torpedoing Anton's shin, at the same time closing his fingers. Anton brought his arms in a circular motion, pulling back, then went low, going for a second uppercut, his moves almost graceful, the kind that came with training. Tom ducked, responding in kind with an uneven right hook, finding himself fast running out of energy. Before he knew it, he was in the air, his frame lifted by a great strength as his back cracked over one of his father's dilapidated wooden chairs, the wood frame flipping over. The pain in his burnt hand and in his back at an almost unbearable level, Tom let out a groan. Above him, he could see the light shimmering against Becca's hair. She hadn't moved, oblivious. He watched Anton swipe up the knife from the floor, Tom seeing the face of a man whose life had been defined by murder and mayhem. Had he been the one to take Clare Buchanan's life? However much he wanted him dead, wanted Becca to be free of him, Tom knew he wanted the world to know the name Anton Merrick, Solomon Capricorn's personal thug for hire, as badly.

Anton was stood over him. Tom witnessed him wipe his crooked nose on his sleeve, his mouth hanging open so he could draw breath, a trail of saliva glistening against his stubbled chin, chest rising and falling. Becca had said he didn't like to lose. 'I should have killed you in Argentina,' Anton snarled.

The knife was twirling in his hand. Tom tried to move, the muscles in his back tensed up and frozen. Blood pounded in his ears. On the walk over from Plaza Herrera he had come to terms with the fact that he might meet his death in Old Panama City. The only comfort he took was that Nash would release every piece of information he had given her into the public sphere, with any luck leading to the arrest and incarceration of Charles Ebdon. His only regret was that Becca might die with him, and that he hadn't been able to save her.

'So kill me,' Tom said. 'Kill me, you murdering motherfucking pig. And make it fast.'

Tom looked over. She hadn't stirred. The moment filled him with dread – that perhaps it was all another game and she had faked everything. That perhaps Anton hadn't cut off her fingers at all. That she didn't care if he lived or died. Yet he was left with a bizarre urge to say goodbye.

'Do it,' Tom hissed.

As Anton dipped his head, almost to prepare himself, still out of breath, something shifted in Tom's eyeline. A cry went up, Becca's left arm moving in a circular motion, the thin blade in her fingertips flashing against the sunlight as she buried it deep into Anton's ribcage.

For a moment, the room seemed to come to a standstill. Tom sat up, back on his feet in a half-second, grabbing a stunned Anton Merrick by the collar and propelling him backwards, driving him up against the opposite kitchen wall, wrapping his fingers around the blade and yanking it roughly back out from the point where it was lodged inside his chest. Anton blanched, his own blade clattering to the tiled floor. Becca backed away, the look in Anton's eyes one of disbelief. Tom pressed the blade up against his assailant's throat. He had seen reactions to punctured lungs before, only that time had been in a war zone and the men suffering had been his comrades.

'Who killed Clare Buchanan?' Tom demanded. Anton tried to look down, his breathing turning shallow, his skin taking on a greyish-blue tincture, the lower half of his polo shirt awash with blood.

His body slipped, head lolling. Tom held on to him by his clothes, his own breathing laboured, yanking him back up so that he could see his face.

'I said, who killed Clare Buchanan? Tell me.'

Anton raised his eyes. 'Fuck you,' he managed.

'These are your dying words. Use them wisely. Did you take her life?'

'No.'

'Then who?'

Anton was looking past him, towards Becca. There was a longing there, perhaps for a different kind of life: to be a different kind of man. Tom looked over his shoulder. Becca had collapsed to the floor, back against the lower cupboards, legs outstretched, the same vacant stare, blind to Anton's plight.

'Cap–,' Anton began, before blood came gushing of out of his mouth in a splutter, spraying against the fabric of Tom's shirt. Tom let go, stepped back, watching the Azeri's body slump to the floor, the light in his eyes gone for ever.

Chapter 42

London, England
24 March, 2017

It happened the way her mother had said it would. Clare Buchanan's video statement had been sent to the Metropolitan Police as she was taking off on an evening KLM Airlines flight from Panama City bound for Amsterdam. Over the North Atlantic, Nash had used the plane's Wi-Fi to watch as the story went live on the Insight News website. Two hours before landing at Schiphol Airport, the exposé was already gaining traction: Clare Buchanan's family had released a strongly worded statement that they expected the case to be reopened and re-examined by the Metropolitan Police. She waited for news of Ebdon's arrest.

The moment the wheels touched the runway in Amsterdam, Nash called her mother.

'It looks like he's gone and done a bloody runner,' Diane said, peeved.

Nash felt a bubble of disappointment burst inside her chest. They had waited too long, and allowed Ebdon to plan an exodus. He had left his wife and family, disappearing into the night. The coward.

'When was the last time he was seen by anyone?' she had asked, following the signs for airline transfers.

'Apparently Ebdon told his wife he was going to be out all day yesterday on business. But he didn't come home in the evening and his phone had been switched off. The UK Border Agency has been put on high alert. I've heard the Met are pulling out all the stops.'

'What about the bus CCTV footage and Anton?'

'We're moving forward and releasing the story tonight. I'm briefing Clare's family again later this afternoon. I went through our investigation and gave them a breakdown of what we know. They're livid with the police, as well as being in shock. I have it on good authority that the Met are furious we're in touch with them.'

At West India Quay, near the desks now vacated by the accounts team by order of the boss, Nash hovered beside the vending machine. Despite the hunger pangs, she couldn't bring herself to eat. She had barely swallowed a morsel since the E-fit of Anton Merrick had appeared on the news and all the front pages, wanted for questioning in connection with the disappearance of Clare Buchanan in 2005. Soon after, a security guard at a residential block of flats in Elephant and Castle had contacted the police, claiming that Anton was resident in the building, producing a wealth of CCTV footage of him coming and going. There was no mistaking it was him. The police had raided his flat.

Anton Vasily Moroshkin. Born 1973 in Baku, Azerbaijan. A Home Office document had been able to verify his original identity, on a passport from the Czech Republic. There was now an investigation into how he had managed to change his name to Anton Merrick on an official passport, when there had been no record of a name change recorded at the Deed Poll Office. People weren't talking about Charles Ebdon anymore. They were talking about Solomon Capricorn, and what kind of reach he could have had into the corridors of British officialdom. Nash inserted a coin into the vending machine, purchased a bottle of cola. It would keep her going into the small hours. Her job was now leading a team of young journalists and interns drafted in to work on the Buchanan case. Her mother had given her the choice of people, and most had volunteered their services. At one end of a bank of desks, Miles – whose brush with death had brought him a heap of attention from the opposite sex – was leading on the investigation into the documents Tom had handed her in Panama. It was right up his street: going after offshore accounts and investments, money trails and suspect bank accounts. He had coined them 'The Zodiac Papers' after Capricorn's horoscope-themed alias.

The lawyer's name cropped up a lot, too: Albert Denham, seemingly Ebdon's chief bagman, until he'd been bumped off. The police were reopening that case, too. Nash had wondered if Denham's first wife Belinda had opened her letter yet, and what information it had contained. The demand for copy was increasing every day. Clare Buchanan's face was back on the front pages.

In Nash's mind, there was only one question remaining. Who had killed her?

Had it been Anton? Or Capricorn himself?

Moving back from the vending machine, Nash reclaimed her seat and stared once more at her laptop screen, listening to the chatter of the interns and journalists around her. Around them the TVs were tuned to different twenty-four-hour UK news channels. Miles looked up from his own computer and caught her eye, granting her a smile. She felt grateful to have him there.

On landing in Amsterdam she had sent a message to Tom, asking for an update, checking whether he and Becca were alright. Forty-eight hours later he had finally sent a response:

All OK
In Costa Rica with B
A won't be a problem anymore

The message had troubled her. Anton *wouldn't be a problem?* Did that mean he was dead? If he was, then part of her was pleased, yet another part of her was left frustrated because of the secrets that would have died with him. Had he been responsible for Clare Buchanan's death, then there would be no one to stand trial. Tom had switched off his phone again and wasn't answering her questions. The man from the double-decker bus CCTV from 2005 – the person the Met had once upon a time been attempting to identify, and the individual responsible for snatching Clare Buchanan – who'd had his name and photograph released into the public arena, now looked to be gone. A dead suspect lessened the impact of her story greatly. And she questioned how was she even supposed to begin to report what had taken place in Panama City, the place he had last been seen alive. She was yet to tell Miles or her mother exactly what she knew.

She watched Miles get up from his seat and walk over, clutching his empty coffee mug. He was wearing his black

Nirvana T-shirt that had been washed so many times it was misshapen, yet it suited him.

'How are you doing?' he asked, pushing the hair from his eyes. 'Have you had lunch yet?'

Nash opened her mouth to respond, but there was a commotion behind her as a member of the team shot to her feet.

'Nash!' she blurted, waving her mobile phone.

Nash swivelled around in her chair. 'What is it?'

'The Met's going to give a press briefing at 3 p.m. Outside Scotland Yard. There's been a development in the Buchanan case.'

'Did they say what development? Did they find Ebdon?'

'No word yet.'

Nash looked to Miles. Behind his glasses, his eyes had lit up. 'Come with me.'

Nash moved to the front of the press crowd gathered underneath the revolving triangular sign outside New Scotland Yard on Victoria Embankment, Miles close on her tail. They were surrounded by broadcast vans, a sea of cabling snaking under their feet. On arrival, the group – roughly thirty sleep-starved, ambitious reporters, all with too high levels of cholesterol – let them pass, knowing the pair were the reason they were all present. Nash took in the faces. A few months earlier, none of the journalists or cameramen present would even have had the first clue as to her name, only that she was the daughter of Diane Cambridge. Now at least they were looking past the accusations of nepotism and paying attention, each giving her a nod of acknowledgement as she and Miles passed them by.

The moment the Met's uniformed spokesperson stepped from the Police Headquarters, phones and microphones were raised high. The name on his white shirt read 'Dunwoody'. Nash swiped her phone screen and started recording. She glanced across at Miles doing the same and felt her pulse quicken, expecting a statement on the whereabouts of Ebdon, or that they had made an arrest, possibly overseas. There had been zero information coming out over the wires and her mother was already putting pressure on all her high-level contacts.

'I am here this afternoon,' the spokesman began, clearing his throat, 'to deliver a statement in connection with the disappearance of Clare Buchanan in 2005. I can confirm that Miss Buchanan's family has been fully briefed and I will be able to take a few questions at the end.

'Following recent press activity, I can confirm that the investigation into the death of Clare Buchanan, who disappeared from a London street on the twenty-first of February in 2005, has been officially reactivated and new detectives have been assigned to the case. In addition, three days ago, on the twenty-first of March, the Metropolitan Police Service was in receipt of a package couriered from the United States of America. This package contained two items. The first was a letter, addressed to officers at New Scotland Yard. The second was an item of clothing, sealed in transparent plastic. I can confirm today that the letter was from an individual named Albert Denham, who we now know to have been an associate of Charles Ebdon, the latter of whom you all know is wanted for questioning in this matter. The handwriting has now been verified. I can also confirm today that Albert Denham was attacked and subsequently died in

London on the night of Sunday the thirteenth of November, 2016.

'In his letter, Mr Denham claims that the item of clothing contained within was the green-coloured trench coat that Clare Buchanan was wearing the night she disappeared, saved by him on the night of her murder. DNA tests are now being conducted as a matter of urgency on the coat.'

Nash almost dropped her phone. A ripple went through the crowd, cameras flashing.

'At the request of Clare's family, the full contents of the letter will be released publicly following this press conference. The letter claims that Clare Buchanan was murdered on the night of the twenty-first of February, 2005, the same night she was last seen alive. Detectives from the Metropolitan Police will be naming individuals who they would like to speak to in connection with their enquiries. In addition to Charles Ebdon and Anton Merrick, these will include an individual named Jonas Vázquez, a Spanish citizen, who we believe was in the UK at the time of Clare Buchanan's disappearance. Further information will be released in due course. I can now take one or two questions.'

A swathe of excitable voices surged all at once. The spokesman waited a few moments for calm before a reporter from the *Telegraph* was singled out.

'What was the origin of this letter and how has it been sent after Albert Denham's death?'

'More information on that will follow. We can confirm it was dispatched from a solicitor's office in Miami, Florida. We are looking into why and how it was sent.'

Dunwoody's assistant made eyes at Nash.

Nash raised her voice. 'Does Denham claim to know who killed Clare Buchanan?'

'As I said, the full contents of the letter will be released in the next hour. There are persons of interest wanted for questioning at this time.'

Dunwoody took one further question before bringing the brief press conference to a close. Over the hubbub, Nash tried to take in everything that had been read out in the statement, looking urgently towards Miles.

'Talk about the bolt from the blue,' he breathed.

Nash's mind was ticking. Something, or *someone*, had triggered the sending of Denham's letter, from a law firm in Miami, after his death. Denham's connection to Florida: his first wife, to whom he had left a house in his last will and testament.

'What?' Miles was saying to her, reading her expression. 'What is it?'

'I think Belinda Channing finally opened the letter from her first husband.'

'She did?'

A pulse of excitement rattled through Nash's chest.

Somehow, Albert Denham had kept hold of Clare's trench coat. Even in death, he was exacting his revenge on the men who had screwed him over. Nash wondered how quickly she could track down Belinda Channing, before the rest of the press pack cottoned on to her existence.

'We need to be getting back,' she said to Miles, seeing that her mother was already calling her, every journalist around her already on his or her phone. The story kept on spiralling, and showed no signs of slowing down. 'It's going to be a long night.'

Chapter 43

Panama
22 March, 2017

Becca stirred, sensing pressure against her shoulder. The dream she'd been having wilted away to a black void. She tried to cling on to it. Opening her eyes, she squinted into the orange sunlight filtering through the smeared passenger side window of the car. She noted that the engine wasn't running.

Then it hit her again.

Richie was dead.

So was Anton.

Her stomach clenched, intestines coiled tight. She felt warm saliva charge her mouth, panic overwhelming her senses, as though she was still back in the kitchen. Grabbing at the handle, she elbowed the car door open, dry-heaving onto the edge of the cracked road surface.

After a moment, she felt a hand at her back: Tom's.

She couldn't look at him, tears threatening to breach the edges of her eyelids for another round of ugly sobbing. Life had always had its cruelties, but to witness a blade landing in Richie's chest, killing him, had crushed what remained of her soul.

In the car, after several moments had passed, she leaned back into her seat, pulling the door to, taking in her surroundings and wiping a line of drool from her cheek. Up ahead, through the windscreen, was a goliath building with a corrugated roof, the early morning sky tinged a shade of candy floss pink.

When she spoke, her voice was hoarse. 'Where are we?'

'This is Paso Canoas,' Tom said. 'We're at the border.'

Becca blinked. On the other side of the building was Costa Rica.

'What time is it?'

'Ten past six.'

'How long was I out for?'

She remembered a petrol station, taking a loo break in a bathroom that smelled strongly of urine and smoked weed; Tom encouraging her to drink some water if she wasn't going to eat anything.

'We arrived here around 10 p.m. You were already asleep so I didn't wake you.'

She didn't respond. They had spent the previous night in Miguel's apartment, exhausted and drained. They had left Panama City the next day around lunch-time in Oliver Holt's Camaro, leaving Miguel to deal with the two dead bodies inside the apartment.

Crossing over high above the canal, heading west over a road bridge, Tom at the wheel, it felt strangely reminiscent of leaving Anil behind in the house in Uruguay five months earlier, a bullet lodged in his brain, only this time, the people she had left behind were the only world she had ever known.

'To get across we have to go inside to immigration,' Tom was saying, nodding through the car windscreen. His words were gentle, almost distant. 'You're going to have to keep your hand inside your pocket,' he added.

She glanced down. The moment he said the words she remembered the throb. Blood had seeped through the gauze that was now wrapped around the space where her two fingers had once been, the stain more brown than red. Underneath were two open wounds, pulsating at the points at which the bones had been severed.

She allowed her eyes to slip shut again, recalling the moment her knife blade had pierced Anton's chest, the fingers on her left hand letting go of the handle, leaving it lodged inside his lung. She remembered him staring down at the object protruding from between his ribs in disbelief. When he'd finally raised his eyes to her, there was a sad quality to them: a look she barely recognised in him. Tom had slammed him against the wall until Anton's knees gave out from under him and he had slid to the floor, coughing up blood, gone in a matter of seconds, the man who had taught her everything. Yet, growing up, he had drawn the line at showing her how to take a life.

Anton Merrick had been her first kill.

She felt numb. The events that followed were jumbled, hazy, Tom on his feet, holding her, urging her to come back to life. Her thrusting him away and stumbling down the corridor, to Richie, to another wail trapped in her throat. Blood had pooled around his body on the floorboards; the bottom of her boots drenched in it. She had attempted resuscitation, yet Tom had once more held her back, containing her wrestling that had seen her hammering her fists against his chest. Then the sobs had started, soaking the front of Tom's shirt, her body trembling. One glance down and she knew by the appearance of Richie's skin, the pallid, grey cheeks and sunken eyes, that he was not coming back, that the time she might have been able to save him had passed.

She remembered asking what would happen to Richie. She'd never received an answer. In the car, she wasn't sure she wanted one. The guilt of abandoning him sat in a leaden stomach. She knew it would never leave.

At the border, inside the immigration building, the Panamanian official gave them a suspicious once-over through the glass at the counter. Becca glanced over at Tom, face haggard, shirt crumpled, a split, fat lip. The official gave them exit stamps. Judging by his glower, had they been coming the other way, Becca thought it might have been a different story. As it was, he seemed content enough to hand them over to be Costa Rica's problem.

Returning to the car, Tom started the engine.

'Where do we go from here?' she asked.

Tom waited, looked towards the immigration building and the road that crossed over on to the other side.

'This is the Pan-American Highway,' he said. 'If we stay on this road it will take us all the way to Mexico.'

Becca glanced down, slowly patting down her pockets with her good hand. Lifting her hips and reaching inside, she pulled out the key she had stolen from Anton's flat, still on her person.

'It's your choice,' Tom said, reaching over and squeezing her wrist. 'So long as we leave Panama.'

The guilt simmered inside her chest, its fiery tendrils

within reach of her heart. Leaving Panama meant leaving Richie for good, the notion that she would never see her brother again causing her bottom lip to quake once more.

'We keep going,' she whispered, the dam breaking, tears gushing forth.

Tom reached for her good hand. She looked down; salt water splashing down onto his scratched and bruised knuckles.

When she looked back at him, he gave her a single nod.

Becca nodded back, wiping her cheeks, grateful not to be alone.

Chapter 44

Guatemala City, Guatemala
27 March, 2017

The Hotel Sinaloa set them back a hundred and fifty-five quetzales, or approximately twenty dollars, for a single night. It was basic but would do the job. Once they had been handed the keys, Becca had crawled into one of the single beds, curling into a foetal position, closing her eyes, without bothering to shower or to sample any food. Since leaving Panama, she had barely eaten, in five days the lack of sustenance starting to show on her already delicate frame.

Tom sat on the edge of the bed, elbows resting on his knees, watching her breathe in and out. A dim evening light shone through the set of red block-striped net curtains, her auburn hair flat against the fabric of the pillow. He'd never known her level of pain, the agony of losing a loved one, a younger sibling at that. She'd been made an orphan and now she had no one. For Becca, sleep seemed to be the only way she could shut down the pain at its source, from deep within.

In Uvita, on the Pacific Coast of Costa Rica, they had bribed a local pharmacist for some antibiotics to treat Becca's wounds. He'd used the wad of US *dolares* thrust upon him by Miguel before they had departed Panama City in his father's Camaro. The rest he had spent on fast food and petrol. At the

Sinaloa, Becca asleep, he had ventured out, purchasing the cheapest second hand android phone he could find, together with some fast food.

Inserting the local SIM card, he logged on to the hotel's Wi-Fi, scrolling through the British news headlines, a solid lump lodged in the base of his throat.

He stopped scrolling.

Ebdon had fled the UK, or so it was believed. He had disappeared into the night almost a week earlier, leaving his wife and daughters behind.

So now Capricorn was the one running.

The news was flooded with articles about Ebdon, Anton, and, to his surprise, Albert Denham, all of them in the context of the missing Clare Buchanan. Speculation was rife. The case had been reopened. Denham had sent a letter from the grave.

It took him an hour to get through them all. He saw no mention of his name. Becca and Richie weren't featured. Nash hadn't gone that far. Not yet.

The question loomed large in the press: *Who Killed Clare Buchanan?*

Denham's letter named three possible culprits: Ebdon, Anton, and a third man, Jonas Vázquez, a Spaniard, the name he had heard on Becca's lips. There was a picture of him, a grainy passport photograph.

So had Denham been trying to cleanse his sins?

He glanced over at Becca. She hadn't stirred.

Tom took the key and went back downstairs. There were bars, painted a marine blue, lining a corridor leading to the lobby. 'Despacito' played over a set of shoddy speakers. Tom used the hotel Wi-Fi to dial Miguel via WhatsApp.

'Where are you?' asked the Panamanian.

'Leaving Panama for dust.'

Miguel didn't understand him.

'Have you heard from my father? Did he make it to England?'

Miguel tutted. 'You know Oliver Holt. He may like those old French books but he prefers the Latin lifestyle.'

Tom winced. 'Please tell me he left.'

'He left. He went to Puerto Rico. Think he's set on the Virgin Islands.'

Tom closed his eyes, wiping the sweat from the back of his neck. It did not come as a surprise. 'I wish him luck. Maybe he should find a rich wife to pay for that Caribbean lifestyle.'

There was a silence.

'Did you do as we agreed?' Tom asked.

'Relax, my friend. It is done.'

'Where?'

'Lake Gatún. On the Colón side. I weighted both of them down; the fish will see to them. The apartment is going up for sale. I'll wire any profits to your father. You know that guy had a Walkman in his pocket? Remember those? I'm going to keep it to show my grandkids.'

Tom thanked him, bid him a grateful farewell. He thought it unlikely they would see one another again. As for the bodies, he vowed to tell Becca only if she asked for the whereabouts of her brother's final resting place.

Becca was awake when he returned to the room, digging into the now cold burger he'd left out for her. She looked up, licking her fingertips.

409

'Are you alright?' he asked.

Becca nodded. 'Thank you for the food.'

He showed her the phone, the latest headline from the UK. Becca took the handset, scrolled through the text of the article, engrossed.

When she was done, she handed it back, still eating. Tom lowered himself to the bed.

'Tell me more about Jonas Vázquez,' he said. 'Tell me what you refused to tell Nash.'

Becca swallowed. 'He's a business associate of my uncle. I've not met him. Their ties go back a while. Jonas is related to Anton. They're half-brothers. Jonas hated Anton.'

'Why?'

'They share a father. But Anton's mother was a foreign whore. Jonas thought he should have been tossed away. Not saved and presented to my uncle's family as a gift. As someone who could solve their problems. Jonas thought he was vermin.'

'The newspapers are saying he's from Spain.'

'That's what he'd like them to think,' Becca said.

'Do you know where your uncle might have gone?'

She was quiet for a moment. 'I have some idea, yes.'

'Where?'

'Jonas lives in Buenos Aires. If anybody's hiding him, it'll be Jonas and his family.'

Tom puffed out his cheeks. He didn't want to probe further, at least not yet. Not whilst she was hurting. He still didn't know what they were going to find in Mexico.

He nodded towards the bandage on her hand. She would need some fresh dressings before they set out on the next leg of their journey.

'Do they still hurt?' he asked.

'Not as much,' Becca replied. 'I've decided I don't think I'll miss them.'

He frowned. 'What do you mean?'

'My fingers,' Becca shrugged. 'I don't need them. I'm left-handed.'

'You're left-handed? I hadn't noticed.'

The colour was returning to her cheeks. She seemed more like herself again. Tom felt glad that she wasn't in England, where the press could find her.

'Neither did Anton,' Becca said, placing the last of the burger in her mouth.

He pocketed the phone, walked to the en-suite bathroom, switched on the tap and splashed his face.

'What now?' Tom asked over the sound of the running water, reaching for a towel. 'I mean, after Mexico, what then?'

He thought he heard her say something, couldn't decipher it. When he switched off the tap he glanced back at her. She was sitting up on the bed, alert, as though food had given her a new lease of life.

He wiped his face. 'I didn't hear what you said.'

Becca looked his way, her eyes no longer brimming with remorse. He found different emotions there. Anger and determination.

'I said I'm going to kill my uncle,' she replied. 'And you're going to help me do it.'

Acknowledgements

I have to start by thanking anyone who read *Intruders*, and who decided to pick up *Evaders* as a result. It means the world to me that you have chosen to do so.

To the team at RedDoor Press: Heather Boisseau, Clare Christian, Lizzie Lewis and Anna Burtt, I am greatly indebted to you all. Thank you for choosing to work with me again, and continuing to make my dreams come true.

To Paul Bennett, grateful thanks for your help in shaping the manuscript, for your honesty, the extra commas, and reminding me that I am not so good on the light relief!

To Laura Gerrard, a huge thank you for your outstanding work and your impeccable attention to detail.

To Tim Barber at Dissect Designs, a heartfelt thank you for the incredible covers, both for *Intruders* and for *Evaders*. I could not be more pleased with both.

To Jen Parker at Fuzzy Flamingo, a special thank you for making what is inside the cover look so stunning.

A big thank you to my fellow authors for the support; Penny Batchelor, A. A. Chaudhuri, Cat Walker, Amanda Weinberg, Adam Hamdy, Bryony Mathew, to name but a few. To all the talented writers from my Faber Academy course, I hope to be able to meet you all in person one day and share a bottle or two of wine.

Thank you to Surjit Parekh for not only championing my books across social media but also for your amazing support.

Thank you to my husband, Paul, for not minding when I abandoned you to Netflix every evening to work on my novel.

And lastly, *muchas gracias* to the whole gang at the British Embassy, Panama City, and to the friends that I made whilst living in wonderful Panamá. I miss you guys. *Abrazos*.

www.thrillerwomen.co.uk

Also by E.C. Scullion

'A tense, twisting, international thriller.
Deftly written and engrossing'
Adam Hamdy

E. C. SCULLION
INTRUDERS

BREAKING IN IS ONLY THE BEGINNING

Chapter 1

Monday 4 July, 2016. 10 a.m.

'My client would expect you to commit a crime,' the lawyer with unruly eyebrows, who called himself Albert Denham, said, 'and under no circumstances get caught doing it.'

There was a silence. Tom Holt swallowed the brittle lump in his throat.

'I don't expect an answer right away,' the lawyer continued, leaning forward and placing his now empty coffee cup on the surface of the table. 'But I have a team waiting in Buenos Aires who require some direction.'

Denham got to his feet. Tom followed, rising from his sofa, shaking Denham's hulking hand when it was offered.

'Perhaps you could show me out,' the lawyer said.

Tom followed him on the stairs to street level. In the hallway, he opened the door. The driver of the BMW Denham had arrived in had returned and now parked kerb-side.

'I just have one question,' Tom managed. 'Why me?'

Denham pushed his hands further into his pockets. He'd worn an overcoat even in the July heat. 'Because on paper it seems that no one would miss you,' he said. 'And it is my opinion that you care little for anyone but yourself. My number is on my card.'

The lawyer left without giving him a backward glance.

Tom closed the door, retreating to his flat, allowing the events of the previous thirty minutes to wash over him.

Albert Denham had arrived without fanfare at 09.35. Before the shriek of the doorbell had echoed through his North London flat, Tom had been standing beside the Venetian blinds, wearing the previous day's underwear and three-day-old stubble. The foul, meaty stench drifting past his nostrils had been that of his own body odour. From his vantage point, he had watched the silver BMW estate pull up. For forty minutes, no one got in or out.

He had felt it in his gut. He was being watched.

In the living room, dim light emanated from his laptop. On the screen was Roxy Palace Online Casino; one of three online gambling sites he'd frequented since his dismissal. The sofa cushions, like memory foam, had still been in the shape of his vegetative self, definition enhanced by a line of toast crumbs.

He had let go of the slats, showered and shaved. Within fifteen minutes he was back in his living room wearing only a towel, peering outside.

The BMW was still parked.

When the lawyer finally emerged, glancing up at the window, Tom let go of the blind a fraction of a second too late.

He'd had time to pull on jeans and a shirt from the wardrobe, his frame slender for six foot two, and check that his sand-blonde hair wasn't doing anything wacky.

Denham was tall, barrel-chested, with dark, slicked-back hair. From the looks of it he was fifty or thereabouts. He had deep frown lines, chasms in his forehead that spoke of untold years of stress, or that he'd seen a thing or two. No one with a happy life had lines like that.

'Can I help you?' Tom had asked, voice still hoarse from the two-thirds' bottle of Rioja he had polished off the previous evening.

The lawyer introduced himself, handing over a business card containing a name, job title and a contact phone number.

'What is it you want to talk to me about?'

'I have a job offer to discuss.'

'How did you find me?'

'My client came to me with your name. I was given your address.'

'Who's your client?'

'I'm afraid I'm not at liberty to disclose that information. My client is a powerful man. He would like to keep this discreet.'

Curiosity got the better of him.

'Well you'd better come in then,' he had said.

The lawyer Denham had a prior knowledge of things. He had known Tom was ex-military, completing two tours in Helmand in '06 and '07. Knew his date of birth: 6th of February 1976. Knew he wasn't married, nor currently in a relationship. He had even known about his parents' divorce when Tom was eleven, Oliver Holt walking out on his mother, taking with him only a backpack and a bottle of rum. He'd known about South Africa, though Tom acknowledged that that part of his history wouldn't have been so hard to unearth. The story had featured in the Cape Town local press five months earlier, concerning his dismissal from Vlok

Petersen and Associates after having been caught gambling company funds at the Grand West Casino, something he had managed to do for weeks without detection.

The lawyer knew about Eden: eight months prior still calling herself his fiancée, the oldest daughter of Hendrick, his immediate boss. Eden Van de Vlok, whose pleas to her father had been the sole reason he hadn't pressed criminal charges.

He paced, kept the blinds closed, wiped the sweat from his upper lip, going over in his mind what he could recall from the conversation.

'I know that you and Mr Van de Vlok have come up with a system of repayment for his lost assets,' Denham had said, 'one that will probably cripple you financially for the next twenty years.'

He hadn't denied it. The arrangement he and Van de Vlok had made was substantial on his part, a form of punishment for the upset he had caused both to Hendrick's family and business.

'I understand you can speak Spanish,' Denham had said.

'I studied Spanish at university. Completed a placement in South America.'

'Where in South America?'

'Mendoza, Argentina. Six months with a homestay family.'

'Have you ever been to Uruguay?'

'Uruguay? No.'

'Do you know anything about Uruguay?'

He had given a shrug. 'The Argies like to spend their summers there on account of the better beaches.'

'So you know what a *Barrio Privado* is?'

'It's a private neighbourhood. A gated community.'

Denham had gulped the coffee Tom had made him. 'The job you did for Hendrick Van de Vlok, tell me about it.'

'I was a consultant, Hendrick's deputy. Our business was badged as secure living. We devised housing communities based around high security, secure compounds, implementing security measures to protect domestic properties, that sort of thing. One in ten South Africans will still choose a house in a gated community given the choice.'

'So you know all about the systems people put in place; locks, fences, CCTV, that sort of thing. The things that are supposed to keep other people… out.'

Tom gave a nod.

'Why did Van de Vlok give you the job in the first place?'

'He thought I had the right background. Thought he could train me up. He liked army men. He liked Brits.'

'He just didn't know you were a gambler. In more ways than one.'

The coffee Tom had been drinking tasted bitter at the back of his throat. The story of his dismissal wasn't a topic he had been fond of sharing with the world outside his flat.

'Why didn't you stay in the army?'

He had sat back into the cushions, brain flooded with so many different memories. 'My commanding officer believed I could lead, and that I'd make a sound colonel one day. If only I hadn't enjoyed spending time playing cards with the soldiers. We came to the mutual decision that it was better if I moved on.'

'My client came to me with your name,' Denham said. 'He

likes to keep a close-knit circle of trusted individuals who work for him. He needs someone he can trust to lead a small team.'

Tom had waited for more. It had not been forthcoming. 'To do what exactly?'

'We would expect you to sign a non-disclosure agreement to cover the duration of the project,' Denham continued unabated. 'You would be handsomely rewarded, if successful.'

'And if unsuccessful?'

'You would still be adequately compensated for your time and effort.'

He had searched Denham's features for any sign he might be lying, quelling the momentary rush of exhilaration in his chest. 'This job, is it legal?'

'Technically, no.'

'And you would expect me to travel to where... to Uruguay?'

'The team is currently based in Buenos Aires, but yes. To Montevideo, the capital of Uruguay.'

'This team... who are they? Are they British?'

'Yes, all of them.'

There was another silence before he had asked the question, a hot lump already forming in his throat, unsure of his precise reaction if Denham were to confirm his suspicions.

'And we are to commit a crime?'

*****

He sat facing Denham on the other side of a chintzy-looking desk in Butler's Wharf on the south side of the Thames, brick walls painted off-white. It was an office of sorts, above a flower shop with partial views of Tower Bridge, a room with a vaulted ceiling and iron rod supports. He'd worn a suit, no tie. Two chairs, upholstered in a dirty shade of brown tweed, both equally moth-eaten, had been placed opposite one another. A large metal filing cabinet dated back to the seventies, the entire place thrown together as if Denham had looted his childhood family home.

He had said no to Denham. Had avoided one jail sentence in South Africa and wasn't of a mind to set himself up for another. He had sat on his sofa, staring at his iPhone with its abandoned WhatsApp chat groups – *so-and-so has left* – wondering if he had made the most colossal mistake.

At 7 p.m., the same phone started to ring.

'I spoke to my client,' Denham had said. 'If you accept the terms of our employment, he has offered to clear your debt to Hendrick Van de Vlok… in its entirety.'

He had capitulated, perhaps more quickly than he should have. Three hefty lump sums would be paid into the account of Hendrick Van de Vlok of Cape Town, South Africa, from a London-based lawyer over the following three months. He would be free. The South American angle had heavily influenced his decision. The allure of the place was strong, given everything he had left behind. His Spanish was rusty but still buried in the recesses of his mind. *Only a criminal if you get caught*, he had told himself. Life could go on as it was, with no purpose, his family fragmented. Eden, now his ex-fiancée, had changed her phone number, so had some of his friends. Now he didn't have any.

He could start again. Forget about another decent job in the private sector, he'd reasoned with himself. The moment anyone carried out a background check, *Christ*, even a Google search on his name, it was all over.

Nothing like uncertainty to get the adrenaline pumping, a commanding officer in the army had once said.

He had googled Denham's name, come up with a rough history: a former corporate lawyer now with his own small firm in Canary Wharf. The man seemed genuine enough. Tom had signed the contract, together with the gag order. He would only be able to discuss the job with those directly involved in it.

In Albert Denham's private office, he sat back in the moth-eaten chair and waited for the lawyer to begin.

Denham turned a laptop around on the surface of the desk so that Tom could see the full image on screen.

'This woman is Sabina Cordero,' Denham said. 'The photograph is about two years old. She's from Argentina, thirty-eight, with two children: Beatriz, eleven, and three-year-old Mateo. She is married to Feliciano Ledesma. He's a surgeon at the British Hospital in Montevideo.'

Tom leaned forward. Sabina Cordero wore sunglasses, white shorts, a shirt tied at the navel, feet splashing in the ocean on some idyllic beach somewhere. She had a hint of Hispanic colouring, an expensive smile.

He nodded once. Denham turned the laptop back around, tapped at the keyboard. Tom was looking at the screen again. 'And this,' Denham said, 'is where they live.'

The front page of a website displayed the aerial view of

a golf course, seemingly built around an expansive series of interlinking roads and houses. It all looked highly familiar, only on a different continent. 'Aves de Las Colinas' swirled across the screen in a sophisticated typeface. *Birds of the Hills*. It was the mirror image of the kind of compound Vlok Petersen had recently designed in Wynberg, a suburban area of Cape Town, though the pictures expertly omitted any evidence of garrison-style fencing.

'Uruguayans, Argentinians, if you have any kind of money along the banks of the River Plate, this is where you build your house, or one of your many houses,' Denham continued. 'Purchase your plot, design your dream home, finish it with a pool and garden and you're living six months of the year in a sun-drenched paradise with no one but a few keen golfers to bother you.'

'Golfers and friendly neighbours all basking under the warm rays of mutual exclusivity,' Tom added. 'So this is the *Barrio Privado* you were talking about.'

'Correct,' Denham nodded. 'Fifteen kilometres east of Montevideo, outside the city limits because inside the city gated communities are unlawful.'

'But this is Latin America,' Tom said. 'You move there for your own personal safety. Or to launder your money.'

'Precisely.'

'But if you do live there, you have guaranteed security. That compound will be surrounded by a towering electric fence, CCTV and controlled vehicle access, more than likely with a fingerprint-recognition entry system.'

'It has a security checkpoint, manned twenty-four seven, only one way in, one way out.'

'Music to Hendrick Van de Vlok's ears,' Tom added with a half-smile.

Denham walked around to Tom's side of the desk, where a coat was hanging up. Tom watched as he rifled around in one of the pockets, pulling out an old-fashioned key. He returned to the other side of the desk, bending to open one of the drawers hidden from Tom's view. Straightening, Denham tossed an envelope on the surface. Tom reached forward, tore it open. He pulled out a credit card and a smart phone.

'I take it your passport is valid and in date?'

He nodded.

'Good. You leave tomorrow night on a flight to Buenos Aires,' Denham said, handing him a printed e-ticket. 'Everything is booked. The phone is for direct contact with me and me only. My number is already plugged in. Use the WhatsApp account – it's encrypted. The credit card can be used for day to day living expenses, supplies, whatever you need. There is no credit limit, it will be paid for each month and I will be scrutinising the bill. Each member of the team has one. Whatever you need to get the job done. The pin is sixty sixty. Six zero six zero, don't forget it, because in five minutes from now I will have forgotten it.'

'Sixty sixty,' Tom repeated, eyes levelled on Denham's. 'So once we are inside the compound, what is it exactly you want us to do?'

There was a moment before Denham replied. 'There is a safe, inside Sabina Cordero's house, house number 8024 inside Las Colinas. Your job… the job of your team, is to bring me the contents of that safe.'

About the Author

Emma Scullion joined the Foreign & Commonwealth Office in 2003. For the past eleven years she has managed to escape Westminster, working in British Embassies in Beijing, Bangkok, Panama City and Montevideo in Uruguay. She is a graduate of the Faber Academy. *Intruders* was her first published novel, followed by *Evaders*. She now lives in Rome with her husband and two children.

Find out more about RedDoor
Press and sign up to our
newsletter to hear about our
latest releases, author events,
exciting **competitions**
and more at

reddoorpress.co.uk

YOU CAN ALSO FOLLOW US:

 @RedDoorBooks

 Facebook.com/RedDoorPress

 @RedDoorBooks